Dionysius Lardner

Hand-Book of Natural Philosophy

SALZWASSER
VERLAG

Dionysius Lardner

Hand-Book of Natural Philosophy

Reprint of the original, first published in 1856.

1st Edition 2024 | ISBN: 978-3-37517-644-0

Salzwasser Verlag is an imprint of Outlook Verlagsgesellschaft mbH.

Verlag (Publisher): Outlook Verlag GmbH, Zeilweg 44, 60439 Frankfurt, Deutschland
Vertretungsberechtigt (Authorized to represent): E. Roepke, Zeilweg 44, 60439 Frankfurt, Deutschland
Druck (Print): Books on Demand GmbH, In de Tarpen 42, 22848 Norderstedt, Deutschland

HAND-BOOK

OF

NATURAL PHILOSOPHY.

ELECTRICITY, MAGNETISM, AND ACOUSTICS.

HAND-BOOK

OF

NATURAL PHILOSOPHY.

BY

DIONYSIUS LARDNER, D.C.L.

FORMERLY PROFESSOR OF NATURAL PHILOSOPHY AND ASTRONOMY IN UNIVERSITY COLLEGE,
LONDON.

ELECTRICITY, MAGNETISM, AND ACOUSTICS.

WITH THREE HUNDRED AND NINETY-FIVE ILLUSTRATIONS.

LONDON:

WALTON AND MABERLY,

UPPER GOWER STREET, AND IVY LANE, PATERNOSTER-ROW.

1856.

RAMSDEN'S ELECTRICAL MACHINE.

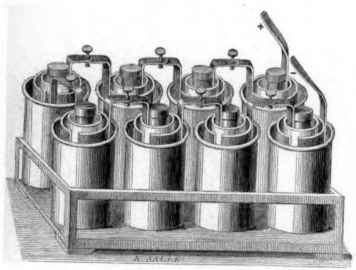

BUNSEN'S BATTERY.

PREFACE.

THIS work is intended for all who desire to attain an accurate knowledge of Physical Science, without the profound methods of Mathematical investigation. Hence the explanations are studiously popular, and everywhere accompanied by diversified elucidations and examples, derived from common objects, wherein the principles are applied to the purposes of practical life.

It has been the Author's especial aim to supply a manual of such physical knowledge as is required by the Medical and Law Students, the Engineer, the Artisan, the superior classes in Schools, and those who, before commencing a course of Mathematical Studies, may wish to take the widest and most commanding survey of the field of inquiry upon which they are about to enter.

Great pains have been taken to render the work complete in all respects, and co-extensive with the actual state of the Sciences, according to the latest discoveries.

Although the principles are here, in the main, developed and demonstrated in ordinary and popular language, mathematical symbols are occasionally used to express results more clearly and concisely. These, however, are never employed without previous explanation.

The present edition has been augmented by the introduction of a vast number of illustrations of the application of the various branches of Physics to the Industrial Arts, and to the practical business of life. Many hundred engravings have also been added to those, already numerous, of the former edition.

For the convenience of the reader the series has been divided into Four Treatises, which may be obtained separately.

MECHANICS	. One Volume.
HYDROSTATICS, PNEUMATICS, and HEAT	. One Volume.
OPTICS	. One Volume.
ELECTRICITY, MAGNETISM, and ACOUSTICS .	One Volume.

The Four Volumes taken together form a complete course of Natural Philosophy, sufficient not only for the highest degree of School education, but for that numerous class of University Students who, without aspiring to the attainment of Academic honours, desire to acquire that general knowledge of these Sciences which is necessary to entitle them to graduate, and, in the present state of society, is expected in all well educated persons.

CONTENTS.

BOOK I.

Electricity.

BOOK II.

Voltaic Electricity.

CHAPTER I.

SIMPLE VOLTAIC COMBINATION.

BOOK III.

Magnetism.'

a

CONTENTS.

BOOK IV.

Acoustics.

CHAP. I.

THEORY OF UNDULATIONS.

CHAP. II.

PRODUCTION AND PROPAGATION OF SOUND.

CHAP. III.

PHYSICAL THEORY OF MUSIC.

CONTENTS.

ELEMENTARY COURSE

OF

ELECTRICITY, MAGNETISM, AND ACOUSTICS.

BOOK THE FIRST.

ELECTRICITY.

~~~~~~~~~~

CHAPTER I.

ELECTRICAL ATTRACTIONS AND REPULSIONS.

1. **Electrical effects.** — If a glass tube, being well dried, be briskly rubbed with a dry woollen cloth, the following effects may be produced :—

The tube, being presented to certain light substances, such as feathers, metallic leaf, bits of light paper, filings of cork, or pith of elder, will attract them.

If the friction take place in the dark, a bluish light will be seen to follow the motions of the cloth.

If the glass be presented to a metallic body, or to the knuckle of the finger, a luminous spark accompanied by a sharp cracking sound, will pass between the glass and the finger.

On bringing the glass near the skin, a sensation will be produced like that which is felt when we touch a cobweb.

The same effects will be produced by the cloth, with which the glass is rubbed, as by the glass itself.

In an extensive class of bodies, when submitted to the same kind of mutual friction, similar effects are produced.

The physical agency from which these and like phenomena ar
has been called *electricity*, from the Greek word ἤλεκτρον (ele

tron), **signifyi
amber, that su
stance having be
the first in whi
the property w
observed by t
ancients.

To study the la
which govern ele
trical forces, let
apparatus be pr
vided, called
electric pendulu
consisting of a sm
ball A, *fig.* I., ab
the tenth of an i
in diameter, tur

Fig. I.

from the pith of elder, and suspended, as represented in
figure, by a fine silken thread attached to a convenient stand.
    If the glass tube B, after being rubbed as above described,
brought into contact successively with two pith balls thus su
pended, and then separated from them, a property will be impart
to the balls, in virtue of which they will be repelled by the gla
tube when it is brought nearer them, and they will in like mann
repel each other when brought into proximity.

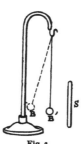

Fig. 2.

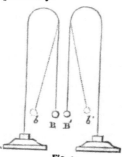

Fig. 3.

    Thus, if the glass tube s, *fig.* 2., be brought nearer the ball
the ball will depart from its vertical position, and will incline its
from the tube in the position B.
    If the two balls, being previously brought into contact with t
tube, be placed near each other, as in *fig.* 3., they will incline fro

each other, departing from the vertical positions B and B', and taking the positions b and b'.

2. **The electric fluid.** — These effects are explained by the supposition that a subtle and imponderable fluid, which is self-repulsive, has been developed upon the glass tube ; that by touching the balls, a portion of this fluid has been imparted to them, which is diffused over their surface, and which, for reasons that will hereafter appear, cannot escape by the thread of suspension ; that the fluid remaining on the glass tube repels this fluid diffused on the balls, and therefore repels the balls themselves which are invested by the fluid ; and, in fine, that the fluid diffused on the one ball repels and is repelled by the fluid diffused on the other ball, and that the balls being covered by the fluid are reciprocally repelled.

A vast body of phenomena, the most important of which will be described in the following chapters, have converted this supposition into a certainty, accepted by all scientific authorities.

The fluid producing these effects is called the *electric fluid.*

3. **Positive and negative electricity.** — If the hand which holds the cloth be covered with a dry silk glove, the cloth, after the friction with the glass, will exhibit the same effects as above described. If it be brought into contact with the balls and then separated from them, it will repel them, and the balls themselves will repel each other. It appears, therefore, that by the friction the electric fluid is at the same time developed on the glass and on the cloth. If after friction the glass be brought into contact with one ball B, *fig.* 3., and the cloth with the other B', other effects will be observed. The glass, when presented to the ball B', will attract it, and the cloth presented to the ball B will attract it.

The balls, when brought near each other, will now exhibit mutual attraction instead of repulsion. It follows, therefore, that the electric fluid developed by friction on the cloth differs from that developed on the glass, inasmuch as instead of being characterised by reciprocal repulsion they are mutually attractive. The supposition, therefore, which has been briefly stated above will require modification.

4. **Hypothesis of a single fluid.** — According to some, the effect of the friction is to deprive the cloth of a portion of its natural charge of electricity, and to surcharge the glass with what the cloth loses ; and accordingly the glass is said to be *positively*, and the cloth *negatively* electrified.

On this supposition, bodies in their natural state have always a certain charge or dose of the electric fluid, the repulsive effect of which is neutralised by the attraction exercised by the body upon it. The electric equilibrium which constitutes this natural state may be deranged, either by overcharging the body with the electric fluid, or by withdrawing from it a part of what it naturally possesses. In the former case, the repulsion of the surplus charge, not being neutralised by the attraction of the body, takes effect. In the latter case, the attraction of the body, being more than equal to the repulsion of the charge of electricity upon it, will take effect upon any electricity which may come within the sphere of its action.

This, which is called the *single fluid theory*, was the hypothesis adopted by *Franklin,* and after him by most English electricians until recently, when phenomena were developed in experimental researches, of which it failed to afford a satisfactory explanation ; and, accordingly, the hypothesis of two fluids, which was generally received on the Continent, has found more favour also in England.

5. **Hypothesis of two fluids.** — According to this theory, bodies in their natural or unelectrified state are charged with a compound electric fluid consisting of two constituents, called by some the *vitreous* and *resinous*, and by others the *positive* and *negative*, fluids. These fluids are each self-repulsive, but are mutually attractive. When they pervade a body in equal quantity, their mutual attractions, neutralising each other, keep them in repose, like equal weights suspended from the arms of a balance. When either is in excess, the body is positively or negatively electrified, as the case may be, the attraction or repulsion of the surplus of the redundant fluid being effective.

6. **Results of scientific research independent of these hypotheses.** — Since the language in which the phenomena of electricity are described and explained, must necessarily have relation to these hypotheses, it has been necessary, in the first instance, thus briefly to state them. It must, however, be remembered, that the question of the validity of these theories does not affect the conclusions, which will be deduced from observation, the proper use of hypotheses being limited to their convenience in supplying a nomenclature to the science, and in grouping and classifying the phenomena.

7. The hypothesis of two fluids supplying, on the whole, the most complete and satisfactory explanation of the phenomena, is that which we shall here generally adopt ; but we shall retain the terms *positive* and *negative* electricity, which, though they are derived originally from the theory of a single fluid, are generally adopted by scientific writers who adhere to the other hypothesis.

8. **Explanation of the effects produced by pith balls.** — We are then to consider that when the glass tube and woollen cloth are

submitted to mutual friction, their natural electricities are decomposed, the positive fluid passing to the glass, and the negative to the cloth. The glass thus becomes surcharged with positive, and the cloth with negative, electricity.

The pith ball B (*fig.* 3.), touched by the glass, receives the positive fluid from it, and the pith ball B', touched by the cloth, receives the negative fluid from it. The ball B therefore becomes positively, and the ball B' negatively, electrified by contact.

Since the contrary electricities are mutually attractive, the balls B and B' in this case attract each other; and, since like electricities are mutually repulsive, the glass rod repels the ball B, and the cloth repels the ball B'.

9. **Electricity is developed by various bodies, when submitted to friction.** — If a stick of resin or sealing wax be rubbed by a woollen cloth, like effects will follow : but, in this case, the electricity of the wax or resin will be contrary to that of the glass, as may be rendered manifest by the pith balls. If B be electrified by contact with the glass, and B' by contact with the resin or wax, they will attract each other, exactly as they did when B' was electrified by contact with the cloth rubbed upon the glass. It appears, therefore, that while glass is positively, resin is negatively, electrified by the friction of woollen cloth.

It was owing to this circumstance that positive electricity came to be called vitreous, and negative electricity resinous.

This nomenclature, is, however, faulty; inasmuch as there are certain substances by the friction of which glass will be negatively electrified, and others by which resin will be positively electrified.

When a woollen cloth is rubbed on resin or wax which, as has been stated, it electrifies negatively, it is itself electrified positively; since the natural fluid being decomposed by the friction, and the negative element going to the resin, the positive element must be developed on the cloth. Thus it appears that the woollen cloth may be electrified by friction, either positively or negatively, according as it is rubbed upon resin or upon glass.

There is no certain test to determine, previous to experiment, which of the bodies submitted to friction receives positive, and which negative, electricity. In general, when any two bodies are rubbed together, electricity is developed, one of them being charged with the positive, and the other with the negative, fluid. A great number of experimental researches have from time to time been undertaken, with a view to the discovery of the physical law, which determines the distribution of the constituent electric fluids in such cases between the two bodies, so that it might in all cases be certainly known which of the two would be positively and which negatively electrified. These inquiries, however, have hitherto been attended with no clear or certain general consequences.

It has been observed, that hardness of structure is generally attended with a predisposition to receive positive electricity. Thus, the diamond, submitted to friction with other stones or with glass, becomes positively electrified. Sulphur, when rubbed with amber, becomes negatively electrified, the amber being consequently positive ; but if the amber be rubbed upon glass or diamond, it will be negative.

It is also observed that when heat is developed by the friction of two bodies, that which takes most heat is negatively, and the other positively, electrified.

In short, the decomposition of the electricity and its distribution between the rubbing bodies is governed by conditions infinitely various and complicated.

An elevation of temperature will frequently predispose a body to take negative, which would otherwise take positive electricity. An increase of polish of the surface produces a predisposition for the positive fluid. The colour, the molecular arrangement, the direction of the fibres in a textile substance, the direction in which the friction takes place, the greater or less pressure used in producing it, all affect more or less, in particular cases, the interchange of the fluids and the relative electricities of the bodies. Thus, a black silk ribbon rubbed on one of white silk takes negative electricity. If two pieces of the same ribbon be rubbed transversely, one being stationary and the other moved upon it, the former takes positive, the latter negative, electricity. Æpinus found that copper and sulphur rubbed together, and two similar plates of glass, evolved electricity, but that the interchange of the fluids was not always the same. There are substances, *disthène*, for example, which, when submitted to friction, develop positive electricity at some parts, and negative at other parts of their surface, although their structure and the state of the surface be perfectly uniform.

10. **Classification of positive and negative substances.** — Of all known substances, a cat's fur is the most susceptible of positive, and probably sulphur of negative, electricity. Between these extreme substances others might be so arranged that any substance in the list being rubbed upon any other, that which holds the higher place will be positively, and that which holds the lower place negatively, electrified. Various lists of this kind have been proposed, one of which is as follows : —

1. Fur of a cat.	6. Paper.
2. Polished glass.	7. Silk.
3. Woollen cloth.	8. Gum-lac.
4. Feathers.	9. Rough glass.
5. Wood.	

Pfaff gives the following :—

1. Fur of a cat.	8. White silk.
2. Diamond.	9. Black silk.
3. Fur of a dog.	10. Sealing-wax.
4. Tourmaline.	11. Colophon.
5. Glass.	12. Amber.
6. Wool.	13. Sulphur.
7. Paper.	

Ritter proposes the following :—

1. Diamond.	6. Silver.
2. Zinc.	7. Black silk.
3. Glass.	8. Grey silk.
4. Copper.	9. Grey manganeseous earth.
5. Wool.	10. Sulphur.

11. **Method of producing electricity by glass and silk with amalgam.** — Experience has proved that the most efficient means of developing electricity in great quantity and intensity is by the friction of glass upon a surface of silk or leather smeared with an amalgam composed of tin, zinc, and mercury, mixed with some unctuous matter. Two parts of tin, three of zinc, and four of mercury, answer very well. Let some fine chalk be sprinkled on the surface of a wooden cup, into which the mercury should be poured hot. Let the zinc and tin melted together be then poured in, and the box being closed and well shaken, the amalgam may be allowed to cool. It is then finely pulverised in a mortar, and, being mixed with unctuous matter, may be applied to the rubber.

CHAP. II.

CONDUCTION.

12. **Conductors and nonconductors.** — Bodies differ from each other in a striking manner in the freedom with which the electric fluid moves upon them. If that fluid be imparted to the surface of glass or wax, it will be confined strictly to that portion of the surface which originally receives it; but if it be imparted to a portion of the surface of a metallic body, it will instantaneously diffuse itself uniformly over the entire extent of such metallic surface, exactly as water would spread itself uniformly over a level surface on which it is poured.

The former class of bodies, which do not give free motion to the electric fluid on their surface, are called *nonconductors;* and the latter, on which unlimited freedom of motion prevails, are called *conductors.*

13. **Degrees of conduction.** — Of all bodies the most perfect conductors are the metals. These bodies transmit electricity in-

stantaneously, and without any sensible obstruction, provided their dimensions are not too small in relation to the quantity of electricity imparted to them.

The bodies named in the following series possess the conducting power in different degrees in the order in which they stand, the most perfect conductor being first, and the most perfect nonconductor last in the list. The black line divides the most imperfect conductors from the most imperfect nonconductors; but it must be observed that the position of this line is arbitrary, the exact relative position of many of the bodies composing the series not being certainly ascertained. The series, however, will be useful as indicating generally the bodies which have the conducting and nonconducting property in a greater or less degree:—

All the metals.	Moist earth and stones.	Dry vegetable bodies.
Well-burnt charcoal.	Powdered glass.	Baked wood.
Plumbago.	Flowers of sulphur.	Dry gases and air.
Concentrated acids.		Leather.
Powdered charcoal.	Dry metallic oxides.	Parchment.
Dilute acids.	Oils, the heaviest the best.	Dry paper.
Saline solutions.	Ashes of vegetable bodies.	Feathers.
Metallic ores.	Ashes of animal bodies.	Hair.
Animal fluids.	Many transparent crystals, dry.	Wool.
Sea-water.		Dyed silk.
Spring-water.	Ice below 13° Fahrenheit.	Bleached silk.
Rain-water.	Phosphorus.	Raw silk.
Ice above 13° Fahrenheit.	Lime.	Transparent gems.
Snow.	Dry chalk.	Diamond.
Living vegetables.	Native carbonate of barytes.	Mica.
Living animals.		All vitrifactions.
Flame.	Lycopodium.	Glass.
Smoke.	Caoutchouc.	Jet.
Steam.	Camphor.	Wax.
Salts soluble in water.	Some siliceous and argillaceous stones.	Sulphur.
Rarefied air.		Resins.
Vapour of alcohol.	Dry marble.	Amber.
Vapour of ether.	Porcelain.	Gum-lac.

14. **Insulators.**—Good nonconductors are also called insulators, because when any body suspended by a nonconducting thread, or supported on a nonconducting pillar, is charged with electricity, such charge will be retained, since it cannot escape by the thread or pillar, which refuses a passage to it in virtue of its nonconducting quality. Thus, a globe of metal supported on a glass pillar, or suspended by a silken cord, being charged with electricity will retain the charge; whereas, if it were supported on a metallic pillar, or suspended by a metallic wire, the electricity would pass away by its free motion over the surface of the pillar or the wire.

15. **Insulating stools** are formed with glass legs, so that any body charged with electricity and placed upon them will retain its electric charge.

16. **Electrics and non-electrics obsolete terms.**—Conducting bodies were formerly called *non-electrics*, and nonconducting bodies were called *electrics*, from the supposition that the

latter were capable of being electrified by friction, but the former not.

The incapability of conductors to be electrified by friction was, however, afterwards shown to be only apparent, and accordingly the use of these terms has been discontinued.

If a rod of metal be submitted to friction, the electricity evolved is first diffused over its entire surface in consequence of its conducting property, and thence it escapes by the hand of the operator which holds it, and which, though not as perfect a conductor as the metal, is sufficiently so to carry off the electricity, so as to leave no sensible trace of it on the metal. But if the metal rod be suspended by a dry silken thread (which is a good nonconductor), or be supported on a pillar of glass, and then be struck several times with the fur of a cat, it will be found to be negatively electrified, the fur which strikes it being positively electrified.

17. **Two persons reciprocally charged with contrary electricity being placed on insulating stools.** — If one strike the other two or three times with the fur of a cat, he that strikes will have his body positively, and he that is struck negatively, electrified, as may be ascertained by the method already explained, of presenting to them successively the pith ball B, *fig.* 2., previously charged with positive electricity. It will be repelled by the body of him that strikes, and attracted by that of him who is struck. But if the same experiment be made without placing the two persons on insulating stools, the same effects will not ensue; because, although the electricities are developed as before by the action of the fur, it immediately escapes through the feet to the ground.

18. **The atmosphere is a nonconductor,** for if it gave a free passage to electricity, the electrical effects excited on the surface of any body surrounded with it would soon pass away; and no electrical phenomena of a permanent nature could be produced, unless the bodies were removed from the contact of the air. It is found, however, that resin and glass, when excited by friction, retain their electricity for a considerable time.

19. **Rarefied air is a conductor,** for an electrified body soon loses its electricity if placed in the exhausted receiver of an air-pump. The electric fluid may, therefore, be considered as forming a coating upon the surface of electrified bodies, and as being held upon them by the tension or pressure of the surrounding air.

20. **Use of the silk string which suspends pith balls.** — In the experiments described in (1.) *et seq.* with the pith balls, the silken string by which they are suspended acts as an insulator.

The pith of elder being a conductor, the electric fluid is diffused over the ball; but the silk being a nonconductor, it cannot escape. If the ball were suspended by a metallic wire attached to a stand composed of any conducting matter, the electricity would escape, and the effects described would not ensue. But if the metallic wire were attached to a glass rod or other nonconductor, the same effects would be produced. In that case the electricity would be diffused over the wire as well as over the ball.

21. **Water a conductor.**—Water, whether in the liquid or vaporous form, is a conductor, though of an order greatly inferior to the metals. This fact is of great importance in electrical phenomena. The atmosphere contains suspended in it always more or less aqueous vapour, the presence of which impairs its nonconducting property. Hence, electrical experiments always succeed best in cold and dry weather. Hence it appears why the most perfect nonconductors lose their virtue if their surface be moist, the electricity passing by the conducting power of the moisture.

22. **Insulators must be kept dry.**—This circumstance also shows why it is necessary to dry previously the bodies, on which it is desired to develop electricity by friction. It will be apparent from what has been explained, that it would be more correct to designate bodies as good and bad conductors in various degrees, than as conductors and nonconductors. There exists no body which, strictly speaking, is either an absolute conductor or absolute nonconductor.

23. **There is no certain test to distinguish conductors from nonconductors.**—Electricity is transmitted, not like light and heat, through the interior dimensions of bodies, but only on their surfaces. Glass, which is an almost perfect conductor of light, is a nonconductor of heat and electricity. Sealing-wax, which is a nonconductor of electricity, is also a nonconductor of light and heat. The metals, on the other hand, are conductors of heat and electricity, but are nonconductors of light. Water is a conductor of electricity and light, but a nonconductor of heat.

24. **The conducting power is variously affected by temperature.**—In the metals it is diminished by elevation of temperature; but in all other bodies, and especially in liquids, it is augmented. Some substances, which are nonconductors in the solid state, become conductors when fused. Sir H. Davy found that glass raised to a red heat became a conductor; and that sealing-wax, pitch, amber, shell-lac, sulphur, and wax become conductors when liquefied by heat. The manner in which electricity is communicated from one body to another, depends on the conducting property of the body imparting and the body receiving it.

25. Effects produced by touching an electrified body by a conductor which is not insulated.—If the surface of a nonconducting body, glass, for example, be charged with electricity, and be touched over a certain space, as a square inch, by a conducting body which is not insulated, the electricity which is diffused on the surface of contact will pass away by the conductor, but no other part of the electricity with which the body is charged will escape. A *patch* of the surface corresponding with the magnitude of the conductor will alone be stripped of its electricity. The nonconducting property of the body will prevent the electricity, which is diffused over the remainder of its surface, from flowing into the space thus drained of the fluid by the conductor. But if the body thus charged with electricity, and touched by a conductor not insulated, be a conductor, the effects produced will be very different. In that case, the electricity which covers the surface of contact will first pass off; but the moment the surface of contact is thus drained of the fluid which covered it, the fluid diffused on the surrounding surface will flow in and likewise pass off, and thus all the fluid diffused over the entire surface of the body will rush to the surface of contact, and escape. These effects, though, strictly speaking, successive, will be practically instantaneous; the time which elapses between the escape of the fluid which originally covered the surface of contact, and that which rushes from the most remote parts to the surface of contact, being inappreciable.

26. Effect produced when the touching conductor is insulated.—If a conducting body, which is insulated and charged with electricity, be brought into contact with another conducting body, which is also insulated and in its natural state, the electricity will diffuse itself over the surfaces of both conductors in proportion to their relative magnitudes.

If s express the superficial magnitude of an insulated conducting body, E the quantity of electricity with which it is charged, and s' the superficial magnitude of the other insulated conductor with which it is brought into contact, the charge E will, after contact, be shared between the two conductors in the ratio of s to s'; so that

$$E \times \frac{s}{s+s'} = \text{the charge retained by } s;$$

$$E \times \frac{s'}{s+s'} = \text{the charge received by } s'.$$

27. Why the earth is called the common reservoir.—If the second conductor s' be the globe of the earth, s' will bear a proportion to s which, practically speaking, is infinite; and consequently the quantity of electricity remaining on s, expressed by

$$E \times \frac{s}{s+s'},$$

will be nothing.   Hence the body s loses its entire charge when
put in conducting communication with the ground.

An electrified body being a conductor, is therefore reduced to
its natural state when put into electric communication with the
ground, and the earth has been therefore called the *common reser-*
voir, to which all electricity has a tendency to escape, and to which
it does in fact always escape, unless its passage is intercepted by
nonconductors.

28. **Electricity passes by preference on the best con-**
ductors. — If several different conductors be simultaneously placed
in contact with an insulated electrified conductor so as to form a
communication between it and the ground, the electricity will
always escape by the best conductor.   Thus, if a metallic chain
or wire be held in the hand, one end touching the ground and the
other being brought into contact with the conductor, no part of
the electricity will pass into the hand, the chain being a better
conductor than the flesh of the hand.   But if, while one end of the
chain touch the conductor, the other be separated from the ground
then the electricity will pass into the hand, and will be rendered
sensible by a convulsive shock.

CHAP. III.

INDUCTION.

29. **Action of electricity at a distance.** — If a body
charged with electricity of either kind, be brought into proximity
with another body B in its natural state, the fluid, with which A
surcharged, will act by attraction and repulsion on the two constituents of the natural electricity of B; attracting that of the contrary, and repelling that of the same kind.   This effect is precisely
similar to that produced on the natural magnetic fluid in a piece
of iron, when the pole of a magnet is presented to it, as will be
explained hereafter.

If the body B in this case be a nonconductor, the electric fluid
having no free mobility upon its surface, its decomposition will
be resisted, and the body B will continue in its natural state, notwithstanding the attraction and repulsion exercised by A on the
constituents of its natural electricity.   But if B be a conductor
the fluids having freedom of motion on its surface, the fluid similar

to that with which B is charged will be repelled to the side most
distant from B, and the contrary fluid will be attracted to the side
next to B. Between these regions a neutral line will separate
those parts of the body B, over which the two opposite fluids are
respectively diffused.

30. **Induction** is the action of an electrified body exerted at
a distance upon the electricity of another body, and is evidently
analogous to that which produces similar phenomena in the magnetic bodies.

31. **Experimental exhibition of its effects.** — To render it
experimentally manifest, let s and s', *fig.* 4., be two metallic balls

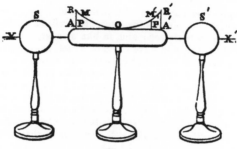

Fig. 4.

supported on glass pillars; and let A A' be a metallic cylinder similarly mounted, whose length is ten or twelve times its diameter,
and whose ends are rounded into hemispheres. Let s be strongly
charged with positive, and s' with negative electricity, the cylinder
A A' being in its natural state.

Let the balls s and s' be placed near the ends of the cylinder A A', their
centres being in line with its axis, as represented in the figure. The positive
electricity of s will now attract the negative, and repel the positive constituent of the natural electricity of A A', so as to separate them, drawing the
negative fluid towards the end A, and repelling the positive fluid towards the
end A'. The negative electricity of s' will produce a like effect, repelling the
negative electricity of A A' towards A, and drawing the positive towards A'.

Since the cylinder A A' is a conductor, and therefore the fluids have freedom
of motion on its surface, this decomposition will take effect, and the half O A
of the cylinder next to s will be charged with negative, and the half O A'
next to s' with positive electricity.

That such is in fact the condition of A A' may be proved by presenting a
pith ball (1.) pendulum charged with positive electricity to either half of the
cylinder. When presented to O A' it will be repelled, and when presented to
O A it will be attracted.

If the two balls s s' be gradually removed to increased but equal distances
from the ends A and A', the recomposition of the fluids will gradually take
place; and when the balls are altogether removed the cylinder A A' will
recover its natural state, the fluids which had been separated by the action
of the balls being completely recombined by their mutual attraction.

Fig. 5.

Let a metallic ring *n'*, *fig.* 5., be supported on a rod or hook of glass *n*, and let two pith balls *b b'* be suspended from it by fine wires, so that when hanging vertically they shall be in contact. Let a ball of metal *r*, strongly charged with positive electricity, be placed over the ring *n'* at a distance of eight or ten inches above it. The presence of this ball will immediately cause the pith balls to repel each other, and they will diverge to increased distances the nearer the ball *r* is brought to the ring *n'*. If the ball *r* be gradually raised to greater distances from the ring, the balls *b b'* will gradually approach each other, and will fall to their position of rest vertically under the ring when the ball *r* is altogether removed.

If the charge of electricity of the balls s and s', *fig.* 4., or of the ball *r*, *fig.* 5., be gradually diminished, the same effect will be produced as when the distance is gradually increased; and, in like manner, the gradual increase of the charge of electricity will have the same effect, as the gradual diminution of the distance from the conductor on which the action takes place.

If the ring *n'*, the balls *b b'*, and the connecting wire, be first feebly charged with negative electricity, and then submitted to the inductive action of the ball *r* charged with positive electricity, placed, as before, above the ring, the following effects will ensue. When the ball *r* approaches the ring, the balls *b b'*, which previously diverged, will gradually collapse until they come into contact. As the ball *r* is brought still nearer to *n'*, they will again diverge, and will diverge more and more, the nearer the ball *r* is brought to the ring.

These various effects are easily and simply explicable by the action of the electricity of the ball *r* on that of the ring. When it approaches the ring, the positive electricity with which it is charged decomposes the natural electricities of the ring, repelling the positive fluid towards the balls. This fluid combining with the negative fluid with which the balls are charged, neutralises it, and reduces them to their natural state: while this effect is gradually produced, the balls *b b'* lose their divergence and collapse. But when the ball *r* is brought still nearer to the ring, a more abundant decomposition of the natural fluid is produced, and the positive fluid repelled towards the balls is more than enough to neutralise the negative fluid with which they are charged; and the positive fluid prevailing, the balls again diverge with positive electricity.

These effects are aided by the attraction exerted by the positive electricity of the ball *r* on the negative fluid, with which the balls *b b'* are previously charged.

If the electrified ball, instead of being placed above the ring, be placed at an equal distance below the balls *b b'*, a series of effects will be produced in the contrary order, which the student will find no difficulty in analysing and explaining.

If the ball *r* be charged with negative electricity, it will produce the same effects when presented above the ring as when, being charged with positive electricity, it is presented below it.

32. Let three copper cylinders, A B, A' B', A" B", *fig.* 6., rounded at the ends, be supported on insulating pillars, and the pith ball pendulums be inserted at their extremities, the pith balls being supported by wires or other conducting threads on rods which are also conductors. Let the cylinders, placed end *to end*, as shown in the figure, be brought near to a conductor c, charged, *for example, with* positive electricity; the electricity of c will decompose the

natural electricity of A, attracting to the end near it the negative, and repelling to the remote end the positive fluid. The positive fluid thus collected

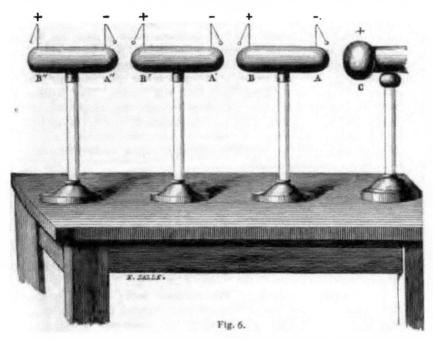

Fig. 6.

at the remote end B, will act by induction in a similar manner upon the
natural electricity of A′ B′; attracting the negative electricity to the near end,
and repelling the positive to the remote end, as indicated in the figure, whose
+ indicates the positive, and − the negative electricity.

This distribution of the two fluids will be shown by the pith balls, as indicated in the figure; the pith balls, charged with each kind of electricity,
being repelled by the rods similarly charged.

In all cases whatever, the conductor, whose electrical state has
been changed by the proximity of an electrified body, returns to
its primitive electrical condition when the disturbing action of
such body is removed; and this return is either instantaneous or
gradual, according as the removal of the disturbing body is instantaneous or gradual.

33. **Effects of sudden inductive action.**—It appears, therefore, that sudden and violent changes in the electrical condition
of a conducting body may take place, without either imparting to
or abstracting from such body any portion of electricity. The
electricity with which it is invested before the inductive action
commences, and after such action ceases, is exactly the same;
nevertheless, the decomposition and recomposition of the constituent fluids, and their motion more or less sudden over it and

through its dimensions, are productive often of mechanical effects of a very remarkable kind. This is especially the case with imperfect conductors, which offer more or less resistance to the reunion of the fluids.

34. **Example in the case of a frog.** — Let a frog be suspended by a metallic wire which is connected with an insulated conductor, and let a metallic ball, strongly charged with positive electricity, be brought under, without, however, touching it. The effects of induction already described will ensue. The positive fluid will be repelled from the frog towards the insulated conductor, and the negative fluid will be attracted towards it, so that the body of the frog will be negatively electrified; but this, taking place gradually as the electrified ball approaches, is attended with no sensible mechanical effect.

If the electrified ball, however, be suddenly discharged, by connecting it with the ground by a conductor, an instantaneous revulsion of the electric fluids will take place, between the body of the frog and the insulated conductor with which it is connected; the positive fluid rushing from the conductor, and the negative fluid from the frog, to recombine in virtue of their mutual attraction. This sudden movement of the fluids will be attended by a convulsive motion of the limbs of the frog.

35. **Inductive shock of the human body.** — If a person stand close to a large conductor strongly charged with electricity, he will be sensible of a shock when this conductor is suddenly discharged. This shock is in like manner produced by the sudden recomposition of the fluids in the body of the patient, decomposed by the previous inductive action of the conductor.

36. **Development of electricity by induction.** — A conductor may be charged with electricity by an electrified body, though the latter shall not lose any of its own electricity or impart any to the conductor so electrified. For this purpose, let the conductor to be electrified be supported on a glass pillar so as to insulate it, and let it then be connected with the ground by a metallic chain or wire. If it be desired to charge it with positive electricity, let a body strongly charged with negative electricity be brought close to it without touching it. On the principles already explained, the negative electricity of the conductor will be repelled to the ground through the chain or wire; and the positive electricity will, on the other hand, be attracted from the ground to the conductor. Let the chain or wire be then removed, and, afterwards, let the electrified body by whose inductive action the effect is produced be removed. The conductor will remain charged with positive electricity.

It may in like manner be charged with negative electricity, by the inductive action of a body charged with positive electricity.

CHAP. IV.

ELECTRICAL MACHINES.

37. **An electrical machine** is an apparatus, by means of which electricity is developed and accumulated, in a convenient manner for the purposes of experiment.

All electrical machines consist of three principal parts, the rubber, the body on whose surface the electric fluid is evolved, and one or more insulated conductors, to which this electricity is transferred, and on which it is accumulated.

38. **The rubber** is a cushion stuffed with hair, bearing on its surface some substance, which by friction will evolve electricity. The body on which this friction is produced is glass, so shaped and mounted as to be easily and rapidly moved against the rubber with a continuous motion. This object is attained by giving the glass the form either of a cylinder revolving on its geometrical axis, or of a circular plate revolving in its own plane on its centre.

39. **The conductors** are bodies having a metallic surface and a great variety of shapes, and always mounted on insulating pillars, or suspended by insulating cords.

40. **The common cylindrical machine.** — A hollow cylinder of glass A B, *fig.* 7., is supported in bearings at C, and made to revolve by means of the wheels C and D connected by a band, a handle E being attached to the greater wheel.

The cushion H, represented separately in *fig.* 8., is mounted on a glass pillar, and pressed with a regulated force against the cylinder by means of springs fixed behind it. A chain, *fig.* 7., connects the cushion with the ground. A flap of black silk equal in width to the cushion covers it, and is carried over the cylinder, terminating above the middle of the cylinder on the opposite side.

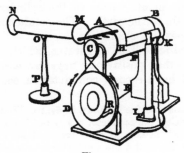
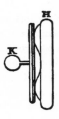

Fig. 7.   Fig. 8.

The conductor is a cylinder of thin brass M N, the ends of which are parts of spheres greater than hemispheres. It is supported by a glass pillar O P.

To the end of the conductor next the cylinder is attached a row of points represented separately in *fig.* 9., which are presented close to the surface of the cylinder, but without touching it. The extent of this row of points corresponds with that of the rubber.

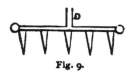

Fig. 9.

As the efficient performance of the machine depends in a great degree on the good insulation of the several parts, and as glass is peculiarly liable to collect moisture on its surface which would impair its insulating virtue, it is usual to cover the insulating pillars of the rubber and conductor, and all that part of the cylinder which lies outside the cushion and silk flap, with a coating of resinous varnish, which, while its insulating property is more perfect than that of glass, offers less attraction to moisture.

To explain the operation of the machine, let us suppose that the cylinder is made to revolve by the handle R. Positive electricity is developed upon the cylinder, and negative electricity on the cushion. The latter passes by the conducting chain to the ground. The former is carried round under the flap, on the surface of the glass, until it arrives at the points projecting from the conductor. There it acts by induction (30.) on the natural electricity of the conductor, attracting the negative electricity to the points and repelling the positive fluid. The negative electricity issuing from the points combines with and neutralises the positive fluid diffused on the cylinder, the surface of which, after it passes the points, is therefore restored to its natural state, so that when it arrives again at the cushion it is prepared to receive by friction a fresh charge of the positive fluid.

It is apparent, therefore, that the effect produced by the operation of this machine is a continuous decomposition of the natural electricity of the conductors, and an abstraction from it of just so much negative fluid as compensates for that which escapes by the cushion and chain to the earth. The conductor is thus as it were drained of its negative electricity by a stream of that fluid, which flowing constantly from the points passes to the cylinder, and thence by the cushion and chain to the earth. The conductor is therefore left surcharged with positive electricity.

41. **Nairne's cylinder machine.** — This apparatus, which is adapted to produce at pleasure either positive or negative electricity, is similar to the last, but has a second conductor in connection with the cushion.

A geometrical drawing in outline of this machine is shown in *fig.* 10. When it is desired to collect positive electricity, the conductor M F is put in connection with the ground, and the machine acts as that described above. When it is desired to collect negative electricity, the conductor M' B is put in connection with the ground, and the conductor M F is insulated. In this case a stream of positive electricity flows continually from M F through the cushion to the cylinder, and thence by the conductor M' B to the ground;

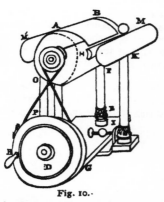

Fig. 10.

leaving the conductor M F charged with negative electricity.

A perspective drawing of the same machine, with some unimportant modifications of form and arrangement, is given in *fig.* 11. In this, C is the conductor which carries the rubber D, and B that which collects the positive electricity; the cylinder A, between these, is worked by a winch M having an insulating handle. The rods attached to the positive and negative conductors, terminate in copper balls, between which, when brought near to each other, a series of electric sparks constantly pass, proceeding from the tendency of the opposite electricities to attract each other and combine.

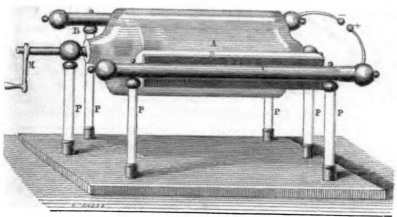

Fig. 11.

42. The common plate machine, known as Van Marum's, is represented in geometrical outline in *fig.* 12.

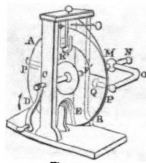

Fig. 12.

It consists of a circular plate of glass A B, *fig.* 12., mounted as represented in the figure. It is embraced between two pair of cushions at E and E', a corresponding width of the glass being covered by a silk sheathing extending to F', where the points of the conductors are presented. The handle being turned in the direction of the arrow, and the cushions being connected by conducting chains with the ground, positive electricity is developed on the glass, and neutralised as in the cylinder machine, by the negative electricity received by induction from the conductors, which consist of a long narrow cylinder, bent into a form to adapt it to the plate. It is represented at M N, a branch M O being carried parallel to the plate and bent into the form M O P Q, so that the part P Q shall be presented close to the plate under the edge of the silk flap. A similar branch of the conductor extends on the other side, terminating just above the edge of the lower silk flap.

The principle of this machine is similar in all respects to that of the common cylinder machine. With the same weight and bulk, the extent of rubbing surface, and consequently the evolution of electricity, is much greater than in the cylinder machines.

Fig. 13.

Fig. 14.

A perspective view of this machine is given in *fig.* 13., where the arc of copper Y Y', connected with the handle is placed vertically, and in *fig.* 14.

the same arc x x' is exhibited horizontally, being then in contact with the cushions. On the other side of the plate is the large copper ball G, standing on an insulating pillar to which the arc x x' *fig.* 13. and Y Y' *fig.* 14. is fixed, being placed horizontally in *fig.* 13., and vertically in *fig.* 14.

When the two arcs Y Y' and x x' are placed as in *fig.* 13., Y Y' being vertical, and x x' horizontal, the two branches x x' are in contact with the cushions, while those of Y Y' approach the plate without touching it; consequently, if by the aid of the handle the plate is turned, the cushions, which are negatively electrified, charge the ball G with the negative fluid, while the positive electricity of the plate, acting by induction upon Y Y', draws from the ground the negative fluid, which it neutralises.

On the other hand, if the branches Y Y' and x x' be disposed as in *fig.* 14., the cushions communicating with the ground by x x' lose all their electricity, while the plate which is positively electrified, acting by induction upon Y Y', and the ball G, drains them of the negative fluid, and leaves them positively electrified.

43. Ramsden's plate machine. — One of the earliest electric apparatus of this form which was constructed is represented in *fig.* 15.

Fig. 15.—RAMSDEN'S ELECTRICAL MACHINE.

The large glass plate G, is mounted between wooden supports M m, and turned by a handle x. It is pressed between two pairs of rubbers, C C. In the direction of its horizontal diameter it passes between two curved brass tubes D D', which collect the electricity from it by points in the usual way. These are

connected with two large conductors s s, supported on insulating pillars
p p, and connected at the remote end by a cylindrical tube, from the middle
of which another tube s proceeds at right angles, terminated in a knob.

After what has been explained of the other machines the theory
of this will be readily understood.

++ **Armstrong's hydro-electrical machine.** — A new species
of electric machine has resulted from the accidental observation
of an electric shock, produced by the contact of a jet of high
pressure steam issuing from a boiler at Newcastle-on-Tyne in
1840. Mr. Armstrong of that place took up the inquiry, and
succeeded in contriving a machine for the production and accumulation of electricity, by the agency of steam. Professor Faraday
investigated the theory of the apparatus, and showed that the
origin of the electrical development was the friction of minute
aqueous particles, produced by the partial condensation of the
steam against the surface of the jet, from which the steam issued.

The hydro-electrical machine has since been constructed in
various forms and dimensions.

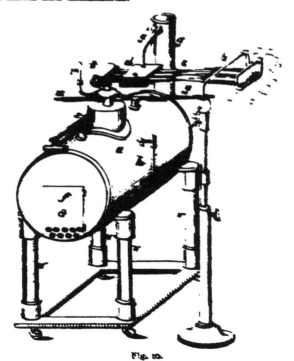

Fig. 10.

Let a cylindrical boiler a, fig. 10, whose length is about twice its diameter,
be mounted on glass legs a, so as to be in a state of insulation.

f is the furnace door, the furnace being a tube within the boiler.

s is the safety-valve.

h is the water-gauge, a glass tube indicating the level of the water in the boiler.

r a regulating valve, by which the escape of steam from the boiler may be controlled.

t a tube into which the steam rushes as it escapes from *r*.

e three or more jet pipes, through which the steam passes from *t*, and from the extremities of which it issues in a series of parallel jets.

d a condensing box, the lower half of which contains water at the common temperature.

g the chimney.

g' an escape pipe for the vapour generated in the condensing box *d*.

b the conductor which takes from the steam the electricity which issues with it from the jet pipes *e*.

k the knob of the conductor from which the electricity may be received and collected for the purpose of experiment.

The jet pipes *e* traverse the middle of the condensing box *d*, above the surface of the water contained in it. Meshes of cotton thread surround these tubes within the box, the ends of which are immersed in the water. The water is drawn up by the capillary action of these threads, so as to surround the tubes with a moist coating, which, by its low temperature, produces a slight condensation of the steam as it passes through that part of the tube.

The fine aqueous particles thus produced within the tube are carried forward with the steam, and, on issuing through the jet pipe, rub against its sides. This friction decomposes the natural electricity, the negative fluid remaining on the jet, and the positive being carried out with the particles of water, and imparted by them to the conductor *b*.

It will be apparent that in this arrangement the interior surface of the jet plays the part of the rubber of the ordinary machine, and the particles of water that of the glass cylinder or plate, the steam being the moving power which maintains the friction.

In order to insure the efficiency of the friction, the conduit provided for  the escape of the steam is not straight but angular. A section of the jet pipe near its extremity is represented in *fig.* 17. The steam issuing from the box *d* encounters a plate of metal *m* which intercepts its direct passage to the mouth of the jet. It is compelled to turn downwards, pass under the edge of this plate, and, rising behind it, turn again into the escape pipe, which is a tube formed of partridge wood enclosed within the metal pipe *n*.

Fig. 17.

It is found that an apparatus thus constructed, the length of the boiler being 32 inches and its diameter 16 inches, will develop as much electricity in a given time as three common plate machines, whose plates have a diameter of 40 inches, and are worked at the rate of 60 revolutions per minute.

A machine on this principle, and on a great scale of magnitude, was erected by the Royal Polytechnic Institution of London, the boiler of which was 78 inches long, and 42 inches diameter. The maximum pressure of the steam at the commencement of the operation was sometimes 90 lbs. per sq. inch.

This, however, fell to 40 lbs. or less. Sparks have been obtained from the conductor at the distance of 22 inches.

Another view of this machine, rendered more distinct by shading, is shown in *fig.* 14.

Fig. 14.—Armstrong's Hydro-electrical Machine.

45. To facilitate the performance of experiments, various accessories are usually provided with these machines.

46. **Insulating stools.**—Insulating stools, constructed of strong, hard wood, well baked and dried, and supported on legs of glass coated with resinous varnish, are useful when it is required to keep for any time any conducting body charged with electricity. The body is placed on one of these stools while it is being electrified.

Thus, two persons standing on two such stools, may be charged, one with positive, and the other with negative, electricity. If, when so charged, they touch each other, the contrary electricities will combine, and they will sustain a nervous shock proportionate to the quantity of electricity with which they were charged.

47. **Discharging rods.**—Since it is frequently necessary to observe the effects of points and spheres, pieces such as *figs.* 19,

20. are provided, to be inserted in holes in the conductors; also metallic balls, *figs.* 21, 22., attached to glass handles for cases in which it is desired to apply a conductor to an electrified body without allowing the electricity to pass to the hand of the

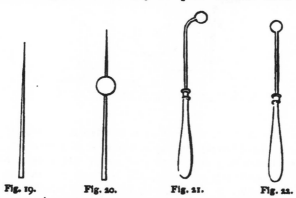

Fig. 19. Fig. 20. Fig. 21. Fig. 22.

operator. With these rods the electricity may be taken from a conductor gradually by small portions, the ball taking by each contact only such a fraction of the whole charge as corresponds to the ratio of the surface of the ball to the surface of the conductor.

48. **Jointed dischargers.** — To establish a temporary connection between two conductors, or between a conductor and the ground, the jointed dischargers, *figs.* 23, 24., are useful. The

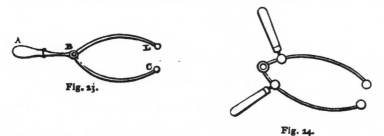

Fig. 23.

Fig. 24.

distance between the balls can be regulated at pleasure by means of the joint or hinge by which the rods are united.

49. **Universal discharger.** — The universal discharger, an instrument of considerable convenience and utility in experimental researches, is represented in *fig.* 25. It consists of a wooden table to which two glass pillars A and A′ are attached. At the summit of these pillars are fixed two brass joints capable of revolving in a horizontal plane. To these joints are attached brass rods c c′, terminated by balls D D′, and having glass handles E E′. These

rods play on joints at B B', by which they can be moved in vertical planes.

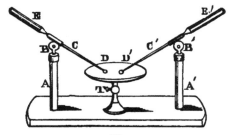

Fig. 25.

The balls D D' are applied to a wooden table sustained on a pillar capable of having its height adjusted by a screw T. On the table is inlaid a long narrow strip of ivory, extending in the direction of the balls D D'. These balls D D' can be unscrewed, and one or both may be replaced by forceps, by which may be held any substance through which it is desired to transmit the electric charge. One of the brass rods c is connected by chain or a wire with the source of electricity, and the other with the ground.

The electricity is transmitted by bringing the balls D D' with the substance to be operated on between them, within such a distance of each other as will cause the charge to pass from one to the other through the introduced substance.

CHAP. V.

CONDENSER AND ELECTROPHORUS.

50. If a conductor A, communicating with the ground, be placed near another conductor B, insulated and charged with a certain quantity of electricity E, a series of effects will ensue by the reciprocal inductive power of the two conductors, the result of which will be that the quantity of electricity with which B is charged, will be augmented in a certain proportion, depending on the distance between the two conductors through which the inductive force acts. The less this distance is the more energetic the induction will be, and the greater the augmentation of the charge of the conductor B.

To explain this, we are to consider that the electricity E, acting on the natural electricity of A, repels a certain quantity of the fluid of the same name to the earth, retaining on the side of A next to B the fluid of the contrary name. This fluid of a contrary name thus developed in A reacts upon the natural electricity of B, and produces a decomposition in the same manner, augmenting the charge E by the fluid of the same name decomposed, and expelling the other fluid to the more remote side of B. This increased fluid in B again acts upon the natural electricity of A, producing a further decomposition; and this series of reciprocal inductive actions producing a succession of decompositions in the two conductors, and accumulating a *tide* of contrary electricities on the sides of the conductors which are presented towards each other, goes on through an indefinite series of reciprocal actions, which, nevertheless, are accomplished in an inappreciable interval of time; so that, although the phenomenon in a strict sense is *physically* progressive, it is *practically* instantaneous.

To obtain an arithmetical measure of the amount of the augmentation of the electrical charge produced in this way, let us suppose that a quantity of electricity on B, which we shall take as the unit, is capable of decomposing on A a quantity which we shall express by m, and which is necessarily less than the unit, because nothing short of actual contact would enable the electricity of B to decompose an equal quantity of the electricity of A.

If, then, the unit of positive electricity act from B upon A, it will decompose the natural electricity, expelling a quantity of the positive fluid expressed by m, and retaining on the side next to B an equal quantity of the negative fluid. Now this negative fluid m, acting on the natural electricity of B at the same distance, will produce a proportionate decomposition, and will develop on the side of B next to A an additional quantity of the positive fluid, just so much less than m as m is less than 1. This quantity will therefore be $m \times m$, or m^2.

This quantity m^2 of positive fluid, again acting by induction on A, will develop, as before, a quantity of negative fluid expressed by $m^2 \times m$, or m^3. And in the same manner this will develop on B an additional quantity of positive fluid expressed by $m^3 \times m$, or m^4. These inductive reactions being indefinitely repeated, let the total quantity of positive electricity developed on B be expressed by P, and the total quantity of negative electricity developed on A by N, we shall have

$$P = 1 + m^2 + m^4 + m^6 + \ldots \ldots \text{ \&c. } ad \ inf.$$
$$N = m + m^3 + m^5 + m^7 + \ldots \ldots \text{ \&c. } ad \ inf.$$

Each of these is a geometrical series; and, since m is less than 1, they are decreasing series. Now it is proved in arithmetic, that although the number of terms in such series be unlimited, their sum is finite, and that the sum of the unlimited number of terms composing the first series is $\dfrac{1}{1-m^2}$, and that of the second $\dfrac{m}{1-m^2}$. We shall therefore have

$$P = \frac{1}{1-m^2}, \quad N = \frac{m}{1-m^2}.$$

In this case we have supposed the original charge of the conductor B to be the unit. If it consist of the number of units expressed by E, we shall have

$$P = \frac{E}{1-m^2}, \quad N = \frac{m \times E}{1-m^2}.$$

It follows, therefore, that the original charge E of the conductor B has been augmented in the ratio of 1 to $1-m^2$ by the proximity of the conductor A.

The less is the distance between the conductors A and B, the more nearly m will be equal to 1, and therefore the greater will be the ratio of 1 to $1-m^2$, and consequently the greater will be the augmentation of the electrical charge of B produced by the presence of A.

For example, suppose that A be brought so near B, that the positive fluid on B will develop nine tenths of its own quantity of negative fluid on A. In that case $m=\frac{9}{10}=0\cdot9$. Hence it appears, that $1-m^2=1-0\cdot81=0\cdot19$; and, consequently, the charge of B will be augmented in the ratio of 1 to $0\cdot19$, or of 100 to 19.

51. **The condenser.**—In such cases the electricity is said to be *condensed* on the conductor B by the inductive action of the conductor A, and apparatus constructed for producing this effect are called *condensers*.

52. **Dissimulated or latent electricity.** — The electricity developed in such cases on the conductor A is subject to the anomalous condition of being incapable of passing away, though a conductor be applied to it. In fact, the conductor A in the preceding experiment is supposed to be connected with the earth by conducting matter, such as chain, metallic column, or wire. Yet the charge of electricity N does not pass to the earth, as it would immediately do if the conductor B were removed.

In like manner, all that portion of the positive fluid P which is developed on B by the inductive action of A, is held there by the influence of A, and cannot escape even if the conductors be applied in contact with it.

Electricity thus developed upon conductors and retained there by the inductive action of other conductors, is said to be *latent* or *dissimulated*. It can always be set *free* by the removal of the conductors by whose induction it is dissimulated.

53. **Free electricity** is that which is developed independently of induction, or which, being first developed by induction, is afterwards liberated from the inductive action.

In the process above described, that part of the charge P of the conductor B which is expressed by E, and which was imparted to B before the approach of the conductor A, is *free*, and continues to be free after the approach of A. If a conductor connected with the earth be brought into contact with B, this electricity E will escape by it; but all the remaining charge of B will remain, so long as the conductor A is maintained in its position.

If, however, E be discharged from B, the charge which remains will not be capable of retaining in the dissimulated state so great a quantity of negative fluid on A as before. A part will be accordingly set free, and if A be maintained in connection with the ground it will escape. If A be insulated, it will be charged with *it still, but in a free state.*

If this free electricity be discharged from A, the remaining charge will not be capable of retaining in the latent state so large a quantity of positive fluid on B as previously, and a part of what was dissimulated will accordingly be set free, and may be discharged.

In this manner, by alternate discharges from the one and the other conductor, the dissimulated charges may be gradually liberated and dismissed, without removing the conductors from one another or suspending their inductive action.

54. **Condensers** are constructed in various forms, according to the strength of the electric charges they are intended to receive. Those which are designed for strong charges require to have the two conductors separated by a nonconducting medium of some considerable thickness, since, otherwise, the attraction of the opposite fluids diffused on A and B would take effect; and they would rush to each other across the separating space, breaking their way through the insulating medium which divides them. In this case the distance between A and B being considerable, the condensing power will not be great, nor is it necessary to be so, since the charges of electricity are by the supposition not small or feeble.

In case of feeble charges, the space separating the conductors may be proportionally small, and, consequently, the condensing power will be greater.

Condensers are usually constructed with two equal circular plates, either of solid metal or having a metallic coating.

55. **Collecting and condensing plates.** — The plate corresponding to the conductor A in the preceding paragraphs is called the *condensing plate*, and that which corresponds to B the *collecting plate*. The collecting plate is put in communication with the body whose electrical state it is required to examine by the agency of the condenser, and the condensing plate is put in communication with the ground.

56. **Cuthbertson's condenser** is represented in *fig.* 26.

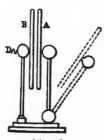

Fig. 26.

The collecting plate B is supported on a glass pillar, and communicates by a chain attached to the hook D with the source of electricity under examination. The condensing plate A is supported on a brass pillar, movable on a hinge, and communicating with the ground. By means of the hinge the disc A may be moved to or from B. The space between the plates in this case may be merely air, or, if strong charges are used, a plate of glass may be interposed.

When used for feeble charges, it is usual to cover the condensing plate with a thin coating of varnished silk, or simply with a coating of resinous varnish. An instrument thus arranged is represented in *fig.* 27., where *b b'*, the condensing plate, is a disc of wood coated with varnished silk *t t'*. The collecting plate *c c'* has a glass handle *m*, by which it may be

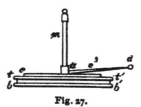

Fig. 27.

raised, and a rod of metal *a d* by which it may be put in communication with the source of electricity under examination.

The condensing plate in this case has generally sufficient conducting power when formed of wood, but may be also made of metal, and instead of varnished silk, it may be coated with gum-lac, resin, or any other insulator.

When the plate *c c'* has received its accumulated charge, its connection with the source of electricity is broken by removing the rod *a d*; and the plate *c c'* being raised from the condensing plate, the entire charge upon it becomes free, and may be submitted to an electroscopic test.

57. **The electrophorus** is an expedient by which a small charge of free electricity may be made to produce a charge of indefinite amount, which may be imparted to any insulated conductor This instrument consists of a circular cake, composed of a mixture of shell-lac, resin, and Venice turpentine, cast in a tin mould (*fig. 29.*). Upon this is laid a circular metallic disc B, rather less in diameter than A, having a glass handle.

Before applying the disc B, the resinous surface is electrified negatively by striking it several times with the fur of a cat. The disc B being then applied to the cake A, and the finger being at the same time pressed upon the disc B (*fig. 28.*), to establish a

Fig. 28.—ELECTROPHORUS.

communication with the ground through the body of the operator, a decomposition takes place by the inductive action of the negative fluid on the resin. The negative fluid escapes from the disc B through the body of the operator to the ground, and a positive charge remains, which is prevented from passing to the resin partly by the thin film of air which will always remain between them even when the plate B rests upon the resin, and partly by the non-*conducting* virtue of the resin.

When the disc B is thus charged with positive electricity kept latent on it by the influence of the negative fluid on A, the finger

Fig. 29.—ELECTROPHORUS.

being previously removed from the disc B, let it be raised from the resin and the electricity upon it, before dissimulated, will become free, and may be imparted to any insulated conductor adapted to receive it.

The charge of negative electricity remaining undiminished on the resin A, the operation may be indefinitely repeated; so that an insulated conductor may be charged to any extent, by giving to it the electric fluid drop by drop thus evolved on the disc B by the inductive action of A.

This is the origin of the name of the apparatus.

CHAP. VI.

ELECTROSCOPES

58. **Electroscopes** in general consist of two light conducting bodies freely suspended, which hang vertically and in contact, in their natural state. When electricity is imparted to them they repel each other, the angle of their divergence being greater or

less according to the intensity of the electricity diffused on them. These electroscopic substances may be charged with electricity either by direct communication with the electrified body, in which case their electricity will be similar to that of the body; or they may be acted upon inductively by the body under examination, in which case their electricity may be either similar or different from that of the body, according to the position in which the body is presented to them. In some cases the electroscope consists of a single light conductor, to which electricity of a known species is first imparted, and which will be attracted or repelled by the body under examination when presented to it, according as the electricities are like or unlike.

These instruments vary infinitely in form, arrangement, mode of application, and sensitiveness, according to the circumstances under which they are placed, and the intensities of the electricities of which they are expected to detect the presence, measure the intensity, or indicate the quality. In electroscopes, as in all other instruments of physical inquiry, the most delicate and sensitive is only the most advantageous, in those cases in which much delicacy and precision are required. A razor would be an ineffectual instrument for felling timber.

59. **Pith ball electroscope.**— One of the most simple and generally useful electroscopic instruments is the pendulous pith ball already mentioned (I.), the action of which may now be more fully explained. When an electrified body is presented to such a ball suspended by a silken thread, it acts by induction upon it, decomposing its natural fluid, attracting the constituent of the contrary name to the side of the ball nearest to it, and repelling the fluid of the same name to the side most remote from it. The body will thus act at once by attraction and repulsion upon the two fluids; but since that of a contrary name which it attracts is nearer to it than that of the same name which it repels, and equal in quantity, the attraction will prevail over the repulsion, and the ball will move towards the electrified body. When it touches it, the fluid of a contrary name, which is diffused round the point of contact, combining with the fluid diffused upon the body, will be neutralised, and the ball will remain charged with the fluid of the same name as that with which the body is electrified, and will consequently be repelled by it. Hence it will be understood why, as already mentioned, the pith ball in its neutral state is first attracted to an electrified body, and after contact with it repelled by it.

60. **The needle electroscope.** — The electric needle is an electroscopic apparatus, somewhat less simple, but more sensitive than the pendulum. It consists of a rod of copper terminated by

Fig. 30.

two metallic balls B and B', *fig*. 30., which are formed hollow in order to render them more light and sensitive. At the middle point of the rod which connects them is a conical cup, formed of steel or agate, suspended upon a fine point, so that the needle is exactly balanced, and capable of turning freely round the point of support in a horizontal plane, like a magnetic needle. A very feeble electrical action exerted upon either of the balls B or B' will be sufficient to put the needle in motion.

61. **Coulomb's electroscope.** — The electroscope of Coulomb, better known as the balance of torsion, is an apparatus still more sensitive and delicate, for indicating the existence and intensity of electrical force. A needle *g g'*, *fig*. 31., formed of gum-lac, is suspended by a fibre of raw silk. At one extremity it carries a small disc *e*, coated with metallic foil, and is so balanced at the point of suspension, that the needle resting horizontally is free to turn in either direction round the point of suspension. When it turns it produces a degree of torsion or twist of the fibre which suspends it, the reaction of which measures the force which turns the needle. Upon the glass cage *v v'*, which is cylindrical, is a graduated circle *d d'*,

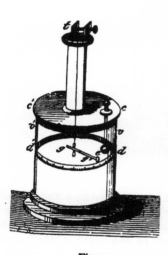

Fig. 31.

which measures the angle through which the needle is deflected. In the cover of the cage an aperture is made, through which may be introduced the electrified body whose force it is desired to indicate and measure by the apparatus.

62. **Quadrant electrometer.** — This instrument, which is generally used as an indicator on the conductors of electrical machines, consists of a pillar A B, *fig*. 32., of any conducting substance, terminated at the lower extremity by a ball B. A rod, also a conductor, of about half the length, terminated by a small pith ball D, plays on a centre C in a vertical plane, having behind it an ivory

Fig. 32.

D

semicircle graduated. When the ball B is charged with electricity, it repels the pith ball D, and the angle of repulsion measured on the graduated arc supplies a rough estimate of the intensity of the electricity.

. 63. **Gold leaf electroscope.** — A glass cylinder A B C D, *fig.* 33., is fixed on a brass stand E, and closed at the top by a.

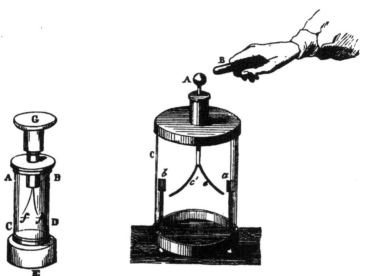

Fig. 33.   Fig. 34.

circular plate A B. The brass top G is connected by a metallic rod with two slips of gold leaf *f*, two or three inches in length, and half an inch in breadth. In their natural state they hang in contact, but when electricity is imparted to the plate G, the leaves becoming charged with it indicate its presence, and in some degree its intensity, by their divergence. On the sides of the glass cylinder opposite the gold leaves are attached strips of tinfoil, communicating with the ground. When the leaves diverge so much as to touch the sides of the cylinder, they give up their electricity to the tinfoil, and are discharged. This instrument may also be affected inductively. If an electrified body B (*fig.* 34.), be brought near to the knob A, its natural electricity will be decomposed; the fluid of the same name as that with which the body is charged will be repelled, will accumulate in the gold leaves *e e'*, and will cause them to diverge.

. 64. **The condensing electroscope** is an instrument which has the same analogy to the common electroscope, as the compound has to the simple microscope. An electroscope with such an appendage is represented in *fig. 35.* The condenser is screwed on the top, the condensing plate communicating with the electroscope, and the collecting plate being laid over it. When the collecting plate is put into communication with the source of electricity to be examined, a charge is produced by induction in the condensing plate under it, and a charge of a contrary name is collected in the electroscope, the leaves of which will diverge, in this case, with an electricity similar in name to that of the body under examination.

Fig. 35.

In the use of instruments of such extreme sensitiveness, many precautions are necessary to guard against disturbances, which would interfere with their indications, and expose the observer to errors. The plates of the condenser in some experiments may be exposed to chemical action, which, as will hereafter appear, is always combined with the development of electricity. In such cases, the condenser of the

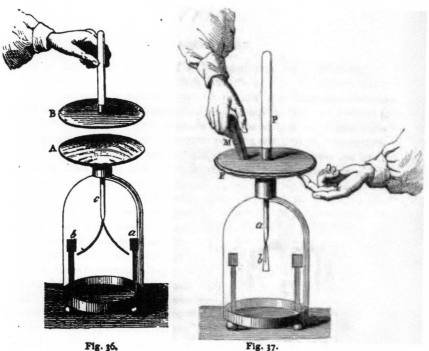

Fig. 36.   Fig. 37.

electroscope should be composed of gilt plates. The apparatus is sometimes included in a glass case, to protect it from atmospheric vicissitudes; and to preserve it from hygrometric effects, a cup of quicklime is placed in the case to absorb the humidity.

The instrument and the manner of experimenting with it is represented on a larger scale in *figs.* 36. and 37.

The plates of the condenser attached to electroscopes vary from four to ten inches in diameter. When greater dimensions are given to them it is difficult to make them with such precision as to ensure the exact contact of their surfaces.

Becquerel used plates of glass twenty inches in diameter, accurately ground together with emery, and coated with thin tinfoil. This apparatus had great sensibility, but as the metal was very oxidable, the results were disturbed by chemical effects not easily avoided. A coating of platinum or gold would have been more free from disturbing action.

CHAP. VII.

THE LEYDEN JAR.

65. THE inductive principle which has supplied the means, in the case of the condenser, of detecting and examining quantities of electricity so minute and so feeble as to escape all common tests, has placed, in the Leyden jar, an instrument at the disposal of the electrician, by which artificial electricity may be accumulated in quantities so unlimited, as to enable him to copy in some of its most conspicuous effects the lightning of the clouds.

To understand the principle of the Leyden jar, which at one time excited the astonishment of all Europe, it is only necessary to investigate the effect of a condenser of considerable magnitude placed in connection, not with feeble, but with energetic sources of electricity, such as the prime conductor of an electrical machine. In such case it would be evidently necessary, that the collecting and condensing plates should be separated by a non-conducting medium, of suffi-

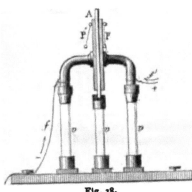

Fig. 38.

cient resistance to prevent the union of the powerful charges, with which they would be invested.

Let P, *fig.* 38., represent the collecting plate of such a condenser, connected by a chain *f'* with the conductor of an electric machine; and let P' be the condensing plate connected by a chain *f* with the ground. Let A be a plate of glass interposed between P and P'.

Let *e* express the quantity of electricity with which a superficial unit of the conductor is charged. It follows that *e* will also express the *free* electricity on every superficial unit of the collecting plate P; and if the total charge on each superficial unit of P, free and dissimulated, be expressed by *a*, we shall, according to what has been already explained, have

$$a = \frac{e}{1-m^2}.$$

The charge on the superficial unit of the condensing plate P' being expressed by *a'*, we shall have

$$a' = m \times a = \frac{m \times e}{1-m^2},$$

which will be wholly dissimulated.

If *s* express the common magnitude of the two plates P' and P, and E express the entire quantity of electricity accumulated on P, and E' that accumulated on P', we shall have

$$E = s \times a = \frac{s \times e}{1-m^2},$$

$$E' = s \times a' = \frac{s \times m \times e}{1-m^2}.$$

It is evident, therefore, that the quantity of electricity with which the plates P and P' will be charged, will be augmented, firstly, with the magnitude (*s*) of the plates; secondly, with the intensity (*e*) of the electricity produced by the machine upon the conductor; and thirdly, with the thinness of the glass plate A which separates the plates P' and P. The thinner this plate is, the more nearly equal to 1 will be the number *m*, and consequently the less will be $1-m^2$, and the greater the quantity E.

When the machine has been worked until *e* ceases to increase, the charge of the plates will have attained its maximum. Let the chains *f* and *f'* be then removed, so that the plates P and P' shall be insulated, being charged with the quantities of electricity of contrary names expressed by E and E'.

If a metallic wire, or any other conductor, be now placed so as to connect the plate P with the plate P', the free electricity on the former passing along the conductor will flow to the plate P' where it will combine with or neutralise a part of the dissimulated fluid. This last, being thus diminished in quantity, will retain by its attraction a less quantity of the fluid on P' a corresponding quantity of which will be liberated, and will therefore pass along the wire to the plate P', where it will neutralise another portion of the dissimulated fluid; and this process of reciprocal neutralisation, liberation, and conduction will go on until the entire charge E' upon the plate P' has been neutralised by a corresponding part of the fluid E originally diffused on the plate P.

Although these effects are strictly progressive, they are practically instantaneous. The current of free electricity flows through the wire, neutralises the charge ʀ′, and liberates all the dissimulated part of ʀ in an interval so short as to be quite inappreciable. In whatever point of view the power of conduction may be regarded, a sudden and violent change in the electrical condition of the wire must attend the phenomenon. If the wire be regarded merely as a channel of communication, a sort of pipe or conduit through which the electric fluid passes from ᴘ to ᴘ′, as some consider it, so large an afflux of electricity may be expected to be attended with some violent effects. If, on the other hand, the opposite fluids are reduced to their natural state, by decomposing successively the natural electricity of the parts of the wire, and taking from the elements of the decomposed fluid the electricities necessary to satisfy their respective attractions, a still more powerful effect may be anticipated from so great and sudden a change.

It appears, from what has been stated, that all the negative electricity collected upon the plate ᴘ′ is dissimulated by the attraction of the greater portion of positive fluid collected upon ᴘ; and that, on the other hand, the negative electricity on ᴘ′, dissimulating an equal quantity of the positive fluid on ᴘ, leaves the excess free; and this excess acting upon the electric pendulum, repels the ball from ᴘ. But if the apparatus be so arranged, as

Fig. 39.

shown in *fig.* 39., that the two plates may be withdrawn from each other, and from the intermediate plate A, the chief part or the whole of the fluids upon ᴘ and ᴘ′ may be rendered free. For this purpose, after the plates have been charged in the manner described above, let the wire *f′*, connecting ᴘ with the electrical machine, and the wire *f*, connecting ᴘ′ with the ground, be both detached from the pillars, so as to leave the plates ᴘ and ᴘ′ at once insulated and charged. This being done, if the plates be removed from A, as shown in *fig.* 39., the electric pendulum on P′, as well as that on P, will be immediately repelled, showing that the negative fluid on P′, or part of it, is rendered free by the removal of the plate P.

The plates, P and P′, being charged in the manner described, and the wires *f* and *f′* being detached, so as to leave them thus charged upon the insulating pillars, they may be discharged either by slow degrees or instantaneously.

To discharge them by slow degrees, let a metallic knob, which is in connection with the ground, be applied to P, and it will draw off from it all the positive fluid which is not dissimulated by the negative fluid on P′. But the plate P being at some distance, however small, from the plate P′, can only dissimulate upon P′ a portion of fluid somewhat less than its own quantity.

It will, therefore, follow, that after the knob has been applied to P, the quantity of negative fluid on P′ will exceed the quantity of positive fluid on P, and, consequently, a certain portion of the negative fluid on P′ will be free; and this will be, accordingly, rendered manifest by the repulsion of the electrical pendulum on P′. Meanwhile all the positive electricity on P being dissimulated, the pendulum on P will not be repelled.

It appears, therefore, that the relative electrical conditions of the two plates P and P′ have been interchanged, P′ being now that which repels the pendulum by its surplus free electricity, while P does not affect it.

If the conducting knob connected with the ground be now applied to P′, it will draw off the free electricity, and the pendulum on P′ will be no longer repelled. It will at the same time liberate a portion of the electricity on P, which will be indicated by the repulsion of the pendulum.

The same process may then be repeated upon P, and so on alternately until all the electricity upon the two plates has been drained off, as it were, drop by drop.

To discharge the plates instantaneously, it is only necessary to connect them electrically by any conductor, such as a rod or wire of metal placed in contact with each. The effect of such a conduction will be, to produce in an inappreciable instant of time all the interchanges which have been just described. At first the free electricity of P will rush towards P′, and a portion of the dissimulated fluid on P′, being thus liberated, will rush towards P; a further portion of the fluid on which being thereby liberated, will rush towards P′; and so on. Although these effects, regarded theoretically, must be considered as taking place successively, they will be practically instantaneous, the whole interval of their accomplishment being inappreciable.

66. **The fulminating pane** was one of the final and most simple forms given to the condenser.

This consisted of a glass plate, *fig.* 40., enclosed in a frame, and having a square leaf of tinfoil attached to each side of it, the leaf on one side being connected with the frame by a ribbon of foil. To charge this, the operator places the side on which the foil is connected with the frame by the ribbon downwards, and connects the ribbon with the ground by a chain or other conductor. He then connects the upper leaf of foil E with the prime conductor of the machine by means of a jointed discharger C, as shown in the figure. The machine being worked, the upper leaf becomes charged with positive electricity, which, acting upon the natural electricities of the lower leaf, decomposes them, and produces the same effects as have been described in the case of the apparatus *fig.* 39.; and the two leaves of tinfoil will become charged with opposite electricities, as in the former case, and may be discharged either gradually or instantaneously, in the manner already described.

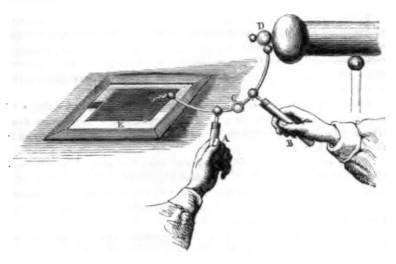

Fig. 40.

The class of phenomena evolved by these expedients has been attended with some of the most remarkable effects presented in the whole domain of physical research. If two such conductors as the plates of tinfoil attached to the fulminating pane, being strongly charged in the manner just described, be put in communication by the human body, which may be done by touching one plate with the fingers of one hand, and the other with the fingers of the other, the two electric fluids, in rushing towards each other, pass through the body, producing the phenomenon now rendered so familiar, called the *electric shock*, and which, though so little regarded at present, produced, when first experienced, the most extraordinary impressions.

Like many other important scientific facts, the discovery of the electric shock, and of the apparatus by which it is most commonly produced, was the result of accident. In 1746 the celebrated Musschenbroeck, having fixed a metallic rod in the cork of a bottle filled with water, he presented it to the electrical machine for the purpose of electrifying the water, holding at the same time the bottle in his hand by its external surface, without touching the metallic rod by which the electricity was conducted to the water. By this accidental circumstance a real condenser was formed, of which the experimenter was totally unconscious, and the principle of which was then wholly unknown. The water in contact with the internal surface of the bottle, and receiving the electricity by the metallic rod from the machine, corresponded to the plate P (*fig.* 38.), and the metallic rod to the conducting wire *f*. The hand of the operator applied to the external surface of the bottle corresponded to the plate P′, and the body of the operator communicating with the ground corresponded to the wire *f*. In the same manner exactly, therefore, as in the case of the apparatus shown in *fig.* 39., the inside of the bottle acquired a strong charge of positive, and the outside an almost equally strong charge of negative, electricity. The operator, then ignorant of the effects, withdrawing the bottle from the machine, and desiring to remove from the mouth of it the wire by which it was charged, applied his left hand to the latter for that purpose, still holding the bottle by its exterior surface in his right hand. His arms and body, therefore, becoming a conductor between the interior and exterior surfaces of the bottle, the electric fluids, in reuniting, passed through him, and inflicted, for the first time, the nervous commotion now known as the electric shock. Nothing could exceed the astonishment and consternation of the operator at this unexpected sensation, and in describing it in a letter addressed immediately afterwards to Reaumur, he declared that for the whole kingdom of France he would not repeat the experiment.

The experiment, however, was soon repeated in different parts of Europe, and the apparatus by which it was produced received a more convenient form, the water being replaced by tinfoil attached to the interior of the jar, which received the name of the Leyden jar, or Leyden phial, the city of Leyden being the place where its remarkable effects were first exhibited.

67. **The Leyden Jar.** — In experimental researches, therefore, the form which is commonly given to the apparatus, with a view to develop the above effects, is that of a cylinder or jar, A B (*fig.* 41.), having a wide mouth and a flat bottom

Fig. 40.

The shaded part terminating at c is a coating of tinfoil placed on the bottom and sides of the jar, a similar coating being situated on the corresponding parts of the interior surface. To improve the insulating power of the glass, it is coated above the edge of the tinfoil with a varnish of gum-lac, which also renders it more proof against the deposition of moisture. A metallic rod, terminated in a ball D, descends into the jar, and is fixed in contact with the inner coating.

To understand the action of this apparatus it is only necessary to consider the inner coating and the metallic rod as representing the metallic surface P, fig. 38, and the outer surface P, the jar itself forming the part of the intervening non-conducting medium. If the ball D be put in communication by a metallic chain with the conductor of the electric machine, and the external coating c with the ground, the jar will become charged with electricity, in the same manner and on the same principles exactly as has been explained in the case of the metallic surfaces P and P, fig. 38.

If, when a charge of electricity is thus communicated to the jar, the communication between D and the conductor be removed, the charge will remain accumulated on the inner coating of the jar. If in this case a metallic communication be made between the ball D and the outer coating, the two opposite electricities on the inside and outside of the jar will rush towards each other, and will suddenly combine. In this case there is no essential distinction between the functions of the outer and inner coating of the jar, as may be shown by connecting the inner coating with the ground and the outer coating with the conductor. For this purpose it is only necessary to place the jar upon an insulating stand, surrounding it by a metallic chain in contact with its outer coating, which should be carried to the conductor of the

Fig. 41.

machine; while the ball D, which communicates with the inner coating, is connected by another chain to the ground. In this case the electricity will flow from the conductor to the outer coating, and will be accumulated there by the inductive action of the inner coating, and all the effects will take place as before.

If, after the jar is thus charged, the communication between the outer coating and the conductor be removed, and a metallic communication be made between the inner and outer coating, the electricities will, as before, rush towards each other and combine, and the jar will be restored to its natural state.

To charge the jar internally, it will be sufficient to hold it with the hand in contact with the external coating, *fig.* 42., presenting the ball c to the conductor of the machine. The electricity will flow from the conductor to the inner coating, and the external coating will act inductively, being connected through the hand and body of the operator with the earth.

Like the apparatus shown in *fig.* 38., the Leyden jar may be discharged either gradually or instantaneously. To discharge it instantaneously, without suffering the electric shock, let the jar A, *fig.* 43., be placed with its ex-

Fig. 43.

ternal coating in communication with the ground, and let the operator, applying one knob c' of a jointed discharger D to the external coating, bring the other c near to the knob B of the jar. Under these circumstances, the two fluids rushing towards each other, along the arms of the discharger, will reunite, and the jar will be discharged.

The process of slow discharge may be executed in the following manner. The rod which enters the jar has attached to the top of it a small bell, I, *fig.* 44.; placed near the bottle, upon a convenient stand, is a metallic rod. P, supporting a similar bell, E, level with I; and an electric pendulum, consisting of a small copper ball, suspended by a silken thread, hangs between

Fig. 44.

the two bells, so that it can be attracted and repelled by the one and the other. Supposing the jar to be charged, and its external coating connected with P by a conductor *e*, and the stand to be insulated, the free part of the positive electricity on the interior of the jar will attract the copper ball, which will strike the bell I; and becoming charged with positive electricity, will be repelled by I, and attracted by E; it will, therefore, strike against E, and will impart to it the positive electricity, and receive from it a charge of negative electricity, proceeding from the outside coating of the jar through the pillar P. The copper ball being negatively electrified, will then be repelled by E, and attracted by I, against which it will strike, and will convey to the interior of the jar the negative fluid which it carries, receiving in exchange an equal charge of the positive fluid.

In this way the pendulum will oscillate between the two bells, conveying successive portions of positive electricity from the interior to the exterior, and of negative electricity from the exterior to the interior.

Effect of the metallic coatings.—The metallic coatings of the jar have no other effect than to conduct the electricity to the surface of the glass, and when there to afford it a free passage from point to point. Any other conductor would, abstractedly considered, serve the same purpose; and metallic foil is selected only for the facility and convenience with which it may be adapted to the form of the glass, and permanently attached to it. That like effects would attend the use of any other conductor may be easily shown.

68. **Experimental proof that the charge adheres to the glass, and not to the coating.**—The electricity with which the jar is charged in this case resides, therefore, on the glass, or on the conductor by which it passes to the glass, or is shared by these.

To determine where it resides, it is only necessary to provide means of separating the jar from the coating after it has been charged, and examining the electrical state of the one and the other. For this purpose let a glass jar B, *fig.* 45., be provided, having a loose cylinder of metal c fitted to its interior, which can be placed in it or withdrawn from it at pleasure, and a similar loose cylinder A fitted to its exterior. The jar being placed in the external cylinder A, and the internal cylinder c being inserted in it, as shown at D, let it be charged with electricity by the machine in the manner already described. Let the internal cylinder be

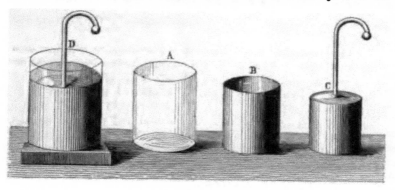

Fig. 45.

then removed, and let the jar be raised out of the external cylinder. The two cylinders, being then tested by an electroscopic apparatus, will be found to be in their natural state. But if an electroscope be brought within the influence of the internal or external surface of the glass jar, it will betray the presence of the one or the other species of electricity. If the glass jar be then inserted in another metallic cylinder made to fit it externally, and a similar metallic cylinder made to fit it internally be inserted in it, it will be found to be charged as if no change had taken place. On connecting by metallic communication the interior with the exterior, the opposite electricities will rush towards each other and combine. It is evident, therefore, that the seat of the electricity, when a jar is charged, is not the metallic coating, but the surface of the glass under it.

Fig. 46.

69. **Improved form of the Leyden jar.—** An improved form of the Leyden jar is represented in *fig.* 46. Besides the provisions which

have been already explained, there is attached to this
hollow brass cup c. cemented into a glass tube. This
passes through the wooden disc which forms the cone of th
and is fastened to it. It reaches to the bottom of the jar. A
munication is formed between c and the internal coating by a
wire terminating in the knob D. This wire, passing loosely th
a small hole in the top, may be removed at pleasure for the p
of cutting off the communication between the cup and the
rior coating. This wire does not extend quite to the bott
the jar, but the lower part of the tube is coated with t
which is in contact with the wire, and extends to the inner c
of the jar.

At the bottom of the jar a hook is provided, by which a
may be suspended so as to form a communication between th
ternal coating and other bodies. When a jar of this kind i
charged, the wire may be removed or allowed to fall out l
verting the jar, in which case the jar will remain charged, sin
communication exists between its internal and external co
and as the internal coating is protected from the contact c
external air, the absorption of electricity in this case is prev
An electric charge may thus be transferred from place to
and preserved for any length of time.

In the construction of cylindrical jars it is not always possi
obtain glass of uniform thickness, for which reason jars are
times provided of a spherical form.

70. **Lane's discharging electrometer.**—*Fig.* 47. cons

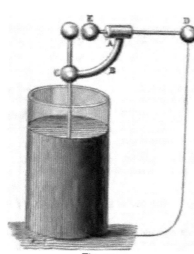

a bent glass rod, A B C, a
end, c, of which a soc
placed, by which it m
attached to a conduct
to the rod of a Leyde
as shown in the figure
the other end is attac
short cylindrical rod A p
by a hole, through wl
brass rod D E slides, l
balls D and E at its extrei
When the instrument is
one of the balls, D fc
ample, is put in commu
tion with the ground, o
the external coating c
jar. The rod D E is the
vanced through the l
until it comes so near

Fig. 47.

ball of the jar that a spark passes between them, and the jar is discharged. The force of the charge is estimated by the distance between the balls at which the spark passes.

The indications of this instrument are modified by so many causes, that as a measure of the electric force of the charge it has but little value. The distance through which the spark will be projected will vary with the hygrometric state of the air, with its temperature, and probably with other physical conditions. It will also vary with the magnitude and form of the conductor, or the knob of the jar to which it is presented.

71. **Cuthbertson's discharging electrometer.**—*Fig.* 48. consists of two glass pillars supported on a wooden table; upon these

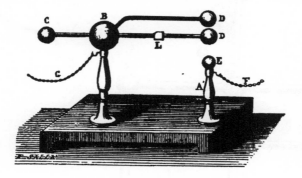

Fig. 48.

are fixed two brass balls B and E. Through the ball B an opening is cut, in which the lever C D' terminated in brass balls is inserted, and in which it is balanced on a knife edge. A small sliding weight L is placed on the arm B D', by the adjustment of which any desired preponderance can be given to the opposite arm C D, which is the heavier when B D' is unloaded. The arm B D' is graduated to indicate the number of grains weight at the centre of the ball D', which would be in exact equilibrium with the preponderance which C has in each position of L. Another arm B D, fixed to the ball B, is terminated in a ball D, which is in contact with D', when the lever C D' is horizontal. By the chain G the balls C, D, and D' can be put in communication with the internal coating of the jar, the free electricity of which will therefore charge the balls D and D', and the ball E is put in communication with the external coating by the chain F, the electricity of which, being dissimulated, will not affect the ball E. The balls D and D', being similarly electrified, will repel each other, and as soon as the charge of the jar is so great that the repulsive force given to the balls D and D′ is sufficient to overcome the preponderance of the ball C, the ball D′ will be repelled by D; and when the former comes into contact with E, the jar will be discharged.

Another form of this instrument, with a quadrant electrometer attached, is shown in *fig.* 49., the corresponding parts being indi-

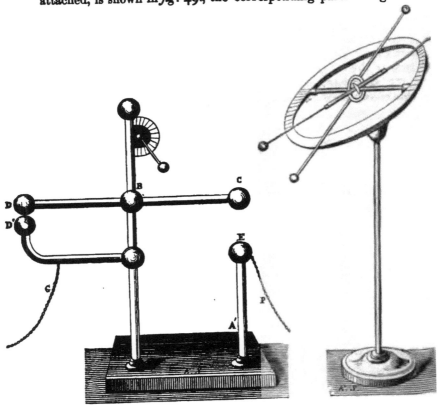

Fig. 49.   Fig. 50.

cated by the same letters. In this case D and D′, receiving electricity from the inner coating, repel each other. The knife edge is within B, and the repulsion depresses C until it touches E, when the discharge is effected.

72. **Harris's circular electrometer.** — *Fig.* 50. is an instrument which is often substituted with advantage for the quadrant. It depends on the same principle, but is more sensitive and accurate.

73. **Charging a series of jars by cascade.** — In charging a single jar, an unlimited number of jars, connected together by *conductors*, may be charged with very nearly the same quantity

ctricity. For this purpose let the series of jars be placed on
ting stools, as represented in *fig.* 51. and let c be metallic

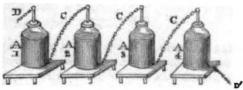

Fig. 51.

s connecting the external coating of each jar with the in-
l coating of the succeeding one. Let D be a chain connecting
st jar with the conductor of the machine, and D' another chain
cting the last jar with the ground. The electricity con-
l to the inner coating of the first jar A acts by induction on
xternal coating of the first jar, attracting the negative elec-
y to the surface, and repelling the positive electricity through
ain c to the inner coating of the second jar. This charge of
ve electricity in the second jar acts in like manner induc-
on the external coating of this jar, attracting the negative
icity there, and repelling the positive electricity through the
c to the internal coating of the third jar ; and in the same
er the internal coating of every succeeding jar in the series
e charged with positive electricity, and its internal coating
negative electricity. If, while the series is insulated, a dis-
er be made to connect the inner coating of the first with the
coating of the last jar, the opposite electricities will rush
ds each other, and the series of jars will be restored to their
al state.

Electric battery. — When several jars are thus combined
ain a more energetic discharge than could be formed by a
jar, the system is called an *electric battery*, and the method
rging it, explained above, is called *charging by cascade.*
er the jars have been thus charged, the chains connecting
uter coating of each jar with the inner coating of the suc-
ng one are removed, and the knobs are all connected one
another by chains or metallic rods, so as to place all the in-
l coatings in electric connection, and the outer coatings are
rly connected. By this expedient the system of jars is ren-
equivalent to a single jar, the magnitude of whose coated
ce would be equal to the sum of all the surfaces of the series
s. The battery would then be discharged, by placing a con-
r between the outer coating of any of the jars and one of the
s.

If s express the total magnitude of the coating of the series of jars, the total charge of the battery will be expressed approximately by

$$\text{E} = \frac{s \times e}{1 - m^2}.$$

75. **Common electric battery.**—It is not always convenient however, to practise this method. The jars composing the battery are commonly placed in a box, as represented in *fig.* 52., coated

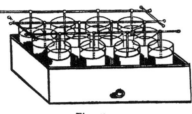

Fig. 52.

on the inside with tinfoil, so as to form a metallic communication between the external coating of all the jars. The knobs, which communicate with their internal coating, are connected by a series of metallic rods in the manner represented in the figure; so that there is a continuous metallic communication between all the internal coatings. If the

Fig. 53.

metallic rods which thus communicate with the inner coating be placed in communication with the conductor of a machine, while the box containing the jars is placed in metallic communication with the earth, the battery will be charged according to the principles already explained in the case of a single jar, and the force of its charge will be equal to the force of the charge of a single jar, the magnitude of whose external and internal coating, would be equal to the sum of the internal and external coating of all the jars composing the battery.

The manner in which a battery is charged by connecting it with a conductor of an electric machine, is shown in *fig.* 53., an electrometer being usually fixed on one of the pivots to indicate the strength of the charge.

The method of discharging the battery and transmitting its charge through an object submitted to experiment, is shown in *fig.* 54. The object under experiment is placed on a convenient

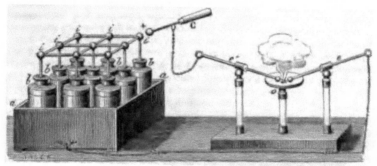

Fig. 54.

stand between the knobs of two insulated conductors, one of which communicates with the outside coating of one of the jars. The other is put in communication with the inside coating of a jar, by means of a jointed discharger.

76. **To estimate the amount of the charge** of a jar or battery, it is to be considered that the internal coating is, in effect, a continuation of the conductor; and if the jars had no external coating, the communication of the internal coating with the conductor would be attended with no other effect, than the distribution of the electricity over the conductor and the internal coating, according to the laws of electrical equilibrium; but the effect of the external coating is to dissimulate or render latent the electricity as it flows from the conductor, so that the repulsion of the part of it which remains free is less than the expansive force of the electricity of the conductor, and a stream of the fluid continues to flow accordingly from the conductor to the internal coating; and this process continues until the increasing force of the free

electricity on the internal coating of the jars becomes so gre
that the force of the fluid on the conductor can no longer ov‹
come it, and thus the flow of electricity to the jars from the c‹
ductor will cease.

It follows, therefore, that during the process of charging the jars,
depth or tension of the electricity on the conductor, is just so much grea
than that of the free electricity on the interior of the jars, as is sufficient
sustain the flow of electricity from the one to the other; and as this
necessarily so extremely minute an excess as to be insensible to any meas
which could be applied to it, it may be assumed that the depth of electric
on the conductor is always equal to that of the free electricity on the
terior of the jars. If e therefore express the actual depth of the elect
fluid at any time on the interior coating $(1-m^2) \times e$ will express the dep
of the free electricity; and since, throughout the process, m does not chan
its value, it follows that the actual depth of electricity, and therefore t
actual magnitude of the charge, is proportionate to the depth of free el‹
tricity on the interior of the jar, which is sensibly the same as the depth
free electricity on the conductor. It follows, therefore, that the magnitu
of the charge, whether of a single jar or several, will always be proportion‹
to the depth of electricity on the conductor of the machine from which t
charge is derived. If, therefore, during the process of charging a jar
battery, an electrometer be attached to the conductor, this instrument w
at first give indications of a very feeble electricity, the chief part of the flu
evolved being dissimulated on the inside of the jars; but as the charge i
creases, the indications of an increased depth of fluid on the conduc‹
become apparent; and at length, when no more fluid can pass from the c‹
ductor to the jars, the electrometer becomes stationary, and the fluid evolv
by the machine escapes from the points or into the circumjacent air.

The quadrant electrometer, described in (62.), is the indicat
commonly used for this purpose, and is inserted in a hole on t
conductor. When the pith ball attains its maximum elevation, t
charge of the jars may be considered as complete. The char‹
which a jar is capable of receiving, besides being limited by t
strength of the glass to resist the mutual attraction of the opposi
fluids, and the imperfect insulating force of that part of the j
which is not coated, is also limited by the imperfect insulati‹
force of the air itself. If other causes, therefore, allowed ‹
unlimited flow of electricity to the jar, its discharge would ‹
length take place, by the elasticity of the free electricity within
surmounting the confining pressure of the air, and accordingly tl
fluid of the interior would pass over the mouth of the jar, a‹
unite with the opposite fluid of the exterior surface.

CHAP. VIII.

LAWS OF ELECTRICAL FORCES.

77. Electric forces investigated by Coulomb. — It is not enough to ascertain the principles which govern the decomposition of the natural electricity of bodies, and the reciprocal attraction and repulsion of the constituent fluids. It is also necessary to determine the actual amount of force exerted by each fluid in repelling fluid of the like or attracting fluid of the opposite kind, and how the intensity of this attraction is varied, by varying the distance between the bodies which are invested by the attracting or repelling fluids.

By a series of experimental researches, which rendered his name for ever memorable, *Coulomb* solved this difficult and delicate problem, measuring with admirable adroitness and precision these minute forces, by means of his electroscope or balance of torsion, already described (61.).

78. Proof-plane. — The electricity of which the force was to be estimated was taken up from the surface of the electrified body upon a small circular disc c, *fig.* 55., coated with metallic foil, and attached to the extremity of a delicate rod or handle, A B, of gum-lac. This disc, called a *proof-plane*, was presented to the ball suspended in the electrometer of torsion (61.), and the intensity of its attraction or repulsion was measured, by the number of degrees through which the suspending fibre or wire was twisted by it.

The extreme degree of sensibility of this apparatus may be conceived, when it is stated that a force equal to the 340th part of a grain was sufficient to turn it through 360 degrees ; and since the reaction of torsion is proportional to the angle of torsion, the force necessary to make the needle move through one degree would be only the 122400th part of a grain. Thus this balance was capable of dividing a force equal to a single grain weight into 122400 parts, and rendering the effect of each part distinctly observable and measurable.

Fig. 55.

79. Law of electrical force similar to that of gravitation. — By these researches it was established that the attraction and repulsion of the electric fluids, like the force of gravitation, and other physical influences which radiate from a centre, vary according to the common law of the *inverse square of the distance* ; that is to say, the attraction or repulsion exerted by a body charged with electricity, or, to speak more correctly, by the electricity with which such a body is charged, increases in the same proportion as

the square of the distance from the body on which it acts is dimi
nished, and diminishes as the square of that distance is increased

In general, if f express the force exerted by any quantity o
electric fluid, positive or negative, at the unit of distance, $\dfrac{f}{D^2}$ wil
express the force which the same quantity of the same fluid wil
exert at the distance D.

In like manner, if the quantity of fluid, taken as the unit, exercis
at the distance D the force expressed by $\dfrac{f}{D^2}$, the quantity expresse
by E, will exert at the same distance D the force F expressed by

$$F = \frac{f \times E}{D^2}.$$

These formulæ have been tested by numerous experiments made
under every possible variety of conditions, and have been found to
represent the phenomena with the greatest precision.

80. **The distribution of the electric fluid on conductors** can
be deduced as a mathematical consequence of the laws of attraction
and repulsion, which have been explained above, combined with
the property in virtue of which conductors give free play to these
forces. The conclusions thus deduced may further be verified by
the *proof-plane* and electrometer of torsion, by means of which the
fluid diffused upon a conductor may be *gauged*, so that its depth
or intensity at every point may be exactly ascertained; and such

Fig. 56.

depths and intensities have accordingly been found to accord perfectly with the results of theory.

81. **It is confined to their surfaces.** — If an electrified con-

ductor be pierced with holes, a little greater than the proof-plane, (*fig.* 56.) to different depths, that plane, inserted so as to touch the bottom of these holes, will take up no electricity.

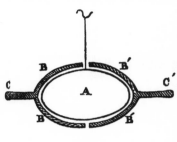

Fig. 57.

If a spheroidal metallic body A (*fig.* 57.), suspended by a silken thread, be electrified, and two thin hollow caps, B B and B' B', made to fit it, coated on their inside surface with metallic foil, and having insulating handles c c' of gum-lac, be applied to it, on withdrawing them the spheroid will be deprived of its electricity, the fluid being taken off by the caps.

The same experiment may be performed conveniently by the apparatus shown in *fig.* 58., consisting of a metallic spheroid sup-

Fig. 58.

ported on an insulating pillar, and two hollow hemispheroids of corresponding magnitude, with insulating handles.

82. **The charge of electricity** upon a conductor being therefore superficial, it follows that its depth or intensity, other things being the same, will be less in proportion as the total surface of the conductor is greater. This may be very elegantly illustrated by means of a band of metallic foil wound round an insulated cylinder, *fig.* 59. A quadrant electrometer is mounted on the end of the insulated cylinder to indicate the varying intensity. The band of foil being completely rolled up, let the conductor be strongly charged by means of a machine. The electrometer will then show a strong charge, the ball being thrown up to 50° or 60°.

The machine being then detached, let the band of foil be gradual unrolled so as to enlarge the surface of the conductor. Accordii

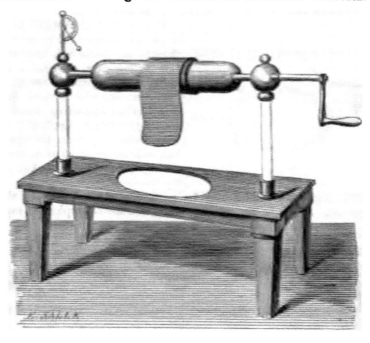

Fig. 59.

as this takes place, the ball of the electrometer will fall to a le: and less angle; and if the band be again coiled up, the ball wi be again repelled, showing that the intensity of the electricit increases as the surface is diminished, and *vice versâ*.

83. **Faraday's apparatus** (*fig.* 60.) also illustrates the super ficial distribution of electricity in a striking manner. A conic muslin bag, like a butterfly net, is attached to an insulated rin of metallic wire. If it be electrified, it will be found that the elec tricity will be confined to its exterior surface. This may be a certained by the proof-plane. By means of two insulated sil threads fixed to the apex of the cone, one within and the othe without, as shown in the figure, the bag may be turned inside ou so that the exterior surface shall become the interior, and *vi versâ*. The electricity will always pass to the exterior surfac the interior being free from it.

The same principle was illustrated by Faraday in several othe ways. A cylinder of metallic gauze, or a trellis of iron wire, tl meshes of which were not very close, was placed upon a hon zontal metal disc, resting on an insulated support. Electricity was then communicated to its inner surface; but on applying the

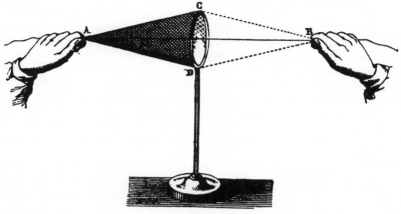

Fig. 60.

proof-plane it was found that the exterior surface alone was electrified. An animal, such as a mouse, placed in the interior, did not suffer any shock even when the entire apparatus was strongly electrified, and vivid sparks taken from it.

A hollow metal cylinder was placed on an insulated metal disc, having a diameter a little larger than its own; being electrified, its exterior surface alone gave signs of electricity. It was surrounded externally with small brass columns, higher than itself, resting by their bases on the same metal disc. The electricity was immediately distributed upon the exterior surface of these small columns.

Faraday, in his lectures, covers his most sensitive gold leaf electroscopes with cotton or linen nets, having loose meshes to protect them from the influence of the surrounding electricity. Notwithstanding the vicinity of powerful electrical machines in action, the sensitive electroscopes thus covered are never affected by electricity, the fluid being exclusively confined to the exterior surface of the tissue with which they are enveloped.

Although it follows, from these and other experimental tests, as well as from theory, that the diffusion of electricity on conductors is nearly superficial, it is not absolutely so. If one end of a metallic rod, coated with sealing wax, be presented to any source of electricity, the fluid will be received as freely from the other end, as if its surface were not coated with a nonconductor. It follows from this that the electricity must pass along the rod sufficiently within the surface of the metal, which is in contact with the wax, to be out of contact with the wax, which, by its insulating virtue, would arrest the progress of the fluid.

84. **How the distribution varies.**—It remains, however, to ascertain how the intensity of the fluid, or its depth on different parts of a conductor, varies.

There are some bodies whose form so strongly suggests the inevitable uniformity of distribution, as to render demonstration needless. In the case of a sphere, the symmetry of form alone indicates the necessity of an uniform distribution. If, then, the fluid be regarded as having an uniform depth on every part of a conducting sphere, exactly as a liquid might be uniformly diffused over the surface of the globe, the total quantity of fluid will be expressed by multiplying its depth by the superficial area of the globe.

85. **Distribution on an ellipsoid.**—If the electrified conductor be not a globe, but an elliptical spheroid, such as A A′ (*fig.* 61.),

Fig. 61.

the fluid will be found to be accumulated in greater quantity at the small ends A and A′ than at the sides B B′, where there is less curvature. This unequal distribution of the fluid is presented by the dotted line in the figure.

It follows from theory, and it is confirmed by observation, that the depth of the fluid at A and A′ is greater than at B B′, in the ratio of the longer axis A A′ of the ellipse to the shorter axis B B′.

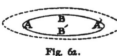

Fig. 62.

If, therefore, the ellipsoid be very elongated, as in *fig.* 62., the depth of the fluid at the ends A and A′ will be proportionally greater.

If a metallic body formed, as shown in *fig.* 63., be supported on an insulating pillar, it will be found by the proof-plane that the depth of the electricity will gradually increase towards the point B, and will decrease towards A.

86. **Effects of edges and points.** — If the conductor be a flat disc, the depth of the fluid will increase from its centre towards its edges. The depth will, however, not vary sensibly near the centre, but will augment rapidly in approaching the edge, as represented in *fig.* 64., where A and B are the edges, and c the centre of the disc, the depth of the fluid being indicated by the dotted line.

It is found in general that the depth of the fluid increases in a rapid proportion in approaching the edges, corners, and extremities, whatever be the shape of the conductor. Thus, when a circular disc or rectangular plate has any considerable magnitude, the depth of the electricity is sensibly uniform at all parts not contiguous to the borders; and whatever be the form, whether round or square, if only it be terminated by sharp angular edges, the depth will increase rapidly in approaching them.

Fig. 63.

If a conductor be terminated, not by sharp angular edges, but by rounded sides or ends, then the distribution will become more

Fig. 64.

uniform. Thus, if a cylindrical conductor of considerable diameter have hemispherical ends, the distribution of the electricity upon it will be nearly uniform; but if its ends be flat, with sharp angular edges, then an accumulation of the fluid will be produced contiguous to them. If the sides of a flat plate of sufficient thickness be rounded, the accumulation of fluid at the edges will be diminished.

The depth of the fluid is still more augmented at corners where the increases of depth, due to two or more edges, meet and are combined; and this effect is pushed to its extreme limit if any part of a conductor have the form of a *point*.

The pressure of the surrounding air being the chief, if not the only force which retains the electric fluid on a conductor, it is evident that if at the edges, corners, or angular points, the depth be so much increased that the elasticity of the fluid exceeds the restraining pressure of the atmosphere, the electricity must escape, and in that case will issue from the edge, corner, or point, exactly as a liquid under strong pressure would issue from a *jet d'eau*.

87. **Distribution of electric fluid varied by induction.**— If a cylindrical conductor with rounded ends be presented to an electrified sphere (*fig.* 65.), its natural electricity will be decom-

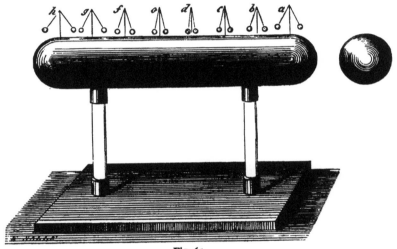

Fig. 65.

posed by induction, the fluid of the same name being repelled, and that of the contrary name attracted, by the sphere, as may be indicated by electric pendulums.

88. **Experimental illustration of the effect of a point.**— Let P, *fig.* 66., be a metallic point attached to a conductor c, and let the perpendicular *n* express the thickness or density of the electric fluid at that place; this thickness will increase in approaching the point P, so as to be represented by perpendiculars drawn from the respective points of the curve n, n', n'' to A P, so that its density at P will be expressed by the perpendicular n'' P.

Experience shows that, in ordinary states of the atmosphere, a very moderate charge of electricity given to the conductor c, will produce such a density of the electric fluid at the point P, as to overcome the pressure of the atmosphere, and to cause the spontaneous discharge of the electricity.

The following experiments will serve to illustrate this escape of electricity from points.

Let a metallic point, such as A P, *fig*. 66., be attached to a conductor, and let a metallic ball of two or three inches in diameter, having a hole in it

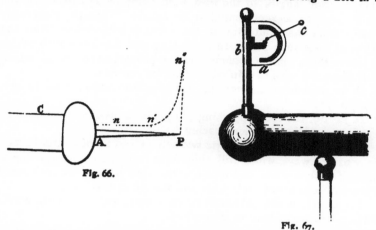

Fig. 66.

Fig. 67.

corresponding to the point P, be stuck upon the point. If the conductor be now electrified, the electricity will be diffused over it, and over the ball which has been stuck upon the point P. The electric state of the conductor may be shown by a quadrant electrometer being attached to it (*fig*. 67.). Let the ball now be drawn off the point P by a silk thread attached to it for the purpose, and let it be held suspended by that thread. The electricity of the conductor C will now escape by the point P, as will be indicated by the electrometer, but the ball suspended by the silk thread will be electrified as before.

89. **Rotation produced by the reaction of points.** — Let

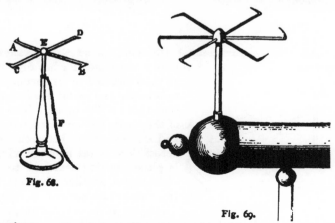

Fig. 68.

Fig. 69.

two wires, A B and C D, *fig*. 68., placed at right angles, be supported by a cap E upon a fine point at the top of an insulating stand, and let them communicate by a chain F with a conductor kept constantly electrified by a machine. Let each of the four arms of the wires be terminated by a point in a horizontal direction, at right angles to the wire, each point being turned in the same direction, as represented in the figure. When the electricity comes from the conductor to the wires, it will escape from the wires at these four points respectively; and the force with which it leaves them will be attended with a proportionate recoil, which will cause the wire to spin rapidly on the centre E.

Other expedients for varying this experiment are shown in *figs.* 69, 70, 71.

In *fig.* 69. the rod supporting the points is inserted in the prime conductor of the electrical machine.

In *fig.* 70. this rod supports two sets (A and B) of points turned in contrary ways, which will, therefore, revolve in contrary directions if both are free and independent; but if they are connected they will counteract each other and remain at rest.

In *fig.* 71. a silk thread sustains a small ball of metal, which strikes a series of bells as it revolves.

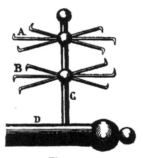

Fig. 70.

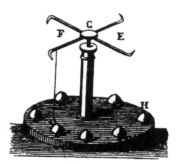

Fig. 71.

90. **Another experimental illustration of this principle** is represented in *fig.* 72. A square wooden stand T has four rods

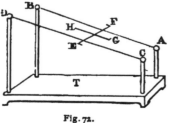

Fig. 72.

of glass inserted in its corners, the rods at one end being less in height than those at the other. The tops of these rods having metal wires A B and C D stretched between them, across these wires another wire E F is placed, having attached to it at right angles another wire G H, having two points turned in opposite directions at its extremities, so that when G H is horizontal these two points shall be vertical, one being presented upwards, and the other downwards. A chain from A communicates with a conductor kept constantly electrified by a machine.

The electricity coming from the conductor by the chain, passes along the system of wires, and escapes at the points G and H. The consequent recoil causes the wire G H to revolve round E F as an axis, and thereby causes E F to roll up the inclined plane.

91. **The electrical orrery** is represented in *fig*. 73. A metallic ball A rests upon an insulating stand by means of a cap within

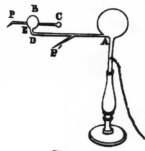

it, placed upon a fine metallic point forming the top of the stand.

From the ball A an arm D A proceeds, the extremity of which is turned up at E, and formed into a fine point.

A small ball B rests by means of a cap on this point, and attached to it are two arms extending in opposite directions, one terminated with a small ball C, and the other by a point P presented in the horizontal direc-

Fig. 73.

tion at right angles to the arm. Another point P', attached at right angles to the arm D A, is likewise presented in the horizontal direction. By this arrangement the ball A, together with the arm D A, is capable of revolving round the insulating stand, by which motion the ball B will be carried in a circle round the ball A. The ball B is also capable at the same time of revolving on the point which supports it, by which motion the ball C will revolve round the ball B in a circle. If electricity be supplied by the chain to the apparatus, the balls A and B and the metallic rods will be electrified, and the electricity will escape at the points P and P'. The recoil produced by this escape will cause the rod D A to revolve round the insulating pillar, and at the same time the rod P C together with the ball B to revolve on the extremity of the arm D A. Thus, while the ball B revolves in a circular orbit round the ball A, the ball C revolves in a smaller circle round the ball B, the motion resembling that of the moon and earth with respect to the sun.

92. **The electrical blow pipe** consists of a metallic point projecting from the conductor of a machine (*fig*. 74.), from which an electric current issues, the effect of which is to produce a current of air directed from the point so strong as to affect the flame of a candle, and even to blow it out.

This experiment may be varied by placing the candle upon the conductor, and presenting to its flame a metallic point, as shown in *fig.* 75., from which a stream of negative electricity will issue, so as to produce a similar current of air.

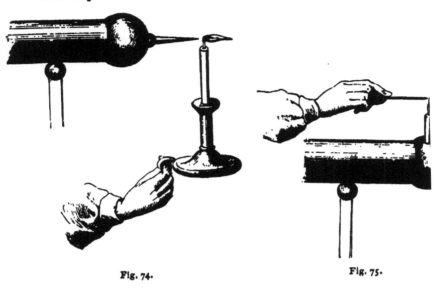

Fig. 74.   Fig. 75.

CHAP. IX.

MECHANICAL EFFECTS OF ELECTRICITY.

93. Attractions and repulsions of electrified bodies. — If a body charged with electricity be placed near another body, it will impress upon such body certain motions, which will vary according as the body thus affected is a conductor or nonconductor ; according as it is in its natural state or charged with electricity ; and, in fine, if charged with electricity, according as the electricity is similar or opposite to that with which the body acting upon it is charged.

Let A, *fig.* 76., be the body charged with electricity, which we shall suppose to be a metallic ball supported on an insulating column. Let B be

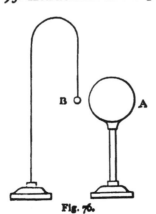

Fig. 76.

the body upon which it acts, which we shall suppose to be a small ball suspended by a fine silken thread. We shall consider successively the cases above mentioned.

94. Action of an electrified body on a nonconductor not electrified.—1°. Let B be a nonconductor in its natural state.

In this case no motion will be impressed on B. The electricity with which A is charged will act by attraction and repulsion on the two opposite fluids, which compose the natural electricity of B, attracting each molecule of one by exactly the same force as it repels the molecule of the other. No decomposition of the fluid will take place, because the insulating property of B will prevent any motion of the fluids upon it, and will therefore prevent their separation. Each compound molecule therefore being at once attracted and repelled by equal forces, no motion will take place.

95. Action of an electrified body on a nonconductor charged with like electricity. — 2°. Let B be charged with electricity similar to that with which A is charged.

In this case B will be repelled from A. For, according to what has been explained above, the forces exerted on the natural electricity of B will be in equilibrium, but the electricity of A will repel the similar electricity with which B is charged; and since this fluid cannot move upon the surface of B because of its insulating virtue, and cannot quit the surface because of the restraining pressure of the surrounding air, it must adhere to the surface, and, being repelled by the electricity of A, must carry with it the ball B in the direction of such repulsion. The ball B therefore will incline from A, and will rest in such a position that its weight will balance the repulsive force.

96. Its action on a nonconductor charged with opposite electricity. — 3°. Let B be charged with electricity opposite to that with which A is charged.

In this case B will be attracted towards A, the distribution of the fluid upon it not being changed, for the same reasons as in the last case.

97. Its action on a conductor not electrified. — 4°. Let B be a conductor in its natural state.

In this case the action of the fluid on A attracting one constituent of the natural electricity of B, and repelling the other, will tend to decompose and separate them; and since the conducting virtue of B leaves free play to the movement of the fluids upon it, this attraction and repulsion will take effect, the attracted fluid moving to the side of B nearest to A, and the repelled fluid to the opposite side.

To render the explanation more clear, let us suppose that A is charged with positive electricity.

In that case, the negative fluid of B will accumulate on the side next A, and the positive fluid on the opposite side. The negative fluid will therefore be nearer to A than the positive fluid; and since the force of the attraction and repulsion increases as the square of the distance is diminished (79.), and since the quantity of the negative fluid on the side next A is equal to the quantity of positive fluid on the opposite side, the attraction exerted on the former will be greater than the repulsion exerted on the latter; and since the fluids are prevented from leaving B by the restraining pressure of the air, the

fluids carrying with them the ball B will be moved towards A, and will rest
equilibrium, when the inclination of the string is such that the weight of
balances and neutralises the attraction.

If A were charged with negative electricity, the same effects would be pr
duced, the only difference being that, in that case, the positive fluid on
would accumulate on the side next A, and the negative fluid on the opposi
side.

Thus it appears that a conducting body in its natural state is alway
attracted by an electrified body, with whichever species of electricity it l
charged.

98. **Its action upon a conductor charged with like electri
city.** — 5°. Let B be a conductor charged with electricity simila
to that with which A is charged.

In this case the effect produced on B will depend on the relative strengt
of the charges of electricity of A and B.

The electricity of A will repel the free electricity of B, and cause it t
accumulate on the side of B most remote from A. But it will also decompos
the natural electricity of B, attracting the fluid of the contrary kind to th
side near A, and repelling the fluid of the same kind to the opposite side. I
will follow from this, that the quantity of the fluid of the same name accu
mulated at the opposite side of B will be greater than the quantity of flui
of the contrary name collected at the side near A. While, therefore, the latte
is more attracted than the former, by reason of its greater proximity, it i
less attracted by reason of its lesser quantity. If these opposite effects ne
tralise each other, — if it lose as much force by its inferior quantity as it gain
by its greater proximity, the attractions and repulsions of A on B will neu
tralise each other, and the ball B will not move. But if the quantity c
electricity with which B is charged be so small that more attraction is gaine
by proximity than is lost by quantity, then the ball B will move towards A
If, however, the quantity of electricity with which B is charged be so grea
that the effect prevail over that of distance, the ball B will be repelled.

It follows, therefore, from this, in order to ensure the repulsion of the ba
B in this case, the charge of electricity must be so strong as to prevail ov
that attraction which would operate on the ball B if it were in its natur
state. A very small electrical charge is, however, generally sufficient for thi

99. **Its action upon a conductor charged with opposit
electricity.** — 6°. Let B be charged with electricity of a contrar
name to that with which A is charged.

In this case B will always be attracted towards A, for the attraction exerte
on the fluid with which it is charged will be added to that which would b
exerted on it if it were in its natural state.

The free electricity on B will be attracted to the side next A, and the na
tural fluid will be decomposed, the fluid of the same name accumulating on
the side most remote from A, and the fluid of the contrary name collecting on
the side nearest to A, and there uniting with the free fluid with which B is
charged. There is therefore a greater quantity of fluid of the contrary name
on that side, than of the same name on the opposite side. The attraction of
the former prevails over the repulsion of the latter therefore at once by
greater quantity and greater proximity, and is consequently effective.

100. **Attractions and repulsions of pith balls explained.—**

What has been explained above will render more clearly understood the attractions and repulsions manifested by pith balls, before and after their contact with electrified bodies (1.). Before contact, the balls, being in their natural state, and being composed of a conducting material, are always attracted, whatever be the electricity with which the body to which they are presented is charged (97.); but after contact, being charged with the like electricity, they are repelled (98.).

When touched by the hand, or any conductor which communicates with the ground, they are discharged and restored to their natural state, when they will be again attracted.

If they be suspended by wire or any other conducting thread, and the stand be a conductor communicating with the ground, they will lose their electricity the moment they receive it.

The electric fluid in passing through bodies, especially if they be imperfect conductors, or if the space they present to the fluid bear a small proportion to its quantity, produces various and remarkable mechanical effects, displacing the conductors sometimes with great violence.

101. Strong electric charges rupture imperfect conductors. — Card pierced by discharge of jar. — A method of exhibiting this effect is represented in *fig.* 77. The chain A communicates with the outside coating of the jar. The card c is placed in such a position that two metallic points touch it on opposite sides, terminating near each other. The pillar G, being glass, intercepts the electricity. The ball of the discharger, being put in communication with the inside coating of the jar, is brought into contact with the ball B, so that the two points which are on opposite sides of the card, being in connection with the two coatings of the jar, are charged with contrary fluids, which exert on each other such an attraction that they rush to each other, penetrating the card, which is found in this case pierced by a hole larger than that produced by a common pin.

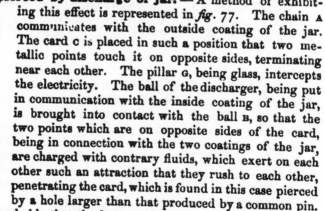

Fig. 77.

It is remarkable that the *burr* produced on the surface of the card is in this case convex *on both sides*, as if the matter producing the hole, instead of passing through the card from one side to the other, had either issued from the middle of its thickness, emerging at each surface, or as if there were two distinct prevailing substances passing in contrary directions, each elevating the edges of the orifice in issuing from it.

The accordance of this effect with the hypothesis of two fluids is apparent.

Another method of exhibiting this phenomenon is shown in *fig*. 78.

Fig. 78.

102. **Curious fact observed by M. Tremery.** — A fact has been noticed by M. Tremery for which no explanation has yet been given. That observer found that when the two points on opposite sides of the card are placed at a certain distance, one above the other, the hole will not be midway between them. When the experiment is made in the atmosphere, the hole will always be nearer to the negative fluid. When the apparatus is placed under the receiver of an air-pump, the hole approaches the positive fluid as the rarefaction proceeds.

If several cards be placed between the knobs of the universal discharger (49.), they may be pierced by a strong charge of a jar or battery, having more than one square foot of coated surface.

103. **Wood and glass broken by discharge.**—A rod of wood half an inch thick may be split by a strong charge transmitted in the direction of its fibres, and other imperfect conductors pierced in the same manner.

If a leaf of writing paper be placed on the stage of the discharger, the electricity passed through it will tear it.

The charge of a ar will penetrate glass. An apparatus for

exhibiting this effect is shown in *fig.* 79. It may also be exhibited by transmitting the charge through the side of a phial, *fig.* 80.

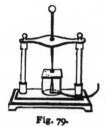

Fig. 79.

Fig. 80.

A strong charge passed through water, scatters the liquid in all directions around the points of discharge, *fig.* 81.

104. **Electrical bells.** — The alternate attraction and repulsion of electrified conductors is prettily illustrated by the *electrical bells.*

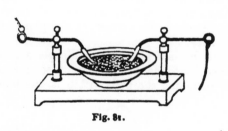

Fig. 81.

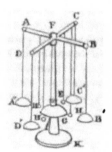

Fig. 82.

A B and C D, *fig.* 82., are two metal rods supported on a glass pillar. From the ends of these rods four bells A' B' C' D' are suspended by metallic chains. A central bell G is supported on the wooden stand which sustains the glass pillar E F, and this central bell communicates by a chain with the ground. From the transverse rods are also suspended, by silken threads, four small brass balls H. The transverse rods being

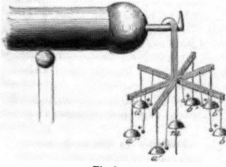

Fig. 83.

put in communication with the conductor of an electrical machine, the four bells A′B′C′D′ become charged with electricity. They attract and then repel the balls H, which when repelled strike the bell G, to which they give up the electricity they received by contact with the bells A′B′C′D′, and this electricity passes to the ground by the chain. The bells will thus continue to be tolled as long as any electricity is supplied by the conductor to the bells A′B′C′D′.

Another form of this apparatus is shown in *fig.* 83.

105. **Repulsion of electrified threads.**—Let a skein of linen thread be tied in a knot at each end, and let one end of it be attached to some part of the conductor of the machine. When the machine is worked the threads will become electrified, and will repel each other, so that the skein will swell out into a form resembling the meridians drawn upon a globe.

106. **Curious effect of repulsion of pith ball.** — Let a metallic point be inserted into one of the holes of the prime conductor, so that, in accordance with what has been explained, a jet of electricity may escape from it when the conductor is electrified. Let this jet, while the machine is worked, be received on the interior of a glass tumbler, by which the surface of the glass will become charged with electricity.

If a number of pith balls be laid upon a metallic plate communicating with the ground, and the tumbler be placed with its mouth upon the plate, including the balls within it, the balls

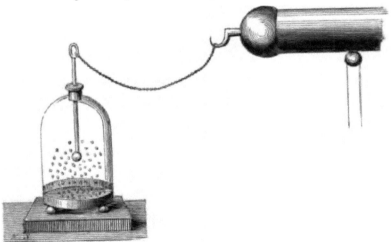

Fig. 84.

will begin immediately leaping violently from the metal and *striking* the glass, and this action will continue till all the

electricity with which the glass was charged has been carried away.

Another form of this apparatus is shown in *fig.* 84.

This is explained on the same principle as the former experiments. The balls are attracted by the electricity of the glass, and when electrified by contact, are repelled. They give up their electricity to the metallic plate, from which it passes to the ground; and this process continues until no electricity remains on the glass of sufficient strength to attract the balls.

107. **Electrical dance.** — Let a disc of pasteboard or wood, coated with metallic foil, be suspended by wires or threads of linen from the prime conductor of an electrical machine, and let a similar disc be placed upon a stand capable of being adjusted to any required height. Let this latter disc be placed immediately under the former, and let it have a metallic communication with the ground. Upon it place small coloured representations in paper, of dancing figures, which are prepared for the purpose. When the machine is worked, the electricity with which the upper disc will be charged will attract the light figures placed on the lower disc, which will leap upwards; and after touching the upper disc and being electrified, will be repelled to the lower disc, and this jumping action of the figures will continue so long as the machine is worked. An electrical dance is thus exhibited for the amusement of young persons.

108. **Curious experiments on electrified water.** — Let a

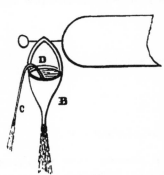

Fig. 85.

small metallic bucket B, *fig.* 85., be suspended from the prime conductor of a machine, and let it have a capillary tube CD of the siphon form immersed in it; or let it have a capillary tube inserted in the bottom; the bore of the tube being so small that water cannot escape from it by its own pressure. When the machine is put in operation, the particles of water, becoming electrified, will repel each other, and immediately an abundant stream will issue from the tube; and as the particles of water after leaving the tube still exercise a reciprocal repulsion, the stream will diverge in the form of a brush.

If a sponge saturated with water be suspended from the prime conductor of the machine, the water, when the machine is first worked will drop slowly from it; but when the conductor becomes strongly electrified, it will descend abundantly, and in the dark will exhibit the appearance of a shower of luminous rain.

109. **Experiment with electrified sealing-wax.** — Let a piece of sealing-wax be attached to the pointed end of a metallic rod; set fire to the wax, and when it is in a state of fusion blow out the flame, and present the wax within a few inches of the prime conductor of the machine. Strongly electrified myriads of fine filaments will issue from the wax towards the conductor, to which they will adhere, forming a sort of network resembling wool. This effect is produced by the positive electricity of the conductor decomposing the natural electricity of the wax; and the latter being a conductor when in a state of fusion, the nega-tive electricity is accumulated in the soft part of the wax near the conductor, while the positive electricity escapes along the metallic rod. The particles of wax thus negatively electrified, being at-tracted by the conductor, are drawn into the filaments above mentioned.

110. **The electrical see-saw,** $a\,b$, *fig.* 86., is a small strip of wood covered over with silver leaf or tinfoil, insulated on c like a

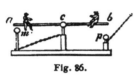

Fig. 86.

balance. A slight preponderance is given to it at a, so that it rests on a wire having a knob m at its top; p is a similar metal ball insulated. Connect p with the inte-rior, and m with the exterior coating of the jar, charge it, and the see-saw motion of $a\,b$ will commence from causes similar to those which excited the movements of the pith balls.

CHAP. X.

THERMAL EFFECTS OF ELECTRICITY.

111. **A current of electricity passing over a conductor raises its temperature.** — If a current of electricity pass over a conductor, as would happen when the conductor of an electrical machine is connected by a metallic rod with the earth, no change in the thermal condition of the conductor will be observed, so long as its transverse section is so considerable as to leave suffi-cient space for the free passage of the fluid. But if its thickness be diminished, or the quantity of fluid passing over it be aug-mented, or, in general, if the ratio of the fluid to the magnitude of

the space afforded to it be increased, the conductor will be found to undergo an elevation of temperature, which will be greater the greater the quantity of the electricity and the less the space supplied for its passage.

112. **Experimental verification.—Wire heated, fused, and burned.**—If a piece of wire of several inches in length be placed upon the stage of the universal discharger (49.), a feeble charge transmitted through it will sensibly raise its temperature. By increasing the strength of the charge, its temperature may be elevated to higher and higher points of the thermometric scale; it may be rendered incandescent, fused, vaporised, and, in fine, burned.

With the powerful machine of the Taylerian Museum at Haarlem, Van Marum fused pieces of wire above 70 feet in length.

Wire may be fused in water; but the length which can be melted in this way is always less than in air, because the liquid robs the metal of its heat more rapidly than air.

A narrow ribbon of tinfoil, from 4 to 6 inches in length, may be volatilised by the discharge of a common battery. The metallic vapour is in this case oxidised in the air, and its filaments float like those of a cobweb.

113. **Thermal effects are greater as the conducting power is less.**—The worst conductors of electricity, such as platinum and iron, suffer much greater changes of temperature by the same charge than the best conductors, such as gold and copper. The charge of electricity, which only elevates the temperature of one conductor, will sometimes render another incandescent, and will volatilise a third.

114. **Ignition of metals.**—If a fine silver wire be extended between the rods of the universal discharger (49.), a strong charge will make it burn with a greenish flame. It will pass off in a greyish smoke. Other metals may be similarly ignited, each producing a flame of a peculiar colour. If the experiments be made in a receiver, the products of the combustion being collected, will prove to be the metallic oxides.

If a gilt thread of silk be extended between the rods of the discharger, the electricity will volatilise or burn the gilding, without affecting the silk. The effect is too rapid to allow the time necessary for the heat to affect the silk.

A strip of gold or silver leaf placed between the leaves of paper, being extended between the rods of the discharger, will be burnt by a discharge from a jar having two square feet of coating. The metallic oxide will in this case appear on the paper as a patch of purple colour in the case of gold, and of grey colour in that of silver

A spark from the prime conductor of the great Haarlem machine burnt a strip of gold leaf twenty inches long by an inch and a half broad.

115. **Effect on fulminating silver.** — The heat developed in the passage of electricity through combustible or explosive substances, which are imperfect conductors, causes their combustion or explosion.

A small quantity of fulminating silver placed on the point of a knife, explodes if brought within a few feet of the conductor of an electrical machine in operation. In this case the explosion is produced by induction.

116. **Electric pistol.** — The electrical pistol or cannon is charged with a mixture of hydrogen and oxygen gases, in the proportion necessary to form water. A conducting wire terminated by a knob is inserted in the touch hole, and the gases are

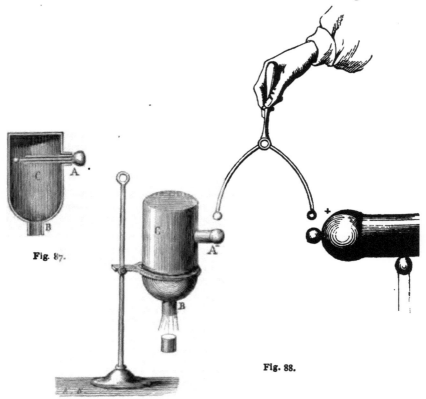

Fig. 87.

Fig. 88.

confined in the barrel by the bullet. An electric spark imparted *to the* ball at the touch hole, causes the explosion of the gases.

This explosion is produced by the sudden combination of the gases, and their conversion into water, which, in consequence of the great quantity of heat developed, is instantly converted into steam of great elasticity, which, by its expansion, forces the bullet from the barrel in the same manner as do the gases which result from the explosion of gunpowder.

One of the forms of this apparatus is represented in section in *fig.* 87. It consists of a metallic vessel c, which is filled with the mixture of the gases, and hermetically closed by a cork. An opening A is made in the side, in which is inserted a metallic rod, terminated in two balls, as shown in *fig.* 87., one interior, and the other exterior, the rod being fixed in the tube by mastic, which, being a nonconductor of electricity, prevents the fluid from escaping from the rod to the sides of the vessel. Thus prepared, the vessel is placed, as shown in *fig.* 88., upon a support, and the ball A is put in electric connection with the conductor of a machine in operation, from which a spark being received a similar spark is transmitted between the internal knob B and the side of the vessel. By this spark the mixture of gases is inflamed, and the cork blown out.

117. **Ether and alcohol ignited.** — Ether or alcohol may be fired by passing through it an electric discharge. Let cold water be poured into a wine glass, and let a thin stratum of ether be carefully poured upon it. The ether being lighter will float on the water. Let a wire or chain connected with the prime conductor of the machine be immersed in the water, and, while the machine is in action, present a metallic ball to the surface of the ether. The electric charge will pass from the water through the ether to the ball, and will ignite the ether. Or, if a person standing on an insulating stool, and holding in one hand a metal spoon filled with ether, present the surface of the ether to a conductor, and at the same time apply the other hand to the prime conductor of a machine in operation, the electricity will pass from the prime conductor through the body of the person to the spoon, and from the spoon through the ether to the conductor to which the ether is presented, and

Fig. 89.

in so passing will *ignite the eth* r.

Another arrangement for performing this experiment is sl
in *fig.* 89.

118. **Resinous powder burned.**—The electric charge tr
mitted through fine resinous powder, such as that of colopl
will ignite it. This experiment may be performed either
spreading the powder on the stage of the discharger (49.), c
impregnating a hank of cotton with it; or, in a still more stri
manner, by sprinkling it on the surface of water contained i
earthenware saucer.

119. **Gunpowder exploded.**—Gunpowder may, in like mai
be ignited by electricity. This experiment is most conveni(
exhibited by placing the powder in a small wooden cup, and
ducting the electric charge along a moist thread, six or seven ir
long, attached to the arm of a discharger, which is connected

the negative coating of a jar, and the charg
its passage from one rod of the discharger t(
other, will ignite the powder.

Fig. 90.

120. **Electric mortars.**—The electric m(
(*fig.* 90.); is an apparatus by which the

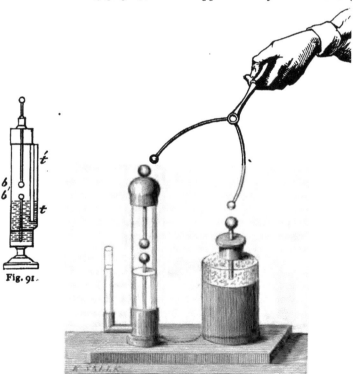

Fig. 91.

Fig. 92.

powder is ignited by passing an electric charge through it. The mixed gases may also be used in this instrument.

Common air or gas, not being explosive, is heated so suddenly and intensely by transmitting through it an electric charge, that it will expand so as to project the ball from the mortar.

121. **Kinnersley's thermometer** (*fig.* 91.) is an instrument intended to measure the degree of heat developed in the passage of an electric charge by the expansion of air. The discharge takes place between the two balls *b b'* in the glass cylinder, and the air confined in the cylinder being heated expands, presses upon the liquid contained in the lower part of the cylinder, and causes the liquid in the tube *t t'* to rise. The variation of the column of liquid in the tube *t t'* indicates the elevation of temperature.

This instrument is shown on a larger scale, and another mode of performing the experiment indicated in *fig.* 92.

CHAP. XI.

LUMINOUS EFFECTS OF ELECTRICITY.

122. **Electric fluid is not luminous.** — An insulated conductor, or a Leyden jar or battery, however strongly charged, is never luminous so long as the electric equilibrium is maintained and the fluid continues in repose. But if this equilibrium be disturbed, and the fluid move from one conductor to another, such motion is, under certain conditions, attended with luminous phenomena.

123. **Conditions under which light is developed by an electric current.** — If the conductor of an ordinary electric machine while in operation be connected with the ground by a thick metallic wire, the current of the fluid which flows along the wire to the ground will not be sensibly luminous; but if the machine be one of great power, such, for example, as the Taylerian machine of Haarlem, an iron wire of 60 or 70 feet long, communicating with the ground and conducting the current, will be surrounded by a brilliant light. The intensity of the electricity necessary to produce this effect, depends altogether on the properties of the medium in which the fluid moves. Sometimes electricity of feeble intensity produces a strong luminous effect, while in other cases electricity of the greatest intensity develops no sensible degree of light.

It has been already explained that the electric fluid with which an insulated conductor is charged is retained upon it only by the pressure of the surrounding air. According as this pressure is increased or diminished, the force necessary to enable the electricity to escape will be increased or diminished, and in the same proportion.

When a conductor A, in communication with the ground, approaches an insulated conductor B charged with electricity, the natural electricity of B will be decomposed, the fluid of the same name as that which charges A escaping to the earth, and the fluid of the opposite name accumulating on the side of B next to A. At the same time, according to what has been explained (97.), the fluid on A accumulates on the side nearest to B. These two *tides* of electricity of opposite kinds exert a reciprocal attraction, and nothing prevents them from rushing together and coalescing, except the pressure of the intervening air. They will coalesce therefore, so soon as their mutual attraction is so much increased as to exceed the pressure of the air.

This increase of mutual attraction may be produced by several causes. *First*, by increasing the charge of electricity upon the conductor A, for the pressure of the fluid will be proportional its depth or density. *Secondly*, by diminishing the distance between A and B, for the attraction increases in the same ratio the square of that distance is diminished; and, *thirdly*, by increasing the conducting power of either or both of the bodies A and for by that means the electric fluids, being more free to move upon them, will accumulate in greater quantity on the sides of and B which are presented towards each other. *Fourthly*, by the form of the bodies A and B, for according to what has been already explained (86.), the fluids will accumulate on the sides presented to each other in greater or less quantity, according as the form of those sides approaches to that of an edge, a corner, or a point.

When the force excited by the fluids surpasses the restraining force of the intervening air, they force their passage through the air, and, rushing towards each other, combine. This movement is attended with light and sound. A light appears to be produced between the points of the two bodies A and B, which has been called the *electric spark*, and this luminous phenomenon is accompanied by a sharp sound like the crack of a whip.

124. **The electric spark.** — The luminous phenomenon called the electric spark does not consist, as the name would imply, of a luminous point which moves from the one body to the other. Strictly speaking, the light manifests no progressive motion. It consists of a *thread of light*, which for an instant seems to connect the two bodies, and in general is not extended between them in

Fig. 93.

one straight unbroken direction like a thread which might be stretched tight between them, but has a zigzag form, resembling more or less the appearance of lightning, *fig.* 93.

125. **Electric aigrette.** — If the part of either of the bodies A or B which is presented to the other have the form of a point, the electric fluid will escape, not in the form of a spark, but as an *aigrette*, or brush light, the diverging rays of which sometimes have the length of two or three inches. A very feeble charge is sufficient to cause the escape of the fluid when the body has this form (87.).

126. **The length of the spark.** — If the knuckle of the finger or a metallic ball at the end of a rod held in the hand be presented to the prime conductor of a machine in operation, a spark will be produced, the length of which will vary with the power of the machine.

By the *length of the spark* must be understood the greatest distance at which the spark can be transmitted.

A very powerful machine will so charge its prime conductor that sparks may be taken from it at the distance of 30 inches.

127. **Discontinuous conductors produce luminous effects.** — Since the passage of the electricity produces light wherever the metallic continuity, or more generally wherever the continuity of the conducting material is interrupted, these luminous effects may be multiplied by so arranging the conductors, that there shall be interruptions of continuity arranged in any regular or desired manner.

128. **Various experimental illustrations.** — If a number of metallic beads be strung upon a thread of silk, each bead being separated from the adjacent one by a knot on the silk so as to break the contact, a current of electricity sent through them will produce a series of sparks, a separate spark being produced between every two successive beads. By placing one end of such a string of beads in contact with the conductor of the machine, and the other end in metallic communication with the ground, a chain of sparks can be maintained so long as the machine is worked.

The string of beads may be disposed so as to form a variety of fancy designs, which will appear in the dark in characters of light.

Similar effects may be produced by attaching bits of metallic foil to glass. Sparkling tubes and plates are contrived in this manner, by which amusing experiments are exhibited. A glass

Fig. 94.

plate is represented in *fig.* 94., by
which a word is made to appear
in letters of light in a dark room
The letters are formed by attaching lozenge-shaped bits of tinfoi
to the glass, disposed in the proper
form.   In the same manner designs may be formed on the inner
surface of glass tubes, *fig.* 95., or plates, *fig.* 96., or, in fine, of glass
vessels of any form, *fig.* 97.

Fig. 95.

In these cases the luminous characters may be made to appear
in lights of various colours, by using spangles of different metals
since the colour of the spark varies with the metal.

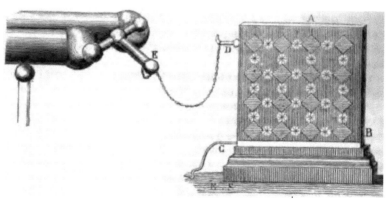

Fig. 96.

129. **Effect of rarefied air.** — When the electric fluid passes
through air, the brilliancy and colour of the light evolved depends
on the density of the air.   In rarefied air the light is more
diffused and less intense, and acquires a reddish or violet colour.
Its colour, however, is affected, as has been just stated, by the

nature of the conductors between which the current flows. When it issues from gold the light is green, from silver red,

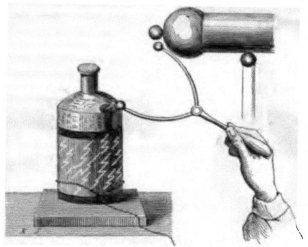

Fig. 97.

from tin or zinc white, from water deep yellow inclining to orange.

It is evident that these phenomena supply the means of constructing electrical apparatus by which an infinite variety of beautiful and striking luminous effects may be produced.

When the electricity escapes from a metallic point in the dark, it forms an aigrette, *fig.* 98., which will continue to be visible so long as the machine is worked.

Fig. 98.

The luminous effect of electricity in rarefied air is exhibited by an apparatus, *fig.* 99. and *fig.* 100., consisting of a glass receiver, which can be screwed upon the plate of an air pump and partially exhausted. The electric current passes between two metallic balls attached to rods, which slide in air-tight collars in the covers of the receiver.

It is observed that the aigrettes formed by the negative fluid are never as long or as divergent as those formed by the positive fluid, an effect which is worthy of attention as indicating a distinctive character of the two fluids.

130. **Experimental imitation of the auroral light.** — This phenomenon may be exhibited in a still more remarkable manner by using, instead of the receiver, a glass tube two or three inches in diameter, and about thirty inches in length. In this

case a pointed wire being fixed to the interior of each of the
one is screwed upon the plate of the air pump, while the ex

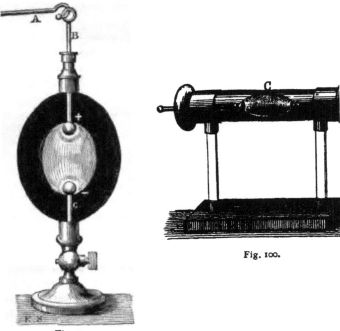

Fig. 99.

Fig. 100.

knob of the other is connected by a metallic chain with the
conductor of the electrical machine. When the machine is w
in the dark, a succession of luminous phenomena will be proc
in the tube, which bear so close a resemblance to the a
borealis as to suggest the most probable origin of that me
When the exhaustion of the tube is nearly perfect, the
length of the tube will exhibit a violet red light. If a
quantity of air be admitted, luminous flashes will be seen to
from the two points attached to the caps. As more and mo
is admitted, the flashes of light which glide in a serpentine
down the interior of the tube will become more thin and v
until at last the electricity will cease to be diffused throug!
column of air, and will appear as a glimmering light at the
points.

131. **Phosphorescent effect of the spark.** — The el
spark leaves upon certain imperfect conductors a trace v
continues to be luminous for several seconds, and sometimes
so long as a minute after the discharge of the spark. The c

of this species of phosphorescence varies with the substances on which it is produced. Thus white chalk produces an orange light. With rock crystal the light, at first red, turns afterwards white. Sulphate of barytes, amber, and loaf sugar render the light green, and calcined oyster shell gives all the prismatic colours.

132. **Leichtenberg's figures.** — The spark in many cases produces effects which not only confirm the hypothesis of two fluids, but indicate a specific difference between them. One of these has been already noticed. The experiment known as Leichtenberg's figures presents another example of this. Let two Leyden jars be charged, one with positive, the other with negative electricity; and let sparks be given by their knobs to the smooth and well dried surface of a cake of resin. Let the surface of the resin be then slightly sprinkled with powder of semen lycopodii, or flowers of sulphur, and let the powder thus sprinkled be blown off. A part will remain attached to the spots where the electric sparks were imparted. At the spot which received the positive spark, the adhering powder will have the form of a radiating star; and at the point of the negative spark it will have that of a roundish clouded spot.

133. **Experiments indicating specific differences between the two fluids.** — If lines and figures be traced in like manner on the cake of resin, some with the positive, and some with the negative knob, and a powder formed of a mixture of sulphur and minium be first sprinkled over the cake and then blown off, the adhering powder will mark the traces of the two fluids imparted by the knobs, the traces of the positive fluid being yellow, and those of the negative red. In this case the sulphur is attracted by the positive electricity, and is therefore itself negative; and the minium by the negative electricity, and is therefore itself positive. The mechanical effects of the two fluids are also different, the sulphur powder being arranged in divergent lines, and the minium in more rounded and even traces.

Let two Leyden jars, one charged with positive and the other with negative electricity, be placed upon a plate of glass coated at its under surface with tinfoil at a distance of six or eight inches asunder, and let the surface of the glass between them be sprinkled with semen lycopodii. Let the jars be then moved towards each other, and let their inner coatings be connected by a discharging rod applied to their knobs. A spark will pass between their outer coatings through the powder, which it will scatter on its passage. The path of the positive fluid will be distinguishable from that of the negative fluid, as before explained, by the peculiar arrangement of the powder; and this difference will disappear near the point where the two fluids meet, where a large round speck is sometimes seen bounded by neither of the arrangements which characterise the respective fluids.

134. **Electric light above the barometric column.** — The
electric light is developed in every form of elastic fluid and vapour when its density is very inconsiderable. A remarkable example of this is presented in the common barometer. When the mercurial column is agitated so as to oscillate in the tube, the space in the tube above the column becomes luminous, and is visibly so in the dark. This phenomenon is caused by the effect of the electricity developed by the friction of the mercury and the glass upon the atmosphere of mercurial vapour which fills the space above the column in the tube.

Fig. 101.

135. **Cavendish's electric barometer.** — The electric barometer of Cavendish, *fig.* 101., illustrates this in a striking manner. Two barometers are connected at the top by a curved tube, so that the spaces above the two columns communicate with each other. When the instrument is agitated so as to make the columns oscillate, electric light appears in the curved tube.

136. **Luminous effects produced by imperfect conductors.** — The electric spark or charge transmitted by means of the universal discharger and Leyden jar or battery through various imperfect conductors, produces luminous effects which are amusing and instructive.

Place a small melon, citron, apple, or any similar fruit on the stand of the discharger; arrange the wires so that their ends are not far asunder, and at the moment when the jar is discharged the fruit becomes transparent and luminous. One or more eggs may be treated in the same manner if a small wooden ledge be so contrived that their ends may just touch, and the spark can be sent through them all. Send a charge through a lump of pipe-clay, a stick of brimstone, or a glass of water, or any coloured liquid, and the entire mass of the substance will for a short time be rendered luminous. As the phosphorescent appearance induced is by no means powerful, it will be necessary that these experiments should be performed in a dark room, and indeed the effect of the other luminous electrical phenomena will be heightened by darkening the room.

137. **Attempt to explain electric light,—the thermal hypothesis.** — No explanation of the physical cause of the electric

spark, or of the luminous effects of electricity, has yet been proposed which has commanded general assent. It appears certain, for the reasons already stated, and from a great variety of phenomena, that the electric fluids themselves are not luminous. The light, therefore, which attends their motion must be attributed to the media, or the bodies through which or between which the fluids move. Since it is certain that the passage of the fluids through a medium develops heat in greater or less quantity in such medium, and since heat, when it attains a certain point, necessarily develops light, the most obvious explanation of the manifestation of light was to ascribe it to a momentary and extreme elevation of temperature, by which that part of the medium, or the body traversed by the fluid, becomes incandescent.

According to this hypothesis, the electric spark and the flash of lightning are nothing more than the particles of air, through which the electricity passes, rendered luminous by intense heat. There is nothing in this incompatible with physical analogies. Flame we know to be gas rendered luminous by the ardent heat developed in the chemical combinations, of which combustion is the effect.

138. **Hypothesis of decomposition and recomposition.** — According to another hypothesis, first advanced by Ritter, and afterwards adopted by Berzelius, Oersted, and Sir H. Davy, the electric fluids have strictly speaking no motion of translation whatever, and never in fact desert the elementary molecules of matter of which, according to the spirit of this hypothesis, they form an essential part. Each molecule or atom composing a body is supposed to be primitively invested with an atmosphere of electric fluid, positive or negative, as the case may be, which never leaves it. Bodies are accordingly classed as electro-positive or electro-negative, according to the fluid attracted to their atoms. Those atoms which are positive attract so much negative fluid, and those which are negative so much positive fluid, as is sufficient to neutralise the forces of their proper electricities, and then the atoms are unelectrised and in their natural state.

When a body is charged with positive electricity, its atoms act by induction upon the atoms of adjacent bodies, and these upon the atoms next beyond them, and so on. The fluids in the series of atoms through which the electricity is supposed to pass, assumes a polar arrangement such as that represented in *fig.* 102.

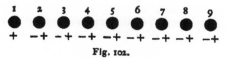

Fig. 102.

The first atom of the series being surcharged with + electricity acts by induction on the second, and decomposes its natural electricity, the negative fluid being attracted to the side near the first atom, and the positive repelled to the side near the third atom. The same effect is produced by atom 2 on atom 3, by atom 3 on atom 4, and so on. The surplus positive fluid on 1 then combines with and neutralises the negative fluid on 2; and, in like manner, the positive fluid on 2 combines with and neutralises the negative fluid on 3, and so on until the last atom of the series is left surcharged with positive electricity.

Such is the hypothesis of decomposition and recomposition which is at present in most general favour with the scientific world.

The explanation which it affords of the electric spark and other luminous electric effects, may be said to consist in transferring the phenomenon to be explained from the bodies themselves to their component atoms, rather than in affording an explanation of the effect in question, inasmuch as the production of light between atom and atom, by the alternate decomposition and recomposition of the electricities, stands in as much need of explanation as the phenomenon proposed.

139. **Cracking noise attending electric spark.**—The sound produced by the electric discharge is obviously explained by the sudden displacement of the particles of the air, or other medium through which the electric fluid passes.

CHAP. XII.

PHYSIOLOGICAL EFFECTS OF ELECTRICITY.

140. **Electric shock explained.** — The material substances which enter into the composition of the bodies of animals are generally imperfect conductors. When such a body, therefore, is placed in proximity with a conductor charged with electricity, its natural electricity is decomposed, the fluid of a like name being repelled to the side more remote from, and the fluid of the contrary name being attracted to the side nearest to, the electrified body. If that body be very suddenly removed from or brought near to the animal body, the fluids of the latter will suddenly suffer a disturbance of their equilibrium, and will either rush towards each other to recombine, or be drawn from each other, being decomposed; and owing to the imperfection of the conducting power of the fluids and solids composing the body, the electricity in passing through it will produce a momentary derangement, as it does in passing through air, water, paper, or any other imperfect conductor. If this derangement do not exceed the power of the parts to recover their position and organisation, a convulsive sensation is felt, the violence of which is greater or less

according to the force of electricity and the consequent derange-ment of the organs; but if it exceed this limit, a permanent injury, or even death, may ensue.

141. **Secondary shock.**—It will be apparent from this, that the nervous effect called the *electric shock* does not require that any electricity be actually imparted to, abstracted from, or passed through the body. The momentary derangement of the natural electricity is sufficient to produce the effect with any degree of violence.

The shock produced thus by induction, without transmitting electricity through the body, is sometimes called the *secondary shock.*

The physiological effects of electricity are extremely various, according to the quantity and intensity of the charge, accord-ing to the part of the body affected by it, and according to the manner in which it is imparted.

142. **Effect produced on the skin by proximity to an electrified body.**—When the back of the hand is brought near to the glass cylinder of the machine, at the part where it passes from under the silk flap, and when therefore it is strongly charged with electricity, a peculiar sensation is felt on the skin, resembling that which would be produced by the contact of a cobweb. The hairs of the skin, being negatively electrified by induction, are attracted and drawn against their roots with a slight force.

143. **Effect of the sparks taken on the knuckle.**—The effect of the shock produced by a spark taken from the prime con-ductor by the knuckle is confined to the hand; but with a very powerful machine, it will extend to the elbow.

144. **Methods of limiting and regulating the shock by a jar.**—The effects of the discharge of a Leyden jar extend through the whole body. The shock may, however, be limited to any desired part or member, by placing two metallic plates con-nected with the two coatings of the jar, on opposite sides of the part through which it is desired to transmit the shock.

145. **Effect of discharges of various force.**—The violence of the shock depends on the magnitude of the charge, and may be so intense as to produce permanent injury. The discharge of a single jar is sufficient to kill birds, and other smaller species of animals. The discharge of a moderate-sized battery will kill rabbits, and a battery of a dozen square feet of coated surface will kill a large animal, especially if the shock be transmitted through the head.

146. **Phenomena observed in the autopsis after death by the shock.**—When death ensues in such cases, no organic lesion or other injury or derangement has been discovered by the

autopsis; nevertheless, the violence of the convulsions which are manifested when the charge is too feeble to destroy life, indicates a nervous derangement as the cause of death.

147. **Effects of a long succession of moderate discharges.** —A succession of electric discharges of moderate intensity, transmitted through certain parts of the body, produce alternate contraction and relaxation of the nervous and muscular organs, by which the action of the vascular system is stimulated and the sources of animal heat excited.

148. **Effects upon a succession of patients receiving the same discharge.** — The electric discharge of a Leyden jar may be transmitted through a succession of persons placed hand in hand, the first communicating with the internal, and the last with the external coating of the jar.

In this case, the persons placed at the middle of the series sustain a shock less intense than those placed near either extremity, — another phenomenon which favours the hypothesis of two fluids.

149. **Remarkable experiments of Nollet, Dr. Watson, and others.** — A shock has in this manner been sent through a regiment of soldiers. At an early period in the progress of electrical discovery, M. Nollet transmitted a discharge through a series of 180 men; and at the convent of Carthusians a chain of men being formed extending to the length of 5400 feet, by means of metallic wires extended between every two persons composing it, the whole series of persons was affected by the shock at the same instant.

Experiments on the transmission of the shock were made in London by Dr. Watson, in the presence of the Council of the Royal Society, when a circuit was formed by a wire carried from one side of the Thames to the other over Westminster Bridge. One extremity of this wire communicated with the interior of a charged jar, the other was held by a person on the opposite bank of the river. This person held in his other hand an iron rod which he dipped in the river. On the other side near the jar stood another person, holding in one hand a wire communicating with the exterior coating of the jar, and in the other hand an iron rod. This rod he dipped into the river, when instantly the shock was received by both persons, the electric fluid having passed over the bridge, through the body of the person on the other side, through the water across the river, through the rod held by the other person, and through his body to the exterior coating of the jar. Familiar as such a fact may now appear, it is impossible to convey an adequate idea of the amazement bordering on incredulity with which it was at that time witnessed.

CHAP. XIII.

CHEMICAL AND MAGNETIC EFFECTS OF ELECTRICITY.

150. **Phenomena which supply the basis of the electro-chemical theory.** — If an electric charge be transmitted through certain compound bodies, they will be resolved into their constituents, one component always going in the direction of the positive, and the other of the negative fluids. This class of phenomena has supplied the basis of the electro-chemical hypothesis already briefly noticed (138.). The constituent which goes to the positive fluid is assumed to consist of atoms which are electrically negative, and that which goes to the negative fluid, as consisting of atoms electrically positive.

151. **Faraday's experimental illustration of this.** — This class of phenomena is more prominently developed by voltaic electricity, and will be more fully explained in the following Book. For the present it will therefore be sufficient to indicate an example of this species of decomposition by the electricity of the ordinary machine. The following experiment is due to Professor Faraday.

Lay two pieces of tinfoil T T', *fig.* 103., on a glass plate, one being connected with the prime conductor of the machine, and the other with the ground. Let two pieces of platinum wire P P', resting on the tinfoil, be placed with their points on a drop of the solution of the sulphate of copper C, or on a piece of bibulous paper wetted with sulphate of indigo in muriatic acid, or iodide of potassium in starch, or litmus paper wetted with a solution of common salt or of sulphate of soda, or upon turmeric paper containing sulphate of soda.

In all these cases the solutions are decomposed: in the first, the copper goes to the positive wire; in the second the indigo is bleached by the chlorine discharged at the same wire; in the third the iodine is liberated at the same

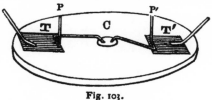

Fig. 103.

wire; in the fourth the litmus paper is reddened by the acid evolved at the positive wire, and when muriatic is used, it is bleached by the chlorine evolved at the same wire; and, in fine, in the fifth case, the turmeric paper is reddened by the alkali evolved at the negative wire.

152. **Effect of an electric discharge on a magnetic needle.** — When a stream of electricity passes over a steel needle

or bar of iron, it produces a certain modification in its magnetic state. If the needle be in its natural state it is rendered magnetic. If it be already magnetic, its magnetism is modified, being augmented or diminished in intensity, according to certain conditions depending on the direction of the current and the position of the magnetic axis of the needle ; or it may have its magnetism destroyed, or even its polarity reversed.

This class of phenomena, like the chemical effects just mentioned, are, however, much more fully developed by voltaic electricity; and we shall therefore reserve them to be explained in the following Book. Meanwhile, however, the following experiments will show how common electricity may develop them.

153. **Experimental illustration of this.** — Place a narrow strip of copper, about two inches in length, on the stage of the universal discharger, and over it a leaf of any insulating material, upon which lay a sewing needle transversely to the strip of copper. Transmit several strong charges of electricity through the copper. The needle will then be found to be magnetised, the end lying on the right of the current of electricity being its north pole.

If the same experiment be repeated, reversing the position of the needle, it will be demagnetised. But by repeating the electric discharges a greater number of times, it will be magnetised with the poles reversed.

BOOK THE SECOND.

VOLTAIC ELECTRICITY.

~~~~~~~~

CHAPTER I.

SIMPLE VOLTAIC COMBINATION.

154. **Discovery of galvanism.**—In tracing the progress of physical science, the greatest discoveries are frequently found to originate, not in the sagacity of observers, but in circumstances altogether fortuitous. One of the most remarkable examples of this is presented by Voltaic Electricity. Speaking of the voltaic pile, Arago, in his "Eloge de Volta," says, that "this immortal discovery arose in the most immediate and direct manner, from an indisposition with which a Bolognese lady was affected in 1790, for which her medical adviser prescribed *frog broth*."

Galvani, the husband of the lady, was Professor of Anatomy in the University of Bologna. It happened that several frogs, prepared for cooking, lay upon the table of his laboratory, near to which his assistant was occupied with an electrical machine. On taking sparks from time to time from the conductor, the limbs of the frogs were affected with convulsive movements resembling vital action.

This was the effect of the inductive action of the electricity of the conductor upon the highly electroscopic organs of the frogs; but Galvani was not sufficiently conversant with this branch of physics to comprehend it, and consequently regarded it as a new phenomenon. He proceeded to submit the limbs of frogs to a course of experiments, with the view to ascertain the cause of what appeared to him so strange. For this purpose, he dissected several frogs, separating the legs, thighs, and lower part of the spinal column from the remainder, so as to lay bare the lumbar nerves. He then passed *copper* hooks through that part of the dorsal column which remained above the junction of the thighs, without any scientific object, but merely for the convenience of suspending them until required for experiment. It chanced, also, that he suspended these *copper* hooks upon the *iron* bar of the balcony of his window, when, to his inexpressible astonishment, he found that whenever the wind or any other accidental cause brought the muscles of the leg into contact with the iron bar, the limbs were affected by convulsive movements similar to those produced by the sparks taken from the conductor of the electric machine.

This fact, reproduced and generalised, supplied the foundation of the theory of animal electricity propounded by Galvani, and for a considerable time universally accepted. In this theory it was assumed that in the animal economy there exists a specific source of electricity ; that at the junction of the nerves and muscles this electricity is decomposed, the positive fluid passing to the nerve, and the negative to the muscle ; and that, consequently, the nerve and muscle are in a state of relative electrical tension, analogous to that of the internal and external coatings of a charged Leyden jar. When, under these circumstances, rods of metal c d, *fig.* 104,

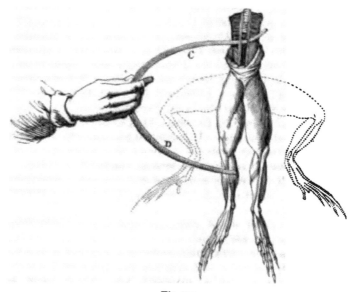

Fig. 104.

are applied, one to the nerve, and the other to the muscle, the opposite electricities rush towards each other along the conducting rods ; a discharge of the nerve and muscle takes place, like that of the Leyden jar ; and this momentary derangement of the electrical condition of the organ produces the convulsive movement.

155. **Volta's correction of Galvani's theory.** — Volta, then Professor of Natural Philosophy at Como, and afterwards at Pavia, repeating the experiments of Galvani, overturned his theory

various ingenious experimental tests, one of which consisted in owing that the effects of the electric shock were equally pro-ced when both metallic rods were applied to the muscle, neither uching the nerve. He contended that Galvani, in taking the rve and muscle to represent the coatings of the Leyden jar, and e metallic rods the discharging conductor, had precisely inverted e truth, for that the rods represented the jar, and the nerve and uscle the conductor.

If the rods, as Galvani supposed, played the part of the metallic nductor, communicating between the opposite electricities im-ated to the nerve and muscle, a single rod of one uniform metal ould serve this purpose, not only as well, but better than two ds of different metals; whereas the presence of *two different etals in contact*, was essential to the development of the pheno-enon.

In fine, Volta maintained, and ultimately proved, that the elec-ricity decomposed was not that of the nerve and muscle, but that f the metallic rods; that the seat of the decomposition was not he junction of the nerve and muscle, but the junction of the two etals; that the positive and negative fluids passed, not upon the erve and muscle, but upon the iron and copper forming the rods owing in opposite directions from their point of junction; and at, in fine, the nerve and muscle, or the latter alone, served erely as the conductor by which the opposite electricities de-eloped on the metals were recomposed, exactly as they would if laced between the internal and external coatings of a charged eyden jar.

156. **Theory of animal electricity exploded.** — After a con-ict of some years' duration, the animal electricity of Galvani fell efore the irresistible force of the reasoning and experiments of olta, whose theory obtained general acceptation. This form of ectric agency has since been denominated indifferently, *gal-tnism* or *voltaic electricity.*

157. **Contact hypothesis of Volta.** — According to the hy-thesis of Volta, now known as the *contact theory,* any two fferent metals, or, more generally, any two different bodies hich are conductors of electricity, being placed in contact, a ontaneous decomposition of their natural electricity will be ected at their surface of contact, the positive fluid moving from ch surface and diffusing itself over the one, and the negative ving in the contrary direction and diffusing itself over the her, the surface of contact constituting a neutral line separating e two fluids.

158. **Electro-motive force.** — This power of electric decom-sition was called by Volta, *electro-motive force.*

Different bodies placed in contact manifest different elec
motive forces, the energy of the electro-motive force being m
sured by the quantity of electricity decomposed.

Its direction and intensity. — The electro-motive force
on the two fluids in opposite directions, but it will be conven
to designate its direction by that of the positive fluid.

To indicate, therefore, the electro-motive force developed, w
any two conductors are placed in contact, it is necessary to as
the energy and direction of such force, which is done by show
the intensity of the electricity developed, and the condu
towards which the positive fluid is directed.

159. **Classification of bodies according to their elect
motive property.** — Although the results of experimental
search are not in strict accordance on these points, the elec
tensions produced by the mere contact of heterogeneous
ductors being in general so feeble, as to elude the usual e
troscopic tests, it has nevertheless been found that bodies ma
arranged so that any one placed in contact with another holdir
lower place in the series, will receive the positive fluid, the lo
receiving the negative fluid, and so that the electro-motive fo
of any two shall be greater the more distant they are from e
other in the series. How far the results of experimental
searches are in accordance on these points, will be seen by cc
paring the following series of electromotors given by Volta, P
Henrici, and Peclet : —

Volta.	Pfaff.	Henrici.	Peclet.
Zinc.	Zinc.	Zinc.	Zinc.
Lead.	Lead.	Lead.	Lead.
Tin.	Cadmium.	Tin.	Tin.
Iron.	Tin.	Antimony.	Bismuth.
Copper.	Iron.	Bismuth.	Antimony.
Silver.	Bismuth.	Iron.	Iron.
Graphite.	Cobalt.	Brass.	Copper.
Charcoal.	Arsenic.	Copper.	Silver.
Crystallised Amber.	Copper.	Silver.	Gold.
	Antimony.	Mercury.	Platinum.
	Platinum.	Gold.	
	Gold.	Platinum.	
	Mercury.		
	Silver.		
	Charcoal.		

To which Pfaff adds the following mineral substances in t
order here given : Argentum vitreum (vitreous silver ore), s
phurous pyrites, cuprum mineralisatum pyritaceum (yellow copp
ore), galena, crystallised tin, niccolum sulphuratum arsenicum p
ritaceum (arsenical mundick), molydena, protoxide of uraniu
oxide of titanium, graphite, wolfram (tungstate of iron a
manganese), gypsum stillatium, crystallised amber, peroxide
lead (?).

It is to be understood, that, according to the results of the experimental researches of the observers above named, the electromotive force produced by the contact of any two of the bodies in the preceding series will be directed from that which holds the lower to that which holds the higher place, and that the energy of such electro-motive force will be greater the more remote the one body is from the other in the series.

160. **Relation of electro-motive force to susceptibility of oxidation.** — The mere inspection of these several series will suggest the general conclusion, that the electro-motive force is directed from the less to the more oxidable body, and that the more the one exceeds the other in its susceptibility of oxidation, the more energetic will be the electro-motive force. Thus, a combination of zinc with platinum produces more electro-motive energy than a combination of zinc with any of the more oxidable metals.

If several electromotors of the series be placed in contact in any order, the total electro-motive force developed is found to be the same, as if the first were immediately in contact with the last. The intermediate elements are therefore in this case inefficient.

161. **Analogy of electro-motive action to induction.** — It appears, therefore, that when two pieces of different metals taken from the series of electromotors, such as zinc and copper, for example, are brought into contact, an electric state is produced in their combined mass similar to that which would be produced by placing an insulated conductor charged with positive electricity near the copper side of the combination. The inductive action of such a conductor would decompose the natural electricity of the combined mass, attracting the negative fluid to the side near the conductor, that is, to the copper element, and repelling the positive fluid to the opposite side, that is, to the zinc element. But this is precisely the effect of the electro-motive force of the two metals as already described.

Let z and c, *fig.* 105., be cylinders of zinc and copper placed end to end. The former will, by the contact, be charged with positive, and the latter with

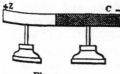

Fig. 105.

negative electricity. Let the two cylinders, being insulated, be separated, and the one will be positively, and the other negatively electrified; but in this case the intensity of the electricity developed upon them will be so feeble, that it cannot be rendered manifest by any of the ordinary electroscopic tests. Let it, however, be imparted to the collecting plate of a powerful condensing electroscope, and, after the two cylinders z and c are discharged, let them be again placed in contact. They will be again charged by their electro-motive action, and their charges may, as before, be imparted to the collecting plates of the electroscopes; and this process may be repeated until the electricities of each kind accumulated in the plates of the electroscopes become sensible.

162. **Electro-motive action of gases and liquids.** — Several German philosophers have recently instituted elaborate experimental researches to determine the electro-motive action of liquids, and even of gases, on solids and on each other. The labours of Pfaff have been especially directed to this inquiry, and have enabled him to arrive at the following general conclusions respecting the electro-motive force developed by the contact of solid with liquid conductors.

The electro-motive force produced by the contact of alkaline liquids with the metals, is generally directed from the metal to the liquid, and its energy is greater, the higher is the place held by the metal in the series of electromotors (159.). Thus, tin, antimony, and zinc, in contact with caustic potash, caustic soda, or ammonia, have a more energetic action than platinum, bismuth, or silver.

The electro-motive force of nitric acid in contact with a metal, is invariably directed from the acid to the metal. In this acid, iron and platinum are the most powerful, and zinc the most feeble electromotors.

Sulphuric and hydrochloric acid, in contact with those metals which stand at the lowest part of the series (159.), develop a force directed from the acid to the metal, and in contact with those at the head of the series, produce a force directed from the metal to the acid. Thus, these acids in contact with the less oxidable metals, as gold, platinum, copper, give an electro-motive force directed from the acid to the metal; but in contact with the more oxidable, as antimony, tin, or zinc, give a force directed from the metal to the acid.

When the metals are placed in contact with weak acid, or saline solutions generally, the electro-motive force is directed from the metal to the liquid, the energy of the force being in general greater the higher is the place of the metal in the series of electromotors (159.). In the case of the metals holding the lowest places in the series, the electro-motive force is in some instances directed with feeble intensity from the liquid to the metal.

163. **Differences of opinion as to the origin of electro-motive action.** — Since the date of the discoveries of Volta to the present day, opinion has been divided in the scientific world as to the actual origin of that electrical excitation which is here expressed by the term electro-motive force, and which, as has been explained, Volta ascribed to the mere mechanical contact of heterogeneous conductors. Some have contended—and among them many of the most eminent recent discoverers in this branch of physics—that the real origin of the electro-motive force is the chemical action which takes place between the solid and liquid conductors; and that, in the cases where there is an apparent development of electricity by the contact of heterogeneous solid

conductors, its real source has been the unperceived chemical action of moisture on the more oxidable electromotor. Others, without disputing the efficacy of chemical action, maintain that it is a secondary agent, merely exciting the electro-motive energy of the solid conductors. Thus, Martens holds that liquids are not properly electromotors at all, but rather modify the electro-motive force of the metals in contact with them; so that they may be considered as sometimes augmenting and sometimes diminishing the effect of the two metals. It is admitted by the partisans of the theory of contact, that the liquids which most powerfully influence the electro-motive force of the solids, are those which act chemically on them with greatest energy. But it is contended that liquids which produce no chemical change on the metal with which they are in contact, do nevertheless affect its electro-motive action.

It fortunately happens, that this polemic can produce no obstacle to the progress of discovery, nor can it affect the certitude of the general conclusions which have been based upon observed facts; while, on the other hand, the spirit of the opposition arising from the conflicting theories, has led to experimental results of the highest importance.

Whatever, therefore, be the origin of the electricity developed under the circumstances which have been described, we shall continue to designate it by the term electro-motive force, by which it was first denominated by its illustrious discoverer; and we shall invariably designate as the direction of this force, that which the positive fluid takes in passing from one element to another in the voltaic combination.

164. **Polar arrangement of the fluids in all electro-motive combinations.** — In every voltaic combination, therefore, the effect of the electro-motive force is a *polar* arrangement of the decomposed fluids ; the positive fluid being driven towards that extremity of the system to which the electro-motive force is directed, and the negative fluid retiring towards the other extremity.

165. **Positive and negative poles.** — These extremities are therefore denominated the *poles* of the system ; that towards which the electro-motive force is directed, and where the positive fluid is collected, being the *positive*, and the other the *negative* pole.

166. **Electro-motive effect of a liquid interposed between two solid conductors.** — When a liquid conductor is placed in contact with and between two solid conductors, an electrical condition is induced, the nature of which will be determined by the quantities and direction of the electro-motive forces developed at the two

surfaces of contact. The several varieties of condition present by such a voltaic arrangement are represented in *fig.* 106. *fig.* 111.

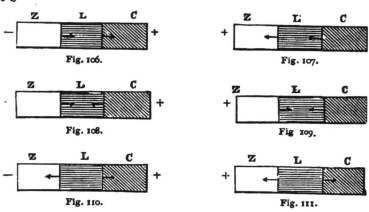

Fig. 106.

Fig. 107.

Fig. 108.

Fig 109.

Fig. 110.

Fig. 111.

Let z and c represent the solid, and L the liquid conductors; and let arrows directed from the two surfaces of contact represent in each case direction of the electro-motive forces. If the electro-motive forces be directed to the same pole, as in *figs.* 106, 107., that pole, receiving all the p tive fluid transmitted by the conductors, will be the positive pole, and other, receiving all the negative fluid transmitted, will be the negative p

The quantity of electricity with which each pole will be charged, will the sum of the quantities developed by the electro-motive forces at the t surfaces, diminished by the sum of the quantities intercepted by reason the imperfect conducting power of the liquid and solids, and by reason of t quantity intercepted in passing from the liquid to the solid conductors at the common surface.

If the electro-motive forces be directed to opposite poles, that pole to whic the more energetic is directed will be the positive pole. The varieties of con ditions presented by this case are represented in *figs.* 108, 109, 110, and 11 Each pole in these cases receives positive fluid from one surface, and negativ from the other. That to which the more energetic electro-motive force directed receives more positive than negative fluid, and is therefore charg with positive fluid equal to their difference, and is, consequently, the positi pole. The other receives more negative than positive fluid, and is, cons quently, the negative pole.

In the case represented in *fig.* 108., the electro-motive force between z and is the more energetic. A greater quantity of positive fluid is received by from the surface z L than of negative fluid from the surface c L, and the su plus of the former above the latter constitutes the free electricity of the po tive pole c. In like manner, the quantity of negative fluid received by t pole z from the surface z L predominates over the quantity of positive flu received from the surface c L, and the surplus of the former over the latt constitutes the free electricity of the negative pole z.

The like reasoning, *mutatis mutandis*, will be applicable to *fig* 109. 111., in which the electro-motive force between z and L is t more energetic, and to *fig.* 110., in which the electro-motive force between c and L is the more energetic.

In all these cases, the quantity of electricity with which the poles are charged is the difference between the actual quantities developed by the two electro-motive forces, diminished by the difference between the quantities intercepted by the imperfection of the conduction of the liquid and solid, and in passing through the surface which separates the liquid and solid conductors.

167. **Electro-motive action of two liquids between two solids.** — The quantity of electricity developed may be augmented by placing different liquid conductors in contact with the two solid conductors. In this case, however, it is necessary to provide some expedient by which the two liquids, without being allowed to intermingle, may nevertheless be in contact, so that the electricities transmitted from the electro-motive surfaces may pass freely from the one liquid to the other. This may be accomplished by separating the liquids by a diaphragm or partition composed of some porous material, which is capable of imbibing the liquids, without being sufficiently open in its texture to allow the liquids to pass in any considerable quantity through it. A partition of unglazed porcelain is found to answer this purpose perfectly. Such an arrangement is represented in *fig.* 112., where z and c are the solid electromotors, L and L′ the two liquids, and P the porous partition separating them.

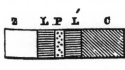

Fig. 112.

168. **Practical examples of such combinations.** — As a practical example of the application of these principles, let the liquid L, *fig.* 106., be concentrated sulphuric acid placed between a plate of zinc z, and a plate of copper c. In this case the electro-motive force is directed from z to L, and from L to c; and, consequently, the tension of the negative electricity on z, and the positive electricity on c, will be the sum of the tensions transmitted from the two surfaces, and z will be the negative, and c the positive pole (166.).

If the liquid be a dilute solution of acid or salt, or a strong alkaline liquid, the electro-motive forces are both directed from the metal to the liquid, but that of the zinc is more energetic than that of the copper; consequently z, *fig.* 108., will in this case be the negative, and c the positive pole, the energy of the combination being proportional to the difference of the two electro-motive forces.

If the liquid be concentrated nitric acid, the electro-motive forces will be both directed from the liquid to the metals. In this case the zinc z, *fig.* 110., being the more feeble electromotor, the copper element c will be the positive, and the zinc z the negative pole.

If two different liquids be interposed between plates of the same metal, th
conditions which affect the development of electricity may be determined b
similar reasoning.

If z and c, *fig.* 112., be two plates of the same metal, and L and L' be tw
liquids, between which and the metal there are unequal electro-motive force
the effect of such an arrangement will be a polar development, the positiv
pole being that to which the electro-motive forces are directed if they have
common direction, and that of the more energetic if they act in opposit
directions. The intensity of the charge at the poles will be in the one cas
the sum, and in the other the difference of the quantities of fluid trans
mitted.

As a practical example of the application of this principle, let the metal
z and c be both platinum, and let L be an alkaline solution, and L' concen
trated nitric acid. In this case the electro-motive forces will be directed from
z to L, and from L' to c, and the effect of the arrangement will be similar t
that represented in *fig.* 106.

169. **Most powerful combinations determined.** — The mos
powerful voltaic arrangements are produced by taking two meta
from the extremes of the electro-motive series (159.), and inte
posing between them two liquids, the electro-motive force of o
being directed from the metal to the liquid, and of the other fr
the liquid to the metal, and so selecting the liquids, subject to t
latter condition, as to have the greatest possible electro-moti
action on the respective metals.

Observing these principles, voltaic combinations of extraordi
nary power have been produced by interposing dilute sulphuric, L
fig. 112., and concentrated nitric acid, L', between zinc z, and car
bon or platinum c. In such a combination, strong electro-motive
forces are developed, directed from the zinc to the acids, and
from the acids to the carbon or platinum. The zinc is therefore
the negative, and the carbon or platinum the positive pole of the
system.

170. **Form of electro-motive combination.** — We have se
lected the form of parallel plates or columns, in the arrangements here described, merely because of the clearness and simplicity which it gives to the exposition of the principles, upon
which all voltaic combinations act. This form, although it was
that of the earliest voltaic systems, and is still in some cases
adhered to, is neither essential to the principle of such arrangements, nor convenient where the development of great force
is required. In order to obtain as great an extent of electro-
motive surface in as small a volume as is practicable, the form of
hollow cylinders of varying diameters, placed concentrically in
cylindrical vessels a little larger, and containing the exciting liquid,
is now generally preferred.

171. **Volta's first combination.** — The simple arrangements
first adopted by Volta consisted of two equal discs of metal, one

of zinc, and the other of copper or silver, with a disc of cloth or bibulous card, soaked in an acid or saline solution, between them. These were usually laid, with their surfaces horizontal, one upon the other.

172. **Wollaston's combination.** — The late Dr. Wollaston proposed an arrangement, in which the copper plate was bent into two parallel plates, a space between them being left for the insertion of the zinc plate, the contact of the plates being prevented by the interposition of bits of cork or other nonconductor. The system thus combined was immersed in dilute acid contained in a porcelain vessel.

173. **Hare's spiral arrangement.** — This consists of two metallic plates, one of zinc and the other of copper, of equal length, rolled together into the form of a spiral, a space of a quarter of an inch being left between them. They are maintained parallel without touching, by means of a wooden cross at top and bottom, in which notches are provided at proper distances, into which the plates are inserted, the two crosses having a common axis. This combination is let into a glass or porcelain cylindrical vessel of corresponding magnitude, containing the exciting liquid.

This arrangement has the great advantage of providing a very considerable electro-motive surface with a very small volume.

The exciting liquid recommended for these batteries when great power is desired, is a solution in water of $2\frac{1}{4}$ per cent. of sulphuric, and 2 per cent. of nitric acid. A less intense but more durable action may be obtained by a solution of common salt, or of 3 to 5 per cent. of sulphuric acid only.

174. **Amalgamation of the zinc.** — Whatever be the form of the arrangement, its force and uniformity of action will be promoted by amalgamating the zinc element, which may be best accomplished in the following manner : —

Immerse the rough plate or cylinder of zinc in a solution of sulphuric acid containing from 12 to 16 per cent. of acid, until the thin film of oxide which usually collects on the surface of the metal be dissolved. Then wash it well in water, and immerse it in a dilute solution of the nitrate of mercury. After a short time a perfectly uniform amalgam will be formed on the surface of the zinc. Let the zinc be then washed in water and rubbed dry with sawdust.

175. **Cylindrical combination with one fluid.** — Voltaic systems of the cylindrical form usually consist of two hollow cylinders of different metals, one of which, however, is always zinc. The exciting liquid being placed in a cylindrical vessel a little longer than the greater of the two hollow metallic cylinders, these are immersed in it concentrically with it and with each other. A

H 3

part of each projecting from the top of the vessel becomes the pole of the system.

Such a combination is represented in vertical section in *fig.* 113., where v v is a vessel of glazed porcelain, containing the acid or saline solution, z z is a hollow cylinder of zinc, and c c a similar hollow cylinder of copper, each being open at both ends, and separated from each other by a space of a quarter to half an inch. Strips of metal c p and z n represent the poles, that connected with the zinc being the negative, and that connected with the copper being the positive pole.

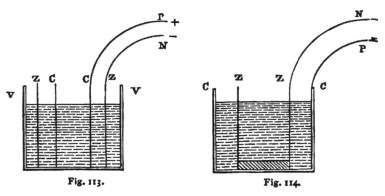

Fig. 113.   Fig. 114.

In some cases the porcelain vessel v v is dispensed with, and the acid solution is placed in a cylindrical copper vessel, in which the hollow cylinder of zinc is immersed, resting upon some nonconducting support. Such an arrangement is represented in *fig.* 114. in vertical section, c c being the copper vessel, z z the zinc cylinder, and p and n the poles.

176. **Cylindrical combinations with two fluids.** — Cylindrical arrangements with two exciting liquids are made in the following manner. The hollow cylinder of zinc z z, open at both ends as already described, is placed in a vessel of glazed porcelain v v (*fig.* 115.). Within this is placed a cylindrical vessel v v, of unglazed porcelain, a little less in diameter than the zinc z z, so that a space of about quarter of an inch may separate their surfaces. In this vessel v v is inserted a cylinder c c of platinum, open at the ends, and a little less than

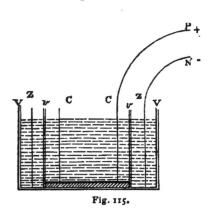

Fig. 115.

v v, so that their surfaces may be about a quarter of an inch asunder. Dilute sulphuric acid is then poured into the vessel v v, and concentrated nitric acid into v v. According to what has been already explained (169.), P proceeding from the platinum will then be the positive, and N proceeding from the zinc the negative pole.

177. **Grove's battery.**—This arrangement is known as *Grove's battery*. Various modifications have been suggested with the view to increase the electro-motive surface of the platinum, and econo- mise expense. Grüel suggests the use of thin platinum, attached by platinum wires to a central axis, from which from 4 to 6 leaves or flaps diverge. Poggendorf proposes a single leaf of platinum, greater in breadth than the diameter of the vessel v v in the ratio of about 3 to 2, and bent into the form of an S, so as to pass freely into it. Pfaff proposes to coat the inner surface of the vessel v v with leaf platinum. Peschel affirms, after having tried this expedient, that it is less effective than the former.

In these systems it is recommended to use a solution of sul- phuric acid containing from 10 to 25 per cent. of acid, and nitric acid of the specific gravity of 1·33.

This arrangement, as usually constructed, is represented in *figs.* 116. and 117., where G is a cylindrical jar of glass or porcelain nearly filled with water,

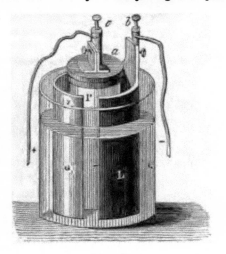

| Fig. 116. | Fig. 117. |

acidulated with sulphuric acid. z is a cylinder of zinc open at both ends, and having an opening in the side passing from end to end. P is a vase of unglazed porcelain or earthenware, filled with nitric acid; and in fine L is a leaf of platinum bent to the form of S, as shown in *fig.* 117., and attached to a cover, a, *fig.* 116., which is placed upon the porous vase P. A metallic rod c, communicating with the leaf of platinum, is connected with a copper wire, which serves as the positive pole, while a second wire, fixed to the zinc at *b*, is the negative pole.

One of the objections to this arrangement is the costly character of the platinum, and the circumstance that when it has been in use for a certain time that metal becomes so brittle that the least accidental disturbance will break it.

178. Bunsen's battery.— The voltaic system known as *Bun-*

Fig. 118.

sen's is similar to the preceding, substituting charcoal for platinum.

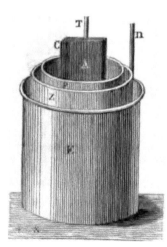

Fig. 119.

The charcoal cylinder used for this purpose is made from the residuum taken from the retorts of gasworks. A strong porous mass is produced by repeatedly baking the pulverised coke, to which the required form is easily imparted. Messrs. Deleuil and Son, of Paris, have fabricated batteries on this principle with great success. I have one at present in use, consisting of fifty pairs of zinc and carbon cylinders, the zinc being 2¼ inches diameter and 8 inches high, which performs very satisfactorily.

The electro-motive forces of Grove's and Bunsen's batteries are considered to be, *cæteris paribus*, equal.

The several parts of this battery, as usually constructed, are shown in *fig.* 118., where A is a cylindrical vessel of glazed earthenware, filled with water acidulated by 8 or 10 per cent. of sulphuric acid. B is the hollow cylinder of amalgamated zinc, to which a copper ribbon is attached, intended to serve as the negative pole, and C is a cylindrical vessel of unglazed porcelain, to be filled with strong nitric acid; and, in fine, D is a solid cylinder of charcoal, to which another copper ribbon is attached, to serve as the positive pole.

The apparatus, with all its parts combined, so as to develop the voltaic current, is shown in *fig.* 119., where the zinc cylinder is placed in the glazed vase E, the unglazed cylinder P within the zinc, and the charcoal cylinder C immersed in the nitric acid contained in P.

179. Daniel's constant battery. — The voltaic arrangement known as Daniel's constant battery consists of a copper cylindrical vessel c c (*fig* 120.), widening near the top *a d.* In this is placed

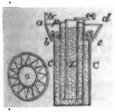

a cylindrical vessel of unglazed porcelain *p.* In this latter is placed the hollow cylinder of zinc z, already described. The space between the copper and porcelain vessels is filled with a saturated solution of the sulphate of copper, which is maintained in a state of saturation by crystals of the salt placed in the wide cup *a b c d,* in the bottom

of which is a grating composed of wire carried in a zigzag direction between two concentric rings, as represented in plan at G. The vessel *p,* containing the zinc, is filled with a solution of sulphuric acid, contain-

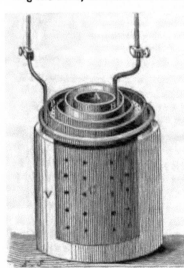

ing from 10 to 25 per cent. of acid when greater electromotive power is required, and from 1 to 4 per cent. when more moderate action is sufficient.

This battery, in its usual form, is represented in perspective in *fig.* 121., where v is a cylinder of glass or porcelain filled with the saturated solution of the sulphate of copper. The copper cylinder c, the sides of which are pierced with holes. is immersed in this. To the upper part of this cylinder is attached the annular gallery, the bottom of which is pierced with small holes, and which is immersed in the solution. This gallery is filled with crystals of the sulphate of copper, which are being

Fig. 121.

constantly dissolved, so as to keep the solution to the point of sat
In fine, in the interior of the cylinder c is contained a smaller cy
unglazed porcelain, filled with water, acidulated with sulphuric
holding in solution common sea salt, in which is plunged the zinc cy
open at both ends and amalgamated. To the cylinder of zinc anc
are attached, by clamping screws, two copper ribbons, which are the
the pile.

180. **Pouillet's modification of Daniel's battery.**
following modification of Daniel's system was adopted
Pouillet in his experimental researches.

A hollow cylinder a, *fig.* 122., of thin copper, having a flat be
and a conical top d, is ballasted with sand b. Above this cone the
the copper cylinder are continued, and terminate in a flange e. I
this flange and the base of the cone, and near the base, is a ring c
This copper vessel is placed in a bladder which fits it loosely like
and is tied round the neck under the flange e. The saturated sol
the sulphate of copper is poured into the cup above the cone, and,

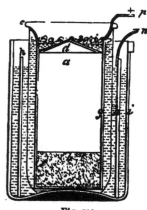

Fig. 122.

through the ring of holes, fills th
between the bladder and the copy
sel. It is maintained in its state of
ration by crystals of the salt depc
the cup.

This copper vessel is then immer
vessel of glazed porcelain i, contai
solution of the sulphate of zinc
chloride of sodium (common salt).
low cylinder of zinc h, split down t
so as to be capable of being enlar
contracted at pleasure, is immersed
solution surrounding the bladder.
poles are indicated by the condu
and n, the positive proceeding fr
copper, and the negative from the j

M. Pouillet states that the
of this apparatus is sustained w
sensible variation for entire

provided the cup above the cone d is kept supplied with th
so as to maintain the solution in the saturated state.

181. **Advantages and disadvantages of these so
systems.**—The chief advantage of Daniel's system is tha
which it takes its name, its *constancy.* Its power, however,
most efficient state, is greatly inferior to that of the carl
platinum systems of Bunsen and Grove. But a serious pr
inconvenience attends all batteries in which concentrated
acid is used, owing to the diffusion of nitrous vapour, ai
injury to which the parties working them are exposed l
spiring it. In my own experiments with Bunsen's batteri
assistants have been often severely affected.

In the use of the platinum battery of Grove, the nuisanc

duced by the evolution of nitrous vapour is sometimes mitigated, by enclosing the cells in a box, from the lid of which a tube proceeds which conducts these vapours out of the room.

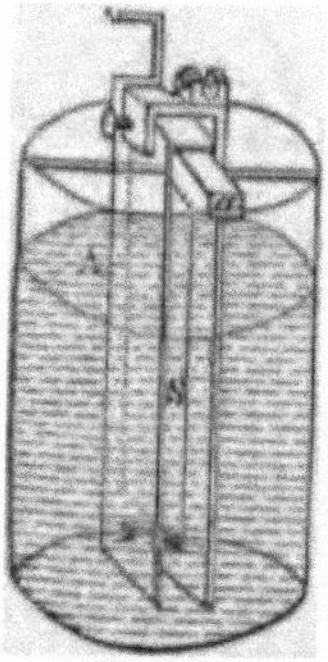

In combinations of this kind, Dr. O'Shaugnessy substituted gold for platinum, and a mixture of two parts by weight of sulphuric acid to one of saltpetre for nitric acid.

Fig. 123.

182. **Smee's battery.** — The voltaic combination called *Smee's battery* consists of a porcelain vessel A, *fig.* 123., containing an acid solution, which may be about 15 per cent. of sulphuric acid in water.

A plate of iron or silver s, whose surfaces are *platinised* by a certain chemical process, is suspended from a bar of wood a, between two plates of zinc z, suspended from the same bar without contact with the plate s. The electro-motive action is explained on the same principle as the combinations already described. Mr. Smee claims, as an advantage for this system, its great simplicity and power, the quantity of electricity evolved being, *cæteris paribus*, very great, and the manipulation easy.

183. **Wheatstone's system.** — Professor Wheatstone has proposed the combination represented in *fig.* 124. A cylindrical vessel *v v*, of unglazed and half-baked red earthenware, is placed in another, v v, larger one of glazed porcelain or glass.

Fig. 124.

The vessel *v v* is filled with a pasty amalgam of zinc, and the space between the two vessels is filled with a saturated solution of sulphate of copper. In the latter solution is immersed a thin cylinder of copper *c c*. A rod or wire of copper N is plunged in the amalgam. The electro-motive forces of this system are directed from the amalgam to the copper solution; so that P proceeding from the copper cylinder is the positive, and N proceeding from the amalgam, is the negative pole.

The action of this system is said to be constant, like that of Daniel, so long at least as the vessel *v v* allows equally free passage to the two fluids, and the state of saturation of the copper solution is maintained.

184. **Bagration's system.** — A voltaic arrangement suggested by the Prince Bagration, and said to be well adapted to galvano-plastic purposes, consists of parallel hollow cylinders, *fig.* 125., of zinc and copper, immersed in sand contained in a porcelain vessel. The sand is kept wet by a solution of hydrochlorate of ammonia.

185. **Becquerel's system.** — M. Becquerel has applied the principle of two fluids and a single metal explained in (168.) in the following manner : —

A porcelain vessel v, *fig.* 126., contains concentrated nitric acid.

A glass cylinder T, to which is attached a bottom of unglazed porcelain, is immersed in it. This cylinder contains a solution of

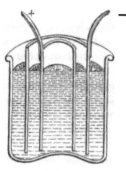
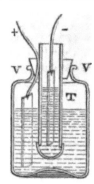

Fig. 125.   Fig. 126.

common salt. Two plates of platinum are immersed, one in the nitric acid, and the other in the solution of salt. The electromotive forces take effect, the conduction being maintained through the porous bottom of the glass vessel T, the positive pole being that which proceeds from the nitric acid, and the negative that which proceeds from the salt.

186. **Schonbein's modification of Bunsen's battery.**—M. Schonbein proposes the following modification of Bunsen's system. In a vessel of cast iron, rendered capable of resisting oxidation by processes which will be explained hereafter, he places a mixture of three parts of concentrated nitric with one of sulphuric acid. In this he immerses the cylindrical vessel of unglazed porcelain which contains the zinc, immersed in a weak solution of sulphuric acid. In this arrangement the cast-iron vessel plays the part of Bunsen's cylinder of charcoal. The positive pole is therefore that which proceeds from the cast-iron vessel, and the negative that which is connected with the zinc.

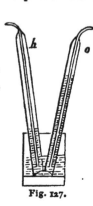

Fig. 127.

187. **Grove's gas electro-motive apparatus.**—We shall conclude this synopsis of the simple voltaic combinations with the gas electro-motive apparatus of Mr. Grove, one of the most curious and interesting that has been contrived. Two glass tubes, h and o, fig. 127., are inverted in a vessel containing water slightly acidulated with sulphuric acid. Hydrogen gas h is admitted into one of these, and oxygen o into the other in the usual way. A narrow strip of platinum passes at the top o

ach tube through an aperture which is hermetically closed around
t, the strip descending near to the bottoms of the tubes.   An
lectro-motive force is developed between the platinum and the
ases, whica is directed from the platinum to the oxygen, and
rom the hydrogen to the platinum.   The end of the platinum
rhich issues from the hydrogen is therefore the positive, and that
rhich issues from the oxygen the negative, pole of the system.

CHAP. II.

VOLTAIC BATTERIES.

188. **Volta's invention of the pile.** — Whatever may be the
efficacy of simple combinations of electromotors compared one with
another, the electricity developed even by the most energetic
among them is still incomparably more feeble than that which
proceeds from other agencies, and indeed so feeble that without
some expedient by which its power can be augmented in a very
high ratio, it would possess very little importance as a physical
agent.   Volta was not slow to perceive this; but having also a
clear foresight of the importance of the consequences that must
result from it if its energy could be increased, he devoted all the
powers of his invention to discover an expedient by which this
object could be attained, and happily not without success.

He conceived the idea of uniting together in a connected and
continuous series, a number of simple electro-motive combinations, in such a manner that the positive electricity developed by
each should flow towards one end of the series, and the negative
towards the other end.   In this way he proposed to multiply the
power of the extreme elements of the series, by charging them with
all the electricity developed by the intermediate elements.

In the first attempt to realise this conception, circular discs of
silver and copper of equal magnitude (silver and copper coin
served the purpose), were laid one over the other, having interposed between them equal discs of cloth or pasteboard soaked in
an acid or saline solution.   A pile was thus formed which was
denominated a *voltaic pile;* and although this arrangement was
speedily superseded by others found more convenient, the original
name was retained.

Such arrangements are still called *voltaic piles,* and sometimes
voltaic batteries, being related to a simple voltaic combination in
the same manner as a Leyden battery is to a Leyden jar.

189. **Explanation of the principle of the pile.**—To
the principle of the voltaic battery, let us suppose several
voltaic combinations, $z^1 L^1 C^1$, $z^2 L^2 C^2$, $z^3 L^3 C^3$, $z^4 L^4 C^4$, *fig.*

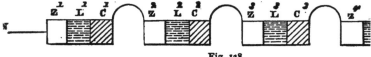

Fig. 128.

be placed, so that the negative poles z shall all look to
and the positive c to the right. Let the metallic plates c
tended, and bent into an arc, so as to be placed in cont:
the plates z. Let the entire series be supposed to stand u]
insulating support, and let the negative pole z^1 of the fir:
bination of the series be put in connection with the grou:
conductor.

If we express by E the quantity of positive electricity developed t
the negative fluid escaping by the conductor, this fluid E will pass t
from thence along the entire series to the extremity c^4. The com
$z^1 L^1 C^1$ acts in this case as the generator of electricity in the same m
the cushion and cylinder of an electrical machine, and the remaind(
series $z^2 L^2 C^2$, &c., plays the part of the conductor, receiving the c
fluid from $z^1 L^1 C^1$.

The second combination $z^2 L^2 C^2$ being similar exactly to the first
an equal quantity of electricity E, the negative fluid passing throug]
and the conductor to the ground. The positive fluid passes from z
the succeeding combinations to the end of the series.

In the same manner, each successive combination acts as a gen(
electricity, the negative fluid escaping to the ground by the precedi:
binations and the conductor, and the positive fluid being diffused (
succeeding part of the series.

It appears, therefore, that the conductor P connected with the last
nation of the series must receive from each of the four combinations
charge E of positive fluid; so that the depth or quantity of electrici
it will be four times that which it would receive from the single com
$z^4 L^4 C^4$ acting alone and unconnected with the remainder of the serie

In general, therefore, the intensity of the electricity received by
ductor attached to the last element of the series, will be as many time:
than that which it would receive from a single combination, as t]
combinations in the series. If the number of combinations compo:
series be n, and E be the intensity of the electricity developed by
combination, then $n \times E$ will be the intensity of the electricity produc(
extremity of the series.

It has been here supposed that the extremity z^1 of the series is co
by the conductor N with the ground. If it be not so connected, an
entire series be insulated, the distribution of the fluids developed wil
ferent. In that case, the conductor P will receive the positive fluid
gated from each of the electro-motive surfaces to the right, and the c(
N will receive the negative fluid propagated from each of these surfa(

left, and each will receive as many times more electricity than it would receive from a single combination, as there are simple combinations in the series. If, therefore, E′ express the quantity of fluid which each conductor P and N would receive from a single combination $z^1 L^1 c^1$, then $n \times E'$ will be the quantity it would receive from a series consisting of n simple combinations.

Since two different metals generally enter with a liquid into each combination, it has been usual to call these voltaic combinations *pairs*; so that a battery is said to consist of so many *pairs*.

On the Continent these combinations are called *elements*; and the voltaic pile is said to consist of so many *elements*, each element consisting of two metals and the interposing liquid.

190. **Effect of the imperfect liquid conductors.** — In what precedes we have considered that all the electricity developed by each pair is propagated without resistance or diminution to the poles P and N of the pile. This, however, could only occur if the materials composing the pile through which the electricity must be transmitted were perfect conductors. Now, although the metallic parts may be regarded as practically perfect conductors, the liquid through which the electricity must be transmitted, in passing from one metallic element to another, is not only an imperfect conductor, but one whose conducting power is subject to constant variation. A correction would therefore be necessary in applying the preceding reasoning, the electricity received by the poles P and N being less than $n \times E'$, by that portion which is intercepted or lost in transmission through the liquid conductors. The amount of the resistance to conduction proceeding from the conductors, liquid and metallic, by which the electricity evolved at the generating surfaces is transmitted to the poles of the pile, has not been ascertained with any clearness or certainty.

Professor Ohm, who has investigated the question of the resistance of the conductors composing a battery to the propagation of the electricity through them, maintains that the intensity of the electricity transmitted to the poles of the pile is "directly as the sum of the electro-motive forces, and inversely as the sum of all the impediments to conduction." We do not find, however, that this law has been so developed and verified by observation and experiment, as to entitle it to a place in elementary instruction.

191. **Method of developing electricity in great quantity.** — If the object be to obtain a great quantity of electricity, the elements of the pile should be combined by connecting the poles of the same name with common conductors. Thus, if all the positive poles be connected by metallic wires with one conductor, and all the negative poles with another, these conductors will be charged with as much electricity as would be produced by a single

combination, of which the generating surfaces would be equal to the sum of the generating surfaces of all the elements of the series; but the intensity of the electricity thus developed would not be greater than that of the electricity developed by a single pair.

192. **Distinction between quantity and intensity important.** — It is of great importance to distinguish between the quantity and the intensity of the electricity evolved by the pile. The quantity depends on the magnitude of the sum of all the surfaces of the electromotors. The intensity depends on the number of pairs composing the series. The quantity is measured merely by the actual quantity of each fluid received at the poles. The intensity is proportional, *cæteris paribus*, to the number of pairs transmitting electricity to the same pole, the fluids being superposed at the poles, and the intensity being produced by such superposition.

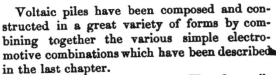

Voltaic piles have been composed and constructed in a great variety of forms by combining together the various simple electromotive combinations which have been described in the last chapter.

193. **Volta's first pile.** — The first pile constructed by Volta was formed as follows:— A disc of zinc was laid upon a plate of glass. Upon it was laid an equal disc of cloth or pasteboard soaked in acidulated water. Upon this was laid an equal disc of copper. Upon the copper were laid in the same order three discs of zinc, wet cloth, and copper, and the same superposition of the same combinations of zinc, cloth, and copper was continued until the pile was completed. The highest disc (of copper) was then the positive, and the lowest disc (of zinc) the negative pole, according to the principles already explained.

It was usual to keep the discs in their places by confining them between rods of glass.

Such a pile, with conducting wires connected with its poles, is represented in *fig.* 129.

194. **The couronne des tasses.** — The next arrangement proposed by Volta formed a step towards the form which the pile definitely assumed, and is known under the name of the *couronne des tasses* (ring of cups): this is represented in *fig.* 130., and consists of a series of cups or glasses containing the acid solution. Rods of

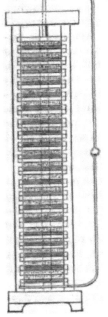

Fig. 129.

zinc and copper z c, soldered together end to end, are bent into the form of arcs, the ends being immersed in two adjacent cups,

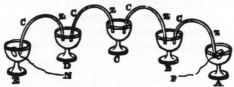

Fig. 130.

so that the metals may succeed each other in one uniform order. A plate of zinc, to which a conducting wire n is attached, is immersed in the first; and a similar plate of copper, with a wire p, in the last cup. The latter wire will be the positive, and the former the negative, pole.

195. **Cruikshank's arrangement.** — The next form of voltaic pile proposed was that of Cruikshank, represented in *fig.* 131. This consisted of a trough of glazed earthenware divided into parallel cells corresponding in number and magnitude to the pairs of zinc and copper plates which were attached to a bar of wood, and so connected that, when immersed in the cells, each

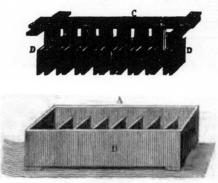

Fig. 131.

copper plate should be in connection with the zinc plate of the next cell. The plates were easily raised from the trough when the battery was not in use. The trough contained the acid solution.

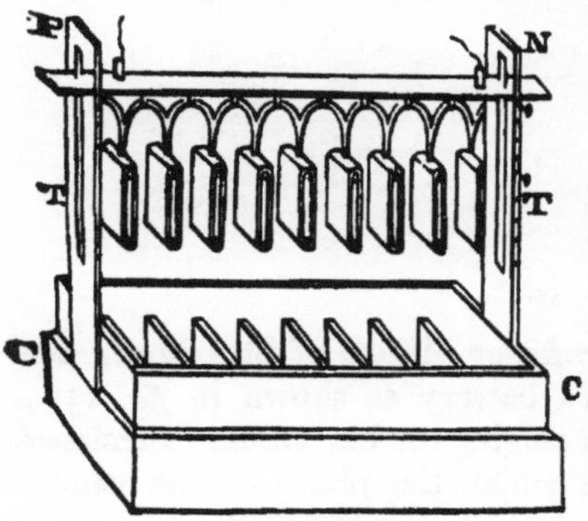

196. **Wollaston's arrangement.** — In order to obtain within the same volume a greater extent of electromotive surface, Dr. Wollaston doubled the copper plate round the zinc plate, without however allowing them to touch. In this case the copper plates have twice the magnitude of the

Fig. 132.

zinc plates. The system, like the former, is attached to a bar of wood, and being similarly connected, is either let down into a trough of earthenware divided into cells, as represented in *fig.* 132., or into separate glass or porcelain vessels, as represented in *fig.* 133. The latter method has the advantage of affording greater facility for discharging and renewing the acid solution.

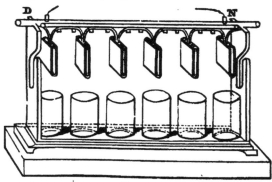

Fig. 133.

Another view of this form of mounting a battery is shown in *fig.* 134.

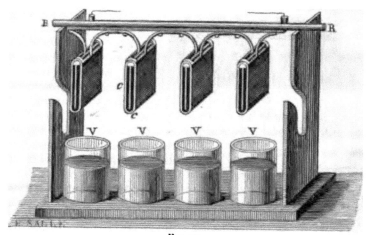

Fig. 134.

197. **Münch's battery.** — Professor Münch of Strasbourg has simplified the form of Wollaston's battery as shown in *fig.* 135. by plunging all the couples in a single wooden trough varnished on the interior. The manner in which the plates of the couples are combined is shown in the figure. This pile has the advantage of small bulk, but its action is not of long continuance.

198. **Helical pile of Faculty of Sciences at Paris.** — The helical pile is a voltaic arrangement adapted to produce

Fig. 135.

electricity of low tension in great quantity. This pile, as constructed for the Faculty of Sciences at Paris under the direction of M. Pouillet, consists of a cylinder of wood *b, fig.* 136., of about

Fig. 136.

four inches diameter and fifteen inches long, on which are rolled spirally two thin leaves of zinc and copper separated by small bits of cloth, and pieces of twine extended parallel to each other, having a thickness a little less than the cloth. A pair is formed in this manner, having a surface of sixty square feet. A single combination of this kind evolves electricity in large quantity, and a battery composed of twenty pairs is an agent of prodigious power.

The method of immersing the combination in the acid solution represented in *fig.* 137.

199. Piles are formed by connecting together a number of any of the simple electro-motive combinations described in the last chapter, the conditions under which they are connected being always the same, the positive pole of each combination being put in metallic connection with the negative pole of the succeeding one.

When the combinations are cylindrical, it is convenient to
them in a framing, which will prevent the accidental fracture

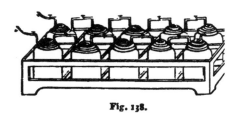

Fig. 138.

Fig. 137.

strain of the connections. A battery of ten pairs of Grove's
Bunsen's is represented with its proper connections in *fig.* 138
A similar battery upon Bunsen's principle is shown in *fig.* 1

Fig. 139.

In *fig.* 140. is represented a convenient form of Daniel's ba
tery, consisting of four pairs. The jars are here made flat, a for

which is more convenient when zinc is used, which is generally manufactured in sheets. The diaphragms are made either of sail cloth, or gold beater's leaf. Each pair is placed in connection by a wire extending from the zinc of one pair to the copper of the other. The terminal wire D attached to the zinc of the first pair is the negative pole, and the wire E attached to the copper of the last pair is the positive pole.

Fig. 140.

200. **Conductors connecting the elements.** — Whatever be the form or construction of the pile, its efficient performance requires that perfect metallic contact should be made and maintained between the elements composing it, by means of short and good conductors. Copper wire, or, still better, strips cut from sheet copper from half an inch to an inch in breadth, are found the most convenient material for these conductors, as well as for the conductors which carry the electricity from the poles of the pile to the objects to which it is to be conveyed. In some cases, these conducting wires or strips are soldered to metallic plates, which are immersed in the exciting liquid of the extreme elements of the pile, and which, therefore, become its poles. In some cases, small mercurial cups are soldered to the poles of the pile, in which the points of the conducting wires, being first scraped, cleaned, and amalgamated, are immersed. Many inconveniences, however, attend the use of quicksilver, and these cups have lately been very generally superseded by simple clamps constructed in a variety of forms, by means of which the conducting wires or strips may be fixed in metallic contact with the poles of the pile, with each other, or with any object to which the electricity is required to be conveyed. Where great precaution is considered necessary to

secure perfect contact, the extremities of the conductors at the points of connection are sometimes gilt by the electrotyping process, which may always be done at a trifling cost. I have not, however, in any case found this necessary, having always obtained

Fig. 140 b.

perfect contact by keeping the surfaces clean, and using screw clamps of the form in *fig.* 140*b*. This is represented in its proper magnitude.

201. Pile may be placed at any distance from place of experiment. — It is generally found to be inconvenient in practice to keep the pile in the room where the experiments are made, the acid vapours being injurious in various ways, especially where nitric acid is used. It is therefore more expedient to place it in any situation where these vapours have easy means of escaping into the open air, and where metallic objects are not exposed to them. The situation of the pile may be at any desired distance from the place where the experiments are made, communication with it being maintained by strips of sheet copper as above described, which may be carried along walls or passages, contact between them being made by doubling them together at the ends which are joined, and nailing the joints to the wall. They should of course be kept out of contact with any metallic object which might divert the electric current from its course. I have myself a large pile placed in an attic connected by these means with a lower room in the house, by strips of copper which measure about fifty yards.

202. Memorable piles: Davy's pile at the Royal Institution. — Among the apparatus of this class which have obtained celebrity in the history of physical science, may be mentioned the pile of 2000 pairs of plates, each having a surface of 32 square inches, at the Royal Institution, with which Davy effected the decomposition of the alkalies, and the pile of the Royal Society of nearly the same magnitude and power.

203. Napoleon's pile at Polytechnic School. — In 1808, the Emperor Napoleon presented to the Polytechnic School at Paris, a pile of 600 pairs of plates, having each a square foot of surface. It was with this apparatus that several of the most important researches of Gay Lussac and Thénard were conducted.

204. Children's great plate battery, consisted of 16 pairs of plates constructed by Wollaston's method, each plate measuring 6 feet in length and 2¾ feet in width, so that the copper surface of each amounted to 32 square feet; and when the whole was connected, there was an effective surface of 512 square feet.

205. Hare's deflagrator was constructed on the helical principle, and consisted of 80 pairs, each zinc surface measuring 54 square inches, and each copper 80 square inches.

206. **Stratingh's deflagrator** consisted of 100 pairs on Wollaston's method. Each zinc surface measured 200 square inches. It was used either as a battery of 100 pairs, or as a single combination (191.), presenting a total electro-motive surface of 227 square feet of zinc and 544 of copper.

207. **Pepys' pile at London Institution** consisted of elements each of which was composed of a sheet of copper and one of zinc, measuring each 50 feet in length and 2 feet in width. These were wound round a rod of wood with horsehair between them. Each bucket contained 55 gallons of the exciting liquid.

208. These and all similar apparatus, powerful as they have been, and memorable as the discoveries in physics are to which several of them have been instrumental, have fallen into disuse, except in certain cases, where powerful physiological effects are to be produced, since the invention of the piles of two liquids, which, with a number of elements not exceeding 40, and a surface not exceeding 100 square inches each, evolve a power equal to the most colossal of the apparatus above described.

The most efficient voltaic apparatus are formed by combining Daniel's, Grove's, or Bunsen's single batteries, connecting their opposite poles with strips of copper as already described. Grove's battery, constructed by Jacobi of St. Petersburgh, consists of 64 platinum plates, each having a surface of 36 square inches; so that their total surface amounts to 16 square feet. This is considered to be the most powerful voltaic apparatus ever constructed. According to Jacobi's estimate, its effect is equal to a Daniel's battery of 266 square feet, or to a Hare's deflagrator of 5500 square feet.

209. **Dry piles.**—The term *dry pile* was originally intended to express a voltaic pile composed exclusively of solid elements. The advantages of such an apparatus were so apparent, that attempts at its invention were made at an early stage in the progress of electrical science. In such a pile, neither evaporation nor chemical action taking place, the elements could suffer no change; and the quantity and intensity of the electricity evolved would be absolutely uniform and invariable, and its action would be perpetual.

210. **Deluc's pile.**—The first instrument of this class constructed was the dry pile of Deluc, subsequently improved by Zamboni. This apparatus is prepared by soaking thick writing-paper in milk, honey, or some analogous animal fluid, and attaching to its surface by gum a thin leaf of zinc or tin. The other side of the paper is coated with peroxide of manganese. Leaves of this

are superposed, the sides similarly coated being all presented
the same direction, and circular discs are cut of an inch diame
by a circular cutter. Several thousands being laid over
another, are pressed into a close and compact column by a scr
and the sides of the column are·then thickly coated with gum-.

The origin of the electro-motive force of the pile is varic
Besides the contact of heterogeneous substances, chemical act
intervenes in several ways. The organic matter acts upon
zinc as well as upon the manganese, reducing the latter to a lo
state of oxidation.

211. **Zamboni's pile.** — Piles, having two elements only, h:
been constructed by Zamboni. These consist of one metal ;
one intermediate conductor, either dry or moist. If the form
the discs are of silvered paper laid with their metal faces all look
the same way ; if the latter, a number of pieces of tinfoil, with
end pointed and the other broad, are laid in two watch-glas
which contain water, in such a manner, that the pointed part
in one glass and the broad part in the other. After some ti
they develop at their poles a feeble electricity, which they ret
for several days, the metal pole being positive in the dry pile, ;
the pointed end of the zinc in the moist one.

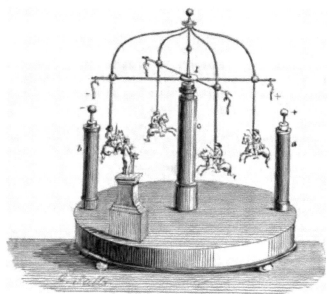

Fig. 141.

212. **Voltaic jeux de bague.** — A pretty voltaic toy has b
constructed upon the principle of dry piles, as shown in *fig.* 14

Two columns of copper a and b, are connected within a circular box on which they stand, by a powerful dry pile placed horizontally between them, the pillar a being its positive, and b its negative pole. Upon a central pivot c is an ivory cup l, with which are connected two horizontal rods at right angles to each other, which support four wires, carrying birds, horses, or goats, upon which stand small figures, holding in their hands rods, aimed, as they pass, at a ring suspended from another figure standing on the same box. From the four extremities of the horizontal rods little flags are suspended, upon which metallic leaf is attached, and as the column revolves these leaves are alternately attracted and repelled by the ball at the top of the columns a and b, and by this attraction and repulsion the apparatus is kept in constant revolution. Galvanic toys constructed on this principle, which continue moving for several years, may be seen in the shops of the opticians.

213. **Piles of a single metal.** — Piles of a single metal have been constructed by causing one surface to be exposed to a chemical action different from the other. This may be effected by rendering one surface smooth and the other rough. A pile of this kind has been made with sixty or eighty plates of zinc of four square inches surface. These are fixed in a wooden trough parallel to each other, their polished faces looking the same way, and an open space of the tenth to the twentieth of an inch being left between them, these spaces being merely occupied by atmospheric air. If one extremity of·this apparatus be put in communication with the ground, the other pole will sensibly affect an electroscope.

In this case, the electro-motive action takes place between the air and the metal.

214. **Ritter's secondary piles.** — The secondary piles, sometimes called *Ritter's piles*, consist of alternate layers of homogeneous metal plates, between which some moist conducting substance is interposed. When they stand alone, no electro-motive force is developed; but, if they be allowed to continue for a certain time in connection with the poles of a battery, and then disconnected, positive electricity will be found to be accumulated at that end which was connected with the positive pole, and negative electricity at the other end; and this polar condition will continue for a certain time, which will be greater, the less the electrical tension imparted. This phenomenon has not been satisfactorily explained, but would seem to arise from the low conducting power of the strata of liquid interposed between the plates.

CHAP. III.

VOLTAIC CURRENTS.

215. The voltaic current. — The voltaic pile differs from the electrical machine, inasmuch as it has the power of constantly reproducing whatever electricity may be drawn from it by conductors placed in connection with its poles, without any manipulation, or the intervention of any agency external to the pile itself. So prompt is the action of this generating power, that the positive and negative fluids pass from the respective poles through such conductors, in a continuous and unvarying stream, as a liquid would move through pipes issuing from a reservoir. The pile may indeed be regarded as a reservoir of the electric fluids, with a provision by which it constantly replenishes itself.

If two metallic wires be connected at one end with the poles P and N, *fig.* 142., of the pile, and at the other with any conductor o, through which it is required to transmit the electricity evolved in the pile, the positive fluid will pass from P along the wire to o, and the negative fluid in like manner

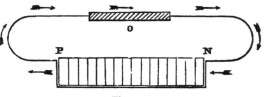

Fig. 142.

from N to o. The positive fluid will therefore form a stream or current from P through o to N, and the negative fluid a contrary current from N through o to P.

It might be expected that the combination of the two opposite fluids in equal quantity would reduce the wire to its natural state; and this would, in fact, be the case, if the fluids were in repose upon the wire, which may be proved by detaching at the same moment the ends of the wires from the poles P and N. The wires and the conductor o will, in that case, show no indication of electrical excitement. If the wire be detached only from the negative pole N, it will be found, as well as the conductor o, to be charged with positive electricity; and if it be detached from the positive pole P, they will be charged with negative electricity, the electricity in each case being in repose. But when both ends of the wire are in connection with the poles P and N, the fluids, being in motion in contrary directions along the wire and intermediate conductors, impart to these, qualities which show that they are not in the natural or unelectrified state, but which have nothing in common with the qualities, which belong to bodies charged with the electric fluid in repose. Thus, the wire or conductor will neither attract nor repel pith balls, nor produce any electroscopic effects. They will, however, produce a great variety of other phenomena, which we shall presently notice.

The state of the electricities in thus passing between the poles of the piles, through a metallic wire or other conductor exterior to the pile, is called a *voltaic current.*

216. **Direction of the current.** — Although, according to what has been stated, this current consists of two streams flowing in contrary directions, it receives its denomination exclusively from the positive fluid; and, accordingly, the *direction of the current* is always from the positive pole through the wire or other conductor to the negative pole.

It is necessary, however, to observe, that in passing through the pile itself from element to element, it moves from the negative pole to the positive pole. The direction and course of the current is indicated in *fig.* 142. by the arrows.

217. **Poles of the pile, how distinguished.** — In designating the poles of the pile, much confusion and obscurity, and consequent difficulty to students, has arisen from identifying the poles of the pile with the extreme plates of metal composing it. In the piles first constructed by Volta, the last plate at the positive end was zinc, and the last at the negative end copper; and such an arrangement was often retained at more recent periods. Hence the positive pole was called the *zinc pole*, and the negative pole the *copper pole*. The extreme plates being afterwards dispensed with, the final plate at the positive end became copper, and that at the negative end zinc; and, consequently, the positive pole was then the copper pole, and the negative pole the zinc pole.

This confusion, however, may be avoided, by observing that the poles, positive or negative, are not dependent on the plates or cylinders of metal with which the pole may terminate, but on the direction of the electro-motive forces of its elements. In general, in a pile composed of zinc and copper elements, the zinc plates of each pair all *look towards* the positive pole, and the copper plates towards the negative pole. It must, however, be observed, that, in the ordinary arrangement, one element of a pair is placed at each extremity of the pile, and constitutes its pole, the pair being only completed when the poles are united by the conducting wire. Thus, the pole to which the copper elements look, terminates in a zinc plate in contact with the exciting liquid, but not with the adjacent copper plate; and the pole to which the zinc plates look terminates in like manner with a copper plate in contact with the exciting liquid, but not with the adjacent zinc plate. The single extreme plates of zinc and copper thus forming the poles of the pile being connected by the conducting wire, form .

fact, a pair through which the current passes exactly as i
through any other pair in the series.

218. **Voltaic circuit.** — When the poles are thus cc
by the conducting wire, the *voltaic circuit* is said to be c
and the current continually flows, as well through the
through the conducting wire. In this state the pile co
evolves electricity at its electro-motive surfaces, to feed ;
tain the current; but if the voltaic circuit be not compl
establishing a continuous conductor between pole and p(
the electricity *will not be in motion*, no current will flow ;
wire or other conductor which is in connection with the
pole will be charged with positive, and that in connecti
the negative pole will be charged with negative electrici
certain feeble tension, and in a state of repose. Since,
case, the electricity with which the pile is charged has ;
escape than by the contact of the surrounding atmosph
electro-motive force is in very feeble operation, having
make good that quantity which is dissipated by the ai
moment, however, the voltaic circuit is completed, the pil
into active operation, and generates the fluid necessary tc
the current.

These are points which it is most necessary that the
should thoroughly study and comprehend ; otherwise, he '
himself involved in great obscurity and perplexity as he ;
to proceed.

219. **Case in which the earth completes the cir**
If the conducting wires connected with the poles P and N,
of being connected with the conductor o, *fig.* 143., be co

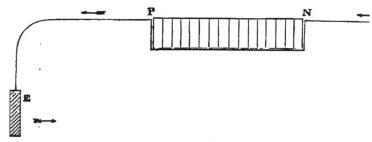

Fig. 143.

with the ground, the *earth itself* will take the place and]
part of the conductor o in relation to the current. The
fluid will in that case flow by the wire P E, *fig.* 143., ;
negative fluid by the wire N E to the earth E ; and the tw
will be transmitted through the earth E E in contrary dii

exactly in the same manner as through the conductor o. In this case, therefore, the voltaic circuit is completed by the *earth itself*.

220. Methods of connecting the poles with the earth. — In all cases, in completing the circuit, it is necessary to ensure perfect contact wherever two different conductors are united. We have already explained the application of mercurial cups and metallic clamps for this purpose, where the conductors to be connected are wires or strips of metal. When the earth is used to complete the circuit, these are inapplicable. To ensure the unobstructed flow of the current in this case, the wire is soldered to a large plate of metal, having a surface of several square feet, which is buried in the moist ground, or, still better, immersed in a well or other reservoir of water.

In cities, where there are extensive systems of metallic pipes buried for the convenience of water or gas, the wires proceeding from the poles P and N may be connected with these.

There is no practical limit to the distance over which a voltaic current may in this manner be carried, the circuit being still completed by the earth. Thus, if while the pile P N, *fig.* 143., is at London, the wire P E is carried to Paris or Vienna (being insulated throughout its entire course), and is put in communication with the ground at the latter place, the current will return to London through the earth E E, as surely and as promptly as if the points E E were only a foot asunder.

221. Various denomination of currents. — Voltaic currents which pass along wires are variously designated, according to the form given to the conducting wire. Thus they are *rectilinear currents* when the wire is straight; *indefinite currents* when it is unlimited in length; *closed currents* when the wire is bent so as to surround or enclose a space; *circular* or *spiral currents* when the wire has these forms.

222. The electric fluid forming the current not necessarily in motion. — Although the nomenclature, which has been adopted to express these phenomena, implies that the electric fluid has a motion of translation along the conductor, similar to the motion of liquid in a pipe, it must not be understood that the existence of such motion of the electric fluid is necessarily assumed, or that its nonexistence, if proved, could disturb the reasoning or shake the conclusions which form the basis of this branch of physics. Whether an actual motion of translation of the electric fluid along the conductor exist or not, it is certain that the *effect* which would attend such a motion is propagated along the conductor; and this is all that is essential to the reasoning. It has been already stated, that the most probable hypothesis which has been advanced for the explanation of the phenomena, rejects the motion of **trans-**

lation, and supposes the effect to be produced, by a series of decompositions and recompositions of the natural electricity of the conductor (138.).

223. Method of coating the conducting wires.—When the wires by which the current is conducted are liable to touch other conductors, by which the electricity may be diverted from its course, they require to be coated with some nonconducting substance, under and protected by which the current passes. Wires wrapped with silk or linen thread may be used in such cases, and they will be rendered still more efficient if they are coated with a varnish of gum-lac.

When the wires are immersed in water, they may be protected by enclosing them in caoutchouc or gutta percha.

If they are carried through the air, it is not necessary to surround them with any coating, the tension of the voltaic electricity being so feeble, that the pressure of the air and its nonconducting quality are sufficient for its insulation.

224. Supports of conducting wire.—When the wire is carried through the air to such distances as would render its weight too great for its strength, it requires to be supported at convenient intervals upon insulating props. Rollers of porcelain or glass, attached to posts of wood, are used for this purpose in the case of telegraphic wires.

225. Ampère's reotrope to reverse the current.——In experimental inquiries respecting the effects of currents, it is frequently necessary to reverse the direction of a current, and sometimes to do so suddenly, and many times in rapid succession. An apparatus for accomplishing this, contrived by Ampère, and which has since undergone various modifications, has been denominated a *commutator*, but may be more appropriately named a *reotrope*, the Greek words ῥέος (*reos*) signifying a current, and τρόπος (*tropos*), a turn.

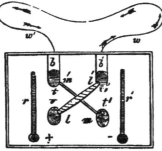

Fig. 144.

Let two grooves r r' (*fig.* 144.), about half an inch in width and depth, be cut in a board, and between them let four small cavities v, t, v', t' be formed. Let these cavities be connected diagonally in pairs by strips of copper l l' and m m', having at the place where they cross each other a piece of cloth or other nonconducting substance between them, so as to prevent the electricity from passing from one to the other. Let the grooves r and r', and the four cavities, be varnished on their surfaces with resin, so as to render them nonconductors.

These grooves and cavities being filled with mercury, let the apparatus represented in *fig.* 145. be placed upon the board.

Fig. 145.

A horizontal axis *a a'* moves in two holes *o o'* made in the upright pieces *p p'*. It carries four rectangular pieces of metal *c*, *c'*, *d*, *d'*, so adapted that when they are pressed downwards one leg of each will dip into the mercury in the groove, and the other into the adjacent cavity. The arms uniting the rectangular metallic pieces are of varnished wood, and are therefore non-conductors. When this apparatus is in the position represented in the figure, it will connect the groove *r* with the cavity *v*, and the groove *r'* with the cavity *t'*. When the ends *d d'* are depressed, and therefore *c c'* elevated, it will connect the groove *r* with the cavity *t*, and the groove *r'* with the cavity *v'*.

The conductor which proceeds from the positive pole of the pile is immersed in the mercury in *r*, and that which comes from the negative pole is immersed in the mercury in *r'*. Two strips of copper *b*, *b'* connect the mercury in the cavities *t* and *v'* with the wire *w w'* which carries the current.

The apparatus being arranged as represented in *fig.* 145., the current will pass from the pile to the mercury in *r*; thence to *v* by the conductor *c*; thence to *v'* by the diagonal strip of metal *l l'*; thence to *w* by the metal *b'*, and will pass along the wire as indicated by the arrows to *b*; thence it will pass to the mercury in *t*; thence by the diagonal strip *m' m* to *t'*; thence by the conductor *c'* to the mercury in the groove *r'*; and thence, in fine, to the negative pole of the pile.

If the ends *d d'* be depressed, and the ends *c c'* elevated, the course of the current may be traced in like manner, as follows: — from *r* to *t*; thence by *b* to *w'*; thence along the conducting wire in a direction contrary to that of the arrows to *b'*: thence to *v'*; thence to *r'*; and thence to the negative pole of the pile.

226. **Pohl's reotrope.** — Various forms have more recently been given to reotropes, one of the most convenient of which is that of Pohl, in which the use of mercury is dispensed with.

Four small copper columns A, B, C, D, *fig.* 146., about ¼ inch diameter, are set in a square board, and connected diagonally, A with D, and B with C, by

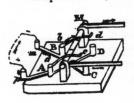

Fig. 146.

two bands of copper, which intersect without contact. These pillars correspond to the four cavities *v*, *v'*, *t*, *t'* in Ampère's reotrope. A horizontal axis crosses the apparatus similar to Ampère's; the ends of which are copper, and the centre wood or ivory. On each of the copper ends a bow *a c*, *b d* of copper rests, so formed, that when depressed on the one side or the other, it falls into contact with the copper pillars A, B, C, D. Two metallic bands connect the pillars A and B with clamps or binding screws *p* and *m*, to which the ends of the wire carrying the current are attached. The ends of the horizontal axis are attached to conductors which proceed from the poles of the pile. The course of the current may be traced exactly as in the reotrope of Ampère.

Fig. 147.

The arrangement and mode of operation of the metallic bows, by depressing one end or the other of which the direction of the current is changed, is represented in *fig.* 147., where *a c* is the bow, A and C the two copper pillars with which it falls into contact on the one side or the other, and *p* the binding screw connected with the wire which carries the current.

227. **Electrodes.** — The designation of *poles* being usual limited to the extreme elements of the pile, and the necessi often arising of indicating a sort of secondary pole, more or le remote from the pile by which the current enters and lea certain conductors, Dr. Faraday has proposed the use of the te *electrodes* to express these. Thus in the reotrope of Ampè the electrodes would be the mercury in the grooves *r r'*, *fig.* 1 In the reotrope of Pohl, the electrodes would be the ends of horizontal axis P and M.

This term electrode has reference, however, more especiall the chemical properties of the current, as will appear hereafter

228. **Floating supports for conducting wire.** — It hap en frequently in experimental researches, respecting the effect of forces affecting voltaic currents or developed by them, that the wire upon which the current passes requires to be supported or suspended in such a manner, as to be capable of changing its position or direction in accordance with the action of such forces. This object is sometimes attained by attaching the wire, together with a small vessel containing zinc and copper plates immersed in dilute acid, to a cork float, and placing the whole apparatus on water or other liquid, on which it will be capable of floating and assuming any position or direction, which the forces acting upon it may have a tendency to give to it.

229. **Ampère's apparatus for supporting movable currents.** — A more convenient and generally useful apparatus for this purpose, however, is that contrived by Ampère; which consist of two vertical copper rods v v' *fig.* 148., fixed in a wooden sta T T', the upper parts being bent at right angles and terminated two mercurial cups y y', one below the other in the same vertic line. The horizontal parts are rolled with silk or coated wi gum-lac, to prevent the electricity passing from one to the oth Two small cavities *r r'* filled with mercury, being connected w the poles of a battery, become the electrodes of the apparat These may be connected at pleasure with two mercurial cups which are in metallic communication with the rods v v'. reotrope may be applied to this apparatus, so as to reverse connections when required.

The wire which conducts the current is so formed at its e

mities as to rest on two points in the cups yy', and to balance itself so as to be capable of revolving freely round the vertical line passing through yy' as an axis.

A wire thus arranged is represented in *fig.* 149., having its

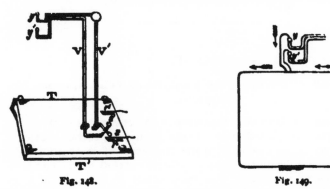

Fig. 148.   Fig. 149.

Is resting in the cups yy', the current passing from the cup y rough the wire, and returning to the cup y'. If the reotrope be rersed, it will pass from y' through the wire and return to y.

230. **Velocity of electricity.** — Numerous experiments have en made, to determine the velocity with which the voltaic curnt is propagated on a conducting wire. In 1834 Professor heatstone made a series of experiments for this purpose with volving reflectors, from which it resulted that a current transitted along a brass wire the twelfth of an inch in diameter was opagated with a velocity of 286000 miles per second, being rater than the velocity of light in the ratio of 286 to 192.

In 1849 Mr. Walker, of the United States, made a series of cperiments with a view to solve the same problem by means of se conducting wires of the electric telegraph. It resulted from is researches that the velocity of the current was not more than 8000 miles per second, being nearly 16 times less than the elocity determined by Professor Wheatstone.

In 1850 Messrs. Fizeau and Gounelle made a similar series of xperiments with the telegraphic wires in France, from which the ollowing results were deduced : —

1°. The velocity on an iron wire the fifth of an inch in diameter ras 62700 miles per second.

2°. On a copper wire the tenth of an inch in diameter it was 110000 miles per second.

3°. The two fluids, positive and negative, are propagated with he same velocity.

4°. The force of the pile and the intensity of the current ha no influence on the velocity of propagation.

5°. Conductors composed of different substances do not gi velocities proportional to their conducting powers.

CHAP. IV.

RECIPROCAL INFLUENCE OF RECTILINEAR CURRENTS AND MAGNETS.

231. Mutual action of magnets and currents. — Whei voltaic current is placed near a magnetic needle, certain moti are imparted to the needle or to the conductor of the current, to both, which indicate the action of forces exerted by the curre on the poles of the needle, and reciprocally by the poles of t. needle on the current. Other experimental tests show that tl magnets and currents affect each other in various ways; that tl presence of a current increases or diminishes the magnetic intei sity, imparts or effaces magnetic polarity, produces temporaj magnetism where the coercive force is feeble or evanescent, ⟨ permanent polarity where it is strong; that magnets reciprocal affect the intensity and direction of currents, and produce or arre them.

232. Electro-magnetism. — The body of these and like phen⟨ mena, and the exposition of the laws which govern them, constitu that branch of electrical science which has been denominatɛ *electro-magnetism.*

To render clearly intelligible the effects of the mutual action a voltaic current and a magnet, it will be necessary to consid separately the forces exerted between the current and each of tl magnetic poles; for the motions which ensue, and the forc actually manifested, are the resultants of the separate actions the two poles.

233. Direction of the mutual forces exerted by a rec¹ linear current and the pole of a magnet. — To simplify t explanation, we shall in the first instance consider only the cɛ of rectilinear currents.

Let c c′, *fig.* 150., represent the wire along which a voltaic current pass directed from c to c′, as indicated by the arrows. Let n n′ be a straight l: which is parallel to the current c c′, and which passes through the magne pole. We shall call this the line of direction of the magnetic pole. Lɛ plane be imagined to pass through these lines c c′ and n n′, and let a line ⅃ be drawn in this plane at right angles to c c′ and n n′.

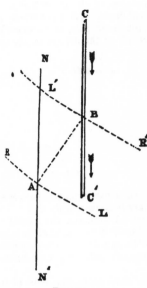

Fig. 150.

The force exerted by the current upon the magnetic pole, and reciprocally the force exerted by the magnetic pole upon the current, will have a direction at right angles to the plane passing through the direction C C′ of the current, and the line of direction N N′ of the magnetic pole.

Thus the line of direction N N′ will be impelled by a force in the direction of the line L R, and the current C C′ by a force in the direction of the line L′ R′; these lines L R and L′ R′ being understood to be drawn at right angles to the plane passing through C C′ and N N′.

But it is necessary to show in which direction on the lines L R and L′ R′ these forces respectively act.

This direction will depend on and vary with the *name* of the magnetic pole and the *direction* of the current on the line C C′.

If we suppose the magnetic pole to be an *austral* or *north* pole, and the current to *descend* on the line C C′, as indicated by the arrows, let an observer be imagined to stand with his person in the direction C C′ of the current, looking towards N N′, and the current consequently passing from his head to his feet. In such case the direction of the force impressed by the current on the line N N′ will be directed to the *right* of such observer, that is, from A towards R.

If the observer stand in the direction of the line of direction N N′ of the magnetic pole, looking towards the current C C′, the force impressed by the magnetic pole upon the current will, as before, be directed to his *right*, that is, from B towards R′.

If the magnetic pole of which N N′ is the line of direction be a *boreal* or *south* pole, these directions will be reversed, each line N N′ and C C′ being impelled to the *left* of the observer, who looks from the other line. Thus, in such case, N N′ will be impelled by a force directed from A towards L, and C C by a force directed from B towards L′.

If the current ascend on the line C C′, the directions of the forces will be the reverse of those produced by a descending current. Thus, when the current ascends, the line N N′ will be impelled to the *left* of the observer at C C′ if the pole be *austral* or *north*, and to his *right* if it be *boreal* or *south*; and in the same case the current C C′ will be likewise impelled to the *left* of the observer at N N′ if the pole be *austral* or *north*, and to his *right* if it be *boreal* or *south*.

To impress the memory with these various effects, it will be sufficient to retain the directions of the forces produced between a descending current and a north magnetic pole. The directions will be the same for an ascending current and a south magnetic pole; they will be reversed for a descending current and south pole, or for an ascending current and north pole.

Thus if the lines of direction of the current and the pole be supposed to be both perpendicular to the surface of this paper, and that the line of direction of the pole pass through the paper at P, and that of the current at c, directions of the forces impressed on the lines of direction of the current the pole for a descending current and north magnetic pole, or an ascend current and a south magnetic pole, are indicated by the arrows in *fig.* x

Fig. 151.   Fig. 152.

and their directions for a descending current and south magnetic pole, or a ascending current and a north magnetic pole, are indicated in *fig.* 152.

For example, if a current descend on a vertical wire, and the austral c north pole of a magnet be placed so that its line of direction shall be to th north of the current, the wire of the current will be impelled by a force directe to the *west*, and the line of direction of the magnetic pole by a force directe to the *east*.

If the current ascend, or if the pole be a south pole, the wire of tl current will be impelled to the *east*, and the line of direction of the pole the *west*.

234. Circular motion of magnetic pole round a fixe current.—If the line of direction of the current be fixed, an that of the magnetic pole be movable, but so connected with tl line of the current as to remain always at the same distance fro it, the line of direction of the pole will be capable only of movin round the surface of a cylinder whose axis is the direction of tl current. In this case the force impressed by the current on tl line of direction of the pole, being always at right angles to th line, and always on the same side of it as viewed from the currer will impart to the line of direction of the pole a motion of co tinued rotation round the current as an axis. This rotation, viewed on the side from which the current flows, will be in tl same direction as the motion of the hand of a watch, where tl pole is north, as represented in *fig* 153., and in the contra direction as represented in *fig.* 154., where the pole is south.

235. Circular motion of a current round a magnet pole.—A similar motion of continued rotation will be impart to the wire conducting the current, if the line of direction of tl magnetic pole be fixed, and the wire be similarly connected wi it. In this case the motion imparted by a north pole on a descen ing current is represented in *fig.* 153., and that impressed by south pole in *fig.* 154.

236. Apparatus to exhibit the direction of the force i

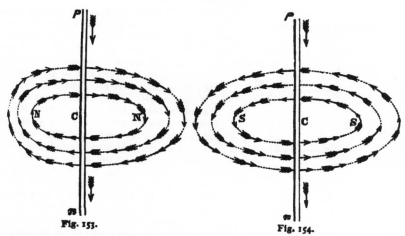

Fig. 153.   Fig. 154.

pressed by a rectilinear current on a magnetic pole.—
To demonstrate the direction of the force impressed by a recti-

Fig. 155.

linear current on a magnetic pole, let a light
bar, *fig.* 155., of ivory, or any other substance
not susceptible of magnetism, made flat at the
upper surface, be balanced like a compass
needle on a fine point, so as to be free to
move round it in an horizontal plane. Let a
magnetic needle, N s, be placed upon one arm
of it, so that one of the poles, the boreal s for example, be exactly
over the point of support; and let a counterpoise, w, be placed
upon the other arm. Let the magnet be rendered astatic, so as
not to be affected by the earth's magnetism by one or other of the
methods which will be hereafter explained.

Let the needle thus suspended be supposed to play round s, *fig.* 156., in the
plane of the paper, and let a voltaic current pass downwards along a wire

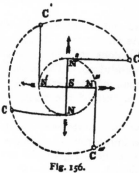

Fig. 156.

perpendicular to the paper, c representing
the intersection of such wire with the paper.
The needle, after some oscillations, will come
to rest in the position s N, so that its direction shall be at right angles to the line c N,
drawn from the current to the pole N, and
so that the centre s shall be to the left of N
as viewed from c.

It follows, from what has been already
explained, that the force exerted by the
current c on the pole N has the direction
indicated by the arrow from s to N. This
force is, therefore, directed to the *right* of N
as viewed from c.

If the wire carrying the current be moved

K 3

round the circle C C' C'' C''', the pole N will follow it, assuming always such positions, N', N'', N''', that S N', S N'', S N''' shall be at right angles to C' N', C'' N'', C''' N'''. It follows, therefore, that whatever position may be given to the current, it will exert a force upon the austral or north pole N of the magnet, the direction of which will be at right angles to the line drawn from the current to the pole, and to the *right* of the pole as viewed from the current.

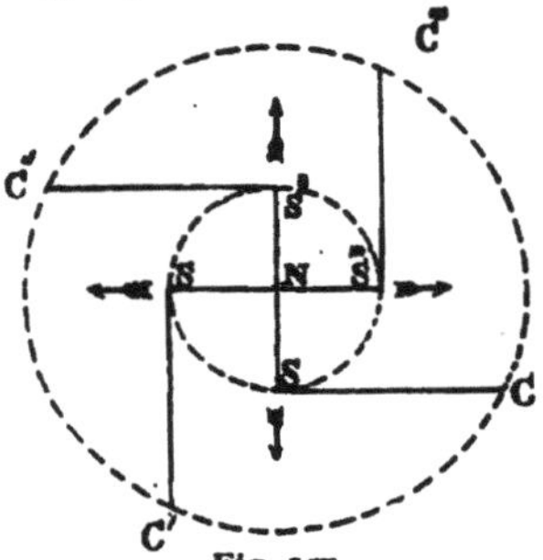

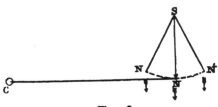

If the position of the needle be reversed, the pole N being placed at the centre of motion, the same phenomena will be manifested, but in this case the needle will place itself to the *right* of the pole S as viewed from the current C, as represented in *fig.* 157. It follows, therefore, in this case, that whatever position be given to the current, it will exert a force upon the boreal or south pole of the magnet, the direction of which will be at right angles to the line drawn from the current to the pole, and to the *left* of the pole as viewed from the current.

Fig. 157.

The current has here been supposed to *descend* along the wire. If it ascend the effects will be reversed. It will exert a force on the austral pole directed to the *left*, and on the boreal pole, one directed to the *right*.

237. Apparatus to measure intensity of this force.— Having indicated the conditions which determine the *directions* of the forces, reciprocally exerted between magnetic poles and a current, it is necessary to explain those which affect their *intensity*.

Let S N, *fig.* 158., be an astatic needle affected by the current C,

Fig. 158.

whose direction is perpendicular to the paper, as already explained. If N be displaced it will oscillate on the one side and the other of its position of rest, and its oscillations will be governed by the laws explained in the case of the pendulum. The intensity of the force impressed on it in the direction of the arrows by the current C, will be proportional to the square of the number of vibrations per minute.

238. Intensity varies inversely as the distance.—If the distance of C from N be varied, it will be found that the square of the number of vibrations per minute will increase, in the same proportion as the distance C N is diminished, and *vice versâ.* It follows, therefore, that the force impressed by the current on the pole is increased in the same ratio,. as the distance of the current from the pole diminishes, and *vice versâ*.

In the case here contemplated, the length of the wire carrying the current being considerable, each part of it exercises a separate force on N, and the entire force exerted is consequently the result-ant of an infinite number of forces, just as the weight of a body is the resultant of the forces separately impressed by gravity on its component molecules. Laplace has shown that the indefinitely small parts into which the current may be supposed to be divided, exert forces which are to each other in the inverse ratio of the squares of their distances from the pole, and that by the compo-sition of these a resultant is produced, which varies in the inverse proportion of the distances, as indicated by observation.

From what has been stated, it is evident that if the current, *fig.* 159., be placed at the centre s of the circle round which the north pole of a magnet is free to move, it will impart to the pole a continuous motion of rotation in that circle. If the current

be supposed to move downwards, the pole N will be constantly driven to the right as viewed from the centre s (233.), and consequently the magnet will move in the direction of the hand of a watch, as indicated by the arrows.

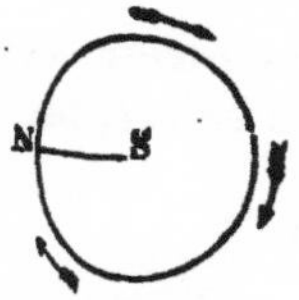

Fig. 159.

If the north pole N be placed at the centre, as in *fig.* 160., the current still descending, the force exerted on the south pole s will be constantly directed to the left as viewed from the centre, and the magnet will accordingly move contrary to the hand of a watch, as indicated by the arrows.

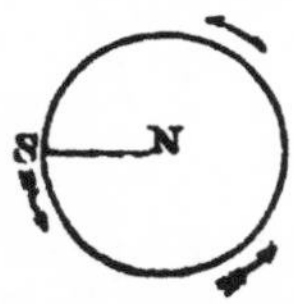

Fig. 160.    Fig. 161. 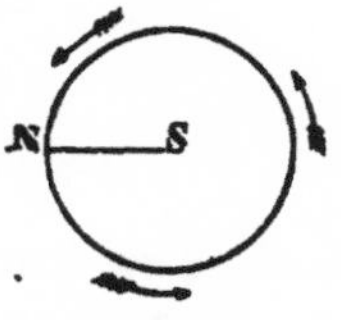   Fig. 162.

If the current ascend, these motions will be reversed, the north pole moving contrary, and the south according to the hand of a watch, as indicated in *figs.* 161, 162.

> Descending current acting on *north* pole (*fig.* 159.).
> Descending current acting on *south* pole (*fig.* 160.).
> Ascending current acting on *south* pole (*fig.* 161.).
> Ascending current acting on *north* pole (*fig.* 162.).

239. **Case in which the current is within, but not at the centre of the circle in which the pole revolves.** — If

the current be within the circle described by the free pole, but not at its centre, the pole will still revolve; but the force which impels it will not be uniform, as it is when the current is at the centre. Since the force exerted by the current on the pole is inversely as its distance from the pole, that force will be necessarily uniform when the current is at the centre, the distance of the pole from it being always the same. But when the current is within the circle

Fig. 163.

at a point c, *fig.* 163., different from the centre, the distance c N will vary, and the force exerted on N will vary in the inverse proportion, increasing as the distance is diminished, and decreasing as the distance is increased. The rotation will nevertheless equally take place, and in the same direction as when the current c is at the centre.

240. **Action of a current on a magnet, both poles being free.** — Having thus explained the mutual action of the current, and each pole of the needle separately, we shall now consider the case in which a magnetic needle, suspended as usual on its centre, is exposed to the action of the current.

241. **Case in which the current is outside the circle described by the poles.** — Let c (*figs.* 164, 165.), as before, be a

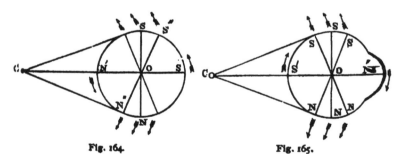

Fig. 164.   Fig. 165.

descending current placed outside the circle in which the poles of the needle N s play. The forces exerted by the current on the two poles N and s have in this case opposite effects on the needle, and consequently it will turn in the direction of that which has the greater effect, and will be in equilibrium when the effects are equal.

If the poles be placed at N' and s' (*fig.* 164.), the force exerted on them will move N' towards N, and s' towards s, and the needle will turn in the direction of the arrows by the combined effects of both forces. When N' arrives at N", the force, being in the direction o N", will be ineffective; but the force acting on s", the opposite pole, will continue to turn the needle towards the position N s, where it is at right angles to c o. After passing N", the force on

N is effective in opposition to that on s, but in a very small degree, so that the effect on s preponderates until the needle arrives at the position s N.   Here the poles N and s being equally distant from c, the forces are equal, and, being equally inclined to s N, have equal effects in opposite directions.   The needle is therefore held in equilibrium.   If the needle be moved beyond this position, the effect of the force on N predominating over that of the force on s, the needle will be brought back to the position s N, and will oscillate on the one side and the other of this direction, showing that it is the position of stable equilibrium.*

If the pole s be placed at s' (*fig.* 165.), the effects on the two poles s' and N' will, as before, combine to turn the needle as indicated by the arrows, moving the south pole toward s, and the north towards N.

It follows, therefore, that a downward current c, acting as in *figs.* 164, 165., outside the circle described by the poles, will throw the needle into a direction s N at right angles to the line c o drawn from the current to the centre of the needle, the north pole being on the *right* as viewed from the current.

An ascending current will produce the contrary effects, the north pole being thrown to the *left* as viewed from the current.

242. **Case in which the current passes through the circle.** — If the current pass through the circle described by the poles,

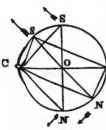

Fig. 166.

the needle will rest indifferently in any direction that may be given to it.   In this case (*fig.* 166.), let c be the current.   The forces it exerts on s and N being in the inverse ratio of the distances, that which affects s will be to that which affects N as c N is to c s.   The moment of the force on s will therefore be c N × c s, and the moment of the force on N will be c s × c N.   These moments being equal, the forces must be in equilibrium †, and the needle will therefore remain at rest whatever position be given to it.

243. **Case in which the current passes within the circle.** — Let the current pass within the circle described by the poles.   In this case the effect of the current on the two poles s and N is opposite in every position.   If the north pole be at N' (*fig.* 167.), the point of the circle nearest to c, the force on N' being greater than the force on s' in the

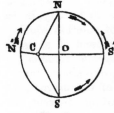

Fig. 167.

* "Mechanics" (298.).   † "Mechanics" (395.).

ratio of c s' to c n' (237.), the effect of the force on n' will p̄edominate, and n' will be moved towards n, and s' towards s. The effects on n will continue to predominate until they arrive at the position n s, where the effects become equal, and the needle is in equilibrium; for here the distances of s and n from c being equal, the forces are equal; and since they are equally inclined to the needle, they have equal effects to turn it in contrary directions. After passing n, the effect on s predominates; the needle will be brought back to the position n s, and will oscillate on the one side and the other, indicating stable equilibrium.

If the needle be placed with the pole s' at the point nearest to c (*fig.* 168.), the effect on s' predominating, s' will be moved towards s, and n' towards n, and the needle will attain the same position as in the former case.

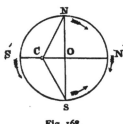

Fig. 168.

It follows, therefore, that when a descending current passes within the circle described by the poles, as represented in *figs.* 167, 168., the needle will be thrown into a direction s n at right angles to the line c o drawn from the current to the centre of the needle, the north pole pointing to the *left* as viewed from the current. An ascending current will produce the contrary effect, throwing the north pole to the right.

It will be observed that the direction of the poles, when the current is *within* the circle, is opposite to its direction when it is *outside* the circle.

244. Apparatus to illustrate electro-magnetic rotation.— A variety of interesting and instructive apparatus has been contrived to illustrate experimentally the reciprocal forces manifested between currents and magnets. These may be described generally as exhibiting a magnet revolving round a current, or a current revolving round a magnet, or each revolving round the other, impelled by the forces which the current and the poles of the magnet exert upon each other. It will be conducive to brevity, in describing these effects, to designate a motion of rotation which from left to right, or according to that of the hand of a watch, as *direct rotation*, and the contrary as *retrograde rotation*. will, therefore, follow from what has been explained, that n and s express the north and south poles of the magnet, and a and d express an ascending and descending current, the rotation of each round the other in every possible case will be follows : —

$$\left.\begin{array}{l} \text{N, D} \\ \text{S, A} \end{array}\right\} \textit{Direct.}$$

$$\left.\begin{array}{l} \text{N, A} \\ \text{S, D} \end{array}\right\} \textit{Retrograde.}$$

We shall classify the apparatus according to the particular manner in which they exhibit the action of the forces.

245. To cause either pole of a magnet to revolve round a fixed voltaic current. — Let two bar magnets be bent into the form shown in *fig.* 169., so that a small part at the middle of their length shall be horizontal. Under this part an agate cup is fixed, by which the magnet is supported on a pivot. Above the horizontal part a small cup containing mercury is fixed. The magnets are thus free to revolve on the pivots. A small circular canal of mercury surrounds each magnet a little below the rect-angular bend, into which the amalgamated point of a bent wire

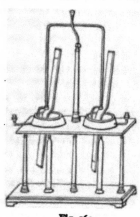

dips. These wires are connected with two vertical rods, which turning at right angles above, terminate in a small cup containing mercury. Two similar mer-curial cups communicate with the circu-lar mercurial canals. If the upper cup be put in communication with the posi-tive pole of a battery, and the lower cups with the negative pole, descending currents will be established on the ver-tical rods ; and if the upper cup be put in communication with the negative, and the lower with the positive, the currents will ascend. The two magnets may be placed either with the same or opposite poles uppermost. The currents pass from

Fig. 169.

the vertical rods to the mercury in the circular canals, thence to the lower cups, and thence to the negative poles.

When the descending current passes on the rods, the north pole of the magnet revolves with direct, and the south pole with retro-grade motion. When the current ascends, these motions are re-versed.

246. To cause a movable current to revolve round the fixed pole of a magnet. — Let a glass vessel, *fig.* 170., be nearly filled with mercury. Let a metallic wire suspended from a hook over its centre be capable of revolving while its end rests upon the surface of the mercury. A rod of metal enters at the bottom of the vessel, and is in contact with a magnetic bar fixed vertically in the centre of the vessel. When one of the poles of

Fig. 170.

the battery is put in communication with the movable wire, and the other with the fixed wire connected with the magnet, a current will pass along the movable wire, either *to* the mercury or *from* it, according to the connection made with the poles of the battery; and the movable wire will revolve round the magnet, touching the surface of the mercury with a motion direct or retrograde, according as the current descends or ascends, and according to the name of the magnetic pole fixed in the centre (244.).

Let $z z'$, *fig.* 171., represent a section of a circular trough containing mercury, having an opening at the centre in which is inserted a metallic rod, terminating at the top in a mercurial cup c. A wire at $a b b' a'$ is bent so as to form three sides of a rectangle, the width $b b'$ corresponding with the diameter of the circular trough $z z'$. A point

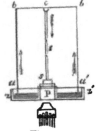

Fig. 171.

is attached to the middle of $b b'$, which rests in the cup c, so that the rectangle is balanced on the rod t, and capable of revolving on the pivot as a centre.

If the mercury in the circular trough be connected by a wire with the negative, while the cup c is connected with the positive pole of a battery, descending currents will be established along the vertical wires $b a$ and $b' a'$; and if the connections be reversed, these currents will ascend.

If, when these currents are established, the pole of a magnet be applied under the centre P, it will act upon the vertical currents, and will cause the rectangular wire $a b b' a'$ to revolve round with a motion direct or retrograde, according to the direction of the current and the name of the magnetic pole (235.).

The points of contact of the revolving wires with the mercury may be multiplied by attaching the ends $a a'$ of the wires to a metallic hoop, the edge of which will rest in contact with the metal; or the wires $a b$ and $a' b'$ may be altogether replaced by a thin copper cylinder balanced on a point in the cup at c.

Another apparatus for illustrating this is represented in *fig.* 172. A bar magnet is fixed vertically in the centre of a circular trough containing mercury. A light and hollow cylinder of copper is suspended on a point resting

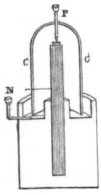

Fig. 172.

in an agate cup placed on the top of the magnet, and having a vertical wire proceeding from it, which terminates in a small mercurial cup P at the top. Another wire connects the mercury in the trough with a mercurial cup N. When the cups P and N are put in communication with the poles of the battery, a current is established on the sides of the copper cylinder c c, and rotation takes place as already described.

A double apparatus of this kind, erected on the two poles of a horse shoe magnet, is represented in *fig.* 173.

247. **Ampère's method.** — Ampère adopted the following method of exhibiting the revolution of a current round a magnet. A double cylinder of copper c c, *fig.* 174., about 2½ inches dia-

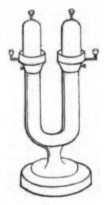

Fig. 173.

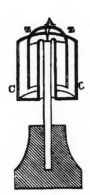

Fig. 174.

meter and 2½ inches high, is supported on the pole of a bar magnet by a plate of metal passing across the upper orifice of the inner cylinder. A light cylinder of zinc z z, supported on a wire arch A, is introduced between the inner and outer cylinders of copper, a steel point attached to the wire arch resting upon the plate by which the copper cylinders are supported. On introducing dilute acid between the copper cylinders, electro-motive action takes place, the current passing from the zinc to the acid, thence to the copper, and thence through the pivot to the zinc. The zinc being in this case free to revolve, while the copper is fixed, and the current descending on the former, the rotation will be direct or retrograde according as the magnetic pole is north or south.

If the copper were free to revolve as well as the zinc, it would turn in the contrary direction, since the current ascends upon it, while it descends on the zinc. Mr. J. Marsh modified Ampère's apparatus, so as to produce this effect by substituting a pivot,

resting in a cup at the top of the magnet, for the metallic ar
which, in the former case, the copper vessel was sustained.

A double arrangement of this kind is given in *fig.* 175., v
the double cylinders are supported on pivots on the two pole
horse shoe magnet. The rotation of the corresponding cyli
on the two opposite magnetic poles will be in contrary direct

248. **To make a magnet turn on its own axis by a
rent parallel to it.** — The tendency of the conductor on v
a current passes to revolve round a magnet will not the less
though the current be so fixed to the magnet as to be inca
of revolving without carrying the magnet with it. In *fig.*
the magnet M is sunk by a platinum weight P; its upper
being fixed to the copper cylinder w w, a current passing
P to N causes the cylinder to rotate, carrying with it the mag

Since a magnetic bar is itself a conductor, it is not necessa
introduce any other; and a current passing along the bar will
rotation to it. An apparatus for exhibiting this effect is r
sented in *fig.* 177., where a magnetic bar is supported i

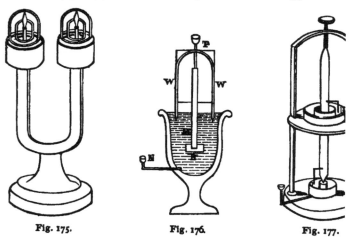

Fig. 175.   Fig. 176.   Fig. 177.

vertical position between pivots which play in agate cups
circular mercurial canal is placed at the centre of the ma
and another round the lower pivot. Mercurial cups commun
with these two canals. When these cups are put in comn
cation with the poles of a battery, the current will pass bet
the two canals along the lower pole of the magnet, in the
direction or the other, according to the mode of connection;
the magnet will turn on its own axis with a direct or retrog
rotation, according to the name of the pole on which the cui
runs, and to the direction of the current.

CHAP. V.

RECIPROCAL INFLUENCE OF CIRCULATING CURRENTS AND
MAGNETS.

If a wire P A B C D N (*figs.* 178, 179.) be bent into the form of any
geometrical figure, the extremities being brought near each other

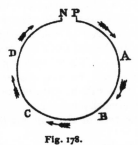

Fig. 178.

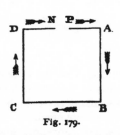

Fig. 179.

without actually touching, a current entering one extremity and
departing from the other, is called a *circulating current.*

249. **Front and back of circulating current.** — If such a
current be viewed on opposite sides of the figure formed by the
wire, it will appear to circulate in different directions, on one side
direct, and on the other *retrograde* (244.). That side on which it
appears *direct* is called the *front,* and the other the *back* of the
current.

250. **Axis of current.** — If the current have a regular figure
having a geometrical centre, a straight line drawn through this
centre perpendicular to its plane is called the *axis* of the current.

251. **Reciprocal action of circulating current and magnetic pole.** — To determine the reciprocal influence of a circulating
current and a magnetic pole placed anywhere upon its axis, let
the axis be X C X' (*fig.* 180.), the plane of the current being at

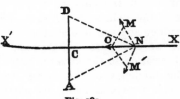

Fig. 180.

right angles to the paper, A
being the point where it ascends, and D the point where
it descends through the paper.

1°. Let N be a *north* magnetic pole placed in *front* of
the current.

The part of the current at
D will exert a force on N in the direction N M' at right angles to
D N, and the part at A will exert an equal force in the direction

N M at right angles to A N. These two forces being compound, will be equivalent to a single force N O* directed from N along the axis *towards* the current.

It may be shown that the same will be true for every two points of the current which are diametrically opposed.

2°. Let a *south* magnetic pole S (*fig.* 181.), be similarly placed in *front* of a circulating current.

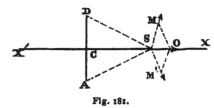

Fig. 181.

The part D will exert upon it a force in the direction S perpendicular to S D and to the left of S as viewed from D and the part A will exert an equal force in the direction S M' to the right of S as viewed from A. These two equal forces will have a resultant S O directed *from* the current ; and the same will be true of every two points of the current which are diametrically opposed.

If the magnetic pole be placed at the *back* of the current, the contrary effects ensue.

The same inferences may be deduced with respect to any circulating current which has a centre, that is, a point within it which divides into two equal parts all lines drawn through it terminating in the current.

It may therefore be inferred generally that *when a magnetic pole is placed upon the axis of a circulating current, attraction or repulsion is produced between it and the current; attraction when* NORTH *pole is before, or a* SOUTH *pole* BEHIND, *and repulsion when a* SOUTH *pole is before, or a north pole* BEHIND.

252. **Intensity of the force vanishes when the distance of the pole bears a very great ratio to the diameter current.** — Since the intensity of the attraction between the component parts of the current and the pole decreases as the square of the distance is increased, and since the lines N M and N M', *fig.* 180., and S M and S M', *fig.* 181., form with each other a greater angle as the distance of the pole from the current is increased, is evident that when the diameter A D of the current bears a inconsiderable ratio to the distance of the pole N or S from it, the attraction or repulsion ceases to produce any sensible effect.

253. **But the directive power of the pole continues.** — This, however, is not the case with relation to the *directive power* of the pole upon the current. The tendency of the forces impressed by the pole upon the current is always to bring the plane of the current at right angles to the line drawn from the pole to

* " Mechanics " (148.).

s centre. There is, in short, a tendency of the line of direction
the pole to take a position coinciding with or parallel to the
tis of the current, and this coincidence may be produced either
r the change of position of the pole or of the plane of the curnt, or of both, according as either or both are free to move.

254. **Spiral and helical currents.** — The force exerted by a
rculating current may be indefinitely augmented by causing the
irrent to circulate several times round its centre or axis. If the
ire which conducts the current be wrapped with silk or coated
ith any nonconducting varnish, so as to prevent the electricity
om escaping from coil to coil when in contact, circulating cur-
nts may be formed round a common centre or axis in a ring, a
iral, a helix, or any other similar form, so that the forces exerted
r all their coils on a single magnetic pole may be combined by
ie principle of the composition of force; and hence an extensive
ass of electro-magnetic phenomena may be educed, which supply
i the same time important consequences and striking experimental
ustrations of the laws of attraction and repulsion which have
een just explained.

255. **Expedients to render circulating currents movable.
-Ampère's and Delarive's apparatus.** — Two expedients have
een practised to render a circulating current movable.

1. By the apparatus of Ampère already described (229.), the wire conduct-
g the current being bent at the ends, as represented in *fig.* 182., may be
ipported in the cups *y y'* as represented in *fig.* 148., so that its plane being
irtical, it shall be capable of revolving round the line *y y'* as an axis. By
is arrangement the plane of the current can take any direction at right
igles to a horizontal plane, but it is not capable of receiving any progres-
ve motion.

Fig. 182.

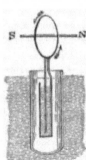

Fig. 183.

2. The latter object is attained by the floating apparatus of M. Delarive.
Let a coated wire be formed into a circular ring composed of several coils.
et one end of it be attached to a copper cell, *fig.* 183., and the other to a slip
f zinc which descends into this cell. The cell being filled with acidulated
ater, a current will be established through the wire in the direction of the

arrows. The copper cell may be inclosed in a glass vessel, or attached t
cork so as to float upon water, and thus be free to assume any position wh
the forces acting upon the current may tend to give it.

256. **Rotatory motion imparted to circular current by
magnetic pole.** — If a magnetic north pole be presented in fr
of a circular current, *fig.* 182., suspended on Ampère's fra
fig. 148., the ring will turn on its points of suspension until
axis pass through the pole. If the pole be carried round in
circle, the plane of the ring will revolve with a correspondir
motion, always presenting the front of the current to the pole, t
axis of the current passing through the pole.

If a south magnetic pole be presented to the back of the cu
rent, like effects will be produced.

If a north magnetic pole be presented to the back, or a sou
to the front of the current, the ring will, on the least disturbanc
make half a revolution round its points of suspension, so as
turn its front to the north and its back to the south magnet
pole.

257. **Progressive motion imparted to it.** — If c, *fig.* 184., r

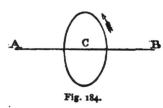

Fig. 184.

present a floating circular current,
north magnetic pole placed anywhe
on its axis will cause the ring co
ducting it to move in that direction
which its front is presented; for if t
pole be before it at A it will attra
the current, and if behind it at B
will repel it (251.). In either ca
the ring will move in the direction

which its front looks.

If a south magnetic pole be similarly placed, it will cause t
current to move in the contrary direction; for if it be place
before the current at A it will repel it, and if behind it at B it wi
attract it. In either case the ring will move in the direction t
which the back of the current looks.

258. **Reciprocal action of the current on the pole.** — If the
magnetic pole be movable and the current fixed, the motion impressed on the pole by the action of the current will have a
direction opposite to that of the motion which would be impressed
on the current, being movable, by the pole being fixed. A north
magnetic pole placed on the axis of a fixed circular current wil
therefore be moved along the axis in that direction in which the
back of the current looks, and a south magnetic pole in tha
direction in which the front looks.

259. **Action of a magnet on a circular floating current.** —
If a bar magnet s N, *fig.* 185., be placed in a fixed position wit

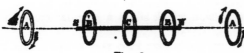

Fig. 185.

the magnetic axis in the direction of a floating circular current A, its north pole N being directed to the front of the current, the current will be attracted by N and repelled by s; but the force exerted by N will predominate in consequence of its greater proximity to A, and the current will accordingly move from A towards N. After it passes N, the bar passing through the centre of the ring, it will be repelled by N and also by s (251.); but so long as it is between N and the centre c of the bar, as at B, the repulsion of N will predominate over that of s in consequence of the greater proximity of N, and the current will move towards c. Passing beyond c to B', the repulsion of s predominates over that of N, and it will be driven back to c, and after some oscillations on the one side and the other, it will come to rest in stable equilibrium, with its centre at the centre of the magnet, its plane at right angles to it, the front looking towards s and the back towards N.

260. **Reciprocal action of the current on the magnet.**— If the current be fixed and the magnetic bar movable, the latter will move in a direction opposite to that with which the current would move, the bar being fixed. Thus, if the current were fixed at A, the bar would move to it in the direction of N A, and the pole N passing through the ring, the bar would come to rest, after some oscillations, with its centre at the centre of the ring.

261. **Case of unstable equilibrium of the current.** — If the ring were placed with its centre at c and its front directed to N, it would be in unstable equilibrium, for if moved through any distance, however small, towards N or s, the attraction of the pole towards which it is moved would prevail over that of the other pole which is more distant, and the ring would consequently be moved to the end of the bar and beyond that point, when, being still attracted by the nearest pole, it would soon be brought to rest. It would then make a half revolution on its axis and return to the centre of the bar, where it would take the position of stable equilibrium.

All these are consequences which easily follow from the general principles of attraction and repulsion established in (251.).

Fig. 186.

262. **Case of a spiral current.**—If the wire which conducts the current be bent into the form of a spiral, *fig.* 186., each convolution will exert the force of a circular current, and the effect of the whole will be the sum of the forces of all the

convolutions. Such a spiral will therefore be subject to the conditions of attraction and repulsion which affect a circular current (251.).

263. **Circular or spiral currents exercise the same action as a magnet.** — In general it may be inferred that circulating currents exercise on a magnetic pole exactly the same effects as would be produced by another magnet, the *front* of the current playing the part of a *south* pole, and the *back* that of a *north* pole.

264. **Case of helical current.** — It has been shown that a helix or screw is formed by a point which is at the same time affected by a circular and progressive motion, the circular motion being at right angles to the axis of the helix, and the progressive motion being in the direction of that axis.* In each convolution the thread of the helix makes one revolution, and at the same time progresses in the direction of the axis through a space equal to the distance between two successive convolutions.

265. **Method of neutralising the effect of the progressive motion of such a current.** — If a current therefore be transmitted on a helical wire, it will combine the characters of a circular and rectilinear current. The latter character, however, may be neutralised or effaced by transmitting a current in a contrary direction to the progression of the screw, on a straight wire extended along the axis of the helix. This rectilinear current being equal, parallel, and contrary in direction to the progressive component of the helical current, will have equal and contrary magnetic properties, and the forces which they exert together on any magnetic pole within their influence will counteract each other.

266. **Right-handed and left-handed helices.** — Helices are of two forms: those in which the wire turns like the thread of a corkscrew, that is, in the direction of the hands of a watch, *fig.* 187.; and those in which it turns in a contrary direction, *fig.* 188.

Fig. 187.

Fig. 188.

267. **Front of current on each kind.** — If a current traverse a right-handed helix, its front will be directed to the end at which it enters, and in the left-handed helix to the end at which it departs.

268. **Magnetic properties of helical currents. — Their poles determined.** — Hence it follows that in a right-handed helical current, the end at which the current enters, and which is the positive pole, has the magnetic properties of a south pole and in the left-handed helix this end has the properties of a north pole.

* "Mechanics" (484.).

269. **Experimental illustration of these properties.** — The magnetic properties of spiral and helical currents may be illustrated experimentally by means of Ampère's arrangement, *fig.* 148., or by a floating apparatus constructed on the same principle as that represented in *fig.* 183.

The manner of forming spiral currents adapted to Ampère's apparatus is represented in *figs.* 189. and 190. In *fig.* 189. the spirals are both in the same

Fig. 189.   Fig. 190.

plane, passing through the axis of suspension y y'. In *fig.* 190. they are in planes parallel to this axis, and at right angles to the line joining their centres, which is therefore their common axis.

270. **The front of a circulating current has the properties of a south, and the back those of a north, magnetic pole.** — According to what has been explained, the front of such a spiral current will have the properties of a south magnetic pole, and will therefore attract and be attracted by the north, and repel and be repelled by the south pole of a magnet. If the spirals in *fig.* 189., therefore, be so connected with the poles of a voltaic system, as to present their fronts on the same side, they will be both attracted by the north pole and both repelled by the south

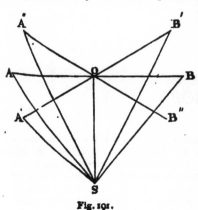

Fig. 191.

pole of a magnet presented to them, that which is nearer to the magnet being more attracted or repelled than the other. If the magnetic pole be equally distant from them, they will be in equilibrium, and the equilibrium will be stable if they are both repelled, and unstable if they are both attracted by the magnet.

To demonstrate this, let s, *fig.* 191., be the south pole of a magnet placed in front of the two spirals, whose centres are at A and B, equally distant from s. It is evident that a perpendicular s o drawn from s to A B will in this case pass through the middle of A B. The pole s will, therefore, according to what has been already explained, repel the two spirals with equal forces. If the spirals be removed from this position to the positions A' B', A', being nearer to s than B', will be repelled by a greater force, and therefore A' will be driven back towards A, and B' towards B. In like manner, if they were removed to the positions A'' B'', the force repelling B'' would be greater than that which repels A'', and therefore B'' will be driven back to B, and A'' to A.

It follows, therefore, that the position of equilibrium of A B is in this case such that the system will return to it after the slightest disturbance on the one side or the other, and is therefore stable.

If the pole s were the north pole, it would attract both currents, and in that case A' would be more strongly attracted than B', and B'' than A'', and consequently the spirals would depart further from the position A after the least disturbance. The equilibrium would therefore be unstable.

It will be found, therefore, that when a *north pole* is presented *before*, or a *south pole behind*, such a pair of spiral currents, the system, *fig.* 189., will, on the least disturbance from the position of unstable equilibrium, turn on its axis *y y'* through half revolution, presenting the fronts of the currents to the south pole, and will there come to rest after some oscillations.

In the position of stable equilibrium, the front of the currents must therefore be presented to the south pole of the magnet, or the back to the north pole.

271. Adaptation of a helical current to Ampère's and Delarive's apparatus. — The manner of adapting a helical current to Ampère's arrangement, *fig.* 148., is represented in *fig.* 192., and the manner of adapting it to the floating method is represented in *fig.* 193.

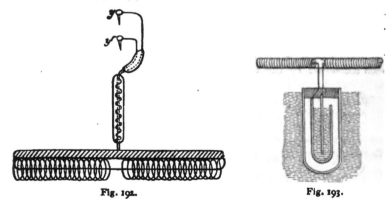

Fig. 192.   Fig. 193.

The positive wire is carried down from *y*, *fig.* 192., and then coiled into an helix from the centre to the extremity. Thence it is carried in a straight direction through the centre of the helix to the other extremity, from whence it is again conducted in helical coils back to the centre, where it is bent upwards and terminates at the negative pole *y'*. In one half of the helix the current, therefore, enters at the centre and issues from the extremity, and in the other half it enters at the extremity and issues from the centre.

If the helices be both right handed, therefore, the end from which the current issues will have the properties of a north, and that at which it enters those of a south, magnetic pole. If they be both left handed, this position of the poles will be reversed (268.).

The wire which is carried straight along the axis neutralises that component of the helical current, which is parallel to the axis, leaving only the circular elements effective (265.).

These properties may be experimentally verified by presenting either pole of a magnetic bar to one or the other end of the helical current. The same attractions and repulsions will be manifested as if the helix were a magnet.

272. **Action of a helical current on a magnetic needle placed in its axis.** — If H H′ (*fig.* 194.) represent a helical

Fig. 194.

current, the front of which looks towards A, a north magnetic pole placed anywhere in its axis, either within the limits of the helix or beyond its extremities, will be urged by a force directed from A towards c. Between A and H it will be attracted by the combined forces of the fronts of all the convolutions of the helix. Between H and H′ it will be attracted by the fronts of those convolutions which are to the left of it, and repelled by the backs of all those to its right. Beyond H′ towards c, it will be repelled by the backs of all the convolutions. In all positions, therefore, it will, if free, be moved from right to left, or in a direction contrary to that towards which the front of the current is directed.

If the pole were fixed and the current movable, the helix would move from right to left, or in that direction towards which the front of the current looks.

If the magnetic needle s N, *fig.* 195., be placed in the centre of the axis of a helical current, with its poles equidistant from the

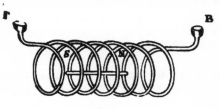

Fig. 195.

extremities, the south pole s being presented towards that end F to which the front of the current looks, it will be in equilibrium, the pole N being repelled towards B, and the pole s towards F by equal forces; for in this case the pole N will be attracted towards B by all the convolutions of the helix between N and B, and will be repelled in the same direction by all the convolutions between N and F; while the pole s will in like manner be attracted towards F by all the convolutions between s and F, and repelled in the same direction by all the convolutions between s and B.

The needle s ʀ, being thus impelled by two equal forces directed *from* its centre, will be in stable equilibrium.

If the directions of the poles were reversed, they would be impelled by two equal forces directed from its extremities towards its centre, and the equilibrium would be unstable.

When the magnetic needle is sufficiently light, and the helical current sufficiently powerful, a curious effect may be observed, if the needle be placed within the helix so as to rest upon the lower parts of the wire. Before the current is transmitted, the needle will rest on the wires under the position s ʀ represented in *fig.* 195.; but the moment the connection with the battery is made, and the current established, it will start up and place itself in the middle of the axis of the helix, as in the figure, where it will remain suspended in the air without any visible support.

CHAP. VI.

ELECTRO-MAGNETIC INDUCTION.

273. **Inductive effect of a voltaic current upon a magnet.** — The forces which a voltaic current impresses upon the poles of a permanent magnet, being similar in all respects to those with which the same poles would be affected by another magnet, it may be expected that the natural magnetism of an unmagnetised body would be decomposed, and polarity imparted to it by the approach of a voltaic current, in the same manner as by the approach of a magnet. Experiment accordingly confirms this consequence of the analogy suggested by the phenomena. It is, in fact, found that a voltaic current is capable of decomposing the natural magnetism of magnetic bodies, and of magnetising them as effectually as the most powerful magnets.

Soft iron rendered magnetic by voltaic currents. — If the wire upon which a voltaic current flows be immersed in filings of soft iron, they will collect around it, and attach themselves to it in the same manner as if it were a magnet, and will continue to adhere to it so long as the current is maintained upon it; but the moment the connections with the battery are broken, and the current suspended, they will drop off.

Sewing needles attracted by current. — Light steel sewing needles being presented to the wire conducting a current will *instantly* become magnetic, as will be apparent by their assuming

tion at right angles to the wire, as a magnetic needle would
der like circumstances. When the current is suspended or
ved, the needles will in this case retain the magnetism im-
d to them.

274. **Magnetic induction of a helical current.**
— To exhibit these phenomena with greater effect and
certainty, the needles should be exposed to the influence
not of one, but of several currents, or of several parts of
the same current flowing at right angles to them. This
is easily effected by placing them within a helical
current.

Let a metallic wire coated with silk or other nonconductor be
rolled helically on a glass tube, *fig.* 196., and the current being
made to pass along the wire, let a needle or bar of steel or hard
iron be placed within the tube. It will *instantaneously* acquire all
the magnetism it is capable of receiving under these circumstances.

On testing the needle it will be found that its boreal or south
pole is at that end to which the front of the current is presented ;
and, consequently, for a right-handed helix, it will be towards
the positive, and for a left-handed helix towards the negative
pole. It appears, therefore, that the needle acquires a polarity
identical with that which the helix itself is proved to possess.

5. **Polarity produced by the induction of helical current.** — In the case of the right-handed helix,
represented in *fig.* 196., the current passes in
the direction indicated by the arrows, and consequently the austral pole will be at *a* and the
boreal pole at *b*. In the case of the left-handed helix *fig.* 197., the position of these poles *a* and *b* is
reversed in relation to the direction of the current, but the boreal pole *b* is in both cases at
that end to which the front of the current looks.

276. **Consequent points produced.** — If the
helix be reversed once or oftener in passing
along the tube, being alternately right-handed
and left-handed, as represented in *fig.* 198., a
consequent point will be produced upon the bar
at each change of direction of the helix.

277. **Inductive action of common electricity produces polarity.** — It is not only by
the induction of the voltaic current that mag-
polarity may be imparted. Discharges of common elec-
y transmitted along a wire, especially if it have the form
helix, will produce like effects. If the wire be straight, the
nce is feeble. Sparks taken from the prime conductor pro-

Fig. 198.

duce sensible effects on very fine needles; but if the wire be placed in actual contact with the conductor at one end and the cushion at the other, so that a constant current shall pass along it from the conductor to the cushion, no effect is produced. The effect produced by the spark is augmented as the spark is more intense and taken at a greater distance from the conductor.

If the wire be formed into a helix, magnetic polarity will be produced by a continuous current, that is, by actually connecting the ends of the wire with the conductor and the cushion: but these effects are much more feeble than those produced under like circumstances by the spark.

All these effects are rendered much more intense when the discharge of a Leyden jar, and still more that of a Leyden battery, is transmitted along the wire. When these phenomena were first noticed, it was assumed that the polarity thus imparted by common electricity must necessarily follow the law which prevails in the case of a voltaic current, and that in the case of helices the boreal or south pole would be presented towards the front of the current. Savary, however, showed that the effects of common electricity obey a different principle, and thus established a fundamental distinction between the voltaic current and the electric discharge.

278. **Conditions on which a needle is magnetised positively and negatively.** — When an electric discharge is transmitted along a straight wire, a needle placed at right angles to the wire acquires sometimes the polarity of a magnetic needle, which under the influence of a voltaic current would take a like position; that is to say, the austral or north pole will be to the right of an observer who looks at the needle from the current, his head being in the direction from which the current flows. The needle is in this case said to be magnetised *positively*. When the opposite polarity is imparted to the needle, it is said to be magnetised *negatively*.

279. **Results of Savary's experiments.** — Savary showed that needles are magnetised by the discharge of common electricity, positively or negatively, according to various conditions, depending on the intensity of the discharge, the length of the conducting wire, supposing it to be straight, its diameter, the thickness of the needles, and their coercive force. In a series of experiments, in which the needles were placed at distances from the current increasing by equal increments, the magnetisation was alternately positive and negative; when the needle was in contact with the wire, it was positive; at a small distance negative; at a greater distance no magnetisation was produced; a further increase of distance produced positive magnetism; and

after several alternations of this kind, the magnetisation ended in being positive, and continued positive at all greater distances.

The number and frequency of these alternations are dependent on the conditions above mentioned, but no distinct law showing their relation to those conditions has been discovered. In general it may be stated that the thinner the wire which conducts the current, the lighter and finer the needles, and the more feeble their coercive force is, the less numerous will be those periodical changes of positive and negative magnetisation. It is sometimes found that when these conditions are observed, the magnetisation is positive at all distances, and that the periodic changes only affect its intensity.

Similar effects are produced upon needles placed in tubes of wood or glass, upon which a helical current is transmitted. In these cases, the mere variation in the intensity of the discharge produces considerable effect.

280. **Magnetism imparted to the needle affected by the nonmagnetic substance which surrounds it.** — Savary also ascertained a fact which, duly studied, may throw much light on the theory of these phenomena. The quantity of magnetism imparted to a needle by an electric discharge, and the character of its polarity, positive or negative, are affected by the nonmagnetic envelope by which the needle is surrounded. If a needle be inserted in the axis of a very thick cylinder of copper, a helical current surrounding the cylinder will not impart magnetism to it. If the thickness of the copper envelope be gradually diminished, the magnetisation will be manifested in a sensible degree, and it will become more and more intense as the thickness of the copper is diminished. This increase, however, does not continue until the copper envelope disappears, for when the thickness is reduced to a certain limit, a more intense magnetisation is produced than when the uncovered needle is placed within the helix.

Envelopes of tin, iron, and silver placed around the needle are attended with analogous effects, that is to say, when they consist of very thin leaf metal they increase the quantity of magnetism which can be imparted to the needles by the current; but when the metallic envelope is much thicker, they prevent the action of the electric discharge altogether. Cylinders formed of metallic filings do not produce these effects, while cylinders formed of alternate layers of metallic and nonmetallic substances do produce them. It is inferred from this that solutions of continuity at right angles to the axis of the needle, or to that of the cylinder, have an influence on the phenomena.

281. **Formation of powerful electro-magnets.** — The inductive effect of a spiral or helical current on soft iron is still

more energetic than on steel or other bodies having more or less coercive force. The property enjoyed by soft iron, of suddenly acquiring magnetism from any external magnetising agent, and as suddenly losing its magnetism upon the suspension of such agency, has supplied the means of producing the temporary magnets which are known under the name of *electro-magnets*.

The most simple form of electro-magnet is represented in *fig.* 199. It is composed of a bar of soft iron bent into the form of

Fig. 199.

a horse shoe, and of a wire wrapped with silk, which is coiled first on one arm, proceeding from one extremity to the bend of the horse shoe, and then upon the other from the bend to the other extremity; care being taken that the convolutions of the spiral shall follow the same direction in passing from one leg to the other, since, otherwise, consequent points would be produced. An armature is applied to the ends of the horse shoe which will adhere to them so long as a voltaic current flows upon the wire,

ut which will drop off the moment that such current is dis-
>ntinued.

282. **Conditions which determine the force of the magnet.**
— The force of the electro-magnet will depend on the dimensions
f the horse shoe and the armature, the intensity of the current, and
ae number of convolutions with which each leg of the horse shoe is
rapped.

283. **Electro-magnet of Faculty of Sciences at Paris.** —
n 1830 an electro-magnet of extraordinary power was constructed
under the superintendence of M. Pouillet at Paris. This ap-
aratus, represented in *fig.* 200., consists of two horse shoes, the
ags of which are presented to each other, the bends being turned
a contrary directions. The superior horse shoe is fixed in the

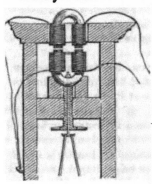

frame of the apparatus, the inferior being attached to a cross piece
which slides in vertical grooves
formed in the sides of the frame. To
this cross piece a dish or plateau
is suspended, in which weights are
placed, by the effect of which the attraction which unites the two horse
shoes is at length overcome. Each
of the horse shoes is wrapped with
10000 feet of covered wire, and they
are so arranged that the poles of
contrary names shall be in contact.
With a current of moderate inten-

Fig. 200.

y the apparatus is capable of supporting a weight of several
ns.

284. **Form of electro-magnets in general.** — It is found
ore convenient generally to construct electro-magnets of two
raight bars of soft iron, united at one end by a straight bar
ansverse to them, and attached to them by screws, so that the
rm of the magnet ceases to be that of a horse shoe, the end at
hich the legs are united being not curved but square. The con-
uctor of the helical current is usually a copper wire of extreme
nuity.

285. **Electro-magnetic power applied as a mechanical
agent.** — The property of electro-magnets, by which they are
apable of suddenly acquiring and losing the magnetic force, has
applied the means of obtaining a mechanical agent which may be
pplied as a mover of machinery. An electro-magnet and its
mature, such as that represented in *fig.* 199., or two electro-
agnets, such as those represented in *fig.* 200., are placed so that
hen the electric current is suspended they will rest at a certain

distance asunder, and when the current passes on the wire they
will be drawn into contact by their mutual attraction. When the
current is again suspended they will separate. In this manner, by
alternately suspending and transmitting the current on the wire
which is coiled round the electro-magnet, the magnet and its
armature, or the two magnets, receive an alternate motion to
and from each other similar to that of the piston of a steam engine, or the foot of a person who works the treddle of a lathe.
This alternate motion is made to produce one of continued rotation
by the same mechanical expedients as are used in the application
of any other moving power.

The force with which the electro-magnet and its armature
attract each other determines the power of the electro-motive
machine, just as the pressure of steam on the piston determines the
power of a steam engine. This force, when the magnets are given
varies with the nature and magnitude of the galvanic pile which is
employed.

286. **Electro-motive power applied in the workshop of
M. Froment.**—The most remarkable and beautiful application of
electro-motive power as a mechanical agent which has been hither-
witnessed, is presented in the workshops of M. Gustave Froment
of Paris, so celebrated for the construction of instruments of precision. It is here applied in various forms to give motion to the
machines contrived by M. Froment, for dividing the limbs of astro-
nomical and surveying instruments and microscopic scales. The
pile used for the lighter description of work is that of Daniel, consisting of about 24 pairs. Simple arrangements are made by
means of commutators, reometers, and reotropes, for modifying
the current indefinitely in quantity, intensity, and direction. By
merely turning an index or lever in one direction or another, any
desired number of pairs may be brought into operation, so that a
battery of greater or less intensity may be instantly made to act,
subject to the major limit of the number of pairs provided. By
another adjustment the copper elements of two or more pairs, and
at the same time their zinc elements, may be thrown into connection, and thus the whole pile, or any portion of it, may be made to
act as a single pair, of enlarged surface. By another adjustment
the direction of the current can be reversed at pleasure. .Other
adjustments, equally simple and effective, are provided, by which
the current can be turned on any particular machine, or directed
into any room that may be required.

The pile used for heavier work is a modification of Bunsen
charcoal battery, in which dilute sulphuric acid is used in the
porous porcelain cell containing the charcoal, as well as in the cell
containing the zinc. By this expedient the noxious fumes of the

nitric acid are removed, and although the strength of the battery is diminished, sufficient power remains for the purposes to which it is applied.

The forms of the electro-motive machines constructed by M. Froment are very various. In some the magnet is fixed and the armature movable; in some both are movable.

In some there is a single magnet and a single armature. The power is in this case intermittent, like that of a single acting steam engine, or of the foot in working the treddle of a lathe, and the continuance of the action is maintained in the same manner by the inertia of a fly wheel.

In other cases two electro-magnets and two armatures are combined, and the current is so regulated that it is established on each, during the intervals of its suspension on the other. This machine is analogous in its operation to the double acting steam engine, the operation of the power being continuous, the one magnet attracting its armature during the intervals of suspension of the other. The force of these machines may be augmented indefinitely by combining the action of two or more pairs of magnets.

Another variety of the application of this moving principle presents an analogy to the rotatory steam engine. Electro-magnets are fixed at equal distances round a wheel, to the circumference of which the armatures are attached at corresponding intervals. In this case the intervals of action and intermission of the currents are so regulated, that the magnets attract the armatures obliquely as the latter approach them, the current, and consequently the attraction, being suspended the moment contact takes place. The effect of this is, that all the magnets exercise forces which tend to turn the wheel, on which the armatures are fixed, constantly in the same direction, and the force with which it is turned is equal to the sum of the forces of all the electro-magnets which act simultaneously.

This rotatory electro-motive machine is infinitely varied, not only in its magnitude and proportions, but in its form. Thus in some the axle is horizontal, and the wheel revolves in a vertical plane; in others the axle is vertical, and the wheel revolves in a horizontal plane. In some the electro-magnets are fixed, and the armatures movable with the wheel; in others both are movable. In some the axle of the wheel which carries the armatures is itself movable, being fixed upon a crank or excentric. In this case the wheel revolves within another, whose diameter exceeds its own by twice the length of the crank, and within this circle it has a hypocycloidal motion.

Each of these varieties of the application of this power, as yet

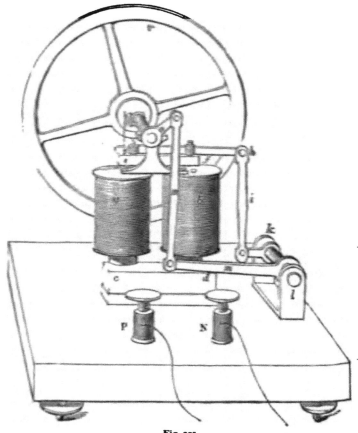

novel in the practical operations of the engineer and manufacturer possesses peculiar advantages or convenience, which render it more eligible for special purposes.

237. **Electro-motive machines constructed by him.** — To render this general description of M. Froment's electro-motive machines more clearly understood, we shall add a detailed explanation of two of the most efficient and useful of them.

In the machine represented in *fig.* 201, *a* and *b* are the two legs of the electro-magnet; *c d* is the transverse piece uniting them, which replaces the

Fig. 201.

bend of the horse shoe; *e f* is the armature confined by two pins on the summit of the leg *a* (which prevent any lateral deviation), the end *f* being jointed to the lever *g h*, which is connected with a short arm -projecting from an axis *k* by the rod *i*. When the current passes round the electro-magnet, the lever *f* is drawn down by the attraction of the leg *b*, and draws with it the lever $g\,k$, by which i and the short lever projecting from the axis k are also driven down. Attached to the same axis k is a longer arm, m, which acts by a connecting rod n upon a crank o and a fly wheel v. When the machine is in motion, the lever $g\,k$ and the armature f attached to it recover their position by the momentum of the fly wheel, after having been attracted downwards. When the current is again established, the armature f and the lever $g\,k$ are again attracted downwards, and the same effects ensue. Thus, during each half-revolution of the crank o, it is driven by the force of the electro-magnet acting on f, and during the other half-revolution it is carried round by the momentum of the fly wheel. The current is suspended at the moment the crank o arrives at the lowest point of its play, and is re-established when it returns to the highest point. The crank is therefore impelled by the force of the magnet in the descending half of its revolution, and by the momentum of the fly wheel in the ascending half.

The contrivance called a *distributor*, by which the current is alternately established and suspended at the proper moments, is represented in *fig.* 202.,

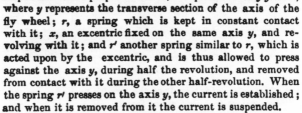

where y represents the transverse section of the axis of the fly wheel; r, a spring which is kept in constant contact with it; x, an excentric fixed on the same axis y, and revolving with it; and r' another spring similar to r, which is acted upon by the excentric, and is thus allowed to press against the axis y, during half the revolution, and removed from contact with it during the other half-revolution. When the spring r' presses on the axis y, the current is established; and when it is removed from it the current is suspended.

Fig. 202.

It is evident that the action of this machine upon the lever attached to the axis k is exactly similar to that of the foot on the treddle of a lathe or a spinning wheel; and as in these cases, the impelling force being intermittent, the action is unequal, the velocity being greater during the descending motion of the crank o than during its ascending motion. Although the inertia of the fly wheel diminishes this inequality by absorbing a part of the moving power in the descending motion, and restoring it to the crank in the ascending motion, it cannot altogether efface it.

Another electro-motive machine of M. Froment is represented in elevation in *fig.* 203., and in plan in *fig.* 204. This machine has the advantage of producing a perfectly regular motion of rotation, which it retains for several hours without sensible change.

A drum, which revolves on a vertical axis $x\,y$, carries on its circumference eight bars of soft iron a placed at equal distances asunder. These bars are attracted laterally, and always in the same direction, by the intermitting action of six electro-magnets b, mounted in a strong hexagonal frame of cast iron, within which the drum revolves. The intervals of action and suspension of the current upon these magnets are so regulated, that it is established upon each of them at the moment one of the bars of soft iron a is approaching it, and it is suspended at the moment the bar begins to depart from it. Thus the attraction accelerates the motion of the drum upon the approach of the piece a towards the magnet b, and ceases to act when the piece a arrives in front of b. The action of each of the six impelling forces upon each of the eight bars of soft iron attached to the drum is thus intermitting. During each revolution of the drum, each of the eight bars a receives six impulses, and therefore the drum itself receives forty-eight impulses. If we suppose the drum to make one revolution in four seconds, it will therefore receive a

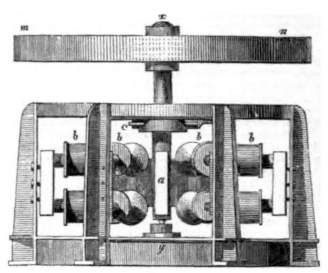

Fig. 203.

succession of impulses at intervals of the twelfth part of a second, which is practically equivalent to a continuous force.

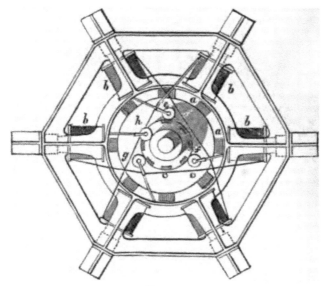

Fig. 204.

The intervals of intermission of the current are regulated by a sim ingenious apparatus. A metallic disc c is fixed upon the axis of l

irface consists of sixteen equal divisions, the alternate divisions being
d with nonconducting matter. A metallic roller *h*, which carries the
nt, presses constantly on the surface of this disc, to which it imparts the
nt. Three other metallic rollers *e f g* press against the edge of the
and, as the disc revolves, come alternately into contact with the con-
ng and nonconducting divisions of it. When they touch the conducting
ions, the current is transmitted; when they touch the nonconducting
.ons, the current is interrupted.

ch of these three rollers *e f g* is connected by a conducting wire with the
icting wires of two electro-magnets diametrically opposed, as is indi-
in *fig.* 204., so that the current is thus alternately established and sus-
id on the several electro-magnets, as the conducting and nonconduct-
ivisions of the disc pass the rollers *e, f,* and *g.*

Froment has adapted a regulator to this machine, which plays the part;
e governor of the steam engine, moderating the force when the action.
e pile becomes too strong, and augmenting it when it becomes too
ì

Fig. 205.

divided circle *m n*, *fig.* 203., has been annexed to the machine at the
estion of M. Pouillet, by which various important physical experiments
be performed.

iother form of this machine, in which the drum carrying the bars of soft
revolves upon a horizontal axis, is shown in *fig.* 205.

and G are the points where the current enters and leaves the machine, these being connected by wires with the voltaic battery; A B C D are four pairs of powerful electro-magnets; F the bars of soft iron upon which they act.

287*. The electro-motive machine of M. Bourbouze, *fig.* 206., consists of four hollow cylinders A *a*, B *b*, round which the conducting wire is coiled. Into the cores of these cylinders pass

Fig. 206.

four rods of soft iron attached to the cross pieces A *a* and B *b*. These cross pieces are themselves attached at their middle points by the rods R and P to the extremities of the working beam F. One arm of this beam, being prolonged, is jointed at I to a connecting rod I H, which is connected with a crank at H. Upon the axis of this crank a fly wheel is fixed by which the varying effect of the crank is equalised. Upon the other extremity of the axis another crank Y is fixed, which is joined by a horizontal connecting rod with a plate which slides to and fro in grooves made in the top of the box N s.

The four soft iron rods attached to the cross pieces A *a* and B *b* extend less than half way down the axes of the four cylinders. Four other similar cast iron rods are similarly connected below by cross pieces K, and pass up the axes of the cylinders less than half way, so that a space remains between the extremities of the two sets of rods above and below.

The sliding plate U consists of a piece of metal in the middle, and slips of ivory at the ends, the middle being always in connection with the positive pole of the voltaic battery. Two conducting wires, each of which is connected with the negative pole of the battery, are connected with the spiral coils which are fixed upon the base; and the ends of these coils are so placed that they press constantly on the sliding plate U. When this plate slides to the right, the end of the wire of the left hand coil rests upon the ivory, and its connection with the battery is broken; but that of the right hand coil rests upon the metal, and its connection with the battery is completed. When the plate U moves to the left, the connections are reversed, and the left hand coil is connected with the battery, the right hand coil being disconnected.

In this way the current is alternately transmitted and suspended on the two wires proceeding from the coils. These wires are connected respectively, one with the wire coiled upon the cylinders A a, and the other with the wire coiled on the cylinders B b. The current is therefore transmitted alternately through the coils upon the pairs of cylinders placed under each extremity of the beam, and renders momentarily magnetic the rods of soft iron inserted in their cores. The coils are so arranged, that the poles of the upper and lower electro-magnets presented to each other have contrary names, and they consequently attract each other. The lower rods being fixed, draw the upper rods towards them when the current passes, and disengage them when it is suspended. In this way the ends of the beam F are alternately drawn down, and a motion of continuous rotation is imparted to the crank shaft, which is equalised by the fly wheel.

288. Applied as a sonometer. — This machine has been applied with much success as a *sonometer*, to ascertain and register directly the number of vibrations made by sonorous bodies in a given time.

289. Momentary current by induction. — If a wire A, on which a voltaic current is transmitted, be brought into proximity with and parallel to another wire B, the ends of which are in metallic contact either with each other, or with some continuous system of conductors, so as to form a *closed circuit*, the electric equilibrium of the wire B will be disturbed by the action of the current A, and a current will be produced upon B in a direction opposite to that which prevails on A. This current will, however, be only momentary. After an instant the wire B will return to its natural state.

If the wire A, still carrying the current, be then suddenly removed from the wire B, the electric equilibrium of B will be again disturbed, and as before, only for a moment; but in this case the current momentarily produced on B will have the same direction as the current on A.

If the contact of the extremities of the wire B, or either of

them with each other, or with the intermediate system of conductors which complete the circuit, be broken, the approach or
removal of the current A will not produce these effects on the
wire B.

If, instead of moving the wire A to and from B, the wires, both
in their natural state, be placed parallel and near to each other,
and a current be then suddenly transmitted on A, the same effect
will be produced on B as if A, already bearing the current, had
been suddenly brought into proximity with B; and in the same
way it will be found that if the current established on A be suddenly suspended, the same effect will be produced as if A, still
bearing the current, were suddenly removed.

These phenomena may be easily exhibited experimentally, by
connecting the extremities of the wire A with a voltaic pile, and
the extremities of B with the wires of a reoscope.   So long as the
current continues to pass without interruption cn A, the needle
of the reoscope will remain at rest, showing that no current passes
on B.   But if the contact of A with either pole of the pile be
suddenly broken, so as to stop the current, the needle of the
reoscope will be deflected for a moment in the direction which
indicates a current similar in direction to that which passed on
A, and which has just been suspended; but this deflection will
only be momentary.   The needle will immediately recover its
position of rest, indicating that the cause of the disturbance has
ceased.

If the extremity of A be then again placed suddenly in contact
with the pile, so as to re-establish the current on A, the needle of
the reoscope will again be deflected, but in the other direction,
showing that the current produced on B is in the contrary direction to that which passes on A, and, as before, the disturbance
will only be momentary, the needle returning immediately to its
position of rest.

These momentary currents are therefore ascribed to the inductive action of the current A upon the natural electricity of
the wire B, decomposing it and causing for a moment the positive
fluid to move in one direction, and the negative in the other.   It
is to the *sudden presence* and the *sudden absence* of the current
A, that the phenomena must be ascribed, and not to any action
depending on the commencement of the passage of the current
on A, or on its discontinuance, because the same effects are produced by the *approach* and *withdrawal* of A while it carries the
current, as by the *transmission* and *discontinuance* of the current
upon it.

290. **Experimental illustration.** — The most convenient form
of apparatus for the experimental exhibition of these momentary

Fig. 207.

currents of induction, consists of two wires wrapped with silk, which are coiled round a cylinder or roller of wood or metal, as represented in *fig.* 207. The ends are separated in leaving the roller, so that those of one wire may be carried to the pile, and those of the other to the reoscope. The effect of the inductive action is augmented in proportion to the length of the wires brought into proximity, other things being the same. It is found that the wire B, which receives the inductive action, should be much finer and longer than that, A, which bears the primary current. Thus, for example, while 150 feet of wire No. 18. were used for A, 2000 feet of No. 26. were used for B.

The effect of the induction is greatly augmented by introducing a cylinder of soft iron, or, still better, a bundle of soft iron wires, into the core of the roller. The current on A renders this mass of soft iron magnetic, and it reacts by induction on the wires conducting the currents.

291. **Momentary currents produced by magnetic induction.** — Since, as has been shown, a magnetic bar and a helical current are interchangeable, it may naturally be inferred that if a helical current produces by induction momentary currents upon a helical wire placed in proximity with it, a magnet must produce a like effect. Experiment has accordingly confirmed this inference.

292. **Experimental illustrations.** — Let the extremities of a covered wire coiled on a roller, *fig.* 208., be connected with a reoscope, and let the pole of a magnet be suddenly inserted in the core of the coil.

A momentary deflection of the needles will be produced, similar to that which would attend the sudden approach of the end of a helical current having the properties of the magnetic pole which is presented to the coil. Thus the *boreal* pole will produce the same deflection as the *front*, and the *austral* pole as the *back* of a helical current.

· In like manner, the sudden removal of a magnetic pole from proximity with the helical wire will produce a momentary current on the wire, similar to that which would be produced by the sudden removal of a helical current having like magnetic properties.

The sudden presence and absence of the magnetic pole within the coil of wire on which it is desired to produce the induced current may be caused more conveniently and efficiently by means of the effects of magnetic in-

M 4

duction on soft iron. The manner of applying this principle to the pr——
duction of the induced current is as follows:—

Fig. 203

Fig. 209.

Let *a b*, *fig.* 209., be a powerful horse shoe magnet, over which is placed a similar shoe of soft iron, round which the conducting wire is coiled in the usual manner, the direction of the coils being reversed in passing from one leg of the horse shoe to the other, so that the current in passing on each leg may have its front presented in opposite directions. The extremities of the wire are connected with those of a reoscope at a sufficient distance from the magnet to prevent its indications from being disturbed by the influence of the magnet.

If the poles *a b* of the magnet be suddenly brought near the ends of the legs of the horse shoe *m c n*, the needle of the reoscope will indicate the existence of a momentary current on the coil of wire, the direction of which will be opposite to that which would characterise the magnetic polarity imparted by induction to the horse shoe *m c n*. If the magnet *a b* be then suddenly removed, so as to deprive the horse shoe *m c n* of its magnetism, the reoscope will again indicate the existence of a momentary current, the direction of which will now, however, be that which characterises the polarity imparted to the horse shoe *m c n*.

It appears, therefore, as might be expected, that the sudden decomposit and recomposition of the magnetic fluids in the soft iron contained within the coil has the same effect as the sudden approach and removal of a magnet.

293. **Inductive effects produced by a permanent magnet revolving under an electro-magnet.** — If the magnet *a b* were mounted so as to revolve upon a vertical axis passing through the centre of its bend, and therefore midway between its legs, its poles might be made to come alternately under the ends of the horse shoe *m c n*, the horse shoe *m c n* being stationary. During each revolution of the magnet *a b*, the polarity imparted by magnetic induction to the horse shoe would be reversed. When the austral pole *a* passes under *m*, and therefore the boreal pole under *n*, *m* would acquire boreal and *n* austral polarity. After making half a revolution *b* would come under *m*, and *a* under *n*, and *m* would acquire by induction austral and *n* boreal polarity. The momentary currents produced in the coils of wire would suffer corresponding changes of direction consequent as well on the commencement as on the cessation of each polarity, austral and boreal.

To trace these vicissitudes of the inductive current produced upon the wire, it must be considered that the commencement of austral polarity in the leg *m*, and that of boreal polarity in the leg *n*, give the same direction to the momentary inductive current, inasmuch as the wire is coiled on the legs in contrary directions. In the same manner it follows that the commencement of boreal polarity in *m*, and of austral polarity in *n*, produce the same inductive current.

The same may be said of the direction of the inductive currents consequent on the cessation of austral and boreal polarity in each of the legs. The cessation of austral polarity in *m*, and of boreal polarity in *n*, or the cessation of boreal polarity in *m*, and of austral polarity in *n*, produce the same inductive current. It will also follow, from the effects of the current and the reversion of the coils in passing from one leg to the other, that the inductive current produced by the cessation of either polarity on one leg of *m c n* will have the same direction as that produced by the commencement of the same polarity in the other.

If the magnet *a b* were made to revolve under *m c n*, it would therefore follow that during each revolution four momentary currents would be produced in the wire, two in one direction during one semi-revolution, and two in the contrary direction during the other semi-revolution. In the intervals between these momentary currents the wire would be in its natural state.

It has been stated that if the extremities of the wire were not in metallic contact with each other, or with a continuous system of conductors, these inductive currents would not be produced. This

condition supplies the means of producing in the wire an intermitting inductive current constantly in the same direction. To
accomplish this, it will be only necessary to contrive means to
break the contact of either extremity of the coil with the intermediate conductor during the same half of each successive revolution of the magnet. By this expedient the contact may be
maintained during the half revolution in which the commencement
of austral polarity in the leg *m*, and of boreal in the leg *n*, and the
cessation of boreal polarity in the leg *m*, and of austral in the leg
n, respectively take place. All these changes produce momentar-
currents having a common direction. The contact being broken
during the other semi-revolution, in which the commencement
boreal polarity in *m*, and of austral in *n*, and the cessation
austral polarity in *m*, and of boreal in *n*, respectively take place,
the contrary currents which would otherwise attend these changes
will not be produced.

294. **Use of a contact breaker.** — If it be desired to reverse
the direction of the intermitting current, it will be only necessary
to contrive a *contact breaker*, which will admit of such an adjustment that the contact may be maintained at pleasure, during either
semi-revolution of the magnet *a b*, while it is broken during the
other.

295. **Magneto-electric machines.** — Such are the principles
on which is founded the construction of magneto-electric machines,
one form of which is represented in *fig.* 210. The purpose of this
apparatus is to produce by magnetic induction an intermitting
current constantly in the same direction, and to contrive means by
which the intervals of intermission shall succeed each other so
rapidly that the current shall have practically all the effects of a
current absolutely continuous.

A powerful compound horse shoe magnet A is firmly attached by bolts
and screws upon an horizontal bed, beyond the edge of which its poles *a* and
b extend. Under these is fixed an electro-magnet X Y, with its legs vertical, and mounted so as to revolve upon a vertical axis. The covered wire
is coiled in great quantity on the legs X Y, the direction of the coils being
reversed in passing from one leg to the other; so that if a voltaic current
were transmitted upon it, the ends X and Y would acquire opposite po-
larities.

The axis upon which this electro-magnet revolves has upon it a small
grooved wheel *f*, which is connected by an endless cord or band *n*, with a
large wheel R driven by a handle *m*. The relative diameters of the wheels
R and *f* is such that an extremely rapid rotation can be imparted to X Y by
the hand applied at *m*.

The two extremities of the wire proceeding from the legs X and Y are
pressed by springs against the surfaces of two rollers, *c* and *d*, fixed upon
the axis of the electro-magnet. These rollers themselves are in metallic

connection with a pair of handles P and N, to which the current evolved in the wire of the electro-magnet X Y will thus be conducted.

If the electro-magnet X Y be now put in rotation by the handle *m*, the

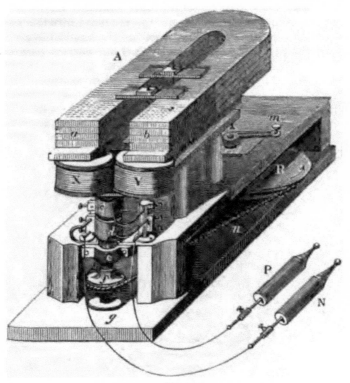

Fig. 210

handles P and N being connected by any continuous conductor, a system of intermitting and alternately contrary currents will be produced in the wire and in the conductor by which the handles P and N are connected. But if the rollers *c* and *d* are so contrived that the contact of the ends of the wire with them shall be only maintained during a semi-revolution, in which the intermitting currents have a common direction, then. the current transmitted through the conductor connecting the handles P and N will be intermitting, but not contrary; and by increasing the velocity of rotation of the electro-magnet X Y, the intervals of intermission may be made to succeed each other with indefinite celerity, and the current will thus acquire all the character of a continuous current.

The contrivances by which the rollers *c* and *d* are made to break the contact, and re-establish it with the necessary regularity and certainty, are various. They may be formed as *excentrics*, so as to approach to and recede from the ends of the wire as they revolve, touching them and retiring from them at the proper moments. Or, being circular, they may consist alternately of conducting and nonconducting materials. Thus one half of the surface of such roller may be metal, while the other is wood, horn, or ivory. When the end of the wire touches the latter the current is suspended, when it touches the former it is maintained.

296. **Effects of this machine—Its medical use.**—All the usual effects of voltaic currents may be produced with this apparatus. If the handles P and N be held in the hands, the arms and body become the conductor through which the current passes from

Fig. 211.

P to N. If x y be made to revolve, shocks are felt, which become insupportable when the motion of x y acquires a certain rapidity.

be desired to give local shocks to certain parts of the body,
ds of the operator, protected by nonconducting gloves,
he knobs at the ends of the handles to the parts of the
etween which it is desired to produce the voltaic shock.

Clarke's apparatus.—In another form of this apparatus,
tructed by Mr. Clarke, of London, the magnet M, *fig.* 211.,
d vertically, and the electro-magnets E E' revolve on a
tal axis, upon which the contact breaking apparatus *a c* is
In other respects this does not differ in principle from that
ed above.

manner of applying it to the decomposition of water is
in *fig.* 212. This phenomenon will be more fully explained
er.

Fig. 212.

roduce and apply physiological effects the wire rolled upon
ctro-magnet must be very fine, and have a total length of
2000 feet. To produce physical effects, on the contrary, the

Fig. 213.

Fig. 214.

hould be thick, about 100 feet being rolled on each arm of
ctro-magnet. In *fig.* 213. is shown the arrangement of the
utator necessary to show the effect of the current in setting

fire to ether, and in *fig.* 214. the arrangement necessary to al
its effect in rendering metallic wire incandescent. These phe
mena will be explained more fully hereafter.

298. **Matteucci's apparatus.**—This apparatus serves to ex
bit experimentally currents produced by induction, not only in
electricity of the pile, but also those produced by the electricity
the machine.

It consists of two circular discs of glass, N and M (*fig.* 215.), each abou
inches diameter, mounted in brass frames, and placed vertically on mova

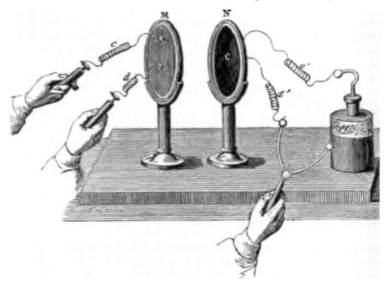

Fig. 215.

stands, so as to be capable of being moved towards or from each other. U
the face of the plate N a copper wire, wrapped with silk, about the twe
of an inch in diameter, is rolled spirally, its extremities being passed thro
two holes in the plate, one at the centre and the other at the circumferenc
the top of the disc. To insulate still more effectually the current, each cir
of the spiral is covered with a thick coating of gum·lac, a condition wh
though not necessary for the voltaic current, is indispensable when the ap
ratus is used to exhibit the effects of a current produced by the discharge
Leyden jar.

A similar wire, but much finer, is coiled spirally upon the face of the ot
plate M, which looks towards that of N; and its extremities are brough
like manner through holes at the centre and circumference of the plate
shown at *a* and *b*.

The arrangement shown in the figure is that which is necessary to
hibit the effect of the current produced by the discharge of a Leyden
Two wires, *c'* and *d'*, clamped to the extremities of the spiral wire on N,
connected, one with the inner coating of the Leyden jar, and the other pla

so that the operator can touch it at will with a discharger, such contact producing immediately the transmission of the electric charge of the jar through the spiral wire on the disc N. At the moment the contact is made, the positive fluid on the inside of the jar rushes along the conducting wire c′, and from thence to the extremity of the spiral wire which passes through the centre of the plate N, and then circulating round the spiral, passes along the wire d′ to the outer coating of the jar.

If the plate M be brought near and parallel to the plate N, and at the same time the extremities, a and b, of the spiral wire upon it be connected, as shown in the figure, by a person holding the conducting handles of the wires c and d, an inductive current will be produced in the circuit of the wire upon M, which will impart a corresponding shock to the person holding the handles.

The intensity of the shock thus imparted may be varied at pleasure, by moving the discs N and M nearer to or further from each other.

To exhibit the inductive current similarly produced by voltaic electricity, it is only necessary to connect the wire c′ and d′ with the voltaic battery, and the wires c and d with a reoscope, when the existence, direction, and intensity of the induced current will be immediately indicated by the deflection of the needle.

299. **Ruhmkorff's apparatus to produce currents of tension.** —By this apparatus inductive currents are produced which have a tension bearing more analogy to that evolved by the electrical machines than to ordinary voltaic currents.

The apparatus which is shown in *fig.* 216. consists of a powerful bobbin c, placed vertically upon a thick plate of glass, which insulates it. This bobbin, which is about 14 inches high, is composed of two wires, one about the twelfth of an inch in diameter, making 300 coils, and the other the eighth of an inch rolled upon the former, making 10000 coils. These wires are not only wrapped with silk, but each coil is insulated from the adjacent ones by a coat of gum-lac. A current produced by one couple of Bunsen's battery is transmitted through the thicker wire. The positive pole being in communication with the wire p G, the current passes from it through E to the commutator D, from which it descends along the metallic plate to a ribbon of copper, which conducts it to one of the extremities, a, of the thick wire of the bobbin. The other extremity of this wire, being connected with one of the copper legs which support the plate of glass, the current coming out of the bobbin passes to a second ribbon c, from whence it mounts along an iron column, b B. Thence it arrives at an oscillating hammer, e, which is sometimes in contact with d, and sometimes removed from it. When the contact takes place, the current follows the conductors, d and F, and mounts to the commutator D, from whence it returns to the pile.

The alternate motion of the hammer e is produced by a cylinder of soft iron, placed in the axis of the bobbin. When the current of the pile passes along the thick wire, this rod of soft iron becomes magnetic, and attracts upwards the little hammer e, which is also iron. The current being then interrupted, and not being capable of passing to the piece d, the rod of soft iron loses its magnetism, and the hammer e falls back upon d. The current then recommences, the hammer e being again raised, and so on.

While the current in this way passes with intermission along the thick wire of the bobbin at each interval of suspension an inductive current is produced in the fine wire in alternately opposite directions. This being completely insulated, the induced current acquires a tension so great as to be capable of producing various phenomena similar to those produced by the common electrical machine. Thus, the current being imparted to two con-

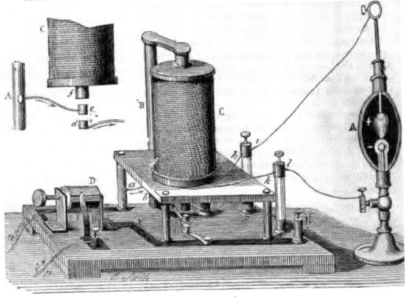

Fig. 216.

ducting wires $h\,i$ and $k\,l$, which are connected with the two rods of such a globe A as has been already described, the same electric light will be produced as was produced by the electrical machine as described in (129.).

The apparatus with the hammer above described, placed under the great bobbin C, is represented on a larger scale to the left of the upper part of the figure, where e represents the hammer, and A e the wire which conducts the current to it. It oscillates between the pieces f and d. It will be observed in this experiment that the greatest brightness will be at the positive pole where the light will have a fiery red colour, that at the negative pole having a violet tint, and being much more feeble. It will be further observed that while the light round the positive pole is confined to its extremity, that round the negative pole is extended along the metal rod to the point where it enters the globe.

300. **Stratification of electric light.** — Experiments made with the above apparatus by M. Quet exhibited the following remarkable phenomena. If the rarefaction of the interior of the globe is preceded by the introduction of the vapour of turpentine, pyroligneous acid, alcohol, sulphurate of carbon, &c., the appearance of the light is modified in a remarkable manner. It assumes then the form of a series of horizontal zones, alternately bright and dark, ranged one above the other, as shown in *fig.* 217.

In this experiment the light is not continuous, but consists of a

on of discharges which follow each other more or less rapidly according to the rate of the oscil
lation of the hammer *a*, *fig.* 216. The
luminous zones, *fig.* 217., then appear
animated with a double movement of
gyration and undulation, which however
M. Quet considers as an optical illusion,
since by causing the hammer *a* to oscillate slowly with the hand, the zones appear
distinct and fixed. It may, however, be
objected that in that case the development of the light is too momentary to
render manifest the effects in question.

As to the quality of the light developed
in this experiment, though that round the
positive pole is most frequently red, and
that round the negative pole violet, this
is subject to some variation, depending on
the nature of the vapour or gas which has
been introduced into the globe.

Fig. 217.

It has been observed by M. Despretz,
that the phenomena exhibited by MM.
Ruhmkorff and Quet, with an intermitting
current, are also produced with a common
us current, but with this important difference, that the
us current requires a strong battery consisting of many
Bunsen's system, while the intermitting current requires
gle pair. It is worthy of remark also that the effect of
nitting current is very little increased by increasing the
the battery.

isfactory explanation appears to have been hitherto pro-
· these phenomena.

**'eculiar properties of the direct and inverse in-
vurrents.**— Notwithstanding the momentary character
equent intermission of induced currents, they are found
s all the physical properties of ordinary voltaic currents.
y impart the same shock to the nervous system, they pro-
same luminous, thermal, and chemical phenomena, they
.agnetism to soft iron, they affect the reoscope in the same
and, in fine, reproduce other currents of induction.
.ock produced by induced currents is however much more
:han that which results from common voltaic currents.
·r the shock imparted by the latter sensible, a battery con-
f many pairs is necessary, while a single pair with the
s above described is sufficient to produce a shock, the

N

continuance of which would be insupportable with an induce
current.

The effects of the direct and inverse induced currents have bee
compared by means of commutators, by which they can be sepa
rately exhibited. So far as respects their effects upon the reoscop
they are nearly alike ; but while the direct current produces a
strong shock, that produced by the inverse current is scarcely
sensible. In like manner, while the direct current is capable of
imparting strong magnetism, the inverse current imparts none.

302. **Statham's apparatus.** — This consists of a copper wire
A B (*fig.* 218.), covered with a thick coating of sulphuretted
gutta percha.

Fig. 218.

At the end of some months a stratum of sulphuret of copper, having a
conducting power over the current, is formed at the surface of contact of the
metal and its envelope. If at any point whatever of the circuit a section be
made through the upper half of the envelope, so as to divide the wire, and
remove about a quarter of an inch of its length, as shown at *a b*, an intense
current, which being transmitted along the wire would be interrupted at *a b*,
finds its way nevertheless at that point along the coating of sulphuret of
copper not divided by the section ; and because of its imperfect conducting
power this part of the envelope becomes incandescent, so that it would
ignite gun cotton or other inflammable substance.

To perform this experiment with an ordinary current a powerful battery
is necessary; but an induced current produced by a single pair of Bunsen
and Ruhmkorff's apparatus will be sufficient for it.

It appears from some recent experiments of Dr. Faraday that
the effects produced by a current which passes along such wires
are very feeble when they are surrounded by air, like those of
telegraphic wires sustained on posts, but that on the contrary
such effects are very intense when the wires are either buried
under ground or carried through water, as is the case in certain
telegraphic arrangements on land and in that of the submarine
cables. Dr. Faraday explains these effects by the supposition
that such a wire surrounded by water or earth, the latter being
always more or less moist, is placed under conditions analogous to
that of a Leyden jar, the conducting wire in the centre corresponding to the internal, and the water or moist earth the external coating, while the same wire suspended in the air is like a
jar having an internal but no external coating.

303. **Inductive effects of the successive convolutions of the same helix.** — The inductive effect produced by the commencement or cessation of a current upon a wire, forming part of a closed circuit placed near and parallel to it, would lead to the inference that some effect may be produced by one coil of a helical current upon another at the moment when such current commences or ceases. At the moment when the current commences, it might be expected that the inductive action of one coil upon another, having a tendency to produce a momentary current in a contrary direction, would mitigate the initial intensity of the actual current, and that at the moment the current is suspended the same inductive action, having a tendency to produce a momentary current in the same direction, would, on the contrary, have a tendency to augment the intensity of the actual current.

The phenomena developed when the contact of a closed circuit is made or broken, are in remarkable accordance with these anticipations.

If the wires which connect the poles of an ordinary pile, consisting of a dozen pairs, be separated or brought together, a very feeble spark will be visible, and no sensible change in the intensity of this spark will be produced when the length of the wire compassing the circuit is augmented so much as to amount to 150 or 200 yards. If this wire be folded or coiled in any manner, so long as the parts composing the folds or coils are distant from each other by a quarter of an inch or more, no change of intensity will be observed. But if the wire be coiled round a roller or bobbin, so that the successive convolutions may be only separated from each other by the thickness of the silk which covers them, a very remarkable effect will ensue. The spark produced when the extremities of the wire are brought together will still be faint ; but that which is manifest when, after having been in contact, they are suddenly separated, will have an incomparably greater length, and a tenfold or even a hundredfold greater splendour. The shock produced, if the ends of the wire be held in the hands when the contact is broken, has also a greater intensity.

304. **Effects of momentary inductive currents produced upon revolving metallic discs. — Researches of Arago, Herschel, Babbage, and Faraday.** — It was first ascertained by Arago that if a circular disc of metal revolve round its centre in its own plane under a magnetic needle, the needle will be deflected from the magnetic meridian, and the extent of its deflection will be augmented with the velocity of rotation of the disc. By increasing gradually that velocity, the needle will at length be turned to a direction at right angles to the magnetic meridian. If the velocity of rotation be still more increased, the needle will

receive a motion of continuous rotation round its centre in the same direction as that of the disc, *fig.* 219.

Fig. 219.

That this does not proceed from any mechanical action of the disc upon the intervening stratum of air, is proved by the fact that it is produced in exactly the same manner, where a screen of thin paper is interposed between the needle and the disc.

Sir John Herschel and Mr. Babbage made a series of experiments to determine the relative power of discs composed of different metals to produce this phenomenon. Taking the action of copper, which is the most intense, as the unit, the following are the relative forces determined for discs of other metals : —

Copper				1·00	Lead				0·25
Zinc				0·93	Antimony				0·09
Tin				0·46	Bismuth				0·02

Professor Barlow ascertained that iron and steel act more energetically than the other metals. The force of silver is considerable, that of gold very feeble. Mercury holds a place between antimony and bismuth.

Herschel and Babbage found that if a slit were made in the direction of a radius of the disc it lost a great part of its force; but that when the edges of such a slit were soldered together with any other metal, even with bismuth, which itself has a very feeble force, the disc recovered nearly all its force.

The motion of rotation of the needle, is an effect which would result from a force impressed upon it parallel to the plane of the disc and at right angles to its radii. It was also ascertained, however, that the disc exercises on the needle forces parallel to its own plane in the direction of its radii, and also perpendicular to its plane.

A magnetic needle, mounted in the manner of a dipping needle, so as to play on a horizontal axis in a vertical plane, was placed over the revolving disc, so that the plane of its play passed through the centre of the disc.   The pole of the needle which was presented downwards was attracted to or repelled from the centre of the disc according to its distance from that point.   Placed immediately over the centre, no effect, either of attraction or repulsion, was manifested.   As it was moved from the centre along a radius, attraction to the centre was manifested.   This attraction was diminished rapidly as the distance from the centre was increased, and, at a certain point, it became nothing, the pole of the needle resting in its natural position.   Beyond this distance repulsion was manifested, which was continued even beyond the limits of the disc.   These phenomena indicate the action of a force directed parallel to the plane of the disc and in the direction of its radii.

A magnetic needle was suspended vertically by one of its extremities, and, being attached to the arm of a very sensitive balance, was accurately counterpoised.   It was then placed successively over different parts of the disc, and was found to be everywhere *repulsed*, whichever pole was presented downwards. These phenomena indicate the action of a repulsive force directed at right angles to the plane of the disc.

All these phenomena have been explained with great clearness and felicity by Dr. Faraday, by the momentary inductive currents produced upon the disc by the action of the poles of the magnet, and the reaction of those currents on the movable poles themselves.   By the principles which have been explained (285.), it will be apparent that upon the parts of the disc which are approaching either pole of the magnet, momentary currents will be produced in directions contrary to those which would prevail upon an electro-magnetic helix substituted for the magnet, and having a similar polarity; while upon the parts receding from the pole, momentary currents will be produced, having the same direction.

These currents will attract or repel the poles of the magnet according to the principles explained and illustrated in (285.); and thus all the motions, and all the attractions and repulsions described above, will be easily understood.

CHAP. VII.

INFLUENCE OF TERRESTRIAL MAGNETISM ON VOLTAIC CURRENTS.

305. **Direction of the earth's magnetic attraction.** — The laws which regulate the reciprocal action of magnets and currents in general being understood, the investigation of the effects produced by the earth's magnetism on voltaic currents becomes easy, being nothing more than the application of these laws to a particular case. It has been shown that the magnetism of the earth is such, that in the northern hemisphere the austral pole of a magnet freely suspended is attracted in the direction of a line drawn in the plane of the magnetic meridian, and inclined below the horizon at an angle which increases gradually in going from the magnetic equator, where it is nothing, to the magnetic pole, where it is 90°. In this part of Europe the direction of the lower pole of the dipping needle, and therefore of the magnetic attraction of the earth, is that of a line drawn in the magnetic meridian at an angle of about 70° below the horizon, and therefore at an angle of about 20° with a vertical line presented downwards.

306. **In this part of the earth it corresponds to that of the boreal or southern pole of an artificial magnet.** — Since the magnetism of the earth attracts the austral pole of the needle, to determine, therefore, its effects upon currents, it will be sufficient to consider it as a southern magnetic pole, placed below the horizon in the direction of the dipping needle, at a distance so great that the directions in which it acts on all parts of the same current are practically parallel.

307. **To ascertain the direction of the force impressed by terrestrial magnetism on a current,** let a line be imagined to be drawn from any point in the current parallel to the dipping needle, and let a plane be imagined to pass through this line and the current. According to what has been explained of the reciprocal action of magnets and currents, it will follow that the direction of the force impressed on the current, will be that of a line drawn through the same point of the current perpendicular to this plane.

Let cc', *fig.* 220., be the line of direction of the current, and draw or parallel to the direction of the dip. Let L O R be a line drawn through O, at right angles to the plane passing through O P and cc'. This line will be the direction of the force impressed by the magnetism of the earth on the current cc'. If the current pass from c to c', this force will be directed from O towards L, since the effect produced is that of a southern magnetic pole placed in the line O P. If the current pass from c' to c, the direc-

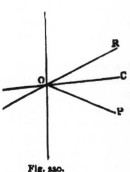

Fig. 220.

tion of the force impressed on it will be from o towards R (227.).

It follows, therefore, that the force which acts upon the current is always in a plane perpendicular to the dipping needle. This plane intersects the horizontal plane in a line directed to the magnetic east and west, and therefore perpendicular to the magnetic meridian; and it intersects the plane of the magnetic meridian in a line directed north and south, making, in this part of the earth, an angle with the horizon of 20° elevation towards the north, and depression towards the south.

If the current be vertical, the plane passing through ction and that of the dipping needle will be the magnetic n. The force impressed upon the current will therefore right angles to the plane of the magnetic meridian, and d *eastward* when the current *descends*, and *westward* when it .

If the current be horizontal, and in the plane of the io meridian, and therefore directed in the line of the magorth and south, the force impressed on it will be directed to gnetic east and west, and will therefore be also horizontal. be directed to the *east,* if the current pass from *north* to and to the *west,* if it pass from *south* to *north.* This will be nt, if it be considered that the effect of the earth's magis that of a *south* magnetic pole placed *below the current.*

If the current be horizontal and at right angles to gnetic meridian, the force impressed on it will be directed and south in the plane of the magnetic meridian, and l to the horizontal plane at an angle of 20° in this part of rth. This may be resolved into two forces, one vertical e other horizontal. The former will have a tendency to the current from the horizontal plane, and the latter will he horizontal plane in the direction of the magnetic north th. It will be directed from the *south* to the *north,* if the t pass from *west* to *east,* and from the *north* to the *south,* if rent pass from *east* to *west.* This will also be apparent, by ring the effect produced upon a horizontal current by a nagnetic pole placed below it.

If a horizontal current have any direction inter- to between the magnetic meridian and a plane at right to it, the force impressed on it, being still at right angles dipping needle, and being inclined to the horizontal plane angle less than 20°, may be resolved into other forces, one of which will be at right angles to the current, and will be directed to the left of the current, as viewed from below by an observer whose head is in the direction from which the current passes (227.).

312. **Effect of the earth's magnetism on a vertical current which turns round a vertical axis.** — It follows, from what has been here proved, that if a *descending* vertical rectilinear current be so suspended as to be capable of turning freely round a vertical axis, the earth's magnetism will impress upon it a force directed from west to east in a plane at right angles to the magnetic meridian ; and it will therefore move to such a position, that the plane passing through the current and the axis round which it moves shall be at right angles to the magnetic meridian, the current being to the *east* of the axis.

If the current *ascend*, it will for like reasons take the position in the same plane to the *west* of the axis, being then urged by a force directed from *east* to *west*.

313. **Effect on a current which is capable of moving in a horizontal plane.** — If a vertical current be supported in such a manner that, retaining its vertical direction, it shall be capable of moving freely in a horizontal plane in any direction whatever, as is the case when it floats on the surface of a liquid, the earth's magnetism will impart to it a continuous rectilinear motion in a direction at right angles to the plane of the magnetic meridian, and directed *eastward* if the current *descend*, and *westward* if it *ascend*.

If a horizontal rectilinear current be supported, so as to be capable of revolving in the horizontal plane round one of its extremities as a centre, the earth's magnetism will impart to it a motion of continued rotation, since it impresses on it a force always at right angles to the current, and directed to the same side of it. If in this case the current flow *towards* the centre round which it revolves, the rotation imparted to it will be *direct;* if *from* the centre, retrograde, as viewed from above (229.).

314. **Experimental illustrations of these effects. — Pouillet's apparatus.** — A great variety of experimental expedients have been contrived to verify these consequences of the principle of the influence of terrestrial magnetism on currents.

To exhibit the effects of the earth's magnetism on vertical currents, M. Pouillet contrived an apparatus consisting of two circular canals, represented in their vertical section in *fig.* 221., one placed above the other, the lower canal having a greater diameter than the upper. In the opening in the centre of these canals a metallic rod *t* is fixed in a vertical position, supporting a mercurial cup *c*. A rod *h h'*, composed of a nonconducting substance, is supported in the cup *c* by a point at its centre. The vertical wires *v v'* are attached to the ends of the rod *h h'*, and terminate in points,

h are turned downwards, so as to dip into the liquid contained in the
r canal, while their lower extremities dip into the liquid contained in

Fig. 221.

the lower canal. A bent wire connects the mercury
contained in the cup *c* with the liquid in the upper
canal.

The liquid in the upper and lower canals is acidulated water or mercury. If the liquid in the lower
canal be put in communication with the positive, and
the rod *t* with the negative pole, the current will pass
from that canal up the two vertical wires *v v'*, thence
to the liquid in the upper canal, thence by the connecting wire to the mercury in the cup *c*, and thence
by the rod *t* to the negative pole.

By this arrangement the two vertical currents *v v'*,
which both ascend, are movable round the rod *t* as
an axis.

hen this apparatus is left to the influence of the earth's magnetism, the
nts *v v'* will be affected by equal and parallel forces directed westward
ght angles to the magnetic meridian (308.). The equal and parallel
s, being at equal distances from the axis *t*, will be in equilibrium in all
ions, and the wires will therefore be astatic; that is to say, not affected
te earth's magnetism.

the point of the wire *v'* at *h'* be raised from the upper canal, the current
will be suspended. In that case, the wire *v* being impelled by the
strial magnetism westward at right angles to the magnetic meridian
ystem will take a position at right angles to that meridian, the wire on
h the current passes being to the west of the axis *t*. If the point at *h'*
rned down so as to dip into the liquid, and the point at *h* be turned up
to suspend the current on *h* and establish that on *h'*, the system will
half a revolution and will place the wire *h'* on which the current runs
s west of *t*.

by the *reotrope* the connections with the poles of the battery be re-
d, the currents on *v v'* will descend instead of ascending. In that case
ystem will be astatic as before, so long as both currents are established
e wires *v v'*. But if the connection of either with the superior canal be
ved, the wire on which the remaining current passes being impelled
ards, the system will take a position in the plane of the magnetic
lian, the wire on which the current runs being east of the axis *t*.

ien the currents on the wires *v v'* are both passing, the system will be
c only so long as the currents are equally intense, and both in the same
with the axis *t*. If while the latter condition is fulfilled one of the
be even in a small degree thicker than the other, it will carry a
ger current, and in that case it will turn to the magnetic east or west,
ling as the currents descend or ascend, just as though the current on
her wire were suppressed; for in this case the effective force is that
the difference of the intensities of the currents acting on that which
stronger.

he two wires be not in the same plane with the axis, the forces which
on them being equal, and parallel to the plane of the magnetic meri-
the position of equilibrium will be that in which the plane passing
gh them will be parallel to the latter plane.

position of equilibrium will be subject to an infinite variety of changes,
ing as the plane of the wires *v v'*, their relative thickness, and their

distances from the axis of rotation are varied, and in this way a great num
ber of interesting experiments on the effects of the earth's magnetism m
be exhibited.

315. **Its application to show the effect of terrestrial mag
netism on a horizontal current.**—To show experimentally th
effect of the earth's magnetism on a horizontal current, M. Pouill
contrived an arrangement on a similar principle, consisting of

Fig. 222.

circular canal, the vertical section
which is represented in *fig.* 222.
horizontal wire *a b* is supported by
point at its centre which rests in
mercurial cup fixed upon a metal
rod, like *t, fig.* 221. Two points *a* and
project from the wire, and dip into the liquid in the canal, 1
small weights *e* and *d* being so adjusted as to keep the wire *
exactly balanced.

If the central rod be connected with the positive, and the liqui
in the canal with the negative pole, the current will ascend on th
central rod, and will pass along the horizontal wire in both direc·
tions from its centre to the points *a* and *b*, by which it will pass to
the liquid in the canal, and thence to the negative pole. If by the
reotrope the connections be reversed and the names of the pole:
changed, the current will pass from *a* and *b* to the centre, and
thence by the central rod to the negative pole.

In the former case, the wire *a b* will revolve with *retrograde*
and in the latter with *direct* rotation, in accordance with what ha
been already explained (227.).

316. **Its effect on vertical currents shown by Ampère'
apparatus.**—If a rectangular current, such as that represente
in *fig.* 168., be suspended in Ampère's frame, *fig.* 137., it will, whe
left to the influence of terrestrial magnetism, take a position a
right angles to the magnetic meridian, the side on which the cu
rent descends being to the east. For in this case the horizont
currents which pass on the upper and lower sides of the rectangl·
being contrary in direction, will have a tendency to revolve, on
with direct, and the other with retrograde motion round *y s*
These forces, therefore, neutralise each other. The vertical de
scending current will be attracted to the east, and the ascendin
current to the west (312.).

317. **Its effect on a circular current shown by Ampère'
apparatus.** — If a circular current, such as that represented i
fig. 167., be suspended in Ampère's frame, *fig.* 137., and sub
mitted to the influence of terrestrial magnetism, each part of it
may be regarded as being compounded of a vertical and horizontal
component. The horizontal components in the upper semicircle,

flowing in a direction contrary to those in the lower semicircle, their effects will neutralise each other. The vertical components will descend on one side and ascend on the other. That side on which they *descend* will be attracted to the *east*, and that at which they *ascend* to the *west*; and, consequently, the current will place itself in a plane at right angles to the magnetic meridian, its front being presented to the south.

318. **Its effect on a circular or spiral current shown by Delarive's floating apparatus.** — If a circular or spiral current be placed on a floating apparatus, it will assume a like position at right angles to the magnetic meridian, with its point to the south; and the same will be true of any circulating current.

319. **Astatic currents formed by Ampère's apparatus.** — To construct a system of currents adapted to Ampère's frame, which shall be astatic, it is only necessary so to arrange them that there shall be equal and similar horizontal currents running in contrary directions, and equal and similar vertical currents in the

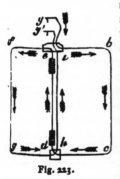

Fig. 223.

same direction, and that the latter shall be at equal distances from the axis on which the system turns; for in that case the horizontal elements, having equal tendencies to make the system revolve in contrary directions, will equilibrate, and the vertical elements being affected by equal and parallel forces at equal distances from the axis of rotation, will also equilibrate.

By considering these principles, it will be evident that the system of currents represented in *fig.* 223., adapted to Ampère's frame, *fig.* 137., is astatic.

320. **Effect of earth's magnetism on spiral currents shown by Ampère's apparatus.** — If the arrangement of spiral currents represented in *fig.* 189. be so disposed that the current after passing through one only of the two spirals shall return to the negative pole, the earth's magnetism will affect it so as to bring it into such a position that its plane will be at right angles to the magnetic meridian. If the descending currents be on the side of the spiral more remote from the axis of motion, the system will arrange itself so that the spiral on which the current flows shall be to the *east* of the axis. If the descending currents be on the side nearer to the axis, the spiral on which the current flows will throw itself to the *west* of the axis. In each case, the front of the current is presented to the magnetic south, and the descending currents are on the east side of the spiral.

If the current pass through both spirals in *fig.* 189., and their fronts be on the same side, the earth's magnetism will throw them into the plane at right angles to the magnetic meridian, their fronts being presented to the south.

If their fronts be on different sides, the system will be astatic, and will rest in any position independent of the earth's magnetism, which in this case will produce equal and contrary effects on the two spirals.

If the system of spiral currents represented in *fig.* 189. be suspended in Ampère's frame, subject to the earth's magnetism, the fronts of the currents being on the same side of the two spirals, it will take such a position that the centres of the two spirals will be in the magnetic meridian, their planes at right angles to it, and the fronts of the currents presented to the south. If in this case the fronts of the currents be on opposite sides, the system will be astatic.

321. **Effect on a horizontal current shown by Pouillet's apparatus.**—The rotation of the horizontal current produced with the apparatus, *fig.* 222., may be accelerated, retarded, arrested, or inverted by presenting the pole of an artificial magnet above or below it, at a greater or less distance. A south magnetic pole placed below it, or a north magnetic pole above, producing forces identical in direction with those produced by terrestrial magnetism, will accelerate the rotation in a greater or less degree, according to the power of the artificial magnet, and the greater or less proximity of its pole to the centre of rotation of the current.

A north magnetic pole presented below, or a south pole above the centre of rotation, producing forces contrary in their direction to those resulting from the earth's magnetism, will retard, arrest, or reverse the rotation according as the forces exerted by the magnet are less than, equal to, or greater than those impressed by terrestrial magnetism.

If the system of currents represented in *fig.* 224., be suspended on Pouillet's apparatus, represented in *fig.* 221., it will receive a motion of continued rotation from the influence of the earth's magnetism. In this case the vertical currents being in the same direction will be in equilibrium (314.) ; and the horizontal currents passing either from the centre of the upper horizontal wire to the extremities, or *vice versâ*, according to the mode of connection, will receive a motion of rotation direct or retrograde (315.).

Fig. 224.

This motion of rotation may be affected in the manner above described, by the pole of a magnet applied in the centre of the lower circular canal, *fig.* 221.

2. **Effect of terrestrial magnetism on a helical** **as shown by Ampère's apparatus.** — A helical cur- such as that represented in *fig.* 192., being mounted on re's frame, or arranged upon a floating apparatus, *fig.* 193., e acted on by the earth's magnetism. The several convo- s will, like a single circulating current, take a position at angles to the magnetic meridian, their fronts being pre- l to the south. The axis of the helix will consequently be ed to the magnetic north and south ; and it will, in fine, it all the directive properties of a magnetic needle, the end ich the front of the currents is directed being its south pole. such a current were mounted on a horizontal axis at right s to the plane of the magnetic meridian, it would, under the nce of the earth's magnetism, take the direction of the ng needle, the front of the currents corresponding in direc- o the south pole of the needle.

3. **The dip of a current illustrated by Ampère's rect-** s. — The phenomenon of the dip may also be experimentally rated by Ampère's electro-magnetic rectangle, *fig.* 225.,

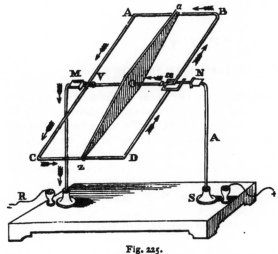

Fig. 225.

h consists of a horizontal axis *x* v, which is a tube of wood or ' non-conductor, at right angles to which is fixed a lozenge- d bar *a z*, composed also of a non-conductor. Upon this is fixed the rectangle A B D C, composed of wire. The rect- rests by steel pivots at M and N on metallic plates, which ıunicate by wires with the mercurial cups at s and R. These ' being placed in connection with the poles of a voltaic battery, the current will pass from the positive cup s up the pillar and round the rectangle, as indicated by the arrows. At *x* it passes along a wire through the tube *x*v to v, and thence by the steel point, the plate m, and the pillar, to the negative cup r.

The axis mn being placed at right angles to the magnetic meridian, and the connections established, the rectangle will be immediately affected by the earth's magnetism, and after some oscillations, will settle into a position at right angles to the direction of the dipping needle.

In this case the forces impressed by the earth's magnetism on the parts of the current forming the sides AC and BD, will pass through the axis mn, and will therefore be resisted. The forces impressed on AB and CD will be equal, and will act at the middle points *a* and *z*, at right angles to AB and CD, and in a plane at right angles to the direction of the dip. These forces will therefore be in directions exactly opposed to each other when the line *az* takes the direction of the dip, and will therefore be in equilibrium.

CHAP. VIII.

RECIPROCAL INFLUENCE OF VOLTAIC CURRENTS.

324. **Results of Ampère's researches.**— The mutual attraction and repulsion manifested between conductors charged with the electric fluids in repose, would naturally suggest the inquiry whether any analogous reciprocal actions would be manifested by the same fluids in motion. The experimental analysis of this question led Ampère to the discovery of a body of phenomena which he had the felicity of reducing to general laws. The mathematical theory raised upon these laws has supplied the means by which phenomena, hitherto scattered and unconnected, and ascribed to a diversity of agents, are traced to a common source.

Although the limits, within which a treatise so elementary as this manual is necessarily confined, exclude any detailed exposition of these beautiful physico-mathematical researches, they cannot be altogether passed over in silence. We shall therefore give as brief an exposition of them as is compatible with their great importance, and that clearness without which all exposition would be useless.

325. **Reciprocal action of rectilinear currents.** — If two

currents be parallel, they will attract or repel each
:ding as they flow in the same or opposite directions.

rified experimentally by the apparatus represented in *fig.* 226.,
the principle of Ampère's frame. The mercurial cup marked +

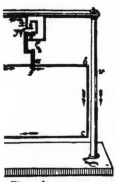

Fig. 226.

receives the current from the positive
pole. The current passes as indicated
by the arrows upwards on the pillar *t*,
and thence to the cup *x*, from which
it flows round the rectangle, returning
to the cup *y*, and thence to the pillar
v, by which it descends to the cup
which is connected with the negative
pole.

If the rectangle thus arranged be
placed with its plane at an angle with
the plane of the pillars *t* and *v*, upon
which the ascending and descending
currents pass, it will turn upon its axis
until its plane coincides with the plane
of the pillars *t* and *v*, the side of the
rectangle *d e* on which the current

ʒ next the pillar *t*, on which it ascends. If by means of the
) the connection be reversed, so that the current shall descend on
shall ascend on *v* and *b c*, it will still maintain its position. But
:ions at *x* and *y* be reversed, the connections of the cups + and —
changed, the current will descend on *e d* while it ascends on *t*, and
ı *b c* while it descends on *v*. In this case *t* will repel *d e* and
ıd *v* will repel *b c* and attract *d e*, and accordingly the rectangle
ıalf revolution, and *b c* will place itself near *t*, and *d e* near *v*.

tion of a spiral or helical current on a rectili-
ınt. — A sinuous, spiral, or helical current, provided
:ions are not considerable in magnitude, impresses on
rent in its neighbourhood the same force as a straight
ıld produce, whose direction would coincide with the
sinuous or spiral current. This is proved experi-
ʼ the fact that a spiral current which has a returning
rrent passing along . its axis, will exercise no force
:raction or repulsion on a straight current parallel to
nce on suspending the spiral current the straight
attract or repel a parallel straight current, it follows
ıiral current exactly neutralises the effect of the
rrent flowing in the opposite direction, and conse-
vill be equivalent to a straight current flowing in the
on.

tual action of diverging or converging rectilinear
- Rectilinear currents which diverge from or converge
ın point mutually attract. Those, one of which di-
the other converges, mutually repel; that is to say,

two rectilinear currents c c' and cc'. fig. 227, which intersec
o, both flow towards or from o, they will mutually attract; bu
one flow towards, and the other from o, they will mutual

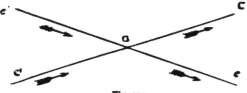

Fig. 227.

repel. The currents, being supposed to flow in the directiocs o
the arrows, oc and oc will mutually attract, as will also oc' and
oc': while oc' and oc will repel, as will also oc and oc'.

If the wires conducting the currents were movable on o as a
pivot, they would accordingly close, the angle coc diminishing
until they would coincide.

328. **Experimental Illustration of this.** — This may be experimentally illustrated by the apparatus
represented in fig. 228. in plan, and in
fig. 229. in section, consisting of a circular canal filled with mercury or acidulated water separated into two parts by
partitions at a and b. Two wires cd and
ef, suspended on a central pivot, move
freely one over and independent of the
other, like the hands of a watch, the
points being at right angles, so as to dip
into the canal. The mercurial cup x being
supposed to be connected with the positive, and y with the negative pole, the
current passing to the liquid will flow along the wires as indicated
by the arrows from the liquid in one section to that of the other

Fig. 228.

and will pass to the negative cup y. Whe
the wires cd and ef thus carrying t
current are left to their mutual influenc
the angle they form will close, and t
directions of the wires will coincide,

Fig. 229.

that the currents shall flow in the same direction upon them.

In these and all similar experiments, the phenomena will ne
sarily be modified by the effects produced by the earth's r
netism. In some cases the apparatus can be rendered ast
and in others, the effect due to the terrestrial magnetism l
known, can be allowed for, so that the phenomena under
mination may be eliminated.

329. Mutual action of rectilinear currents which are not the same plane. — If two rectilinear currents be not in the ne plane, their directions cannot intersect although they are t parallel. In this case a line may always be drawn, which is the same time perpendicular to both. To assist the imagination conceiving such a geometrical combination, let a vertical rod supposed to be erected, and from two different points of this d let lines be drawn horizontally, but in different directions, e, for example, pointing to the north, and the other to the east. voltaic currents pass along two such lines, they will mutually tract, when they flow *both to* or *both from* the vertical rod; they ll mutually repel, when one flows *to* the vertical rod and the her *from* it.

In either case the mutual action of such currents will have a ndency to turn them into the same plane and to parallelism. they mutually attract, their lines of direction turning round e vertical line will take a position parallel to each other, and at e same side of that line. If they mutually repel, they will turn ι the vertical line in contrary directions, and will take a position urallel to each other, but at opposite sides to it.

In *fig.* 230., AB and CD represent two currents which are not in

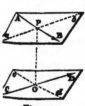

the same plane. Let PO be the line which intersects them both at right angles, and let planes be supposed to pass through their directions respectively, which are parallel to each other, and at right angles to PO. If, in this case, CD be fixed and AB movable, the latter will be turned into the direction *a b* parallel to CD; or if CD were free and AB fixed, CD would take the position *c d*; if both were free ley would take some position parallel to each other; and if free change their planes, they would mutually approach and coalesce. follows from this, that if the direction of either of the two currents be reversed, the directions of the forces they exert on each her will be also reversed; but if the directions of both currents reversed, the forces they exert on each other will be unered.

330. Mutual action of different parts of the same current. —Different parts of the same current exercise on each other 'epulsive force. This will follow immediately as a consequence the general principle which has been just established. Since a pulsive action takes place between o c and o *c'*, *fig.* 227., and ch action is independent of the magnitude of the angle c o *c'*, it ll still take place, however great that angle may be, and will erefore obtain when the angle c o *c'* becomes equal to 180°;

o

that is, when o c′ forms the continuation of c o, or coalesces with o c′. Hence, between o c and o c′ there exists a mutually repulsive action.

331. Ampère's experimental verification of this. — Independently of this demonstration, M. Ampère has reduced the repulsive action of different parts of the same rectilinear current to the following experimental proof :—

Let A B C D, *fig.* 231., be a glass or porcelain dish, separated into two divisions by a partition A C, also of glass ; and let it be filled with mercury

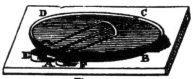

Fig. 231.

on both sides of A C. Let a wire, wrapped with silk, be formed into two parallel pieces united, by a semicircle whose plane is at right angles to that of the straight parallel parts, and let these two parallel straight parts be placed floating on the surface of the mercury at each side of the partition A C, over which the semicircle passes. The mercury in the divisions of the dish is in metallic communication with the mercurial cups E and F placed in the direction of the straight arms of the floating conductor. When the cups E and F are put in connection with the poles of a voltaic battery, a current will pass from the positive cup to the end of the floating conductor, from that along the arm of the conductor, then across the partition by the semicircle, then along the other floating arm, and from thence through the mercury to the negative cup. There is thus on each side of the partition a rectilinear current, one part of which passes upon the mercury, and the other part upon the straight arm of the floating conductor. When the current is thus established, the floating conductor will be repelled to the remote side of the dish. This repulsion is effected by that part of the straight current which passes upon the mercury acting on that part which passes along the wire.

332. Action of an indefinite rectilinear current on a finite rectilinear current at right angles to it. — A finite rectilinear current *ab*, *fig.* 232., which is perpendicular to an indefinite rectilinear current *c d* lying all at the same side of it, will be acted on by a force tending to move it parallel to itself, either in the direction of the indefinite current, or in the contrary direction, according to the relative directions of the two currents.

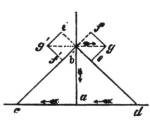

Fig. 232.

If the finite current do not meet the indefinite current, let its line of direction be produced till it meets it at *a*. Take any two points *c* and *d* on the indefinite current at equal distances from *a*, and draw the lines *c b* and *d b* to any point on the finite current.

First case. Let the finite current be directed *towards* the indefinite current. Hence the point *b* will be attracted by *d* and re-

e (327.); and since *d b* = *c b*, the attraction will be equal
pulsion.   Let the equal lines *b e* and *b f* represent this
and repulsion.   By completing the rectangle, the dia-
will represent the resultant of these forces; and this line
illel to *c d*, and the resultant is contrary in direction to
nite current.

ne may be proved of the action of all points on the in-
urrent on the point *b*, and the sum of all these resultants
e total action of the indefinite current on *b*.

ne may be proved respecting the action of the definite
n all the points of the indefinite current.

the current *a b* will be urged by a system of forces acting
its parallel to *c d*, and in a contrary direction.

case.   Let the finite current be directed *from* the inde-
'rent.   The point *b* will then be attracted by *c* and re-
d, and the resultant *b g'* will be contrary to its former

the current *a b* will be urged by a system of forces pa-
d, and in the same direction as the indefinite current.

he action of the two currents is reciprocal, the indefinite
rill be urged by a force in its line of direction, either
 or contrary to its direction, as the finite current runs
nwards it.

ase in which the indefinite current is circular.—
.efinite current *c d* be supposed to be bent into a circular
s to surround a cylinder, on the side of which is placed
cal current *a b*, it is evident that the same reciprocal
ll take place; but in that case the motion imparted will
'rotation round the axis of the cylinder as a centre.

xperimental verification of these principles.—
'inciples are experimentally verified by the apparatus,

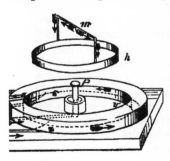

fig. 233., where *a z s b* represents a ribbon of copper
coated with silk and carried
round the copper circular
canal *v*.   A conductor connects the mercurial cup *c*
with the central metallic
pillar which supports a mercurial cup *p*.   In this cup
the metallic point *m* is
placed.   The mercurial cup
d is in metallic communica-

Fig. 233.

the acidulated water in the circular canal *v*.   A hoop of
ı supported by the point *m* by means of the rectangular

wire, and is so adjusted that its lower edge dips into the liquid in the canal *v*.

Let the mercury in *a* be connected with the positive pole of the battery, and the mercury in *d* with the negative pole. The current entering at *a* will pass round the circular canal upon the coated ribbon of copper, and, arriving at *b*, it will pass to *c* by a metallic ribbon or wire connecting these cups. From *c* it will pass to the central pillar and thence to the cup *p*. It will then pass from *m* as a centre in both directions on the wire, and will descend to the hoop *h*, from which it will pass into the liquid in the canal *v*, and thence to the cup *d*, with which the liquid is in metallic communication, and, in fine, from *d* it will pass to the negative pole of the battery.

By this arrangement, therefore, a circular current flows round the exterior surface of the vase *v*, while two descending currents constantly flow upon the wire at right angles to this circular current. The circular current being fixed, and the vertical currents being movable, the latter will receive a motion of continued rotation by the action of the former; and in the case here supposed, this rotation will be in a direction contrary to the direction of the circular current. If the connections be reversed by the reotrope, the direction of the circular current will be reversed, but at the same time that of the vertical currents on the wire will be also reversed; and, consequently, no change will take place in the direction of the rotation. These changes of direction of the two currents neutralise each other. But if, while *d* is still connected with the negative pole, *b* be connected with the positive pole, the connection between *b* and *c* being removed, and a connection between *a* and *c* being established, then the direction of the circular current being from *s* to *z* will be reversed; while that of the vertical currents remains still the same, the direction of the rotation will be reversed.

335. **To determine in general the action of an indefinite rectilinear current on a finite rectilinear current.** — *First.*

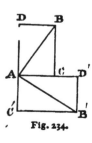

Fig. 234.

Let it be supposed that the finite current A B, *fig.* 234., has a length so limited that all its points may be considered as equally distant from the indefinite current, and therefore equally acted on by it. In this case the current A B may be replaced by two currents, A D perpendicular and A C parallel to the indefinite current, and the action of the indefinite current on A B will be equivalent to its combined actions on A D and A C.

If A be supposed to be the positive end of the finite current, it

o be the positive end of the component currents A D and
upposing the indefinite current parallel to A C to run in the
irection as A C, then A D will be urged in the direction A C
and A C in the direction A C′ by forces proportional to A D
:. Hence, if A D′ = A D, and A C′ = A C, A D′ and A C′ will
ı in magnitude and direction the two forces which act on
nponent currents. The resultant of these two forces A D′
′ will be the diagonal A B′, which is evidently perpendicular
nd equal to it.

idly. Let the finite current have any proposed length, and
ı positive end A, *fig.* 235., let a line A o be drawn perpendicular to the indefinite
current x′x, this current
being supposed to run
from x′ to x.

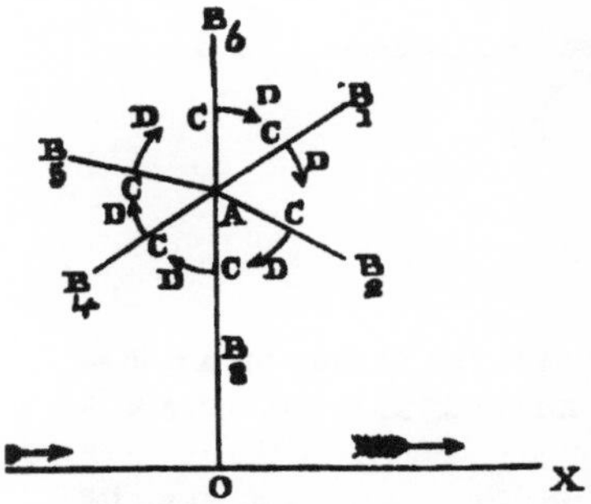

If the distance o A be
greater than A B, that current A B, whatever be its
position, will lie on the
same side of x′x, and the
action of x′x on every
small element of A B will
be perpendicular to A B,
as has been just demon-

Fig. 235.

, The current A B will therefore be acted on by a system
llel forces perpendicular to its direction. The resultant
e forces will be a single force equal to their sum, and
. to their common direction. Hence the indefinite current
ll act on the finite current A B by a single force R in the
m C D.

e current A B be supposed to assume successively different
ıs, B₁, B₂, B₃, &c., around its positive end A, the line C D
›resent in each position the direction of the action of the
; x′x upon it.

evident that when the indefinite current runs from x′ to x,
ion on the finite current is such as would cause it to turn
ts positive end A with a direct, or round its negative end
a retrograde rotation.

e indefinite current run from x to x′, the direction of its
›n A B, and the consequent motions of A B, would be re-

point c of the current A B at which the resultant R acts
'y with the position of the current A B, approaching more
; x′x as A B approaches the position A B₃; but in every
ı this resultant must be between A and B. The force

O 3

producing the rotation therefore having a varying moment, the rotation will not be uniform.

If the distance O A be very great compared with A B, the resultant R will be sensibly constant, and will act at the middle point of A B.

In this case, if the middle point of A B be fixed, no rotation can take place.

If the distance O A be less than A B, the current A B will in certain positions intersect x′x, *fig.* 236., and a part will be at one

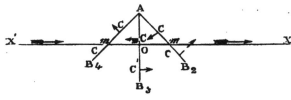

Fig. 236.

side and a part at the other. In this case the action on A B, in all positions in which it lies altogether above x′x, is the same as in the former case.

When it crosses x′x, as in the positions A B₂, A B₃, A B₄, the action is different. In that case the forces which act on A m, and those which act on m B, are in contrary directions, and their resultant is in the one direction or in the other, according as the sum of the forces acting on one part is greater or less than the sum of the forces acting on the other part. If A m be in every position of A B greater than m B, then the resultant will be in every position in the same direction as if the current A B did not cross x′x; and if the point A were fixed, a motion of continued rotation would take place, in the same manner as in the former case, except that the impelling force would be diminished as the line A B would approach the position A B₃.

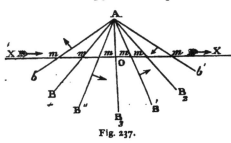

Fig. 237.

But if A O be less than half A B, the circumstances will be different. In that case there will be two positions A B₂ and A B₄, *fig.* 237., at equal distances from A B₃, at which the line A B will be bisected by x′x.

In all positions of A B *not included between* A B₂ and A B₄, the action of the indefinite

:nt upon it takes place in the same direction as in the former
.

it in the positions A B′ and A B″, where m B′ and m B″ are
:er than m A, the forces acting on m B′ and m B″ exceed those
g in the contrary direction on m A, and consequently the rent of the forces on A B in all positions between A B$_2$ and A B$_4$,
ntrary to its direction in every other position of the line A B.

the positions A B$_2$ and A B$_4$ the resultant of the forces in one
:tion on A m is equal and contrary to the resultant of the
:s on B m. There will in these positions be no tendency of

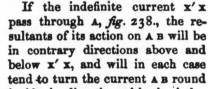

Fig. 238

the current A B to move except
round its middle point.

If the indefinite current x′ x
pass through A, *fig.* 238., the resultants of its action on A B will be
in contrary directions above and
below x′ x, and will in each case
tend to turn the current A B round

)oint A so as to make it coincide in direction with the inde-
: current x′ x.

6. **Experimental illustration of these principles.** —
e effects may be illustrated experimentally by means of the
:ratus, *fig.* 233., already described. The circular current sur-
ding the canal v being removed, and the currents on the wire
ing continued, let an indefinite rectilinear current be con-
:d under the apparatus at different distances from the vertical
)assing through the pivot, and the effects above described will
:hibited.

7. **Effect of a straight indefinite current on a system
verging or converging currents.**—If any number of finite
inear currents diverge from or converge to a common centre,
rstem will be affected by an indefinite current near it, in the
manner as a single radiating current would be affected.
us if a number of straight and equal wires have a common
mity, and are traversed by currents flowing between that
mity and the circumference of the circle in which their
extremities lie, an indefinite current x′ x placed in the plane
e circle, as represented in *fig.* 239., will cause the radiating
n of currents to revolve in the one direction or the other, as
ted by the arrows in the figures.

3. **Experimental illustration of this action.** — These
is may be shown experimentally, by putting a vertical wire,
40., in communication with the centre of a shallow circular
lic vessel of mercury v, and another wire N, communicating

with the outside of the vessel, into communication with the poles of a battery : diverging currents will be transmitted through the

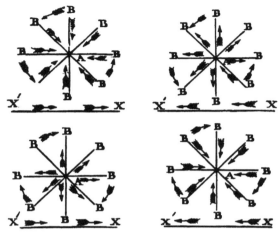

Fig. 239.

mercury in the one direction or the other, according to the con-

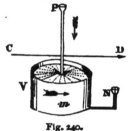

Fig. 240.

nection ; and if a straight conducting wire c D, conveying a powerful electric current, is brought near the vessel, a rotation will be imparted to the mercury, the direction of which will be in conformity with the principles just explained. Davy used a powerful magnet instead of the straight wire.

339. **Consequences deducible from this action.**—The following consequences respecting the action of finite and indefinite rectilinear currents will readily follow from the principles which have been established.

When a finite vertical conductor A B, movable round an axis o o′, is subjected to the action of an indefinite horizontal current M N, the plane A B o′ o will place itself in the position o o′ B′ A′, when the vertical current descends, and the horizontal current runs from N to M, *fig.* 241.

If the direction of the vertical or horizontal current be reversed, the position of equilibrium of the former will be o o′ B A ; but if the direction of *both* be reversed, the position of equilibrium will remain unaltered.

When two vertical conductors A B and A′ B′ are movable round a vertical axis o o′, and connected together, they will remain in equilibrium, whatever be their position, if they are both traversed by currents of the same intensity in the same direction, provided that the indefinite rectilinear current which acts upon them be at such a distance and in such a position that its distances from the

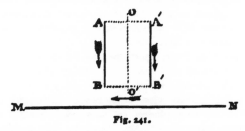

Fig. 241.

points B and B′ may be considered always equal. When the wires A B and A′ B′ are traversed by currents in opposite directions, one ascending and the other descending, the system will then turn on the axis o o′ until the vertical plane through A B and A′ B′ becomes parallel to M N, the descending current being on that side from which the indefinite current flows.

340. **Action of an indefinite straight current on a circulating current.** — The circulating current A, *fig.* 242., is

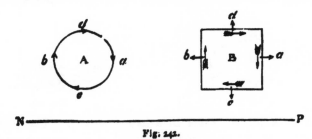

Fig. 242.

affected by the indefinite current P N in the same manner as the rectangular current B would be affected. The current P N affects the *descending* side *a* by a force *contrary* to, and the ascending side *b* by an equal force *according* with, its own direction (332.). In the same manner it affects the sides *c* and *d* with forces in contrary directions, one *towards*, and the other *from* P N. But the side *c*, being nearer to P N than *d*, is more strongly affected; and consequently the attraction, in the case represented in *fig.* 242., will prevail over the repulsion. If the direction of either the rectilinear or circulating current be reversed, the repulsion will prevail over the attraction.

Thus it appears, that an indefinite current flowing from *right* to *left*, under a circulating current having *direct* rotation, or one moving from left to right under a circulating current having retrograde rotation, will produce attraction : and two currents moving in the contrary directions will produce repulsion.

If the current A be fixed upon a horizontal axis $a\,b$ on which it is capable of revolving, that side c at which the current moves in the same direction as P S will be attracted downwards, and the plane of the current will take a position passing through P S, the side c being nearest to that line.

If the current A be fixed upon the line $c\,d$ as an axis, it will turn into the same position, the side b on which the current ascends being on the side towards which the current P S is directed.

341. **Case in which the indefinite straight current is perpendicular to the plane of the circulating current.—** If the rectilinear current A B, *fig.* 243, be perpendicular to the circular current Q S X, and within it, and be movable round the central line $o\,o'$, a motion of rotation will be impressed upon it contrary to that of the circular current. This may be experimentally verified by an apparatus constructed on the principles represented in *fig.* 244, consisting of a wire frame supported and

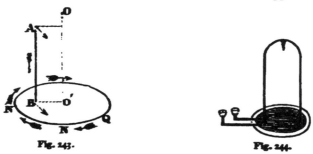

Fig. 243.   Fig. 244.

balanced on a central point in a mercurial cup. The current passing between this point and the liquid in a circular canal will ascend or descend on the vertical wires according to the arrangement of the connections. The circular current may be produced by surrounding the circular canal with a metallic wire, or ribbon coated with a nonconductor, upon which the current may be transmitted in the usual way. The wire frame will revolve upon the central point with direct or retrograde rotation, according to the directions of the currents. If the current ascend on the wires, they will revolve in the same direction as the circular current; if it descend, in the contrary direction.

The circular current may also be produced by a spiral current placed under the circular canal, and the wire frame may be replaced by a light hollow cylinder, supported on a central point. The spiral in this case may be movable and the cylinder fixed, or *vice versâ*, and the reciprocal actions will be manifested.

use in which the straight current is oblique to
e of the circulating current. — Like effects will
be produced when the rec-
tilinear current, instead of being
perpendicular to the plane of
the circular current, is oblique
to it.

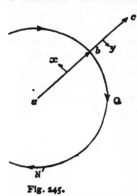

Fig. 245.

Let the rectilinear current *a c*,
fig. 245., be parallel to the plane
of the circular current ɴ ǫ. If
the current flow from *a* to *c*, the
part *a b* which is within the circle will be affected by a force opposite to the direction of the
nearest part of the current ɴ ǫ,
and the part *b c* outside the cir-
affected by a force in the same direction. If the current
c to *a*, contrary effects will ensue.

is case the straight current be limited to *a b*, and be
' resolving round *a* in a plane parallel to that of the
·ill receive a motion of rotation in the same or in a con-
:tion to that of the circulating current, accordingly as it
b to *a*, or from *a* to *b*. If the straight current be limited
ill, under the same circumstances, receive rotation in the
lirection. If, in fine, it extends on both sides of the
ill rotate in the one direction or the other, according
rnal or external part predominates.

»ciprocal effects of curvilinear currents. — The
fluence of rectilinear and curvilinear currents being
l, the reciprocal effects of curvilinear currents may be
ed. Each small part of such current may be regarded
rectilinear current, and the separate effects of such ele-
arts being ascertained, the effects of the entire extent of
.near currents will be the resultants of these partial

ntual action of curvilinear currents in general. —
ı variety of problems arises from the various forms that
· currents may assume, the various positions they may
:lation to each other, and the various conditions which
ıin their motions. The solution of all such problems,
·resents no other difficulties than those which attend the
:ation of the geometrical and mechanical principles,
plained in each particular case.

as an example one of the most simple of the infinite
forms under which such problems are presented, let the,

centres of two circular currents be fixed ; the planes of the currents being free to assume any direction whatever, they will turn upon their centres until they come to the same plane, the parts of the currents which intersect the line joining their centres flowing in the same direction. It is evident that upon the least disturbance from this position, they will be brought back to it by the mutual attraction of the parts of the circles on the sides which are near each other. This is therefore their position of stable equilibrium, and it is evident that the fronts of the currents in this position are on opposite sides of their common plane.

CHAP. IX.

VOLTAIC THEORY OF MAGNETISM.

345. Circulating currents have the magnetic properties.— From what has been proved, it is apparent that a helical current has all the properties of a magnet. Such currents exert the same mutual attraction and repulsion, have the same polarity, when submitted to the influence of terrestrial magnetism have the same directive properties, and exhibit all the phenomena of variation and dip as are manifested by artificial and natural magnets. And it is evident that these properties depend on the *circulating* and not on the *helical* character of the current, inasmuch as the effect of the progression of the helix being neutralised, by carrying the current back in a straight direction along its axis, the phenomena instead of being disturbed are still more regular and certain.

These properties of circulating currents have been assumed by Ampère as the basis of his celebrated theory of magnetism, in which all the magnetic phenomena are ascribed to the presence of currents, circulating round the constituent molecules of natural and artificial magnets, and round the earth itself.

Let a bar magnet be supposed to be cut by a plane at right angles to its length. Every molecule in its section is supposed to be invested by a circulating current, all these currents revolving in the same direction, and consequently their fronts being presented to the same extremity of the bar. The forces exerted by all the currents thus prevailing around the molecules of the same section may be considered as represented by a single current circulating round the bar; and the same being true of all the transverse sections of the bar, it may be regarded as being sur-

unded by a series of circulating currents all looking in the same
rection, and circulating round the bar. That end of the bar
wards which the fronts of .the currents are presented will have
e properties of a south or boreal pole, and the other end those
a north or austral pole.

346. Magnetism of the earth may proceed from currents.
·In this theory the globe of the earth is considered to be tra-
rsed by electric currents parallel to the magnetic equator. The
rces exerted by the currents circulating in each section of the
.rth, like those in the section of an artificial magnet, are con-
lered as represented by a single current equivalent in its effect,
id which is called the *mean current of the earth*, at each place
pon its surface. The magnetic phenomena indicate that the
irection of this mean current at each place is in a plane at right
ngles to the dipping needle, and that it is directed in this plane
:om east to west, and at right angles to the magnetic meridian.

347. Artificial magnets explained on this hypothesis.—
n bodies such as iron or steel, which are susceptible of magnetism,
ut which are not magnetised, the currents which circulate round
he constituent molecules are considered to circulate in all pos-
ible planes and all possible directions, and their forces thus
ieutralise each other. Such bodies, therefore, exert no forces of
.ttraction or repulsion on each other. But, when such bodies are
nagnetised, the fronts of some or all of these currents are turned
n the same direction, and their forces, instead of being opposed,
.re combined. The more perfect the magnetism is, the greater
iroportion of the currents will thus be presented in the same
lirection, and the magnetisation will be perfect when all the
nolecular currents are turned towards the same direction.

348. Effect of the presence or absence of coercive force.
–If the body thus magnetised be destitute of all coercive force,
ike soft iron, the currents which are thus temporarily turned by
he magnetising agent in the same direction will fall into their
riginal confusion and disorder when the influence of that agent
i suspended or removed, and the body will consequently lose the
nagnetic properties which had been temporarily imparted to it.
f, on the contrary, the body magnetised have more or less coer-
ive force, the accordance conferred upon the direction of the
nolecular currents, is maintained with more or less persistence
fter the magnetising agency has ceased; and the magnetic pro-
erties accordingly remain unimpaired until the accordance of the
nrrents is deranged by some other cause.

**349. This hypothesis cannot be admitted as established
ntil the existence of the molecular currents shall be
roved.**—To establish this theory according to the rigorous

principles of inductive science, it would be necessary that the actual existence of the molecular voltaic currents, which form the basis of the theory, should be proved by some other evidence than the class of effects which they are assumed to explain. Until such proof shall be obtained, they cannot be admitted to have the character of a vera causa, and the theory must be regarded as a mere hypothesis, more or less probable, and more or less ingenious, which may be accepted provisionally as affording an explanation of the phenomena, and thus reducing magnetism to the dominion of electricity.

CHAP. X.

EROSCOPES AND REOMETERS.

350. **Instruments to ascertain the presence and to measure the intensity of currents.**—It has been shown that when a voltaic current passes over a magnetic needle freely suspended, it will deflect the needle from its position of rest, the quantity of the deflection depending on the force, and its direction on the direction of the current.

If the needle be astatic, and consequently have no directive force, it will rest indifferently in any direction in which it may be placed. In this case the deflecting force of the current will have no other resistance to overcome than that of the friction of the needle on its pivot; and if the deflecting force of the current be greater than this resistance, the needle will be deflected, and will take a position at right angles to the current, its north pole being to the left of the current (233.).

If the needle be not astatic, it will have a certain directive force, and, when not deflected by the current, will place itself in the magnetic meridian. If, in this case, the wire conducting the current be placed over and parallel to the needle, the poles will be subject at once to two forces; the directive force tending to keep them in the magnetic meridian, and the deflecting force of the current tending to place them at right angles to that meridian. They will, consequently, take an intermediate direction, which will depend on the relation between the directive and reflecting forces. If the latter exceed the former, the needle will incline more to the magnetic east and west; if the former exceed the latter, it will incline more to the magnetic north and south. If these forces be equal, it will take a direction at an angle of 45°

with the magnetic meridian. The north pole of the needle will, in all cases, be deflected to the left of the current (233.).

If while the directive force of the needle remains unchanged the intensity of the current vary, the needle will be deflected at a greater or less angle from the magnetic meridian, according as the intensity of the current is increased or diminished.

351. **Expedient for augmenting the effect of a feeble current.** — It may happen that the intensity of the current is so feeble, as to be incapable of producing any sensible deflection even on the most sensible needle. The presence of such a current may, nevertheless, be detected, and its intensity measured, by carrying the wire conducting it first over and then under the needle, so that each part of the current shall exercise upon the needle a force tending to deflect it in the same direction. By this expedient the deflecting force exercised by the current on the needle is doubled.

Such an arrangement is represented in *fig.* 246. The wire passes

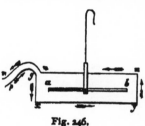

Fig. 246.

from *n* to *z* over, and from *y* to *x* under the needle; and it is evident, from what has been explained (233.), that the part *z n* and the part *y x* exercise deflecting forces in the same direction on the poles of the needle, both tending to deflect the north or austral pole *a* to the left of a person who stands at *z* and looks towards *n*. It may be shown in like manner that the vertical parts of the current *g x* and *y z* have the same tendency to deflect the north pole *a* to the left of a person viewing it from *z*.

352. **Method of constructing a reoscope, galvanometer, or multiplier.** — The same expedient may be carried further. The wire upon which the current passes may be carried any number of times round the needle, and each successive coil will equally augment its deflecting force. The deflecting force of the simple current will thus be multiplied by twice the number of coils. If the needle be surrounded with a hundred coils of conducting wire, the force which deflects it from its position of rest will be two hundred times greater than the deflecting force of the simple current.

The wire conducting the current must in such case be wrapped with silk or other nonconducting coating, to prevent the escape of the electricity from coil to coil.

Such an apparatus has been called a *multiplier*, in consequence of thus multiplying the force of the current. It has been also denominated a galvanometer, inasmuch as it supplies the means of measuring the force of the galvanic current.

We give it by preference the name *reoscope* or *reometer*, as indicating the presence and measuring the intensity of the current.

To construct a *reometer*, let two flat bars of wood or metal be

Fig. 247.

Fig. 248.

united at the ends, so as to leave an open space between them of sufficient width to allow the suspension and play of a magnetic needle. Let a fine metallic wire of silver or copper, wrapped with silk, and having a length of eighty or a hundred feet, be coiled longitudinally round these bars, leaving at its extremities three or four feet uncoiled, so as to be conveniently placed in connection with the poles of the voltaic apparatus from which the current proceeds. Over the bars on which the conducting wire is coiled, is placed a dial, upon which an index plays, which is connected with the magnetic needle suspended between the bars, and which has a common motion with it, the direction of the index always coinciding with that of the needle. The circle of the dial is divided into 360°, the index being directed to 0° or 180°, when the needle is parallel to the coils of the conducting wire.

Such an instrument, mounted in the usual manner and covered by a bell glass to protect it from the disturbance of the air, is represented in *fig.* 247., and in another form, with its appendages more complete, in *fig.* 248.

The needle is usually suspended by a single filament of raw silk. If the length of wire necessary for a single coil be six inches, fifty feet of wire will suffice for a hundred coils. To detect the presence of very feeble currents, however, a much greater number of coils is frequently necessary, and in some instruments of this kind there are several thousand coils of wire.

353. **Nobili's reometer.**—Without multiplying inconveniently the coils of the conducting wire, Nobili contrived a reoscope which possesses a sensibility sufficient for the most delicate experimental researches. This arrangement consists of two magnetic needles fixed upon a common centre parallel to each other, but with their poles reversed as represented in *fig.* 249. If the directive forces

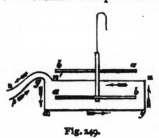

Fig. 249.

of these needles were exactly equal, such a combination would be astatic; and although it would indicate the presence of an extremely feeble current, it would supply no means of measuring the relative forces of two such currents. Such an apparatus would be *reoscopic*, but not *reometric*. To impart to it the latter property and at the same time to confer on it a high degree of sensibility, the needles are rendered a little, and but a little, unequal in their directive force. The directive force of the combination, being the difference of the directive forces of the two needles, is therefore extremely small, and the system is proportionately sensitive to the influence of the current.

354. **Differential reometer.**—In certain researches a differential reometer is found useful. In this apparatus two wires of

exactly the same material and diameter are coiled round the instrument, and two currents are made to pass in opposite directions upon them so as to exercise opposite deflecting forces on the needle. The deviation of the needle in this case measures the difference of the intensities of the two currents.

355. Great sensitiveness of these instruments illustrated. —The extreme sensitiveness and extensive utility of these reoscopic apparatus will be rendered apparent hereafter. Meanwhile it may be observed that if the extremities p and n of the conducting wires be dipped in acidulated water, a slight chemical action will take place, which will produce a current by which the needle will be visibly affected.

In all cases it is easy to determine the direction of the current by the direction in which the north pole of the needle is deflected.

CHAP. XI.

PHOTOMAGNETISM AND DIAMAGNETISM.

356. Faraday's discovery.—About the year 1845 Dr. Faraday made two beautiful discoveries, by one of which the phenomena of magnetism have been placed in relation with those of light, and by the other the domain of magnetic power has been immensely enlarged, by demonstrating its influence in various degrees over almost all natural bodies, whatever be their physical state, whether solid, liquid, or gaseous.

357. The photomagnetic phenomena, which have been developed by these remarkable researches, are briefly noticed in Hand Book, "Optics," Chap. XII. We shall here, however, resume the subject, and shall explain more fully the apparatus by which the phenomena can be exhibited.

358. Apparatus for their exhibition.—Two rods of soft iron, wrapped in the usual manner with covered wire, are mounted so that their axes are horizontal and in the same direction as shown in *fig.* 250. An adjustment is provided, by means of which the opposite poles f and e can, within certain limits, be moved to and from each other. The axes of the two rods are perforated from end to end, so that light can be transmitted without interruption from a to b. Any transparent body through which the light is required to be transmitted for the purpose of experiment is placed on a suitable stand d, between e and f. At the extremity *a* of the axial perforation *a* polarising prism is placed, and at the other extremity *b* an analysing prism is mounted so as to be capable

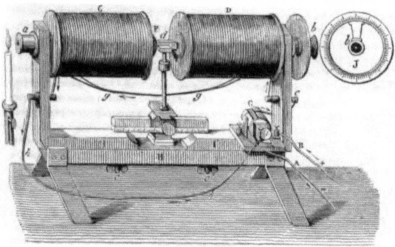

Fig. 250.

of being turned round the axis by an arm which carries an index moving on a graduated circular plate as shown at J. By reference to "Optics," Chap X., it will be seen that, by such a combination of prisms, rays of light can be polarised and the direction of their planes of polarisation determined. If the analysing prism *b* be turned round its axis, the light which passes through it, supposing it to be polarised, will be extinguished in two opposite positions of the analysing prism, and will be seen with its full intensity in two intermediate positions at right angles to these. The plane which passes through the ray in the two latter positions is the plane of polarisation.

It is shown in "Optics," Chap. XII., that a transparent medium which possesses the power of rotatory polarisation, will exert that power in different degrees on the different component parts of solar light; the planes of polarisation being turned more or less from their original position, according as the light is more or less refrangible. If a prism *d* of any transparent medium, having the property of rotatory polarisation, be placed therefore between the poles E and F, a polarised ray of compound solar light transmitted through it will have its plane of polarisation changed in different degrees by the prism *d*; consequently the position in which the analysing prism *b* would extinguish the different constituent rays will be different. This circumstance will be attended with the exhibition of a series of chromatic tints to an eye receiving the light at *b*. Thus, when the prism has that position in which the index is at right angles to the plane of polarisation of the red light that light will be extinguished, and the light received by the eye will have the complementary tint. In like manner, when the index is in the direction of the plane of polarisation of the blue ray, the light transmitted will have the tint complementary to blue, and so on.

These phenomena are purely optical, and have no reference to the magnetic influence. We shall now see, however, how that influence is capable of reproducing the same phenomena with bodies which, in their natural state, have no rotatory polarisation.

For this purpose, after placing the body on which the experiment is made, as described above at *d*, so that a ray of light transmitted along the perforation of the soft iron rods shall pass through it, a voltaic current is transmitted along the wire coiled upon the rods, so as to render them magnetic. This is accomplished by the apparatus shown in the figure in the following manner.

The current produced by a battery consisting of ten or twelve pairs of Bunsen's arrangement, arriving by the wire B, is received by the commutator G, from which it is transmitted, as indicated by the arrow, to the wire coiled upon D, after passing. round which it goes along the wire *g* to the coils on C, after passing which it issues along the wire *h* to the commutator, and thence along the wire A to the negative pole of the battery.

By means of the commutator G the direction of the current may be reversed at pleasure, so that it may be made to enter the coils on C through the wire *h*, to pass from C to D by the wire *g*, and to issue from D to the commutator, and thence by B to return to the battery.

By thus reversing the current the poles E and F can be made to change their names at pleasure.

359. **Photomagnetic phenomena.**—If a rod of flint glass, or, better still, that particular sort of heavy glass used by Professor Faraday, and described in "Optics" (305.), be placed at *d*, between the poles E and F, and a polarised ray of homogeneous light be transmitted through it, the direction of its plane of polarisation will be determined by the analysing prism *b*. Let the index of that prism be placed at right angles to the plane of polarisation, so that the polarised ray will be extinguished. This being done, let the connections of the conducting wires A and B with the battery be established, so that the current may pass through the coils C and D, and render the soft iron bars surrounding the ray magnetic. The moment the current is thus re-established, the ray will be no longer extinguished by the prism *b* in its actual position; and to

extinguish it it will be necessary to turn the index, right or left, through a certain angle.

If the current be reversed, the direction in which the index must be turned to extinguish the ray must be also reversed.

Hence it appears that the current, or the magnetic virtue which it imparts to the bars, exercises upon the ray of light, or upon the transparent medium through which the ray passes, or upon both of these, such an influence as to impart the power of rotatory polarisation to the medium d, and that this rotatory polarisation is positive or negative, according to the position of the magnetic poles E and F relatively to d.

The acquisition of this quality and its removal is absolutely instantaneous. This is proved by the fact of the instantaneous appearance and disappearance of the light at b, at the moment when the connections forming the voltaic circuit are made and broken.

360. **Effects on polarised solar light.**—If, instead of polarised homogeneous light, a ray of polarised solar light be transmitted through d, the light transmitted at b, while the current is established, will not be extinguished in any position which can be given to the index of the prism b, but a series of complementary tints of coloured light will be transmitted as the index is moved from one position to another. This is explained by the fact that the rotatory power produced by the current, is different for the different component parts of the solar light, the planes of polarisation of which being therefore turned through different angles, they will be extinguished in different positions of the index; and when the index has such a position as will extinguish any one ray, the complementary tint will be transmitted at b.

Since the original experiments made by Professor Faraday the investigation has been pursued by M. Bertin, M. Pouillet, M. Edmund Becquerel, and M. Matthiessen, from which it appears that, besides the glass used by Faraday, many other substances, solid and liquid, exhibit, in different degrees, like properties. Among these the principal are the silicates of lead in general, the flint glass of commerce, rock salt, and common glass. And among liquid substances, the bichloride of tin, the sulphuret of carbon, water, olive oil and alcohol, and all aqueous and alcoholic solutions.

361. **Diamagnetic phenomena.**—Dr. Faraday demonstrated, at the epoch above mentioned, that a certain class of substances, or rather bodies placed under certain physical conditions, without being themselves magnetic, are repelled by sufficiently powerful electro-magnets. To such substances he gave the name *diamag-*

netic. and the body of phenomena thus developed has accordingly received the title of diamagnetism.

Bodies possess this remarkable property in all the three states, solid, liquid, and gaseous.

The apparatus by which diamagnetic phenomena can be experimentally exhibited with greatest convenience and facility is that which has been applied to the exhibition of the photomagnetic effects, and which is represented in *fig. 250.*: to adapt it, however, to this purpose the poles s and q are so arranged that pieces of soft iron of various forms, adapted to each class of experiments, can be attached to them, so that these pieces, or their extremities, become in fact the poles of the magnets.

762. **Diamagnetism of solids.** — If two pieces of soft iron, s and q, conical in their form and rounded at the ends, be attached

Fig. 251.

to the poles, as shown in *fig. 251.*, a small ball of iron b or any other substance susceptible of magnetism, resting in contact with them as shown in the figure, will adhere to them with more or less force so long as the current is transmitted through the coils, but will be disengaged from them the moment the current is suspended.

If a similar ball b of any diamagnetic substance, bismuth for example, be similarly suspended, it will be repelled from the magnetic poles the moment the current is established, and will continue to be so repelled so long as the current continues to be transmitted. It will remain during such an interval in the same manner as a pendulum would, if drawn from the perpendicular and retained at the extremity of its arc of vibration. The moment, however, the connections are broken, and the current discontinued, the ball of bismuth will fall down into contact with s and q as before.

Fig. 252.

If a small cube of copper m, be suspended in the space between the magnetic poles, as shown in *fig. 252.*, and be made to revolve rapidly by first twisting the thread by which it is suspended and then letting it untwist, its rotation will be suddenly stopped the moment the poles s and q are rendered magnetic by the transmission of the current, and the rotation will re-commence the moment the connections are broken and the current discontinued.

If a small bar of any magnetic body, such as iron, be similarly suspended, as shown in *fig.* 253., between the poles of the electro-magnets, it will be brought to rest by their attraction in such a

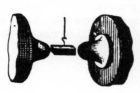

position that its ends shall be presented to the two poles, and consequently its length is in the direction of the axes of the magnets. This position Professor Faraday has called the axial direction.

If a similar bar of bismuth or any other diamagnetic body be similarly suspended, the position in which it will be brought to rest by the repulsion of the magnets, will be that in which its length is at right angles to the axes of the magnets, a position to which Professor Faraday gives the name of the equatorial direction.

Thus it appears that the influence of the magnets is to maintain magnetic bodies in the axial, and diamagnetic bodies in the equatorial position.

363. **Various diamagnetic bodies.**—The number of diamagnetic bodies is very considerable. Among the metals, bismuth is that in which the property is more pronounced; lead and zinc come next, but their action is much more feeble. Among the metaloids which manifest the property are phosphorus, selenium, and sulphur; and among compound bodies water, alcohol, ether, spirit of turpentine, most of the acids and saline solutions, wax, amber, mother o' pearl, tortoise shell, quill, carbon, and many others.

Liquids are submitted to similar experiments by being enclosed in small and very thin tubes of glass. When these tubes are suspended as above described, they are found to assume the axial or equatorial position, according as the liquid is magnetic or diamagnetic.

364. **Diamagnetism varies with the surrounding medium.** —Professor Faraday has shown that the properties of magnetism and diamagnetism cannot be said to belong, in an absolute sense, to all bodies, but that, on the contrary, the same body may be magnetic or diamagnetic, according to the medium with which it is surrounded; and as that medium is changed, it will accordingly assume alternately the axial or equatorial direction when suspended between the magnetic poles. For example, if a weak solution of the protosulphate of iron, included in a thin glass tube, be suspended between the magnetic poles, it will take the axial direction; if it be immersed in water when so suspended it will still keep the axial direction; but if immersed in a stronger solution of the protosulphate of iron than that which is contained in the tube, it will then take the equatorial direction, showing that it

possesses the magnetic or diamagnetic property according to the medium in which it is immersed.

365. **Plücher's apparatus.**—In the prosecution of diamagnetic researches M. Plücher used an experimental apparatus somewhat different in form from that shown in *fig.* 250., which was attended

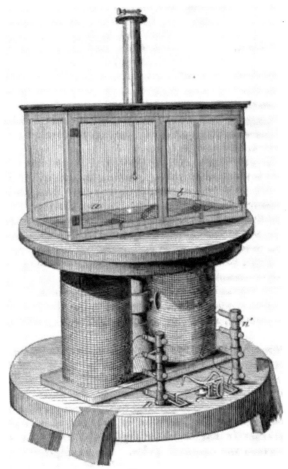

Fig. 254.

with several advantages. This apparatus, which is represented in *fig.* 254., consists of a large electro-magnet, similar to that shown in *fig.* 250., but having the legs vertical and the poles *a* and *b* consequently not presented one to the other, but standing in the same horizontal line. Upon *a* and *b*, as in the case of the apparatus

resented in *fig.* 250., polar pieces of soft iron of various forms,
ording to the experiment to be performed, can be adapted.
ese pieces, placed in various positions with relation to each
er, form a sort of horizontal magnetic area or field, in which
 bodies to be submitted to experiment are suspended by a
k attached to a fine silver wire, having the properties of the
ance of torsion already described (61.). This magnetic stage
covered and enclosed by a glass case, and when the hook is
; used for the measurement of torsional forces it is adapted
support a very sensitive common balance, of which all the parts
: formed of glass — the dishes being watch glasses.
When the dishes are filled with the liquid of which the mag-
:ic or diamagnetic properties are sought, the equilibrium is esta-
shed while the current is being transmitted, the dish containing
: liquid being suspended over the magnetic poles. Upon closing
: circuit the equilibrium no longer subsists, and the dish con-
ning the liquid is either attracted or repelled according as it
magnetic or diamagnetic.
The coils surrounding the electro-magnet consist of several
stinct wires, two or more of which may be put in connection at
easure, so that the current may be transmitted upon them
thout passing on the others. In this way the force of the
ectro-magnet may be varied at will, while the intensity of the
irrent remains the same. The apparatus for making this ad-
stment is shown at *n* and *n'*, the commutator being at *c*.

366. **The diamagnetic properties of liquids** can also be
:hibited in a remarkable manner by means of the apparatus
own in *fig.* 250. For this purpose, pieces D and C of the form
own in *fig.* 255. are attached to the poles, and the liquid under

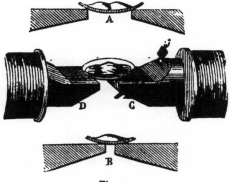

Fig. 255.

:periment, contained in a watch glass, is placed upon them as
own in the figure.

If a solution of chloride of iron be placed thus upon the arma-tures D and C, as soon as the current is established the solution will assume a convex form or two distinct convex forms, according to the distance between the magnetic poles, as shown at A and B. These forms will continue so long as the current is maintained; and the same forms will be assumed by all magnetic liquids.

The forms assumed by diamagnetic liquids, such as mercury, will be the inverse of these.

This experiment can, however, be performed with still greater convenience with the apparatus of M. Plücher, shown in *fig.* 254.

367. **Diamagnetism of flame.** — It was observed by M. Ban-calari that the flame of a candle placed between the poles of the electro-magnet was repelled, as if blown by a current of air, while the current was transmitted, as shown in *fig.* 256. All flames present the same phenomenon, but in different degrees. M. Quet obtained such effects in a very decided manner by submitting the electric light to the effects of the magnetic poles, as shown in *fig.* 257.

Fig. 256.   Fig. 257.

No satisfactory theory has yet been proposed to explain the phenomena of diamagnetism. Various hypotheses have been imagined, but none which has commanded any general assent. Dr. Faraday ascribes the phenomena to induction, assuming that in the diamagnetic body inductive currents are produced which act by repulsion upon the voltaic currents to which, according to the theory of Ampère, the magnetic value is due. MM. Edmund Becquerel and Plücher have each proposed other hypotheses, which suppose the diamagnetic bodies to be arrested by a magnetic medium which exercises the power of repulsion.

CHAP. XII.

THERMO-ELECTRICITY.

68. Disturbance of the thermal equilibrium of conductors reduces a disturbance of the electric equilibrium.—If a

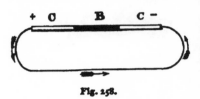

Fig. 258.

piece of metal B, *fig.* 258., or other conductor, be interposed between two pieces, c, of a different metal, the points of contact being reduced to different temperatures, the natural electricity at these points will be decomposed, the positive fluid passing in one direction, and the negative fluid in the other. If the extremities of the pieces c be connected by a wire, a constant current will be established along such wire. The intensity of this current will be invariable so long as the temperatures of the points of contact of B with c remain the same ; and it will in general be greater, the greater the difference of these temperatures. If the temperatures of the points of contact be rendered equal, the current will cease.

These facts may be verified by connecting the extremities of c with the wires of any reoscopic apparatus. The moment a difference of temperature is produced at the points of contact, the needle of the reoscope will be deflected ; the deflection will increase or diminish with every increase or diminution of the difference of the temperatures ; and if the temperatures be equalised, the needle of the reoscope will return to its position of rest, no deflection being produced.

369. **Thermo-electric current.**—A current thus produced is called a *thermo-electric current.* Those which are produced by the ordinary voltaic arrangements are called for distinction *hydro-electric currents*, a liquid conductor always entering the combination.

370. **Experimental illustration.**—A convenient and simple apparatus for the experimental illustration of a thermo-electric current is represented in *fig.* 259. A narrow strip of copper *c d* bent into a rectangular form, and soldered at both ends to a plate of bismuth *e e'*. A magnetic needle *a b* moves freely on its pivot within the rectangle. The apparatus is so placed, that its vertical plane coincides with that of the magnetic meridian ; and the needle, when undisturbed by the current, is at rest in the same direction. Now, if a lamp *f* be applied to one end *e* of the plate of bismuth, so as to raise its temperature above that of the other end, the needle will be immediately deflected, and the deflection will in-

crease as the difference of the temperatures of the ends of the plate of bismuth is increased. If the end *e* of the bismuth be cooled to a

Fig. 259.

temperature below that of the surrounding atmosphere, the needle will be deflected the other way, showing that the direction of the current has been reversed. And by repeating the same experiments with the other end *e'*, these results will be confirmed.

371. Conditions which determine the direction of the current. — When the temperature of the end *e* of the bismuth is more elevated than that of the end *e'*, the north pole of the needle is deflected to the left of a person standing at the end *e*, from which it appears that the current flows round the rectangle in the direction represented by the arrow.

If cold be applied to the end *e*, the needle will be deflected to the right, showing that the direction of the current will be reversed, the positive fluid always flowing towards the warmer end of the bismuth.

372. A constant difference of temperature produces a constant current. — If means be taken to maintain the extremities of the bismuth at a constant difference of temperature, the needle will maintain a constant deflection. Thus, if one end of the bismuth be immersed in boiling water and the other in melting ice, so that their temperatures shall be constantly maintained at 212° and 32°, the deflection of the needle will be invariable. If the temperature of the one be gradually lowered, and the other gradually raised, the deflection of the needle will be gradually diminished; and when the temperatures are equalised, the needle will resume its position in the magnetic meridian.

373. Different metals have different thermo-electric ener-gies. — This property, in virtue of which a derangement of the ectric equilibrium attends a derangement of the thermal equi-)rium, is common to all the metals, and, indeed, to conductors merally; but, like other physical properties, they are endowed ith it in very different degrees. Among the metals, bismuth and ntimony have the greatest thermo-electric energy, whether they e placed in contact with each other, or with any other metal. f a bar of either of these metals be placed with its extremities in ontact with the wires of a reometer, a deflection of the needle will e produced by the mere warmth of the finger applied to one end f the bar. If the finger be applied to both ends, the deflection will e redressed, and the needle will return to the magnetic meridian.

It has been ascertained that if different parts of the same nass of bismuth or antimony be raised to different temperatures, he electric equilibrium will be disturbed, and currents will be established in different directions through it, depending on the relative temperatures. These currents are, however, much less intense than in the case where the derangement of temperature is produced at the points of contact or junction of different conductors.

374. Pouillet's thermo-electric apparatus. — M. Pouillet has with great felicity availed himself of these properties of thermo-electricity, to determine some important and interesting properties of currents. The apparatus constructed and applied by him in these researches is represented in *fig.* 261.

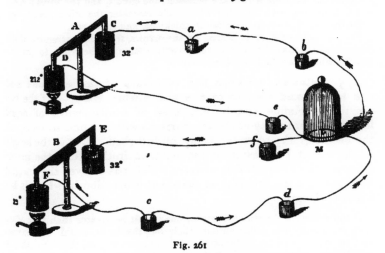

Fig. 261

Two rods, A and B, of bismuth, each about sixteen inches in length and an ch in thickness, are bent at the ends at right angles, and being supported vertical stands are so arranged that the ends C D and E F may be let down into cups. The cups C and E are filled with melting ice, and D and F with boiling water, so that the ends C and E are kept at the constant temperature of 32°, and the ends D and F at the constant temperature of 212°.

A differential reometer (354.) is placed at M. Two conducting circuits are formed either of one or several wires, one commencing from F, and after passing through the wire of the reometer M, returning to E; the other commencing from D, and after passing through the wire of the reometer in a contrary direction to the former, returning to C. The wires conducting the current are soldered to the extremities C, D, E, F of the bismuth rods which are immersed in the cups.

If the two currents thus transmitted, the one between F and E, and the other between D and G, have equal intensities, the needle of the reometer M will be undisturbed; but if there be any difference of intensity, its quantity and the wire on which the excess prevails will be indicated by the quantity and direction of the deflection of the needle.

The successive wires along which the current passes are brought into metallic contact by means of mercurial cups, a, b, c, d, &c., into which their ends are immersed.

The circuits through which the current passes may be simple or compound. If simple, they consist of wire of one uniform material and thickness. If compound, they consist of two or more wires differing in material, thickness, or length.

The wire composing a simple circuit is divided into two lengths, one extending from D or F to the cup e or d, where the current enters the convolutions of the reometer, and the other extending from the cup b or f, where the current issues from the reometer to C or E, where it returns to the thermoelectric source. The wires composing a compound current may consist of a succession of lengths, the current passing from one to another by means of the metallic cups. Thus, as represented in the figure, the wires F c, c d, and f E, forming, with one wire of the reometer, one circuit, and the wires D e, b a, and a C, forming with the other wire of the reometer the other circuit, may differ from each other in material, in thickness, and in length.

The currents pass, as indicated by the arrows, from the extremity of the bismuth which has the higher temperature through the wires to the extremity which has the lower temperature.

375. Relation between the intensity of the current and the length and section of the conducting wire. — If the two circuits be simple and be composed of similar wires of equal lengths, the intensity of the two currents will be found to be equal, the needle of the reometer being undisturbed. But if the length of the circuit be greater in the one than in the other, the intensities will be unequal, that current which passes over the longest wire having a less intensity in the exact proportion in which it has a greater length.

If the section of the wire composing one circuit be greater than that of the wire composing the other circuit, their lengths being equal, the current carried by the wire of greater section will be more intense than the other in exactly the proportion in which the section is greater.

If the wire composing one of two simple circuits have a length less than that composing the other, and a section also less in the same proportion than the section of the other, the currents passing over them will have the same tensity, for the excess of intensity due to the lesser length of the one is compensated by the excess due to the greater section of the other.

In general, therefore, if I and I' express the intensities of the two currents transmitted from D and F (*fig.* 261.) over two simple circuits of wire of the same metal, whose sections are respectively s and s', and whose lengths are L and L', we shall have:—

$$I : I' :: \frac{s}{L} : \frac{s'}{L'};$$

that is to say, the intensities are directly as the sections and inversely as the lengths of the wire.

If two simple circuits be compared, consisting of wires of different metals this proportion will no longer be maintained, because in that case wires of equal length and equal section will no longer give the currents equal intensities, because they will not have equal conducting powers. That circuit which, being alike in other respects, is composed of the metal of greatest conducting power, will give a current of proportionally greater intensity. The relative intensities, therefore, of the currents carried by wires of different metals of equal length and thickness are the exponents of the relative conducting powers of these metals.

In general, if c and c' express the conducting powers of the metals composing two simple circuits, we shall have:—

$$I : I' :: c \times \frac{s}{L} : c' \times \frac{s'}{L'}.$$

376. Conducting powers of metals. — M. Pouillet ascertained on these principles the conducting powers of the following metals relatively to that of distilled mercury taken at 100 :—

Metals.	Conducting Power.	Metals.	Conducting Power.
Mercury	100	Copper	3840
Iron	600 to 700	Gold	3975
Steel	500 to 800	Silver	5150
Brass	200 to 900	Palladium	5790
Platinum	855		

377. Current passing through a compound circuit of uniform intensity. — The current which passes through a compound circuit is found to have an uniform intensity throughout its entire course. In passing through a length of wire, which is a bad conductor, its intensity is neither greater nor less than upon one which is a good conductor, and its intensity on pieces of unequal section and unequal length is in like manner exactly the same.

378. Equivalent simple circuit. — A simple circuit composed of a wire of any proposed metal and of any proposed thickness can always be assigned upon which the current would have the same intensity as it has on any given compound circuit; for by increasing the length of such circuit the intensity of the current may be indefinitely diminished, and by diminishing its length the intensity may be indefinitely increased. A length may therefore be always found which will give the current any required intensity.

The length of such a standard wire which would give the

current of a simple circuit the same intensity as that of a compound circuit, is called the *reduced length* of the compound circuit.

379. **Ratio of intensities in two compound circuits.**—It is evident, therefore, that the intensities of the currents on two compound circuits are in the inverse ratio of their *reduced lengths*, for the wires composing such reduced lengths are supposed to be of the same material and to have the same thickness.

380. **Intensity of the current on a given conductor varies with the thermo-electric energy of the source.**—In all that has been stated above, we have assumed that the source of thermo-electric agency remains the same, and that the changes of intensity of the current are altogether due to the greater or less facility with which it is allowed to pass along the conducting wires from one pole of the thermo-electric source to the other. But it is evident, that with the same conducting circuit, whether it be simple or compound, the intensity of the current will vary either with the degree of disturbance of the thermal equilibrium of the system or with the thermo-electric energy of the substance composing the system.

In the case already explained, the ends of the cylinders A and B have been maintained at the fixed temperatures of 32° and 212°. If they had been maintained at any other fixed temperatures, like phenomena would have been manifested; with this difference only, that with the same circuit the intensity of the current would be different, since it would be increased if the difference of the temperature of the extremities were increased, and would be diminished if that difference were diminished.

In like manner, if, instead of bismuth, antimony, zinc, or any other metal were used, the same circuit and the same temperatures of the ends C and D or E and F would exhibit a current of different intensity, such difference being due to the different degree of thermo-electric agency with which the different metals are endowed.

The relative thermo-electric agency of different sources of these currents, whether it be due to a greater or less disturbance of the thermal equilibrium, or to the peculiar properties of the substance whose temperature is deranged, or, in fine, to both of these causes combined, is in all cases proportional to the intensity of the current which it produces in a wire of given material, length, and thickness, or in general to the intensity of the current it transmits through a given circuit.

The relative thermo-electric energy of two systems may be ascertained by placing them as at A and B, *fig.* 261., and connecting them by simple circuits of similar wire with the differential reometer. Let the lengths of the wires composing the two circuits be so adjusted, that the currents passing upon them shall have the same intensity. The thermo-electric energy of the two systems will then be in the direct ratio of the lengths of the circuits.

381. **Thermo-electric piles.**—The intensity of a thermo-electric current may be augmented indefinitely, by combining together a number of similar thermo-electric elements, in a manner similar to that adopted in the formation of a common voltaic battery. It is only necessary, in making such arrangement, to dispose the elements so that the several partial currents shall all flow in the same direction.

Such an arrangement is represented in *fig.* 262., where the two metals (bismuth and copper, for example) composing each thermo-electric pair

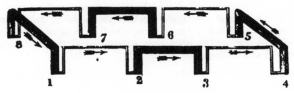

Fig. 262.

are distinguished by the thin and thick bars. If the points of junction marked 1, 3, 5, &c. be raised to 212°, while the points 2, 4, 6, &c. are kept at 32°, a current will flow from each of the points 1, 3, 5, &c. towards the points 2, 4, 6, &c. respectively, and these currents severally overlaying each other, exactly as in the voltaic batteries, will form a current having the sum of their intensities.

382. **Thermo-electric pile of Nobili and Melloni.**—Various expedients have been suggested for the practical construction of such thermo-electric piles, one of the most efficient of which is that of MM. Nobili and Melloni.

This pile is composed of a series of thin plates of bismuth and antimony bent at their extremities, so that when soldered together they have the form and arrangement indicated in *fig.* 263. The spaces between the successive plates are filled by pieces of pasteboard, by which the combination acquires sufficient solidity, and the plates are retained in their position without being pressed into contact with each other. The pile thus formed is mounted in a frame as represented in *fig.* 264., and its poles are connected with two pieces of metal by which the current may be transmitted to any conductors destined to receive it. It will be perceived that all the points of junction of the plates of bismuth and antimony, which are presented at the same side of the frame, are alternate in their order, the 1st, 3rd, 5th, &c. being on one side, and the 2nd, 4th, 6th, &c. on the other. If, then, one side be exposed to any source of heat or cold from which the other is removed, a corresponding difference of temperature will be produced at the alternate joints of the metal, and a current of proportionate intensity will flow between the poles o and p upon any conductor by which they may be connected.

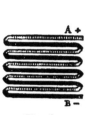

Fig. 263.

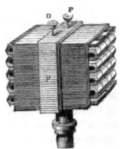

Fig. 264.

It is necessary, in the practical construction of this apparatus, that the metallic plates composing it should be all of the same length, so that when combined the ends of the system where the metallic joints are collected should form an even and plain surface, which it is usual to coat with lamp-black, so as to augment its absorbing power, and at the same time to render it more even and uniform.

The form of electric pile used by Melloni in his experiments on radiant heat, has been already described in "Heat" (577.), and represented there in *fig.* 281. Another view of the apparatus, differently arranged, is given in *fig.* 265., where F and E are the

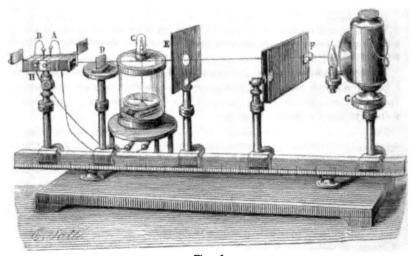

Fig. 265.

screens, D the stage upon which the bodies under experiment are placed, H the thermometric pile, c the galvanometer, and A and B *the* polar wires of the pile.

CHAP. XIII.

ELECTRO-CHEMISTRY.

383. **Decomposing power of a voltaic current.** — When a voltaic current of sufficient intensity is made to pass through certain bodies consisting of constituents chemically combined, it is found that decomposition is produced attended by peculiar circumstances and conditions. The compound is resolved into two constituents, which appear to be transported in contrary directions, one *with* and the other *against* the course of the current. The former is disengaged at the place where the current leaves, and the other at the place where it enters, the compound.

All compounds are not resolvable into their constituents by this agency, and those which are, are not equally so; some being resolved by a very feeble current, while others yield only to one of extreme intensity.

384. **Electrolytes and electrolysis.** — Bodies which are capable of being decomposed by an electric current have been called *electrolytes*, and decomposition thus produced has been denominated *electrolysis*.

385. **Liquids alone susceptible of electrolysis.** — To render electrolysis practicable, the molecules of the electrolyte must have a perfect freedom of motion amongst each other. The electrolyte must therefore be liquid. It may be reduced to this state either by solution or fusion.

386. **Faraday's electro-chemical nomenclature.** — It has been usual to apply the term poles either to the terminal elements of the pile, or to the extremities of the wire or other conductor by which the current passes from one end and enters the other. These are not always identical with the points at which the current enters and leaves an electrolyte. The same current may pass successively through several electrolytes, and each will have its point of entrance and exit; but it is not considered that the same current shall have more than two poles. These and other considerations induced Dr. Faraday to propose a nomenclature for the exposition of the phenomena of electrolysis, which has to some extent obtained acceptation.

387. **Positive and negative electrodes.** — He proposed to call the points at which the current enters and departs from the electrolyte, *electrodes*, from the Greek word όδός (hodos), a path or way. He proposed further to distinguish the points of entrance

and departure by the terms *Anode* and *Kathode*, from the Greek words άνοδοs (anodos), *the way up*, and κάθοδοs (kathodos), *the way down*.

388. **Only partially accepted.** — Dr. Faraday also gave the name *ions* to the two constituents into which an electrolyte is resolved by the current, from the Greek word *ίων* (ion), *going* or *passing*, their characteristic property being the tendency to pass to the one or the other electrode. That which passes to the positive electrode, and which therefore moves against the current, he called the *Anion;* and that which passes to the negative electrode and therefore moves with the current, he called the *Kation.* These terms have not, however, obtained acceptation. Neither have the terms "Anode" and "Kathode," positive and negative electrode, or positive and negative pole, being almost universally preferred.

The constituent of an electrolyte which moves with the current is distinguished as the *positive* element, and that which moves against it as the *negative* element. These terms are derived from the hypothesis that the constituent which appears at the positive electrode, and which moves, or seems to move, towards it after decomposition, is attracted by it as a particle negatively electrified would be; while that which appears at the negative electrode is attracted to it as would be a particle positively electrified.

389. **Composition of water.** — To render intelligible the process of electrolysis, let us take the example of water, the first substance upon which the decomposing power of the pile was observed. Water is a binary compound, whose simple constituents are the gases called oxygen and hydrogen. Nine grains weight of water consist of eight grains of oxygen and one grain of hydrogen.

The specific gravity of oxygen being sixteen times that of hydrogen, it follows that the volumes of these gases which compose water are in the ratio of two to one; so that a quantity of water which contains as much oxygen as, in the gaseous state, would have the volume of a cubic inch, contains as much hydrogen as would, under the same pressure, have the volume of two cubic inches.

The combination of these gases, so as to convert them into water, is determined by passing the electric spark taken from a common machine through a mixture of them. If eight parts by weight of oxygen and one of hydrogen, or, what is the same, one part by measure of oxygen and two of hydrogen, be introduced into the same receiver, on passing through them the electric spark an explosion will take place; the gases will disappear, and the receiver will be filled first with steam, which being condensed, will be presented in the form of water. The weight of water contained in the receiver will be equal precisely to the sum of the weight of the two gases.

These being premised, the phenomena attending the electrolysis of water may be easily understood.

390. **Electrolysis of water.** — Let a glass tube, closed at one end, be filled with water slightly acidulated, and, stopping the open end, let it be inverted and immersed in similarly acidulated water contained in any open vessel. The column in the tube will be sustained there by the atmospheric pressure, as the mercurial column is sustained in a barometric tube; but in this case the tube will remain completely filled, no vacant space appearing at the top, the height of the column being considerably less than that which would balance the atmospheric pressure. Let two platinum wires be connected with the poles of a voltaic pile, and let their extremities, being immersed in the vessel containing the tube, be bent so as to be presented upwards in the tube without touching each other. Immediately small bubbles of gas will be observed to issue from the points of the wires, and to rise through the water and collect in the top of the tube, and this will continue until the entire tube is filled with gas, by the pressure of which the water will be expelled from it. If the tube be now removed from the vessel, and the gas be transferred to a receiver, so arranged that the electric spark may be transmitted through it, on such transmission the gas will be reconverted into water.

The gases, therefore, evolved at the points of the wires, which in this case are the *electrodes*, are the constituents of water; and since they cannot combine to form water, except in the definite ratio of 1 to 2 by measure, they must have been evolved in that exact proportion at the electrodes.

391. **Explanation of this phenomenon by the electro-chemical hypothesis.** — This phenomenon is explained by the supposition that the voltaic current exercises forces directed upon each molecule of the water, by which the molecules of oxygen are impelled or attracted towards the positive electrode, and therefore against the current, and the molecules of hydrogen towards the negative electrode, and therefore with the current. The electro-chemical hypothesis is adopted by different parties in different senses.

According to some, each molecule of oxygen is invested with an atmosphere of negative, and each molecule of hydrogen with an atmosphere of positive electricity, which are respectively inseparable from them. When these gases are in their free and uncombined state, these fluids are neutralised by equal doses of the opposite fluids received from some external source, since otherwise they would have all the properties of electrified bodies, which they are not observed to have. But when they enter into combination, the molecule of oxygen dismisses the dose of positive electricity, and the molecule of hydrogen the dose of negative electricity which previously neutralised their proper fluids; and these latter fluids then exercising their mutual attraction, cause the two gaseous molecules to coalesce and to form a molecule of water.

When decomposition takes place, a series of opposite effects are educed. The molecule of oxygen after decomposition is charged with its natural negative, and the molecule of hydrogen with its natural positive fluid, and these molecules must borrow from the decomposing agent or some other source, the doses of the opposite fluids which are necessary to neutralise them. In the present case, the molecule of oxygen is reduced to its natural state by the positive fluid it receives at the positive electrode, and the molecule of hydrogen by the negative fluid it receives at the negative electrode.

The electro-chemical hypothesis is, however, differently understood and differently stated by different scientific authorities. It is considered by some that the decomposing forces in the case of the voltaic current, are the attractions and repulsions which the two opposite fluids developed at the electrodes exercise upon the atmospheres of electric fluid, which are assumed in this theory to surround and to be inseparable from the molecules of oxygen and hydrogen which compose each molecule of water, the resultants of these attractions and repulsions being two forces, one acting on the oxygen and directed towards the positive electrode, and the other acting on the hydrogen and directed towards the negative electrode. Others, with Dr. Faraday, deny the existence of these attractions, and regard the electrodes as mere paths by which the current enters and leaves the electrolyte, and that the effect of the current in passing through the electrolyte is to propel the molecules of oxygen and hydrogen in contrary directions, the latter in the direction of the current, and the former in the contrary direction; and that this combined with the series of decompositions and recompositions imagined by Grotthus, which we shall presently explain, supplies the most satisfactory exposition of the phenomena.

Our limits, however, compel us to dismiss these speculations, and confine our observations rather to the facts developed by experimental research, using, nevertheless, the language derived from the theory for the purposes of explanation.

392. **Method of electrolysis which separates the constituents.**—The process of electrolysis may be so conducted that

the constituent gases shall be developed and collected in separate receivers.

The apparatus represented in *fig.* 266., contrived by Mitscherlich, is very

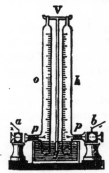

Fig. 266.

convenient for the exhibition of this and other electrolytic phenomena. Two glass tubes *o* and *h*, about half an inch in diameter, and 6 or 8 inches in length, are closed at the top and open at the bottom, having two short lateral tubes projecting from them, which are stopped by corks, through which pass two platinum wires which terminate within the tubes in a small brush of platinum wire, which may with advantage be surrounded at the ends with spongy platinum. The tubes *o h*, being uniformly cylindrical and conveniently graduated, are filled with acidulated water, and immersed in a cistern of similarly acidulated water *g*.

If the external extremities of the platinum wires be connected by means of binding screws *a* and *b*, or by mercurial cups with wires which proceed from the poles of a voltaic arrangement, their internal extremities will become electrodes, and electrolysis will commence. Oxygen gas will be evolved from the positive, and hydrogen from the negative electrode, and these gases will collect in the two tubes, the oxygen in the tube *o* containing the positive, and the hydrogen in the tube *h* containing the negative electrode. The graduated scales will indicate the relative measures of the two gases evolved, and it will be observed that throughout the process the quantity of gas in the tube *h* is double the quantity in the tube *o*. If the gases be removed from the tubes to other receivers and submitted to chemical tests, one will be found to be oxygen and the other hydrogen.

393. **How are the constituents transferred to the electrodes?** — In the apparatus *fig.* 266., the tubes containing the electrodes are represented as being near together. The process of electrolysis, however, will equally ensue when the cistern *g* is a trough of considerable length, the tubes *o* and *h* being at its extremities. It appears, therefore, that a considerable extent of liquid may intervene between the electrodes without arresting the process of decomposition. The question then arises, where does the decomposition take place? At the positive electrode, or at the negative electrode, or at what intermediate point? If it take place at the positive electrode, a constant current of hydrogen must flow from that point through the liquid to the negative electrode; if at the negative electrode, a like current of oxygen must flow from that point to the positive electrode; and if at any intermediate point, two currents must flow in contrary directions from that point, one of oxygen to the positive, and one of hydrogen to the negative electrode. But no trace of the existence of any such currents has ever been found. Innumerable expedients have been contrived to arrest the one or the other gas in its pro-

gress to the electrode without success; and therefore the strongest physical evidence supports the position that neither of these con‑stituent gases does actually exist in the separate state at any part of the electrolyte, except at the very electrodes themselves, at which they are respectively evolved.

If this be assumed, then it will follow that the molecules of oxygen and hydrogen evolved at the two electrodes, were not previously the component parts of the same molecule of water. The molecule of oxygen evolved at the positive electrode must be supplied by a molecule of water contiguous to that electrode, while the molecule of hydrogen simultaneously evolved at the negative electrode must have been supplied by another molecule of water contiguous to the latter electrode. What then becomes of the molecule of hydrogen dismissed by the former, and the molecule of oxygen dismissed by the latter? Do they coalesce and form a molecule of water? But such a combination would again involve the supposition of currents of gas passing through the electrolyte, of the existence of which no trace has been observed.

394. **Solution on the hypothesis of Grotthus.**—The only hypothesis which has been proposed presenting any satisfactory explanation of the phenomena is that of Grotthus, in which a series of decompositions and recompositions are supposed to take place between the electrodes.

Let o h, o′ h′, o″ h″, &c., represent a series of molecules of water ranged between the positive electrode p and the negative electrode n.

$$\text{P} \ldots \text{O H} \ldots \text{O}' \text{H}' \ldots \text{O}'' \text{H}'' \ldots \text{O}''' \text{H}''' \ldots \text{O}'''' \text{H}'''' \ldots \text{N}.$$

When o h is decomposed and o is detached in a separate state at p, the positive fluid inseparable from h, according to the electro-chemical hypo‑thesis, being no longer neutralised by an opposite fluid, attracts the negative fluid of o′, and repels the positive fluid of h′, and decomposing the molecule of water o′ h′, the molecule o′ coalesces with h, and forms a molecule of water. In like manner, h′ decomposes o″ h″, and combines with o″; h″ de‑composes o‴ h‴, and combines with o‴; and h‴ decomposes o⁗ h⁗, and combines with o⁗; and, in fine, h⁗ is disengaged at the negative electrode n. Thus, as the series of decompositions and recompositions proceeds, the molecules of oxygen are disengaged at the positive electrode p, and those of hydrogen at the negative electrode n.

In this hypothesis it is further supposed, as already stated, that the molecule of oxygen o, disengaged at the positive electrode p, receives from that electrode a dose of positive electricity, which being equal in quantity to its own proper negative electricity, neutralises it; and, in like manner, the molecule of hydrogen h⁗, disengaged at the negative electrode n, receives from it a corresponding dose of negative electricity which neutralises its own positive electricity. It is thus that the two gases, when liberated at the electrodes, are in their natural and unelectrified state.

395. **Effect of acid and salt on the electrolysis of water.** —In the electrolysis of water as described above, the acid held in

olution undergoes no change. It produces, nevertheless, an important influence on the development of the phenomena. If the electrodes be immersed in pure water, decomposition will only be produced when the current is one of extraordinary intensity. But if a quantity of sulphuric acid even so inconsiderable as one per cent. be present, a current of much less intensity will effect the electrolysis; and by increasing the proportion of the acid gradually from one to ten or fifteen per cent. the decomposition will require a less and less intense current.

It appears, therefore, that the acid without being itself affected by the current, renders the water more susceptible of decomposition. It seems to lessen the affinity which binds the molecules of oxygen and hydrogen, of which each molecule of water consists.

Various other acids and salts soluble in water produce the same effect.

The electrolyte, properly speaking, is therefore in these cases the water alone. The bath in which the electrodes are immersed, and in which the phenomena of the electrolysis are developed, may contain various substances in solution; but so long as these are not directly affected by the current, they must not be considered as forming any part of the electrolyte, although they not only influence the phenomena as above stated, but are also involved in important secondary phenomena, as will presently appear.

The process of the electrolysis of water has been presented here in its most simple form, no other effect save the mere decomposition of the electrolyte being educed. If, however, the platinum electrodes which have no sensible affinity for the constituents of water be replaced by electrodes composed of any metal having a stronger affinity for oxygen, other phenomena will be developed. The oxygen dismissed by the water at the positive electrode, instead of being liberated, will immediately enter into combination with the metal of the electrode, forming an oxide of that metal. This oxide may adhere to the electrode, forming a crust upon it. In that case, if the oxide be a conductor, it will itself become the electrode. If it be not a conductor it will impede and finally arrest the course of the current, and put an end to the electrolysis. If it be soluble in water it will disappear from the electrode as fast as it is formed, being dissolved by the water; and in that case the water will become a solution of the oxide, the strength of which will be gradually increased as the process is continued.

If the water composing the bath hold an acid in solution, for which the oxide thus formed at the positive electrode has an affinity, the oxide will enter into combination with the acid, and will form a salt which will either be dissolved or precipitated, according as it is soluble or not in the bath.

While the oxygen disengaged from the water at the positive electrode undergoes these various combinations, the hydrogen is frequently liberated in the free state at the negative electrode, and may be collected and measured. In such case it will always be found that the quantity of the hydrogen developed at the negative electrode, is the exact equivalent of the oxygen which has entered into combination with the metal at the positive electrode, and also that the quantity of the metal oxidated is exactly that which corresponds with the quantities of the two gases which are disengaged, and with the quantity of water which is decomposed.

396. **Secondary action of the hydrogen at the negative electrode.**—In some cases the hydrogen is not developed in the form of gas at the negative electrode, but in its place the pure metal, which is the base of the oxide dissolved in the bath, is deposited there. In such cases the phenomena become more complicated, but nevertheless sufficiently evident. The hydrogen developed at the negative electrode, instead of being disengaged in the free state, attracts the oxygen from the oxide, and combining with it forms water, liberating at the same time the metallic base of the oxide which is deposited on the negative electrode.

Thus there is in such cases both a decomposition and a recomposition of water. It is decomposed at the one electrode to produce the oxide, and recomposed at the other electrode to reduce or decompose the same oxide.

397. **Its action on bodies dissolved in the bath.**—This effect of the hydrogen developed at the negative electrode is not limited to the oxide or salt produced by the action of the positive electrode. It will equally apply to any metallic oxide or salt which may be dissolved in the bath. Thus, while the oxygen may be disengaged in a free state and collected in the gaseous form over the positive electrode, the hydrogen developed at the negative electrode may reduce and decompose any metallic salt or oxide, which may have been previously dissolved in the bath.

398. **Example of zinc and platinum electrodes in water.**—To render this more clear, let it be supposed that while the negative electrode is still platinum, the positive electrode is a plate of zinc, a metal eminently susceptible of oxidation. In this case no gas will appear at the zinc, but the protoxide of that metal will be formed. This substance being insoluble in water will adhere to the electrode if the bath contain pure water; but if it be acidulated, with sulphuric acid for example, the protoxide so soon as it is formed will combine with the sulphuric acid, producing the salt called the sulphate of zinc, or more strictly the sulphate

of the oxide of zinc. This being soluble, will be dissolved in the bath.

399. **Secondary effects of the current.** — In all these cases the primary and, strictly speaking, the only effect of the current is the decomposition of water, and the only substances affected by the electric agency are the constituents, oxygen and hydrogen, of the water decomposed. All the other phenomena are secondary and subsequent to the electrolysis, and depend, not on the current, but on the affinities of the electrodes and of the substances held in solution by the electrolyte, for the constituents of the electrolyte and for each other. The phenomena, however, though successive as regards the physical agencies which produce them, are practically simultaneous in their manifestation, and are often so complicated and interlaced in their mutual relations and dependencies, that it is extremely difficult to discover a clear and certain analysis of them.

400. **Compounds which are susceptible of electrolysis.** — The electrolysis of water is, in all its circumstances and conditions, a type and example of the phenomena attending the decomposition of other compounds by the same agency.

Compounds are susceptible of electrolysis or not, according to the nature, properties, and proportion of their constituents.

It has been ascertained by direct experiment that most of the simple bodies are capable of being disengaged from compounds of which they may be constituents by electrolysis, and analogy renders it probable that all of them have this property. Those which have not yet been ascertained to be capable of elimination by this agency, include nitrogen, carbon, phosphorus, boron, silicon, and aluminium. The difficulty of obtaining these substances in compounds of a form adapted to electrolysis, has alone rendered them exceptions to the otherwise universally ascertained law.

401. **Electrolytic classification of the simple bodies.** — Attempts have been made to classify bodies according to the tendencies they manifest to pass to the one or the other electrode, in the process of electrolytic decomposition, those which evince the strongest tendency to go to the positive electrode being considered in the highest degree electro-negative, and those which show the strongest tendency to go to the negative electrode in the highest degree electro-positive. Although experimental research has not yet supplied very extensive or accurate data for such a classification, the following proposed by Berzelius will be found useful, as indicating in a general manner the electrical characters of a large number of simple bodies, subject, however, to such corrections and modifications as further experiment and observation may suggest.

402. I. Electro-negative bodies.

1. Oxygen.	8. Selenium.	15. Antimony.
2. Sulphur.	9. Arsenic.	16. Tellurium.
3. Nitrogen.	10. Chromium.	17. Columbium.
4. Chlorine.	11. Molydeoum.	18. Titanium.
5. Iodine.	12. Tungsten.	19. Silicium.
6. Fluorine.	13. Boron.	20. Osmium.
7. Phosphorus.	14. Carbon.	21. Hydrogen.

403. II. Electro-positive bodies.

1. Potassium.	11. Zirconium.	21. Bismuth.
2. Sodium.	12. Manganese.	22. Uranium.
3. Lithium.	13. Zinc.	23. Copper.
4. Barium.	14. Cadmium.	24. Silver.
5. Strontium.	15. Iron.	25. Mercury.
6. Calcium.	16. Nickel.	26. Palladium.
7. Magnesium.	17. Cobalt.	27. Platinum.
8. Glucinium.	18. Cerium.	28. Rhodium.
9. Yttrium.	19. Lead.	29. Iridium.
10. Aluminium.	20. Tin.	30. Gold.

All the bodies named in the first series are supposed to be negative with relation to those in the second. Each of the bodies in the first series is negative, and each of the bodies in the second positive, with relation to those which follow.

The meaning is, that if an electrolyte composed of any two of the bodies in the first list be submitted to the action of the current, that which stands first in the list will go to the positive electrode; if an electrolyte composed of any body in the first and another in the second list be electrolysed, the former will go to the positive electrode; and, in fine, if an electrolyte composed of any two of the bodies named in the second list be electrolysed, the first named will go to the negative pole.

It has been objected that sulphur and nitrogen occupy too high a place in the negative series, these bodies being less negative than chlorine and fluorine, and that hydrogen ought rather to be placed in the positive series.

404. The order of the series not certainly determined.— It must be observed that the order of the simple bodies in these series has not been determined in all cases by the direct observation of the phenomena of the electrolysis. It has been in many cases only inferred from the analogies suggested by their chemical relations.

405. Electrolytes which have compound constituents.— When the constituents of an electrolyte are compound bodies, the decomposition proceeds in the same manner as with those binary compounds whose constituents are simple. Most of the salts which have been submitted to experiment prove to be electrolytes, the acid constituent appearing at the positive, and the base at the negative electrode. Acids are therefore in general regarded as electro-negative bodies analogous to oxygen, and alkalies and oxides electro-positive bodies analogous to hydrogen.

406. According to Faraday, electrolytes whose constituents are simple can only be combined in a single proportion. — It appears to result from the researches of Faraday, hat two simple bodies cannot combine in more than one proportion so as to form an electrolyte.

When hydrochloric acid, whose constituents are chlorine and rydrogen, is submitted to the current, electrolysis ensues, the chlorine appearing at the positive and the hydrogen at the negative electrode.

The protochlorides of the metals composed of the metallic base and one equivalent of chloride are also easily electrolysed, the chlorine always appearing at the positive electrode; but the perchlorides of the same metals which contain two or more equivalents of chlorine are not susceptible of electrolysation.

In general, compounds which consist of two simple elements are only electrolysable when their constituents are single equivalents. Hence sulphuric acid which has three, and nitric acid which has ive equivalents of oxygen, are neither of them susceptible of electrolysation.

407. Apparent exceptions explained by secondary action. —In the investigation of the chemical phenomena which attend he transmission of the current through liquid compounds, results rill be occasionally observed which will at first seem incompatible ith this law. But in these cases the phenomena are invariably he consequences, not of electrolysis, but of secondary action. hus, nitric acid submitted to the current is decomposed, losing ne equivalent of its oxygen, and reduced to nitrous acid. In is case the real electrolyte is the water, which always exists in ore or less quantity in the acid. This water being decomposed, e oxygen is delivered at the positive electrode, and the hydrogen veloped at the negative electrode attracts from the nitric acid ne equivalent of its oxygen, with which it combines and forms iter, reducing the nitric to nitrous acid.

Ammonia, which consists of one equivalent of nitrogen and ree of hydrogen, is not properly an electrolyte, though in solun it is decomposed by the secondary action of the current. In is case, as in the former, the real electrolyte is the water in iich the ammonia is dissolved. Nitrogen, and not oxygen, is sengaged at the positive electrode. The oxygen, which is the imary result of the electrolysis of the water, attracts the hydron of the ammonia, with which it reproduces water and liberates e nitrogen.

408. Secondary effects favoured by the nascent state of he constituents: results of the researches of Becquerel nd Crosse. — It is a general law in chemistry that substances in the nascent state, that is, when just disengaged from compounds with which they have been united, are in a condition most favourable for entering into combinations. This explains the great facility with which the constituents of electrolytes combine with the electrodes where even a feeble affinity prevails, and also the various secondary effects. When oxygen is evolved against copper, iron, or zinc, chlorine against gold, or sulphur against silver at the electrode, oxides of copper, iron, or zinc, chloride of gold, or sulphuret of silver, are readily formed. If the current producing these changes be of very feeble intensity, so that the new compounds are very slowly formed, so slowly as more to resemble growth than strong chemical action, they will assume the crystalline structure. In this manner Becquerel and Crosse have succeeded in obtaining artificially mineral crystals, and exhibiting on a small scale effects similar to those which are in progress on a scale so vast in the mineral veins which pervade the crust of the globe, and which, doubtless, result from feeble electric currents established for countless centuries in its strata by the vicissitudes of temperature and other physical causes.

409. **The successive action of the same current on different vessels of water.** — If the same current be conducted successively through a series of vessels containing acidulated water, by connecting the water in each vessel with the water in the succeeding vessel by platinum wires ɪ, ɪ′, ɪ″, ɪ‴, &c., as represented in *fig.* 267., the current will enter each vessel at the

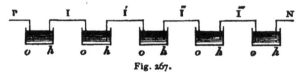

Fig. 267.

extremity *o*, and will depart from it at the extremity *h*. The water in each vessel will in this case constitute a separate electrolyte, and will be decomposed by the current. The ends *o* will be all positive, and the ends *h* all negative electrodes. Oxygen will be disengaged at all the ends *o*, and hydrogen at all the ends *h*; and if the gases disengaged be collected, the same quantity of oxygen will be found to be disengaged at the ends *o*, and the same quantity of hydrogen at the ends *h*, the volume of the latter being double that of the former. The weight of the oxygen produced will be eight times that of the hydrogen, and the weight of the water decomposed will be nine times that of the hydrogen.

410. **The same current has an uniform electrolytic power.** — Since it is ascertained by reometric instruments that the same current has everywhere the same intensity, it follows

that this constant intensity is attended with an electrolytic power of corresponding uniformity. From this and other similar results it is inferred that the quantity of electricity which passes in a current is proportional to the quantity of a given electrolyte which the current decomposes.

411. **Voltameter of Faraday.** — On this ground Faraday gave the name of *voltameter* to an apparatus similar in principle to that described in (392.), taking water as the standard electrolyte by which the quantity of electricity necessary to effect the decomposition of any other electrolytes might be measured. Thus, if it is found that a current which decomposes in a given time an ounce of water, will in the same time decompose two ounces of one electrolyte (A), and three ounces of another electrolyte (B), it is inferred that the quantity of electricity necessary to decompose a given weight of A is half that which would decompose an equal weight of water, and that the quantity necessary to decompose a given weight of B is a third of that which would decompose the same weight of water, and, in fine, that the quantities of electricity necessary to decompose equal weights of A and B are in the ratio of 3 to 2.

412. **Effect of the same current on different electrolytes — Faraday's law.** — If the series of vessels represented in *fig.* 267., connected by metallic conductors I, I′, &c., instead of containing water, contain a series of different electrolytes, each electrolyte will be decomposed exactly as it would be if it were the only electrolyte through which the current passed.

Let us suppose that the first vessel of the series which the current enters from P contains water, and that means are provided by which the quantities of oxygen and hydrogen liberated at o and h shall be indicated, and that in like manner the quantities of the constituents of each of the other electrolytes disengaged at the respective electrodes can be determined. It will then be found that for every grain weight of hydrogen liberated in the first vessel, the number of grains weight of each of the constituents of the several electrolytes disengaged will be expressed by their respective chemical equivalents.

Thus, if e, e', e'', e''', &c. be the chemical equivalents of the several constituents of the series of electrolytes, that of hydrogen being the unit, and if h express the number of grains weight of hydrogen evolved in the voltameter tube over the first vessel in a given time, then the number of grains weight of each of the constituents of the several electrolytes which shall be evolved in the same time will be

$$e \times h, \quad e' \times h, \quad e'' \times h, \quad e''' \times h, \quad \&c., \quad \&c.$$

413. **It comprises secondary results.** — This remarkable law extends not only to the direct results of electrolysis, but also to all the secondary effects of the current.

Thus, it applies to the quantities of the several metallic electrodes which e with the constituents which are the immediate results of the lysis, and also to all combinations and decompositions which result he affinities which may exist between the results, primary or secondary, electrolysis, and any foreign substances which the electrolyte may hold lution.

414. Practical example of its application.—As a practical mple of the application of this electro-chemical law, let us ppose the first vessel which the current enters at P to contain ater, the next iodide of potassium, the succeeding one proto-hloride of tin, the next hydrochloric acid, and the last sulphate f soda. The current will severally decompose these, the oxygen, iodine, chlorine, and acid appearing at the five positive electrodes, and the hydrogen, potassium, tin, and soda at the five negative electrodes. If the electrode against which the oxygen is evolved be zinc, the oxide of zinc will result as a secondary product; and if the electrode against which the chlorine is evolved be gold, the chloride of that metal will likewise be produced by secondary action. The chemical equivalents of the several substances involved in this process are as follows:—

Hydrogen	1·00	Hydrochloric acid	36·47
Oxygen	8·00	Sulphuric acid	40·10
Water	9·00	Soda	31·30
Iodine	126·30	Sulphate of soda	71·40
Potassium	39·26	Zinc	32·30
Iodide of potassium	165·56	Gold	199·20
Chlorine	35·47	Oxide of zinc	40·30
Tin	57·90	Chloride of gold	234·67
Protochloride of tin	93·37		

It will follow, therefore, from the general electrolytic law above stated, that for every grain of hydrogen evolved at the negative electrode in the first vessel, the following will be the quantities of the chemical results produced in the several vessels:—

I. Oxygen evolved at positive electrode - 8·00
   Water decomposed - 9·00
   Zinc oxidated - 32·30
   Oxide of zinc produced - 40·30

II. Iodine evolved at the positive electrode - 126·30
   Potassium evolved at the negative electrode - 39·26
   Iodide decomposed - 165·56

III. Chlorine evolved at the positive electrode - 35·47
   Tin evolved at the negative electrode - 57·90
   Gold combined at positive electrode - 199·20

IV. Chloride of gold produced - 234·67
   Protochloride of tin decomposed - 93·37
   Chlorine evolved at positive electrode - 35·47
   Hydrogen evolved at negative electrode - 1·00
   Hydrochloric acid decomposed - 36·47

V. Sulphuric acid evolved at positive electrode - 40·10
   Soda evolved at negative electrode - 31·30
   Sulphate decomposed - 71·40

415. Sir H. Davy's experiments showing the transfe the constituents of electrolytes through intermediate ? tions.—If the series of vessels containing different electr be connected by liquid conductors by means of capillary si ... the metallic conductors by which they are supp ᴐe connected in the cases just described; phenomena are produced, ᴇspecting which a remarkable discordance has arisen between the ᴜghest scientific authorities.

From some of the early experiments of Sir H. Davy, confirmed ᴐy those of Gautherot, Hesinger, and Berzelius, it appeared that ᴜhe voltaic current was not only capable of decomposing various ᴇlasses of chemical compounds, but of transferring or decanting ᴜheir constituents successively through two or more vessels, to ᴐring them to the respective electrodes at which they are liberated. Davy pushed this inquiry to its extreme limits, and by various experiments, characterised by all that address for which he was so remarkable, arrived at certain general results which we shall now briefly state.

Let a series of cups

P ⇛→ A B C D E ⇛→ N

be connected by capillary siphons, which may be conveniently formed of the fibres of asbestos or amianthus. Let any electrolyte, a solution of a neutral salt for example, be placed in C; and let the other cups be filled with distilled water. Let a plate of platinum connected with the positive pole of a voltaic battery be immersed in the cup A, and a similar plate connected with the negative pole be immersed in E. The voltaic current will then enter the series of cups at A, and passing successively from cup to cup through the siphons, will issue from them at E, as indicated by the arrows. Let the water in the cups A, B, D, and E be tinged by the juice of red cabbage, the property of which is to be rendered *red* by the presence of an acid, and *green* by that of an *alkali*.

The current thus established will, according to Sir H. Davy, decompose ᴜhe salt in the cup C. The acid will be transported through the two siphons, ᴜnd the water in B to the positive electrode in A, where it will be liberated, ᴜnd will enter into solution with the tinged water. At the same time the ᴜlkali will pass through the two siphons, and the cup D to the negative ᴇctrode, and will enter into solution with the water in D.

The presence of the acid in A and of the alkali in E will be rendered ᴍanifest by the red colour imparted to the contents of the former, and the ᴇeen to the latter.

416. While being transferred they are deprived of their ᴜemical property.—Although to arrive at A and E respectively ᴜe acid must pass through B and the alkali through E, their preᴜnce in these intermediate cups is not manifested by any change ᴇ colour. It was therefore inferred by Sir H. Davy, that so long ᴜs the constituents of the salt are under the immediate influence ᴜf the current, they lose their usual properties, and only recover ᴇem when dismissed at the electrodes by which they have been ᴇspectively attracted.

If the direction of the current be reversed, so that it shall enter ᴇ B and issue from A, the constituents of the salt will be transᴇrted back to the opposite ends of the series, the acid which had been deposited in A will be transferred successively through the cups B, C, D, and the intermediate siphons to the cup E, and the alkali in the contrary direction from E through D, C, B, and the siphons to A. This will be manifested by the changes of colour of the infusions. The liquid in A which had been reddened by the acid, will first recover its original colour, and then become green according as the ratio of the acid to the alkali in it is diminished; and in like manner the infusion in E, which had been rendered green by the alkali, will gradually recover its primitive colour, and then become red as the proportion of the acid to the alkali in it is augmented.

During these processes no change of colour will be observed in the intermediate cups B and D.

The intermediate cups B and D being filled with various chemical solutions for which the constituents of the salt had strong affinities, and with which under any ordinary circumstances they would immediately enter into combination, these constituents nevertheless invariably passed through the intermediate vessels without producing any discoverable effect upon their contents. Thus, sulphuric acid passed in this manner through solutions of ammonia, lime, potash, and soda, without affecting them. In like manner hydrochloric and nitric acids passed through concentrated alkaline menstrua without any chemical effect. In a word, acids and alkalis having the strongest mutual affinities, were thus reciprocally made to pass each through the other without manifesting any tendency to combination.

417. Exception in the case of producing insoluble compounds. — Strontia and baryta passed in the same way through muriatic and nitric acids, and reciprocally these acids passed with equal facility through solutions of strontia and baryta. But an exception was encountered when it was attempted to transmit strontia or baryta through a solution of sulphuric acid, or *vice versâ*. In this case the alkali was arrested *in transitu* by the acid, or the acid by the alkali, and the salt resulting from their combination was precipitated in the intermediate cup.

The exception therefore generalised, included those cases in which bodies were attempted to be transmitted through menstrua for which they have an affinity, and with which they would form an insoluble compound.

418. This transfer denied by Faraday. — This transmission of chemical substances through solutions with which they have affinities by the voltaic current, those affinities being rendered dormant by the influence of the current which appeared to be established by the researches of Davy, published in 1807, and since that period received by the whole scientific world as an established principle, has lately been affirmed by Dr. Faraday to be founded in error. According to Faraday no such transfer of the constituents of a body decomposed by the current can or does take place. He maintains that in all cases of electrolysation it is an absolutely indispensable condition that there be a continuous and unbroken series of particles of the electrolyte between the two electrodes at which its constituents are disengaged. Thus, when water is decomposed, there must be a continuous line of water between the positive electrode at which the oxygen is developed, and the negative electrode at which the hydrogen is disengaged. In like manner, when the sulphate of soda, or any other salt is decomposed, there must be a continuous line of particles of the salt between the positive electrode at which the acid appears, and the negative electrode at which the alkali is deposited.

Dr. Faraday affirms, that in Davy's celebrated experiments, in which the acid and alkaline constituents of the salt appear to be drawn through intermediate cups, containing pure water or solutions of substances foreign to the salt, the decomposition and apparent transfer of the constituents of the salt could not have commenced until, by capillary attraction, a portion of the salt had passed over through the siphons, so that a continuous line of saline particles was established between the electrodes. Dr. Faraday admits such a transfer of the constituents, as may be explained by the series of decompositions and recompositions involved in the hypothesis of Grotthus.

419. **Apparent transfer explained by him on Grotthus' hypothesis.** — It is also admitted by Dr. Faraday, that when pure water intervenes between the metallic conductors proceeding from the pile and the electrolyte, decomposition may ensue, but he considers that in this case the true electrodes are not the extremities of the metallic conductors, but the points where the pure water ends and the electrolyte begins, and that accordingly in such cases the constituents of the electrolyte will be disengaged, not at the surfaces of the metallic conductors, but at the common surfaces of the water and the electrolyte. As an example of this he produces the following experiment. Let a solution of the sulphate of magnesia be covered with pure water, care being taken to avoid all admixture of the water with the saline solution. Let a plate of platinum proceeding from the negative pole of a battery be immersed in the water, at some distance from the surface of the solution on which the water rests, and at the same time let the solution be put in metallic communication with the positive pole of the battery. The decomposition of the sulphate will speedily commence, but the magnesia, instead of being deposited on the platinum plate immersed in the water, will appear

at the common surface of the water and the solution. The water, therefore, and not the platinum, is in this case the negative electrode.

420. **Faraday thinks that conduction and decomposition are closely related.** — Dr. Faraday maintains that the connection between conduction and decomposition, so far as relates to liquids which are not metallic, is so constant that decomposition may be regarded as the chief means by which the electric current is transmitted through liquid compounds. Nevertheless, he admits, that when the intensity of a current is too feeble to effect decomposition, a quantity of electricity is transmitted sufficient to affect the reoscope.

In accordance with those principles, Faraday affirms that water which conducts the electric current in its liquid state, ceases to do so when it is congealed, and then it also resists decomposition, and in fine ceases to be an electrolyte. He holds that the same is true of all electrolytes.

421. **Maintains that non-metallic liquids only conduct when capable of decomposition by the current.** — The connection between decomposition and conduction is further manifested, according to Dr. Faraday, by the fact that liquids which do not admit of electro-chemical decomposition, do not give passage to the voltaic current. In short, that electrolytes are the only liquid non-metallic conductors.

422. **Faraday's doctrine not universally accepted — Pouillet's observations.** — These views of Dr. Faraday have not yet obtained general acceptation; nor have the discoveries of Davy of the transfer and decantation of the constituents of electrolytes through solutions foreign to them, been yet admitted to be overthrown. Peschel and other German authorities, in full possession of Faraday's views and the results of his experimental researches still continue to reproduce Davy's experiments, and to refer ᵗ their results and consequences as established facts. Pouillᵉ writing in 1847, and also in possession of Faraday's research which he largely quotes, maintains nevertheless the *transport* the constituents under conditions more extraordinary still, more incompatible with Faraday's doctrine than any imagine Davy. In electro-chemical decomposition he says, — " There once separation and transport. Numberless attempts have made to seize the molecule of water which is decomposed, arrest *en route* the atoms of the constituent gases before arrival at the electrodes, but without success. For exam two cups of water, one containing the positive and the otᵗ negative wire of a battery, be connected by any conduct gular phenomena will be observed. If the intermediate co ᵗetallic, decomposition will take place independently

cups" (as already described), "but if the intermediate conductor be the human body, as when a person dips a finger of one hand into the water in one cup, and a finger of the other hand into the other, the decomposition will sometimes proceed as in the case of a metallic connection; but more generally oxygen will be disengaged at the wire which enters the positive cup, and hydrogen at the wire which enters the negative cup, no gases appearing at the fingers immersed in the one and the other. It would thus appear that one or other of the constituent gases must pass through the body of the operator, in order to arrive at the pole at which it is disengaged. And even when the two cups are connected by a piece of ice, the decomposition proceeds in the same manner, one or other gas appearing to pass through the ice, since they are disengaged at the poles in the separate cups in the same manner." [*]

423. **Davy's experiments repeated and confirmed by Becquerel.** — The experiments of Davy, in which the transfer of the constituents of an electrolyte through water and through solutions for which these constituents have affinities, was demonstrated, have been repeated by Becquerel, who has obtained the same results. The capillary siphons used by Becquerel were glass tubes filled with moistened clay. He also found that the case in which the constituent transferred would form an insoluble compound with the matter forming the intermediate solution, forms an exception to this principle of transfer; but he observed that this only happens when the intensity of the current is insufficient to decompose the compound thus formed in the intermediate solution.[†]

424. **The electrodes proved to exercise different electrolytic powers by Pouillet.** — The question whether the decomposing agency resides altogether at one or at the other electrode, or is shared between them, has been recently investigated by M. Pouillet.

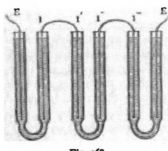

Fig. 268.

Let three tubes of glass having the form of the letter U, *fig.* 268., be prepared, each of the vertical arms being about five inches long, and half an inch in diameter. Let the curved part of the tubes connecting the legs have a diameter of about the twentieth of an inch when the solutions used are good conductors, but the same diameter as the tubes themselves when the

[*] Pouillet, "Elements de Physique," ed. 1847, vol. i. p. 598.
[†] Becquerel, "Traité de Physique," vol. ii. p. 330., ed. 1844.

conducting power is more imperfect. In this latter case, however, the results are less exact and satisfactory.

Let platinum wire E and E′ proceeding from the poles of a
voltaic battery be plunged in the first and last tubes, and let the
intermediate tubes be connected by similar wires I I′ and I″ I‴.
Let acidulated water be poured into the tube E I, and the solutions on which the relative effects of the two electrodes are to be
examined, into the other tubes I I″ and I‴ E′. After the electrolysis has been continued for a certain time, the quantity of the
solution decomposed in each leg may be ascertained by submitting
the contents of each leg to analysis. The quantity remaining un-
decomposed being thus ascertained and subtracted from the
original quantity, the remainder will be the quantity decomposed,
since the fluids are prevented from intermixing to any sensible
extent by the smallness of the connecting tube, and by being
nearly at the same level during the process. It may be assumed
that the decomposing agencies of the two electrodes, will be proportional to the quantities of the solutions decomposed in the legs
in which they are respectively immersed.

425. Case in which the negative electrode alone acts. —
The current being first transmitted ·through a voltameter to indicate the actual quantity of electricity transmitted, the tubes E I,
I′ I″ and I‴ E′ were filled, the first with a solution of the chloride
of gold, the next with the chloride of copper, and the third with
the chloride of zinc. After the lapse of a certain interval the
contents of the tubes were severally examined, and it was found
that the solutions in legs in which the positive electrodes were
immersed had suffered no decomposition. The quantities of the
chlorides contained in them respectively were undiminished,
while the chloride in each of the legs containing the negative
electrodes was diminished by exactly the quantity corresponding
to the metal deposited in the negative wire, and the chlorine
transferred to the positive leg.

It was therefore inferred that in these cases the entire decomposing agency must be ascribed to the negative electrode.

The same results were obtained for the other metallic chlorides.

426. Cases in which the electrodes act unequally. — The
alkaline chlorides showed somewhat different properties. In the
case of the chloride of magnesium the agency of the negative was
found to be greater than that of the positive electrode, but it was
not exclusively efficacious. In the cases of the chlorides of potassium, sodium, barium, &c., the agency was also shared by the true
electrodes, but the agency of the positive electrode was found to
be greater than the negative in the ratio of about three to one.

427. Liquid electrodes. — Series of electrolytes in imme-

diate contact. — In general, the electrodes by which the current enters and departs from an electrolyte, are solid and most frequently metallic conductors. In an experiment already cited (419.), Faraday has shown that water may become an electrode, and Pouillet in some recent experiments has succeeded in generalising this result, and has shown not only that the current may be transmitted to and received from an electrolyte by liquid conductors, but that a series of different electrolytes may become mutual electrodes, the current passing immediately from one to the other without any intermediate conductor, solid or liquid, and that each of them shall be electrolysed. Thus, suppose that the series of electrolytes are expressed by

$$\gg\!\!\!\rightarrow \quad \text{A} \quad \text{B} \quad \text{C} \quad \text{D} \quad \gg\!\!\!\rightarrow$$
$$a\,a' \quad b\,b' \quad c\,c' \quad d\,d'$$

the current as indicated by the arrows entering A, and departing from D, and being supposed to have sufficient intensity to effect the electrolysis of all the solutions. Let the electro-negative constituents be expressed by a, b, c, d, and the electro-positive by a', b', c', d'. It is evident that the points at which any two succeeding solutions touch, will be at the same time the negative electrode of the first, and the positive electrode of the second, and that, consequently, the positive constituent of the first and the negative constituent of the second will be disengaged at this point, and being in the nascent state will be under the most favourable conditions to combine in virtue of their affinities, and so to form new compounds as secondary effects. Thus, the common surface of A and B will be the negative electrode of A, and the positive electrode of B, because it is at this surface that the current departs from A and enters B, and accordingly the electro-positive constituent a' of A, and the electro-negative constituent b of B, will be developed at this common surface, and if they have affinity, will enter into combination.

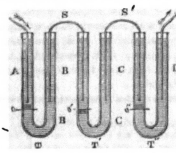

Fig. 269.

428. Experimental illustration of this. — These principles may be experimentally illustrated and verified by placing the electrolytic solutions in U-shaped tubes T, T', T'', as represented in *fig.* 269.

Let two electrolytic solutions A and B be introduced into the first tube T, so carefully as to prevent them from intermixing, and let their common surface be at o. In like manner let the solutions B and C be introduced into the tube T′, and the solutions C and D into the tube T″, their common surfaces being at o′ and o″. Let the legs of the tubes T and T′, which contain the solution B, be connected by a glass siphon containing the same solution, and the legs of the tubes T′ and T″, containing the solution C, be similarly connected. Let the positive wire of a battery be immersed in A, and the negative wire in D, the current being sufficiently intense to electrolyse all the solutions.*

In this case o will be the positive electrode of B, and the negative electrode of A; o′ the positive electrode of C, and the negative electrode of B; and o″ the positive electrode of D, and the negative electrode of C.

If A be pure water, B the chloride of zinc, the water being decomposed, oxygen will be disengaged at the positive wire, and hydrogen at the common surface o. The chloride being also decomposed, the chlorine, its electro-negative constituent, will be disengaged at o, where it will enter into combination with the hydrogen, and form hydrochloric acid, the presence of which may be ascertained by the usual tests. The oxide of zinc, the electro-positive constituent of B, will be disengaged at o′, and will form a compound with the electro-negative constituent of C, and so on.

429. Electrolysis of the alkalis and earths.—The decomposing power of the voltaic current had not long been known before it became, in the hands of Sir H. Davy and his successors, the means of resolving the alkalis and earths, before that time considered as simple bodies, into their constituents. This class of bodies was shown to be oxidised metals. When submitted to such conditions as enabled a strong voltaic current to pass through them, oxygen was liberated at the positive electrode, and the metallic base appeared at the negative electrode.

430. The series of new metals.— A new series of metals was thus discovered, which received names derived from those of the alkalis and earths of which they formed the bases. Thus, the metallic base of potash was called *potassium*, that of soda, *sodium*, that of lime, *calcium*, that of silica, *silicium*, and so on.

In many cases it is difficult to maintain those metals in their simple state, owing to their strong affinity for oxygen. Thus potassium, if exposed to the atmosphere at common temperatures, enters directly into combination with the air, and burns. When it is desired to collect and preserve it in the metallic state it is decomposed by the current in contact with mercury, with which it enters into combination, forming an amalgam. It is afterwards separated by distillation from the mercury, and preserved in the metallic state under the oil of naphtha, in a glass tube hermetically closed, the air being previously expelled.

431. Schœnbein's experiments on the passivity of iron.

---

* This is not the experimental arrangement adopted by M. Pouillet. It has occurred to me, as a method of exhibiting his principle under a more general form and somewhat more clearly and satisfactorily than his apparatus, in which the siphons S, S′ have no place.

—Among the effects of the voltaic current which have been not satisfactorily or not at all explained, are those by which iron, under certain conditions, is enabled to resist oxidation even when exposed to agents of the greatest power ; such, for example, as nitric acid. The most remarkable researches on this subject are those of Schœnbein. In his experiments, the wires proceeding from the poles of the battery were immersed in two mercurial cups, which we shall call P and N. A bath of water B, acidulated with about 8 per cent. of sulphuric acid, was then connected with the cup N by a platinum wire. A piece of iron wire was placed with one extremity in P, and the other in the bath B. No oxidation was manifested at the end immersed in the bath, and no hydrogen was evolved at the platinum wire. In fine, no electrolysis took place.

Several circumstances were found to restore to the iron its oxidable property, and to establish the electrolysis of the liquid in the bath, but only for a short interval of a few seconds. These circumstances were : — 1. The contact for a moment of the platinum and iron wires in the bath. 2. The momentary suspension of the current by breaking the contact at any point of the circuit. 3. The contact of any oxidable metal, such as zinc, tin, copper, or silver, with the iron in the bath. 4. The momentary diversion of a portion of the current, by connecting the cups P and N by a copper wire, without breaking the connections of the original circuit. 5. By agitating the end of the iron wire in the bath.

If in connecting B and P by the iron wire the wire be first immersed in B, oxidation will take place for some seconds after the other acid is immersed in P.

The intensity of the current diverted by connecting the cups P and N by a copper wire, can be varied at pleasure by varying the length and section of the connecting wire (375.). When such a derived current is established, several curious and interesting phenomena are observed. When the derived current has great intensity, no effect is produced upon the iron. Upon gradually diminishing the intensity of the derived current, the iron becomes *active*, that is, susceptible of oxidation. With a less intensity it again becomes *passive*, and the oxidation ceases. As the derived current is gradually reduced to that intensity at which the iron becomes permanently *passive*, there are several successive periods during which it is alternately *active* and *passive*, the intervals between these periods being less and less. In the apparatus of Schœnbein the iron became permanently active when the copper wire conducting the derived current was half a line thick, and from 6 inches to 16 feet long.

These effects are reproduced with all the oxacids, but are not manifested either with the hydracids or the Haloid salts.

432. **Other methods of rendering iron passive.** — Iron may be rendered passive also by placing it as the positive electrode in a solution of acetate of lead with a current of ordinary intensity. The iron should be immersed in the solution for about half a minute to a depth of about half an inch. A wire thus treated, being washed clean, acquires the permanently passive property, even though the part immersed in the solution has not been coated with the peroxide of lead. And in this case the conditions above stated, under which it recovers momentarily its active character, become inoperative.

Iron thus *galvanised* acquires to a great degree the virtue of platinum and the other highly negative metals, and for many purposes may be substituted for them. Thus Schœnbein has constructed voltaic batteries of passive iron and zinc.

The iron wire used for telegraphic purposes is rendered passive by this process.

433. **Tree of Saturn.** — The well known experiment of the *Tree of Saturn* presents a remarkable example of the effect of a feeble current of long continuance. A bundle of brass wires is passed through a hole made longitudinally through the centre of a bottle cork, and fitted tightly in it so as to diverge in a sort of cone from the bottom of the cork. A plate of zinc is then tied round the wires at the point where they diverge from the cork, so as to be in contact with all the wires. The wires and cork are then introduced into a glass flask containing a limpid solution of the acetate of lead, and the top of the cork luted over to prevent the admission of air. The zinc and brass thus immersed in the solution form a voltaic pair, and a current passes through the solution from the zinc to the wire. The water of the solution is slowly decomposed, the oxygen combining with the zinc, and the hydrogen attracting the oxygen from the oxide of lead, and reproducing water, while the metallic lead attaches itself to the wires. The acetic acid, liberated by the secondary decomposition of the acetate of lead, enters into combination with the oxide of zinc, and produces the acetate of that metal, which passes into solution in the water. The contents of the flask are gradually converted into a solution of the acetate of zinc, and the metallic lead, the process being very slow, is crystallised in a variety of beautiful forms upon the divergent brass wire.

434. **Davy's method of preserving the copper sheathing of ships.** — The method proposed by Sir H. Davy to preserve from corrosion the copper sheathing of ships, depends on the long-continued action of feeble currents. The copper is united with a

mass of zinc, iron, or some more oxidable metal, so as to form a voltaic combination. The sea water being a weak solution of salt, a feeble permanent current is established between the more and less oxidable metals, passing through the water from the latter to the former, and causing its slow decomposition. The oxygen combines with the protecting metal, and the hydrogen disengaged on the copper, decomposes the salts held in solution in the sea water, attracting their oxide constituents, such as lime, magnesia, &c., which are deposited upon the copper in a rough crust. Upon the coating thus formed collect marine vegetation, shells, and other substances. Thus, while the copper sheathing is preserved from corrosion, there arises the counteracting circumstance of an appendage to the hull of the ship, which impedes its sailing qualities.

435. **Chemical effects produced in voltaic batteries.** — The fluids interposed between the solid elements of all forms of voltaic arrangements may be regarded as electrolytes, the solid elements in contact with them being the electrodes. In all arrangements in which one acid solution is interposed between two solids, one of which is more oxidable than the other, the primary chemical effect is the decomposition of the water of the solution, the oxygen being disengaged upon the more, and the hydrogen upon the less, oxidable metal. The partisans of the chemical origin of the current contend, that in this case the oxygen gives up its negative electricity to the more oxidable, and the hydrogen its positive to the less oxidable metal, so that if those metals be connected by a metallic wire outside the system, a current will be established on the wire, directed from the less to the more oxidable metal, which is found to be in effect what actually takes place.

The secondary effects are very various and complicated, and are in accordance with the principles of electrolytic action already explained. The first is the production of an oxide of the more oxidable metal. If the liquid element be an acid solution, this oxide will, in general, enter into combination with the acid, forming a salt which will be the next secondary effect. The hydrogen evolved against the less oxidable metal, may either be liberated in the gaseous state, or attract an equivalent of oxygen from one of the substances dissolved in the liquid element, thereby reproducing water, and decomposing the substances thus attacked.

436. **Effect of amalgamating the zinc.** — The advantage which attends the amalgamation of the zinc (174.), in batteries in which that metal is used, is, that it is thus protected from the direct action of the acid by which the metal would be consumed, without contributing to the supply of the current. Zinc, being a metal eminently susceptible of oxidation, would be affected by the acid

even in the weakest solutions, and a portion of the metal, more or less according to the strength of the solution, would be oxidated, a corresponding quantity of the acid being decomposed. This would produce the twofold inconvenience of the ineffectual consumption of both the metal and the acid. By the process of amalgamation the surface of the zinc is coated with a thin stratum of amalgam, which is proof against the acid, and which, on the other hand, increases the susceptibility of the metal to combine with the oxygen disengaged from the water by the current.

437. **Effects in Smee's battery.**—The preceding observations are more or less applicable to all the single fluid arrangements described in (171.) to (175.), as well as to Smee's system (182.). It has been found that the intensity of the current in the system of Smee, has been greatly augmented by *platinisation* of the surface of the metal used as the negative pole of the system. The process by which this effect is produced is as follows. The surface of the metal being scraped quite clean, it is immersed in a solution of the double chloride of potassium and platinum, and being connected with the negative pole of a battery, of which the positive pole is connected with the solution by a plate of platinum immersed in it, electrolysation takes place, platinum being deposited on the negative electrode as a secondary result. The positive platinum electrode is meanwhile attacked by the chlorine, and dissolved so as to maintain the solution in the proper state of saturation.

Mr. Smee, after trying plates of iron and silver, substituted for them plates of platinum, the surface of which was platinised by this process, and an improved action ensued. M. Bouquillon substituted for them a plate of copper, upon the surface of which a rough coating of copper was first deposited by a similar process, and upon this a coating of silver, over which a coating of platinum was deposited. By this means the plate is stated to have acquired in the highest degree the power of liberating the hydrogen, and stimulating the current.

438. **In Wheatstone's battery.** — In the system of Wheatstone (183.), in which a single fluid, a saturated solution of sulphate of copper, is used as the exciting fluid, the water of the solution is electrolysed. The oxygen combines with the zinc of the amalgam, and forms as a secondary result an oxide. The hydrogen disengaged upon the copper acts upon the sulphate, whose constituents are sulphuric acid and the protoxide of copper. It attracts the oxygen from the protoxide, with which it combines, forming water. The metallic copper and the acid are both liberated, the latter entering into combination with the oxide of zinc, and forming the sulphate of that oxide. For each equivalent of

zinc oxidated, there is therefore an equivalent of metallic copper, and an equivalent of the sulphate of the oxide of zinc produced.

439. **In the two fluid batteries.** — In batteries in which two fluids separated by a porous diaphragm are interposed between the solid elements, chemical effects somewhat more complicated are exhibited, and indeed authorities are not in accordance as to the principles on which the phenomena are explicable.

440. **Grove's battery.**—In the case of Grove's battery (177.), the primary phenomenon is the decomposition of the water of the two solutions which is effected through the cylinder of porous porcelain, the oxygen being disengaged upon the zinc, and the hydrogen upon the platinum. The secondary effects are—1. The oxidation of the zinc. 2. The combination of the oxide with the acid, producing sulphate of zinc, which is deposited in the acid solution. 3. The combination of the hydrogen with one equivalent of the oxygen of the nitric acid, by which water is reproduced, and the *nitric* reduced to *nitrous* acid, which is evolved in the gaseous state.

441. **Bunsen's battery.**—The same phenomena are manifested in the battery of Bunsen (178.), which differs from that of Grove only in the substitution of the carbon for the platinum element.

442. **Daniel's battery.** — The theory of the chemical phenomena developed in the operation of Daniel's constant battery (179.), has not been clearly determined. During the performance of the apparatus metallic copper is deposited on the copper cylinder c c, *fig.* 120., which contains the solution of the sulphate of copper. The solution itself would become gradually less concentrated, but it is maintained in a state of saturation by the continual dissolution of the salt, which rests upon the wire grating ʊ, and the sulphate of the oxide of zinc accumulates in the cylinder *p p*. The fluid in this vessel *p p*, which is at the beginning a weak solution of sulphuric acid, is gradually converted into a solution of the sulphate of zinc, which is stated by Pfaff, Paggendorf, and others to be nearly as effective as an exciting fluid as the original acid solution. The electro-motive virtue of the zinc in this case is therefore but little, and that of the copper not at all, impaired by the continued action of the battery.

The chemical changes which are effected in this battery may be explained as follows :—A double electrolysis may be imagined as a primary effect, that of the water contained in the two solutions, the electrolytic action being transmitted through the intermediate porous cylinder and that of the sulphate, the acid constituent being transmitted to the zinc through the porous cylinder and through the solution contained in it, in the same manner as the constituents of the electrolyte in Davy's experiments (415.),

were transmitted through the capillary siphons and the intermediate solutions.   The secondary phenomena would be as follows:
—The hydrogen of the decomposed water developed on the copper
in a nascent state, would attract the oxygen of the oxide of
copper also developed on the copper in a nascent state by the
decomposition of the salt.   Water would thus be reproduced in a
quantity equal to that lost by decomposition, and the metallic
copper of the oxide would be deposited on the copper cylinder.
The solution of the sulphate being reduced below saturation by
the amount of the salt thus decomposed, an equal quantity would
be received by dissolution from the salt in G, which would restore
it to the state of saturation.   Meanwhile the acid constituent of
the salt would be transferred to the zinc, where it would combine
with the oxide of that metal formed by its combination with the
oxygen of the decomposed water developed upon it, and the sulphate of the oxide would be formed, which would be dissolved in
the solution, leaving the amalgamated zinc free to the further
operation of the current.

This interpretation of the phenomena cannot be admitted by
those who, with Dr. Faraday, reject the principle of the transfer
of an electrolyte through a menstruum foreign to it, unless indeed
it be assumed that some small portions of the sulphate must pass
through the porous cylinder, and mix with the acid solution.

However this may be, we are not aware that any other satisfactory explanation has been proposed for the phenomena developed in this battery.

CHAP. XIV.

ELECTRO-METALLURGY.

443. Origin of this art. — The decomposing power of the voltaic
current applied to solutions of the salts and oxides of metals has
supplied various processes to the industrial arts, which inventors,
improvers, and manufacturers have denominated galvano-plastic,
electro-plastic, galvano-type, electrotype, and electro-plating and
gilding.   These processes and their results may be comprehended
under the more general denomination, *Electro-metallurgy.*

**444. The metallic constituent deposited on the negative
electrode.** — If a current of sufficient intensity be transmitted
through a solution of a salt or oxide, having a metallic base, it
will be understood, from what has been already explained, that

while the oxygen or acid is developed at the positive electrode, the metal will be evolved either by the primary or secondary action of the current of the negative electrode, and being in the nascent state, will have a tendency to combine with it, if there be an affinity, or to adhere to it by mere cohesion, if not.

445. Any body may be used as the negative electrode. — The bodies used as electrodes must be *superficially* conductors, since otherwise the current could not pass between them; but subject to this condition, they may have any material form or magnitude which is compatible with their immersion in the solution. If the body be metallic, its surface has necessarily the conducting property. If it be formed of a material which is a non-conductor, or an imperfect conductor, the power of conduction may be imparted to its surface by coating it with finely powdered black lead and other similar expedients. This process is called *metallising* the surface.

446. Use of a soluble positive electrode. — By the continuance of the process of decomposition the solution will be rendered gradually weaker, and the deposition of the metal would go on more slowly. This inconvenience is remedied by using, as the positive electrode, a plate of the same metal, which is to be deposited on the negative electrode. The acid or oxygen liberated in the decomposition, in this case, enters into combination with the metal of the positive electrode, and produces as much salt or oxide as is decomposed at the other electrode, which salt or oxide being dissolved as fast as it is formed, maintains the solution at a nearly uniform degree of strength.

447. Conditions which affect the state of the metal deposited. — The state of the metal disengaged at the negative electrode depends on the intensity of the current, the strength of the solution, its acidity, and its temperature, and the regulation of these conditions in each particular case will require much practical skill on the part of the operator, since few general rules can be given for his direction.

In the case, for example, of a solution of one of the salts of copper, a feeble current will deposit on the electrode a coating of copper so malleable that it may be cut with a knife. With a more intense current the metal will become harder. As the intensity of the current is gradually augmented, it becomes successively brittle, granulous, crystalline, rough, pulverulent, and in fine loses all cohesion, — practice alone will enable the operator to observe the conditions necessary to give the coating deposited on the electrode the desired quality.

448. The deposit to be of uniform thickness. — It is in all cases desirable, and in many indispensable, that the metallic coating deposited on the electrode shall have an uniform thickness. To insure this, conditions should be established which will render the action of the current on every part of the surface of the electrode uniform, so that the same quantity of metal may be deposited in the same time. Many precautions are necessary to attain this object. Both electrodes should be connected at several points with the conductors, which go to the poles of the battery, and they should be presented to each other so that the intermediate spaces should be as nearly as possible equal, since the intensities of the currents between point and point vary with the distance. The deposition of the metal is also much influenced by the form of the body. It is in general more freely made on the salient and projecting parts, than in those which are sunk.

449. **Means to prevent absorption of the solution by the electrode.** — If the body on which the metallic deposit is made be one which is liable to absorb the solution, a coating of some substance must be previously given to it which shall be impervious to the solution.

450. **Nonconducting coating used where partial deposit is required.** —When a part only of a metallic or other conducting body is desired to be coated with the metallic deposit, all the parts immersed not intended to be so coated are protected by a coating of wax, tallow, or other nonconductor.

451. **Application of these principles to gilding, silvering, &c.** — The most extensive and useful application of these principles in the arts is the process of gilding and silvering articles made of the baser metals. The article to be coated with gold being previously made clean, is connected with the negative pole of the battery, while a plate of gold is connected with its positive pole. Both are then immersed in a bath consisting of a solution of the chloride of gold and cyanide of potassium, in proportions which vary with different gilders. Practice varies also as to the temperature and the strength of the solution. The chloride is decomposed, the metallic base being deposited as a coating on the article connected with the negative pole, and the chloride combining with a corresponding portion of the gold connected with the positive pole, and reproducing the chloride which is dissolved in the bath as fast as it is decomposed, thus maintaining the strength of the solution.

A coating of silver, copper, cobalt, nickel, and other metals is deposited by similar processes.

452. **Cases in which the coating is inadhesive.** — When the article on which the coating is deposited is metallic, the coating will in some cases adhere with great tenacity. In others, the result is less satisfactory ; as, for example, where gold is deposited

on iron or steel. In such cases the difficulty may be surmounted by first coating the article with a metal which will adhere to it, and then depositing upon this the definite coating.

453. Application to gilding, silvering, or bronzing objects of art. — The extreme tenuity with which a metallic coating may be deposited by such processes, supplies the means of imparting to various objects of art the external appearance and qualities of any proposed metal, without impairing in the slightest degree their most delicate forms and lineaments. The most exquisitely moulded statuette in plaster may thus acquire all the appearance of having been executed in gold, silver, copper, or bronze, without losing any of the artistic details on which its beauty depends.

454. Production of metallic moulds of articles. — If it be desired to produce a metallic mould of any object, it is generally necessary to mould it in separate pieces, which being afterwards combined, a mould of the whole is obtained. That part intended to be moulded is first rubbed with sweet oil, black lead, or some other lubricant, which will prevent the metal deposited from adhering to it, without separating the mould from the surface, in so sensible a degree as to prevent the perfect correspondence of the mould with the original. All that part not intended to be moulded is invested with wax or other material, to intercept the solution. The object being then immersed, and the electrolysis established, the metal will be deposited on the exposed surface. When it has attained a sufficient thickness the object is withdrawn from the solution, and the metallic deposit detached. It will be found to exhibit, with the utmost possible precision, an impression of the original. The same process being repeated for each part of the object, and the partial moulds thus obtained being combined, a metallic mould of the whole will be produced.

455. Production of objects in solid metal.—To reproduce any object in metal it is only necessary to fill the mould of it, obtained by the process above explained, with the solution of the metal of which it is desired to form the object, the surface of the mould being previously prepared, so as to prevent adhesion. The solution is then put in connection with the positive pole of the pile, while the mould is put in connection with the negative pole. The metal is deposited on the mould, and when it has attained the necessary thickness the mould is detached, and the object is obtained.

In general, however, it is found more convenient to mould the object to be reproduced in metal by the ordinary processes in wax, plaster of paris, or fusible alloy. When they are made in wax, plaster, or any nonconducting material, their inner surfaces must be rubbed with black lead, to give them the conducting

8

power.   When the deposit is made of the necessary thickness, the mould is broken off or otherwise detached.

Statues, statuettes, and bas-reliefs in plaster can thus be reproduced in metal with the greatest facility and precision, at an expense not much exceeding that of the metal of which they are formed.

456. **Reproduction of stereotypes and engraved plates.**— A mould in plaster of paris, wax, or gutta percha, being taken from a wood engraving and a stereotype plate, a stereotype may be obtained from the mould by the processes above described. The pages now before the reader have been stereotyped by this process.

Copper or steel engraved plates may be multiplied by like methods.   A mould is first taken, which exhibits the engraving in relief.   A metallic plate deposited upon this by the electrolytic process will reproduce the engraved plate.

457. **Metallising textile fabrics.**—The electro-metallurgic processes have been extended by ingenious contrivances to other substances besides metal.   Thus a coating of metal may be deposited on cloth, lace, or other woven fabrics, by various ingenious expedients, of which the following is an example :—On a plate of copper attach smoothly a cloth of linen, cotton, or wool, and then connect the plate with a negative pole of a voltaic battery, immerse it in a solution of the metal with which it is to be coated, and connect a piece of the same metal with the positive pole ; decomposition will then commence, and the molecules of metal, as they are separated from the solution, must pass through the cloth in advancing to the copper to which the cloth is attached.   In their passage through the cloth they are more or less arrested by it.   They insinuate themselves into its pores, and, in fine, form a complete metallic cloth.   Lace is metallised in this way by first coating it with plumbago, and then subjecting it to the electro-metallurgic process.

Quills, feathers, flowers, and other delicate fibrous substances may be metallised in the same way.   In the case of the most delicate of these the article is first dipped into a solution of phosphorus and sulphate of carbon, and is well wetted with the liquid. It is then immersed in a solution of nitrate of silver.   Phosphorus has the property of reviving silver and gold from their solutions. Consequently, the article is immediately coated with a very attenuated fibre of the metal.

458. **Glyphography.**—If a thin stratum of wax or other soft substance be spread upon a plate of metal, any subject or design may be engraved upon the coating without more labour than would be expended on a pencil drawing.   When the engraving is

thus made on the wax it is subjected to the electrotype process, by which a sheet of copper or other metal is deposited upon it. When this is detached it exhibits in relief the engraving, from which impressions may be produced in the same manner as from a wood engraving, to which it is altogether analogous.

459. **Reproduction of daguerreotypes.** — One of the most remarkable and unexpected applications of the electrotype process is to daguerreotypes. The picture being taken upon the plate by the usual process of daguerreotype, a small part of the back is cleaned with sand paper, taking care not to allow the face of the plate to be touched. A piece of wire is then soldered to the part of the back thus prepared. The plate is then immersed in a solution of copper, and connected with the battery, the back being protected by a coating of wax. After a deposit of sufficient depth has been made upon the face of the plate, it is withdrawn from the solution, and the plate of copper deposited being detached, exhibits the picture with an expression softer and finer than the original. By this process, when conducted with skill, several copies may be taken from the same daguerreotype.

If the electrotype copy thus obtained be passed through a weak solution of the cyanide of gold and potassium, in connection with a weak battery, a beautiful golden tint will be imparted to the picture, which serves to protect it from being tarnished.

460. **Galvano-plastic apparatus.** — Having thus explained, generally, the principles upon which the galvano-plastic processes are conducted, and the principal expedients by which they are applied in the arts, we shall show the forms given in practice to the apparatus by which the effects described above are produced.

One of the most simple forms consists of a cistern filled with a saturated solution of the sulphate of copper. Two brass rods, communicating one with the positive and the other with the negative pole of a voltaic battery, are placed upon it, from which the mould, which has been previously prepared, is suspended. A plate of pure copper being suspended from the other rod and also immersed in the solution, the decomposition of the sulphate of copper commences the moment the current is established. Its acid and oxygen constituents are attracted to the positive electrode, while the pure copper is deposited on the negative electrode, which is in this case the mould. Several moulds may be suspended from the same rod, and the process will go on simultaneously with all of them. After the lapse of about forty-eight hours, the moulds will be found covered with a solid and compact stratum of copper, the adhesion of which to the mould will be prevented by the means already explained.

The best moulds are those of gutta percha. To make them, the medal or other object to be reproduced is first covered with plumbago, which will prevent its adherence to the gutta percha. The gutta percha being then softened by heating it in warm water, it is applied with a gentle pressure upon the object to be reproduced. After being left to cool and harden, it is detached from the object, of which it will retain a perfect impression. The gutta percha mould thus produced being coated with plumbago to give it the conducting power, it is suspended in the solution, and connected with the negative pole of the battery.

The plate of copper c, which serves as the negative electrode, also maintains the solution at the point of saturation; for the acid and oxygen, which are disengaged in contact with it, enter into combination immediately with the copper, producing the sulphate of that metal, which is dissolved in the solution, replacing that which it has lost by decomposition.

461. **Simple galvano-plastic apparatus.**—A form of apparatus commonly used is represented in *fig.* 271., where A is a

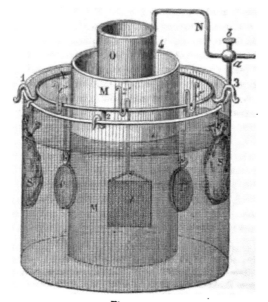

Fig. 271.

brass rod, supported by hooks 1, 2, 3, 4, on the edge of a large cylindrical vessel of glass or porcelain. One of these hooks, 3, supports a vertical rod *a*, on which there is a metallic ball pierced horizontally, in which a conducting rod N is held by the tightening screw *b*.

Supposing the deposit required is copper, the solution of the sulphate of copper is poured into the vessel. In this vessel is immersed a smaller cylindrical vessel M N of unglazed porcelain filled with acidulated water, in which a cylinder o of amalgamated zinc connected with N is plunged.

Let small bags s s, filled with crystals of the sulphate of copper, be suspended upon the edge of the vessel and immersed in the solution, so that as

ion is weakened by decomposition, these crystals shall be dissolved
ore its strength.

ie objects P V T, &c., upon which the copper is to be deposited, be
ended upon the ring A by metallic rods: a complete voltaic combi-
ill thus be formed, since the copper electrodes P V T, &c., will be
llic connection by the ring A, the rod a, and the conductor N,
; zinc cylinder O; so that the whole will form a single pair on
system (179.). This being done, the decomposition of the solution
ceed, copper will be deposited upon P V T, &c., and the strength
olution will be restored by the dissolution of the copper crystals
gs s s.

Spenser's simple apparatus. — A bladder cover D,
:., is tied upon one of the mouths of a cylindrical glass
b, open at top and bottom, so as to form a diaphragm.

ietallic solution being poured into the cylindrical vessel C, R is plunged
h the end covered by the bladder downwards, and is then partially
th acidulated water. This vessel is supported by a brass ring H H
on the edge of the vessel C, to which the conductors E and F are
, one E being connected with a disc of zinc A immersed in the
id water in R, and the other with a similar disc of copper B immersed
lution in C.

pparatus acts upon the same principle as that described above.

Fau's simple apparatus. — This does not differ much
ose above described.

linder C, *fig.* 273., is filled with acidulated water; a smaller cylinder

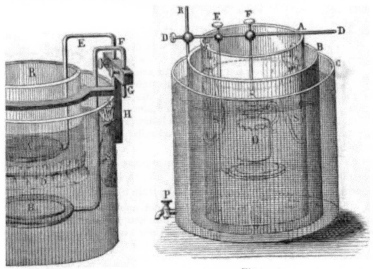

Fig. 272.   Fig. 273.

: is immersed in it. In this latter cylinder B, a still smaller cylinder
zed porcelain A is contained, and the latter is filled with the metallic

solution. The conducting rod D D, in contact with the zinc B, by the rod B, communicates with the object O to be metallised by means of the rods E F. The sacks s s filled with crystals of the sulphate are immersed in the metallic solution as before.

464. **Brandely's simple apparatus.** — In this apparatus the metallic bath is contained in a large cistern of glazed earthenware O, *fig.* 274.

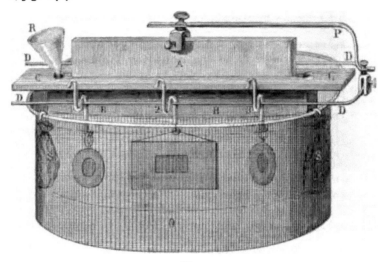

Fig. 274.

A sack made of goldbeaters' skin serving as a diaphragm is nailed to the edge of a long slit made in a beam of wood C C, which rests upon the edge of the cistern O. This sack B B is filled with acidulated water, in which a plate of zinc A is immersed. This zinc is connected by the metallic ribbon P and the rod D D, and the hooks 1, 2, 3, with the objects to be metallised, which are suspended in the metallic bath contained in the cistern O. The strength of this solution is maintained as before by bags of the salt s s suspended in it. The action is in all respects similar to that of those already described.

465. **Compound galvano-plastic apparatus.** — In the arrangements above described, the metallic bath in which the process is conducted constitutes a part of the voltaic apparatus.

In other arrangements, called the compound apparatus, the battery is placed outside and apart from the metallic bath, and may be at any distance from it, or even in another room. Such a compound apparatus is represented in *fig.* 275., where B is the metallic bath, and R the pile. Two metallic rods 1 and 2 communicate with the positive and negative poles of the pile. On the negative rod 2 are suspended the objects to be metallised, and on the positive rod 1 a plate A of the metal which is contained in the solution.

The circuit being closed, the metal decomposed in the solution by the current is deposited upon the objects C D to be metallised, while a corresponding portion of the metal of the plate A combining with the acid enters into the solution, and maintains its strength; an object which is further accomplished by the bags of crystals s s.

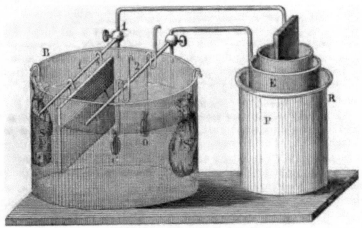

Fig. 275.

In the simple apparatus the continued efficiency is more or less impeded, by the transmission of the two liquid solutions by endosmose through the porous diaphragm. This is avoided in the compound apparatus just described, and others of similar arrangement.

CHAP. XV.

ELECTRO-TELEGRAPHY.

466. **Common principle of all electric telegraphs.** — Of all the applications of electric agency to the uses of life, that which is transcendently the most admirable in its effects, and the most important in its consequences, is the electric telegraph. No force of habit, however long continued, no degree of familiarity, can efface the sense of wonder which the effects of this most marvellous application of science excite.

The electric telegraph, whatever form it may assume, derives its efficiency from the three following conditions : —

1. A power to develop the electric fluid continuously, and in the necessary quantity.

2. A power to convey it to any required distance without being injuriously dissipated.

3. A power to cause it, after arriving at such distant point, to make written or printed characters, or some sensible signs serving the purpose of such characters.

The apparatus from which the moving power by which these effects are produced is derived, is the voltaic pile. This is to the electric telegraph what a boiler is to a steam engine. It is the generator of the fluid by which the action of the machine is produced and maintained.

We have therefore first to explain how the electric fluid generated in the apparatus just explained, can be transmitted to a distance without being wasted or dissipated in an injurious degree *en route*.

If tubes or pipes could be constructed with sufficient facility and cheapness, through which the subtle fluid could flow, and which would be capable of confining it during its transit, this object would be attained. As the galvanic battery is analogous to the boiler, such tubes would be analogous in their form and functions to the steam pipe of a steam engine.

467. **Conducting wires.** — If a wire, coated with a nonconducting substance capable of resisting the vicissitudes of weather, were extended between any two distant points, one end of it being attached to one of the extremities of a galvanic battery, a stream of electricity would pass along the wire — *provided the other end of the wire were connected by a conductor with the other extremity of the battery.*

To fulfil this last condition, it was usual, when the electric telegraphs were first erected, to have a second wire extended from the distant point back to the battery in which the electricity was generated. But it was afterwards discovered that the *earth itself* was the best, and by far the cheapest and most convenient, conductor which could be used for this returning stream of electricity.

Instead, therefore, of connecting the poles of the battery by a second wire, they are connected respectively with the earth by two independent wires, so that the returning current is first transmitted to the earth, and through the earth to a corresponding wire at the distant station, to which a telegraphic communication is made.

This arrangement will be more readily understood by reference to *fig.* 276. If P be the point from which the current is transmitted, it will pass along the wire *p* to a plate of metal, five or six feet square, buried in the earth, from whence it will pass through the earth, as indicated by the arrows, to another plate of metal *s'*,

from thence, by the wire *n*, to the negative pole N of the
ery.
the arrangement, as here represented, the current is trans-

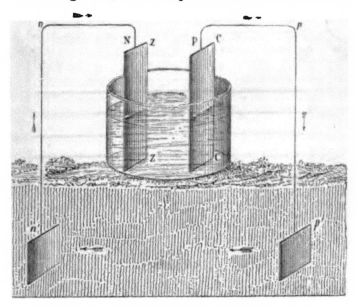

Fig. 276.

d through the wire and the earth from the positive to the
ive pole of the same battery. But the effects will be precisely
ame if P be imagined to represent the positive pole of a
ry at any one station, and N the negative pole of a different
ry at any other station, however distant; provided only that
egative pole of the former battery be connected with the
ve pole of the latter by a wire, or series of wires, or any
continuous conductors.

has not been found necessary in practice to wrap the wires
silk, or to case them with any other nonconductor. They
ly consist of iron, which is recommended at once by its
çth and cheapness, and are coated with zinc, the better to
oxidation, by the galvanic process.

2 wires thus prepared are usually suspended on posts from
1 to thirty feet high, and at intervals of about sixty yards
277.), which is at the rate of about thirty to a mile.

each of these poles are attached as many tubes or rollers of
lain or glass as there are wires to be supported. Each wire
1 through a tube, or is supported on a roller; and the mate-

rial of the tubes or rollers being among the most perfect of the class of nonconducting substances, the escape of the electricity at the point of contact is prevented.

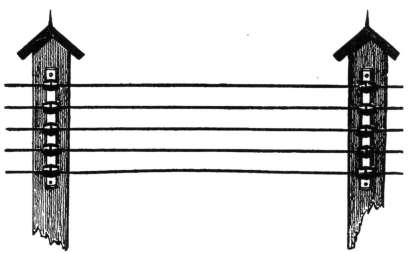

Fig. 277.

468. Although the mode of carrying the conducting wires at a certain elevation on supports above the ground has been the most general mode of construction adopted on telegraphic lines, it has been found in certain localities subject to difficulties and inconvenience, and some projectors have considered that in all cases it would be more advisable to carry the conducting wires under ground.

This underground system has been adopted in the streets of London, and of some other large towns. The English and Irish Magnetic Telegraph Company have adopted it on a great extent of their lines, which overspread the country. The European Submarine Telegraph Company has also adopted it on the line between London and Dover, which follows the course of the old Dover mail-coach road by Gravesend, Rochester, and Canterbury.

469. The methods adopted for the preservation and insulation of these underground wires are various.

The wires proceeding from the central telegraph station in London are wrapped with cotton thread, and coated with a mixture of tar, resin, and grease. This coating forms a perfect insulator. Nine of these wires are then packed in a half-inch leaden pipe, and four or five such pipes are packed in an iron pipe about three inches in diameter. These iron pipes are then laid under the foot pavements, along the sides of the streets, and are thus conducted to the terminal stations of the various railways, where they are united to the lines of wire supported on posts along the sides of the railways already described.

470. Provisions, called *testing posts*, are made at intervals of a quarter of a mile along the streets, by which any failure or accidental irregularity in the buried wires can be ascertained, and the place of such defect always known within a quarter of a mile.

471. **Telegraphic signs.**—The current being by these means transmitted instantaneously from any station to another, connected with it by such conducting wires, it is necessary to select among the many effects which it is capable of producing, such as may be fitted for telegraphic signs.

There are a great variety of properties of the current which supply means of accomplishing this. If it can be made to affect any object in such a manner as to cause such object to produce any effect sensible to the eye, the ear, or the touch, such effect may be used as a *sign*; and if it be capable of being *varied*, each distinct *variety* of which it is susceptible may be adopted as a *distinct sign*. Such signs may then be taken as signifying the letters of the alphabet, the digits composing numbers, or such single words as are of most frequent occurrence.

The rapidity and precision of the communication will depend on the rate at which such signs can be produced in succession, and on the certainty and accuracy with which their appearance at the place of destination will follow the action of the producing cause at the station from which the despatch is transmitted.

These preliminaries being understood, it remains to show what effects of the electric current are available for this purpose.

These effects are:—

I. The power of the electric current to deflect a magnetic needle from its position of rest.

II. The power of the current to impart temporary magnetism to soft iron.

III. The power of the current to decompose certain chemical solutions.

472. **Signs made with the needle system.**—Let us now see how these three properties have been made instrumental to the transmission of intelligence to a distance.

We have explained how a magnetic needle over which an electric current passes will be deflected to the right or to the left, according to the direction given to the current. Now, it is always easy to give the current the one direction or the other, or to suspend it altogether, by merely changing the end of the galvanic trough with which the wires are connected, or by breaking the contact.

A person, therefore, in London, having command over the end of a wire which extends to Edinburgh, and is there connected with a magnetic needle, in the manner already described, can deflect that needle to the right or to the left at will.

Thus a single wire and a magnetic needle are capable of making at least two signals.

By repeating the same signals a greater or less number of times, and by variously combining them, signs may be multiplied; but it is found more convenient to provide two or more wires affecting different needles, so as to vary the signs by combination, without the delay attending repetition.

Such is, in general, the nature of the signals adopted in the electric telegraphs in ordinary use in England, and in some other parts of Europe.

It may aid the conception of the mode of operation and communication if we assimilate the apparatus to the dial of a clock with its two hands. Let us suppose that a dial, instead of carrying hands, carried two needles, and that their north poles, when quiescent, both pointed to twelve o'clock. When the galvanic current is conducted under either of them, the north pole will turn either to three o'clock or to nine o'clock, according to the direction given to the current.

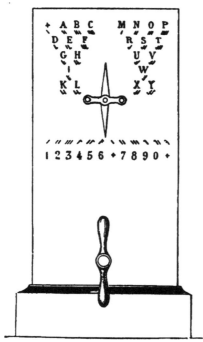

Now, it is easy to imagine a person in London governing the hands of such a clock erected in Edinburgh, where their indications might be interpreted according to a way previously agreed upon. Thus, we may suppose that when the needle No. 1. turns to nine, the letter A is expressed; if it turn to three, the letter B is expressed. If the needle No. 2. turn to nine o'clock the letter C is expressed; if it turn to

Fig. 278.—THE SINGLE NEEDLE TELEGRAPH.

ree, the letter D. If both needles are turned to nine, the letter
is expressed; if both to three, the letter F. If No. 1. be turned
nine, and No. 2. to three, the letter G is expressed; if No. 2.
turned to nine, and No. 1. to three, the letter H, and so forth.
The usual form of a telegraph of this kind which depends on a
ngle needle for its indications, is shown in *fig.* 278., and one on
e double needle system in *fig.* 279. In the former, one con-

Fig. 279—The Double Needle Telegraph.

ting wire between the stations is sufficient, but in the latter
are necessary.

.73. **Telegraphs operating by an electro-magnet.**—Tele-
phs depending on the second and third principles adverted to

above, have been brought into extensive use in America, the needle system being in no case adopted there.

The power of imparting temporary magnetism to soft iron by the electric current, has been applied in the construction of telegraphs in a great variety of forms; and indeed it may be stated generally that there is no form of telegraph whatever, in which the application of this property can be altogether dispensed with.

To explain the manner in which it is applied, let us suppose the conducting wire at the station of transmission, London for example, to be so arranged that its connection with the voltaic battery may, with facility and promptitude, be established and broken at the will of the agent who transmits the despatch. This may be effected by means of a small lever acting like the key of a pianoforte, which being depressed by the finger, transmits the current. The current may thus be transmitted and suspended in as rapid alternation as the succession of notes produced by the action of the same key of a pianoforte.

At the station to which the despatch is transmitted, Edinburgh for example, the conducting wire is coiled spirally round a piece of soft iron, which has no magnetic attraction so long as the current does not pass along the wire, but which acquires a powerful magnetic virtue so long as the current passes. So instantaneously does the current act upon the iron, that it may be made alternately to acquire and lose the magnetic property several times in a second.

Now let us suppose this soft iron to be placed under an iron lever, like the key of a pianoforte, so that when the former has acquired the magnetic property, it shall draw this key down as if it were depressed by the finger, and when deprived of the magnetic property, it will cease to attract it, and allow it to recover its position of rest. It is evident in this case that movements would be impressed by the soft iron, rendered magnetic, on the key at Edinburgh, simultaneous and exactly identical with the movements impressed by the finger of the agent upon the key in London. In fact, if the key in Edinburgh were the real key of a pianoforte, the agent in London could strike the note and repeat it as often and with such intervals as he might desire.

This lever at Edinburgh, which is worked by the agent in London, may, by a variety of expedients, be made to act upon other movable mechanism, so as to make visible signals, or to produce sounds, to ring a bell or strike a hammer, or to trace characters on paper by means of a pen or pencil, so as actually to write the message, or to act upon common movable type so as to print it. In fine, having once the power to produce a certain mechanical effect at a distant station, the expedients are infinitely various by which such mechanical effect may be made subservient to telegraphic purposes.

474. **Morse's system.**—The telegraph of Morse, extensively used in the United States, affords an example of this. To comprehend its mode of operation, let us suppose the lever, on which the temporary magnet acts, to govern the motion of a pencil or style under which a ribbon of paper is moved, with a regulated motion, by means of clockwork. When the current passes, the style is pressed upon the paper, and when the current is suspended, t is raised from it. If the current be maintained for an interval more or less continued, the style will trace a line on the ribbon, the length of which will be greater or less according to the duration of the current. If the current be maintained only for an nstant, the style will merely make a dot upon the ribbon. Lines, therefore, of varying lengths, and dots separated by blank spaces, will be traced upon the ribbon of paper as it passes under the style, and the relative lengths of these lines, their combinations with each other and with the dots, and the lengths of the blank intervening spaces, are altogether under the control of the agent who transmits the despatch.

It is easy to imagine how a conventional alphabet may be formed by such combinations of lines and dots.

Provisions are made, so that the motion of the paper does not begin until the message is about to be commenced, and ceases when the message is written. This is easily accomplished. The cylinders which conduct the band of paper are moved by wheel-work and a weight properly regulated. The motion is imparted by a detent detached by the action of the magnet, which stops the motion when the magnet loses its virtue.

A perspective view of the instrument, omitting the paper roller and ribbon, is given in *fig.* 280.

z. The wooden base upon which the instrument is screwed.

B. The brass base plate attached to the wooden base z.

A. The side frames supporting the mechanism.

h, h. Screws which secure the transverse bars connecting the side frames.

G. The key for winding up the drum containing the mainspring, or supporting the weight, according as the mechanism is impelled by one or the other power.

3, 4. Clock-work.

x. A lock or gauge to regulate the pressure of the rollers on the paper.

c. The pillar supporting the electro-magnet.

p. The adjusting screw passing into the pillar, c, projecting through the armature, to enable the telegraphist to adjust the sound of the back stroke of the armature at pleasure.

o. The spring bar, and

d. the screw to adjust the action of the pen lever.

D. The apparatus for adjusting the paper rollers

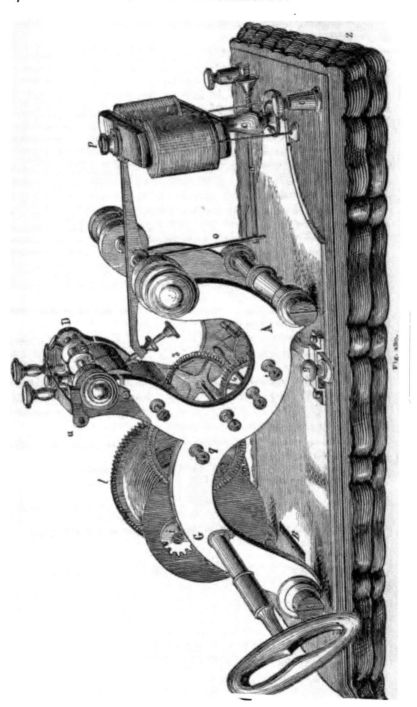

Fig. 180.

475. **Electro-chemical telegraphs.** — The following description of the telegraph of Mr. Bain will convey some idea of the general principle on which all forms of electro-chemical telegraphs are based : —

Let a sheet of writing paper be wetted with a solution of prussiate of potash, to which a little nitric and hydrochloric acid have been added. Let a metallic desk be provided corresponding in magnitude with the sheet of paper, and let this desk be put in communication with a galvanic battery so as to form its negative pole. Let a piece of steel or copper wire forming a pen be put in connection with the same battery so as to form its positive pole. Let the sheet of moistened paper be now laid upon the metallic desk, and let the steel or copper point which forms the positive pole of the battery be brought into contact with it. The galvanic circuit being thus completed, the current will be established, the solution with which the paper is wetted will be decomposed at the point of contact, and a blue or brown spot will appear. If the pen be now moved upon the paper, the continuous succession of spots will form a blue or brown line, and the pen being moved in any manner upon the paper, characters may be thus written upon it as it were in blue or brown ink.

In this manner, any kind of writing may be inscribed upon the paper, and there is no other limit to the celerity with which the characters may be written, save the dexterity of the agent who moves the pen, and the sufficiency of the current to produce the decomposition of the solution in the time which the pen takes to move over a given space of the paper.

The electro-chemical pen, the prepared paper, and the metallic desk being understood, we shall now proceed to explain the manner in which a communication is written at the station where it arrives.

The metallic desk is a circular disc, about twenty inches in diameter. It is fixed on a central axis, with which it is capable of revolving in its own plane. An uniform movement of rotation is imparted to it by means of a small roller, gently pressed against its under surface, and having sufficient adhesion with it to cause the movement of the disc by the revolution of the roller. This roller is itself kept in uniform revolution by means of a train of wheelwork, deriving its motion either from a weight or main spring, and regulated by a governor or fly. The rate at which the disc revolves may be varied at the discretion of the superintendent, by shifting the position of the roller towards the centre ; the nearer to the centre the roller is placed the more rapid will be the motion of rotation. The moistened paper being placed on this disc, we have a circular sheet kept in uniform revolution.

The electro-chemical pen, already described, is placed on this paper at a certain distance from its centre. This pen is supported by a pen-holder, which is attached to a fine screw extending from the centre to the circumference of the disc in the direction of one of its radii.

On this screw is fixed a small roller, which presses on the surface of the disc, and has sufficient adhesion with it to receive from it a motion of revolution. This roller causes the screw to move with a slow motion in a direction from the centre to the circumference, carrying with it the electro-chemical pen. We have thus two motions, the circular motion carrying the moistened paper which passes under the pen, and the slow rectilinear motion of the pen itself directed from the centre to the circumference. By the combination of these two motions, it is evident that the pen will trace upon

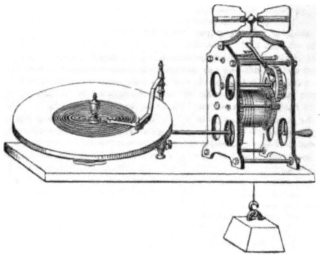

Fig. 281.

the paper a spiral curve, commencing at a certain distance from the centre, and gradually extending towards the circumference. The intervals between the successive coils of this spiral line will be determined by the relative velocities of the circular disc, and of the electro-chemical pen. The relation between these velocities may likewise be so regulated, that the coils of the spiral may be as close together as is consistent with the distinctness of the traces left upon the paper.

Now, let us suppose that the galvanic circuit is completed in the manner customary with the electric telegraph, that is to say, the wire which terminates at the point of the electro-chemical pen is carried from the station of arrival to the station of departure, where it is connected with the galvanic battery, and the returning current is formed in the usual way by the earth itself. When the communication between the wire and the galvanic battery at the station of departure is established, the current will pass through the wire, will be transmitted from the point of the electro-chemical ꞏpen to the moistened paper, and will, as already described, make a blue or brown line on this paper. If the current were continuous and uninterrupted, this line would be an unbroken spiral, such as has been already described ; but if the current be interrupted at intervals, during each such interval the pen will cease to decompose the solution, and no mark will be made on the paper. If such interruption be frequent, the spiral, instead of being a continuous line, will be a broken one, consisting of lines interrupted by blank spaces. If the current be allowed to act only for an instant of time, there will be a blue or brown dot upon the paper ; but if it be allowed to continue during a long interval, there will be a line.

Now, if the intervals of the transmission and suspension of the current be regulated by any agency in operation at the station of departure, lines and

ts corresponding precisely to these intervals will be produced by the
ctro-chemical pen on the paper, and will be continued regularly along
e spiral line already described.   It will be evident, without further expla-
tion, that characters may thus be produced on the prepared paper cor-
sponding to those of the telegraphic alphabet already described, and thus
e language of the communication will be written in these conventional
mbols.

There is no other limit to the celerity with which a message may be thus
ritten, save the sufficiency of the current to effect the decomposition while
e pen passes over the paper, and the power of the agency used at the
ation of departure to produce, in rapid succession, the proper intervals in
e transmission and suspension of the current.

But the prominent feature of this system is the extraordinary celerity of
hich it is susceptible.   In an experiment performed by M. Le Verrier and
yself before Committees of the Institute and the Legislative Assembly at
'aris, despatches were sent a thousand miles, at the rate of nearly 20000
rords an hour.*

CHAP. XVI.

CALORIFIC, LUMINOUS, AND PHYSIOLOGICAL EFFECTS OF THE VOLTAIC CURRENT.

**176. Conditions on which calorific power of current de-
ends.** — When a voltaic current passes over a conductor, an
levation of temperature is produced, the amount of which will
lepend on the quantity and intensity of the electricity trans-
nitted, upon the conductibility of the material composing the
onductor, and upon the magnitude of the space which it offers
or the passage of the electric fluid.   Although the conditions
rhich determine this development of heat are not ascertained
rith much certainty or precision, it may be stated generally that
he quantity of heat produced is augmented with the quantity of
ie fluid transmitted, and the obstacles opposed to its passage.
. given current, therefore, will develop less heat on good than on
ad conductors, and on those having a large than on those having
small transverse section.

The development of heat, so far as it depends on the current
self, appears to increase in a much larger ratio with the quantity,
an with the intensity, of the electric fluid.   Thus, while it is

* Lardner's " Electric Telegraph," § 9.

T 2

greatly augmented by increasing the extent of surface of the elements of the pile, it is very little affected by augmenting their number. For a like reason it is greatly augmented by selecting the elements from the extremes of the electro-motive series (159.), since in that case the quantities of electricity developed are increased in proportion to the electro-motive energy of the exciting surfaces.

When a voltaic current of a certain intensity passes along a metallic wire, the wire becomes heated. If the intensity of the current be increased, the wire will become incandescent, and will, by a further increase of the force of the current, be fused or burned.

The same current which will produce only a slight elevation of temperature upon a wire of a certain diameter, will render a finer wire incandescent, and will fuse or burn one which is still finer.

477. Calorific effects: Hare's and Children's deflagrators. — The calorific power of a battery depending chiefly on the extent of the heating surface, and the electro-motive energy of its elements, those forms which, within a given volume, present the most extensive surfaces, such as Hare's spiral arrangement (173.), and others, on a like principle, contrived by Children and Strating, and denominated *deflagrators*, and the systems of Grove (177.) and Bunsen (178.), in which platinum or carbon is combined with zinc, and excited by two fluids, are the most efficient. With piles of the latter kind, consisting of ten to twenty pairs, the development of heat is so considerable that substances which resist the most powerful blast furnaces are easily fused and burned. Extraordinary effects are produced by this calorific agency. Metallic wire, submerged in water, is rendered incandescent, and may be fused either in vacuo or in an atmosphere of any gas, such as azote or carbonic acid, which is not a supporter of combustion.

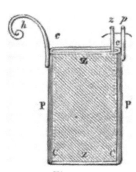

Fig. 282.

478. Wollaston's thimble battery. — A combination thus designated, which has acquired a sort of historical scientific interest, is represented in its actual size in *fig.* 282.

A strip of thin silver or platinum leaf P, is bent double, so as to include between its folds a plate z of amalgamated zinc, the distance between the surfaces being about the twentieth of an inch. The surfaces are kept separated by small bits of cork thrust between them. Two short copper wires, one, z, attached to the zinc, and the other, p, to the platinum, form the poles of the combination, and when these are connected by a wire a voltaic current will pass from p to z. Each of these polar wires has a fine slit made in it, into which an extremely fine platinum wire is inserted, extending between z and p, the intervening length between these points being not more than the tenth of an inch. The wire handle h is provided, to enable the operator to immerse the apparatus in a wine glass, containing a solution composed of three parts of water and one of sulphuric acid. The current which will then be established upon the wire between p and z will render it incandescent.

479. **Experimental illustration of the conditions which effect calorific power of a current.** — If the poles of a powerful battery be connected by iron or platinum wire from two to three feet in length, the metal will become incandescent. If its length or thickness be diminished, it will fuse or burn. If its length or thickness be increased, it will acquire first a darker degree of incandescence, and then will be only heated without being rendered luminous. The same current which will render iron or platinum wire incandescent or fuse it, will only raise the temperature of silver or copper wire of the same length and thickness without rendering it incandescent. If, on the other hand, the iron or platinum be replaced by tin or lead of much greater length or thickness, these metals will be readily fused by the same current.

These phenomena are explained by the different conductibility of these different metals, silver and copper being among the best, and lead and tin being among the worst metallic conductors of electricity.

If two pointed pencils of thick platinum wire, being connected with the poles of the battery, be presented point to point, so that the current may pass between them, they will be fused at the points and united, as though they were soldered together. This effect will equally be produced under water.

480. **Substances ignited and exploded by the current.** — Combustible or explosive substances, whether solid or liquid, may be ignited by the heat developed in transmitting a current through them. Ether, alcohol, phosphorus, and gunpowder, present examples of this.

481. **Application of this in civil and military engineering.** — This property has been applied with great advantage in engineering operations, for the purpose of springing mines, an operation which may thus be effected with equal facility under water. Experiments made by the Russian military engineers at

St. Petersburg, and by the English at Chatham, have demonstrated the advantage of this agency in military operations, more especially in the springing of subaqueous mines.

In the course of the construction of the South Eastern Railway it was required to detach enormous masses of the cliff near Dover, which, by the direct application of human labour, could not have been accomplished, save at an impracticable cost. Nine tons of gunpowder, deposited in three charges, at from fifty to seventy feet from the face of the cliff, were fired by a conducting wire, connected with a powerful battery, placed at 1000 feet from the mine. The explosion detached 600000 tons weight of chalk from the cliff. It was proved that this might have been equally effected at the distance of 3000 feet.

482. **Jacobi's experiments on conduction by water.**— Jacobi instituted a series of experiments, with a view to ascertain how far water might be substituted for a metallic conductor for telegraphic purposes. He first established (as Peschel states) conduction of this nature between Oranienbaum and an arm of the Gulph of Finland, a distance of 5600 feet, one half through water, and the other through an insulated copper wire, three fourths of a line in diameter, which was carried over a dam, so that the entire length of the connection was 11200 feet. The electric current was excited by a Grove's battery of twenty-four pairs, and a common voltaic pile of 150 six-inch plates. A zinc plate of five square feet was sunk in the sea from one pole of the battery, and at the opposite end of the connecting wire a similar plate was sunk in a canal joining the sea. Charcoal points were used for completing the circuit of the Grove's battery; these, and also a fine platinum wire, were made red hot, and these phenomena appeared to be more intense than when copper wires were used as conductors. In a later experiment he employed a similar conduction, the distance in this case being 9030 feet, namely, from the winter palace of the emperor, to the Fontanka near the Obuchowski bridge. One of the conductors was a copper wire carried underground, the other was the Neva itself, in which a zinc plate of five square feet was sunk beneath the surface of the river. At the other extremity a similar zinc plate was immersed in a small pond, whose level was five or six feet above the Fontanka, from which it was separated by a floodgate. The battery consisted of twenty-five small Daniel's constant batteries, by means of which, notwithstanding the great extent of water, all the galvanic and magnetic phenomena were produced. At Lenz's suggestion, a different species of conduction was tried between the same stations. A connection was established with a point of the *iron* roof of the winter palace, which was connected with the

ground by means of conducting rods, and the current was carried equally well along the moist earth.

483. **Combustion of the metals.**—If thin strips of metal or common metallic leaf be placed in connection with the poles of a battery, it will undergo combustion, the colour of the flame varying with the metal, and in all cases displaying very striking and brilliant effects. Gold thus burned gives a bluish-white light, and produces a dark brown oxide. Silver burns with a bright sea-green flame, and copper with a bluish-green flame, mingled with red sparks, and emits a green smoke. Zinc burns with a dazzling white light, tin with red sparks, and lead with a purple flame. These phenomena are produced with increased splendour, if the metal to be burned attached to one pole be brought into contact with mercury connected with the other pole.

484. **Spark produced by the voltaic current.**— Bring nearly together the amalgamated ends of the polar wires, while the battery is in a state of activity; a small, white, starlike spark will be seen accompanied by a crackling noise like that which attends the emission of a feeble electrical spark.

Plunge the end of one of the wires into a small vessel of mercury, and bring the other near the surface of the metal. A similar spark is emitted just before the point touches the mercury, on which a small black speck may be seen where the spark struck it.

The spark obtained from an amalgamated point is visible under water or in the flame of a candle.

Fasten a fine sewing-needle to the end of one of the wires, and touch the other pole with the free end of the needle; a starlike red spark will be emitted. A continued stream of these sparks may be obtained by connecting a small round or triangular file with one pole, and presenting to it and removing from it with great rapidity the point of a copper wire attached to the other pole.

Coat the ends of the connecting wires with soot, by holding them in the flame of an oil lamp, and the sparks will be both larger and brighter; they will be obtained of the greatest intensity by holding the points of the wires in the flame opposite to each other.

Nobili says, that, in performing experiments of this kind, he obtained the brightest sparks by connecting the two ends of the battery with a long spiral copper wire, or with a wire insulated by being wound round with silk.

485. **The electric light.** — Of all the luminous effects produced by the agency of electricity, by far the most splendid is the light produced by the passage of the current, proceeding from a powerful battery, between two pencils of hard charcoal presented

point to point. The charcoal being an imperfect conductor is rendered incandescent by the current, and being infusible at any temperature hitherto attained, the degree of splendour of which its incandescence is susceptible has no other practical limit except the power of the battery.

The charcoal best adapted for this experiment is that which is obtained from the residuum of the coke in retorts of gas works. This is hardened and formed into pencil-shaped pointed cylinders,

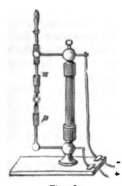

from two to four inches in length, and mounted as represented in *fig.* 283., where *p* and *n*, the two metallic pencil holders, are in metallic connection with the poles of the pile, and so mounted that the charcoal pencils fixed in them can at pleasure be made to approach each other until their points come into contact, or to recede from each other to any necessary distance. When they are brought into contact, the current will pass between them, and the charcoal will become intensely luminous. When separated to a short distance, a splendid flame will pass between them of

Fig. 283.

the form represented in *fig.* 284. It will be observed that the

form of the flame is not symmetrical with relation to the two poles, the part next the positive point having the greatest diameter, and the diameter becoming gradually less in approaching the negative point.

486. Incandescence of charcoal by the current not combustion.—It would be a great error

Fig. 284.

to ascribe the light produced in charcoal pencils to the combustion of that substance. None of the consequences or effects of combustion attend the phenomena, no carbonic acid is produced, nor does the charcoal undergo any diminution of weight save a small amount due to mere mechanical causes. On the contrary, at the points where the calorific action is most intense, it becomes more hard and dense. But what negatives still more clearly the supposition of combustion is, that the incandescence is still more intense in a vacuum, or in any of the gases that do not support combustion, than in the ordinary atmosphere.

Peschel states that, instead of two charcoal pencils, he has laid a piece of charcoal, or well burnt coke, upon the surface of mercury, connected with one pole of the battery, while he has touched it with a piece of platinum connected with the other pole. In this manner he obtained a light whose splendour was intolerable to the eye.

487. **Electric lamps of Messrs. Foucault, Deleuil, and Dubosc-Soleil.**—M. Foucault first applied the electric light produced by charcoal pencils as a substitute for the lime light in the gas microscope.

This apparatus, in the form in which it is now constructed by M. Dubosc of Paris, is represented in *fig.* 285. M. Dubosc has applied to his photo-

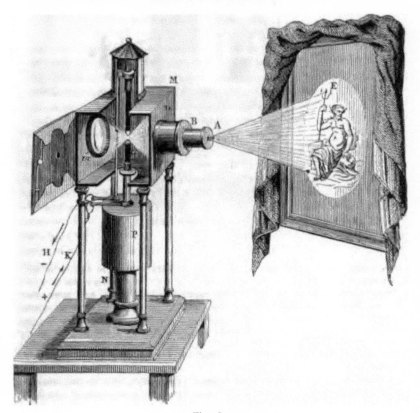

Fig. 285.

electric microscope a self-adjusting apparatus, by which the light is maintained with a nearly uniform brilliancy, notwithstanding the gradual waste of the charcoal. This is accomplished by an electro-magnet, by which the current is re-established, whenever it has a tendency to be suspended.

Photo-electric apparatus of MM. Deleuil.—This apparatus, which is represented in *fig.* 286., has a self-acting adjustment, and is of cheaper construction than that of M. Dubosc. The negative charcoal pencil is supported by a metallic rod which slides with friction in a support D, but being once regulated remains fixed. The positive pole is continually raised by the current itself as the charcoal is wasted. This is accomplished by a regulating

Fig. 286.

apparatus placed under the stage. A lever, attached at one end to a spiral spring, is capable of oscillating through a very small angle on a centre, being maintained at the other end between the points of two screws seen under the stage in the figure, which limit its play. This lever A is drawn upwards by the spring, and in the contrary direction by the electro-magnet. In fine, a small straight spring fixed at the extremity of the lever is pressed upon small teeth ranged like those of a rack on the rod, which carries the positive charcoal pencil, and transmits to this latter the motion of the lever.

This being understood, so long as the current passes with its full intensity, the electro-magnet attracting its armature, which is fixed to the lever, one arm of the lever is raised, and the opposite arm is lowered, and, consequently, the spring is drawn down, so that its upper extremity is lowered from one tooth to another of the rack; when, on the contrary, the distance between the charcoal points being augmented, the current is enfeebled. The electro-magnet being no longer capable of supporting the arm of the lever, the end is drawn upwards by the spiral spring, and the small spring being pressed against a tooth of the wheel, drives it upwards and raises the pencil. The charcoal points are, therefore, again brought into contiguity, and the current is re-established.

I have had an apparatus of this kind in operation with great

y for some years. It is worked by a battery on Bunsen's
e, consisting of fifty pairs.

Method of applying the heat of charcoal to the
of refractory bodies and the decomposition of the
.—This is accomplished by substituting for the charcoal
p, *fig.* 283., a piece of charcoal in the form of a small cup,
sented in *fig.* 287.

all piece of the substance to be acted on is placed in the
charcoal cup s, and the electric flame is made to
play upon it by bringing it into proximity with the
pencil above it. In this way gold or platinum may
be fused, or even burned. If a small piece of soda
or potash be placed in the cup s, its decomposition
will be effected by the flame, and small globules of
sodium or potassium will be produced in the cup,
which will launch themselves towards the point of the
pencil, undergoing at the same time combustion, and
producing the alkali.

Physiological effects of the current.—This class of
s found to consist of three successive phases : *first*, when
ent first commences to pass through the members affected
secondly, during its continuance; and, *thirdly*, at the
of its cessation. A sharp convulsive shock attends the
d last; and the intermediate period is marked by a con-
eries of lesser shocks rapidly succeeding each other. The
f a voltaic battery has been said to be distinguished from
oduced by a Leyden jar, inasmuch as the latter is felt less
affecting only our external organs, and being only instan-
in its duration; while the latter pervades the system,
ting itself through the whole course of the nerves which
between its points of admission and departure.

pears that the physiological effect of the current depends
er on its intensity, and little or not at all upon its quantity.
proved by the fact, that the effect of a battery of small
s as great as one consisting of the same number of large
A single pair, however extensive be its surface, produces
ible shock. To produce any sensible effect, from ten to
airs are necessary. A battery of 50 to 100 pairs gives a
trong convulsive shock. If the hands, previously wetted
lted water, grasp two handles, like those represented at P
fig. 210., connected with such a battery, violent shuddering
fingers, arms, and chest will be produced; and if there be
e or tender parts of the skin, a pricking or burning sensa-
l be produced there.

voltaic shock may be transmitted through a chain of

persons in the same manner as the electric shock, if their hands, which are joined, be well moistened with salted or acidulated water, to increase the conducting power of the skin.

As the strongest phases of the shock are the moments of the commencement and cessation of the current, any expedient which produces a rapid intermission of the current will augment its physiological effect. This may be accomplished by various simple mechanical expedients, by which the contact of the conductors connecting the poles may be made and broken in rapid succession; but no means are so simple and effectual for the attainment of this object as the contrivances for the production of the magneto-electric current described in (295.), which, in fact, is exactly the rapidly intermitting current here required.

490. **Therapeutic agency of electricity.**—Electric excitation has been tried as a curative agent for various classes of maladies from the date of the discovery of the Leyden jar. Soon after the discovery of galvanism, Galvani himself proposed it as a therapeutic agent; but although a great number of scientific practitioners in different countries have devoted themselves to the investigation of its effects, there still remains much doubt, not only as to its curative influence, but as to the classes of maladies to which it may be with advantage applied, and even as to its mode of application. It appears, however, to be generally admitted that voltaic electricity is much better fitted for medical purposes than common electricity, and that of the different forms of voltaic electricity intermitting currents produced by induction are in general to be preferred to the immediate currents produced by the battery. It is even maintained by practitioners who have more especially devoted themselves to the study of its effects, that different induced currents have different therapeutic properties.

A current produced by the immediate induction of another current proceeding directly from the voltaic battery is called an *induced current of the first order.*

If an induced current of the first order be applied to produce, by induction, another current in an independent wire, such current is called an *induced current of the second order.*

It is maintained by practitioners that these two orders of induced currents have different therapeutic effects, and that the effects of both of them differ from those of a primary current. Induced currents, however intense, having only a feeble chemical action, it follows that when they are transmitted through the organs, they do not produce there the effect of primary currents, and consequently do not tend to produce the same disorganisation. Dr. Duchenne, who has made numerous experiments on the medical application of galvanic electricity, has ascertained that induced currents used to electrify the muscles of the face, act but very feebly on the retina, while the primary current proceeding from the battery acts so strongly on that organ as to affect it dangerously, as the effects of practice have proved. The same practitioner holds, that while the induced currents of the first order produce strong muscular contractions, and are attended with little effect on the cutaneous sensibility, induced currents of the second order, on the contrary, exalt the cutaneous sensibility to such a degree, that their application should be avoided in the case of all patients whose skin is very irritable.

It appears to result from the experience of practitioners that the use of voltaic electricity in therapeutics should be guided by a profound knowledge of its physiological properties. Matteucci, in his lectures on the physical phenomena of living bodies, recommends that in the application of voltaic electricity a current of very feeble intensity should be first employed. He mentions the case of a paralytic patient who was seized with strong tetanic convulsions, in consequence of the application of a current produced only by a single pair. He recommends further, that in no case should the voltaic action be prolonged beyond a moderate interval, that the intermitting current should always be preferred to the continued, and that after each series of twenty or thirty shocks the operation should be suspended.

An infinite variety of apparatus have been contrived for the therapeutic application of voltaic electricity. The following may serve as examples of these:—

491. Duchenne's electro-voltaic apparatus.—This apparatus consists of a bobbin wrapped with coils of two wires, like that already explained in (290.).

This bobbin is enclosed in a brass tube G, *fig.* 288. The apparatus is fixed upon a mahogany case containing two drawers. The first contains a compass needle mounted as a reometer, and serving to measure the intensity of the primary current. The second contains in a compact form a charcoal battery. The zinc element M has itself the form of the drawer, and contains a solution of sea salt, and a rectangular piece U made of the charcoal of coke all calcined and prepared in the same manner as for Bunsen's battery. In the central part of the charcoal is a little cavity, in which a small quantity of nitric acid is poured, which is immediately absorbed. Two ribbons of copper proceeding from the poles of the battery are connected with the buttons L and N attached to the front of the drawer. The first of these L connected with the zinc end of the battery, and represents the negative pole; and the second is connected with the charcoal end, and represents the positive pole.

When the drawers are closed, the buttons L and N are put in connection with two pieces connected with the arrangement combined within the cylinder G. One of these pieces is movable, so that the circuit can be closed and broken at pleasure.

The induced current is produced only at the moments when the primary current commences and terminates. It is therefore necessary that the

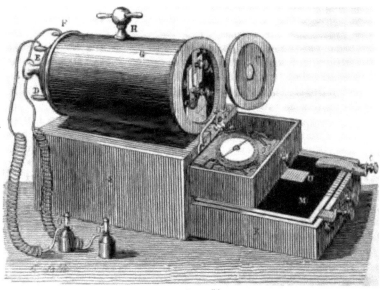

Fig. 288.

latter current should be subject to continued intermission. In the present apparatus, these intermissions may be rendered at pleasure more or less rapid. To render them rapid, the current passes into a piece of soft iron A, which oscillates very rapidly under the influence of a bundle of soft iron wires placed in the axis of the bobbin, and temporarily magnetised by the current. It is this piece A which, by its alternate motion to and fro, interrupts and re-establishes the primary current, and by that means produces the intermission of the induced current.

To produce a slow intermission of the current, the oscillating piece A is rendered fixed by means of a little rod b; and instead of making the current pass through the piece A, it is made to pass through an elastic ribbon e, and through the metal teeth of a wooden wheel with which that ribbon is connected, and which appears in the figure above the needle of the galvanometer. By turning a handle provided for the purpose, but which is not represented in the figure, the current is interrupted as often as the ribbon e ceases to touch a tooth; and as there are four teeth, there are four intermissions in each revolution, so that the operator, by turning a handle more or less rapidly, can vary at will the rate of intermission, and, consequently, the number of shocks imparted in a given time.

To transmit the shocks, the extremities of the wire conducting the induced current are put in connection with two buttons E and F at the end of the cylinder, and these buttons are themselves connected by means of two conducting wires wrapped with silk, with two exciters having glass handles o o. The operator holding them by the glass handles, and applying their bases to the two parts of the body of the patient, between which he intends to transmit the shock, the desired effect is produced, its intensity being regulated by turning the handle already mentioned.

A regulator is also provided by which the intensity of the current can be varied at will. This consists of a copper cylinder which envelopes the bobbin, and which can be drawn from it more or less, like a drawer, by the aid of a graduated rod. The greatest intensity is produced when the regulator is drawn out, so as to uncover the bobbin altogether, and the minimum when it completely covers it. The effect of this cylindrical cover is explained by the induced currents which are produced in its mass.

492. **Duchenne's magneto-electric apparatus.**—This apparatus, represented in *fig.* 289., acts upon the principle explained

Fig 289.

n (297.). The magnet M R has two arms connected at their posterior extremities by an armature of soft iron. In front is another armature X, also of soft iron, which turns upon a horizontal axis, to which motion is imparted by the wheel and pinion A, and the handle B.

Upon the two arms of the magnets a copper wire wrapped with silk is coiled, destined to receive the inductive action of the magnets. Upon this first wire a second F C is coiled, in which an induced current of the second order is produced.

When a motion of rotation is imparted to the armature X, this piece, being magnetised at each moment that it passes the poles of the magnets M R, exercises upon the distribution of magnetism in them an action which produces in the first wire an induced current of the first order, and this wire, reacting upon the second wire, produces in it an induced current of the second order. These currents, however, may be separately developed by means of pieces J and I, each of which is double, but one of which only is shown in the figure. The current passes by them through the covered helical wires to the excitors N N, which are similar to those already described in the former apparatus.

The intermissions necessary for the production of the induced currents are obtained by means of the commutator B, which is analogous to that already described in the case of Clarke's magneto-electric apparatus, *fig.* 211., and by means of a system of metallic pieces, O, L, Y, and T.

The intensity of the shocks is regulated by the button and screw V, which serve to bring the magnets and the armature X nearer to or more distant from each other ; but a more effectual regulator is supplied by two copper cylinders G G, which envelope the bobbins, and, by means of the graduated rod H, can be drawn off or on them to any desired extent. These have the same effect as the similar envelope described in the former apparatus.

The therapeutic effects of these apparatus are reputed, among French medical practitioners, to be beneficial in several classes of maladies, and especially in paralytic cases.

493. **Pulvermacher's galvanic chain.**—This apparatus, which is represented in *fig.* 290., consists of a series of small cylindrical

Fig. 290.

rods of wood, upon which are rolled, one beside the other, without contact, however, a wire of zinc and a wire of copper. One of these rods with the wires rolled upon it is shown upon a larger scale in *fig.* 291.

At each of its ends the zinc wire c d, *fig.* 291., of the cylinder A is jointed to the copper wire of the cylinder B by means of two little rings of copper implanted in the wood. The zinc wire of the cylinder B is then connected, in the same manner, with the copper

vire of the third cylinder, and so on, so that the zinc of one
:ylinder always forms, with the copper of the following cylinder, a
:ouple altogether analogous to the arrangement of the ordinary
galvanic pile.

The combination thus forming a sort of flexible chain is held by the

Fig. 291.

operator, as shown in *fig.* 290.,
and plunged in a vessel containing vinegar and water.
The wooden rods, which are
very porous, imbibing the acidulated liquid, assume the character of the discs of cloth or
pasteboard in the original voltaic pile shown in *fig.* 129.;
and the chemical action which
ensues between the zinc and
the acetic acid of the vinegar
produces a current, the inten-
sity of which is proportional to the number of pairs in the chain. Thus a
chain consisting of 120 pairs will impart a strong shock.

The interruption of the current is produced by two armatures M and N,
fig. 290., to which the two poles of the chain are attached. The armature N
serves only to establish more surely the contact with the hand; but the
armature M, besides this, serves to interrupt the current. For that purpose,
a piece of clockwork is contained within it, which imparts an oscillating
motion to a movable piece, so that the pole of the pile is alternately thrown
into and out of contact with the armature. The rapidity of the oscillations,
and, consequently, the number of shocks imparted in a given time, can be
varied within certain limits by means of a little regulator, which is adjusted by the hand. In fine, the clockwork is wound up by turning the
handle *o, fig.* 290.

494. **Medical application of the voltaic shock.** — The influence of the galvanic shock on the nervous system in certain
classes of malady has been tried with more or less success, and
apparatus have been contrived for its convenient application, both
generally and locally, to the system. The most convenient forms
of apparatus for this purpose are those which have been explained
in the preceding paragraphs, and which have derived great convenience and efficacy from the expedients by which the operator
is enabled to measure and regulate the intensity of the shock with
the greatest certainty and precision by surrounding the rim of
the electro-magnet with loose cylinders or globes of thin copper,
movable upon them in the manner above described, so as to
increase or diminish at will the force of the induced current.

495. **Effects on bodies recently deprived of life.** — This
class of phenomena is well known, and, indeed, was the origin of
the discovery of galvanism. Galvani's original experiment on the
limbs of a frog, already noticed (154.), has often been repeated.

Bailey substituted for the legs of the frog those of the grasshopper, and obtained the same results.

Experiments made on the bodies of men and inferior animals recently deprived of life have afforded remarkable results. Aldini gave violent action in this way to the various members of a dead body. The legs and feet were moved rapidly, the eyes opened and closed, and the mouth, cheeks, and all the features of the face were agitated by distortions. Dr. Ure connected one of the poles of a battery with the supraorbital nerve of a man cut down after hanging for an hour, and connected the other pole with the nerves of the heel. On completing the circuit the muscles are described to have been moved with a fearful activity, so that rage, anguish, and despair, with horrid smiles, were successively expressed by the countenance.

This agency has been used occasionally with success as an expedient for restoring suspended animation.

The bodies and members of inferior animals recently killed are susceptible of the same influence, though in a less degree. The current sent through the claw of a lobster recently torn from the body, will cause its instant contraction.

496. **Effect of the shock upon a leech.** — If a half-crown piece be laid upon a sheet of amalgamated zinc, a leech placed upon the coin will betray no sense of a shock, until, by moving, some part of it comes into contact with the zinc. The connection being thus established, the leech will receive a shock, as will be rendered manifest by the sudden recoil of the part which first touches the zinc.

497. **Excitation of the nerves of taste.** — If a metallic plate, connected with one pole of the battery, be applied to the end of the tongue, and another wetted with salted water, and connected with the other pole, be applied to any part of the face, the metal on the tongue will excite a peculiar taste, acid or alkaline, according as it is connected with the positive or negative pole. This is explained by the decomposition of the saliva by the current.

498. **Excitation of the nerves of sight.** — If a metallic plate, wetted with salted or acidulated water, be applied at or near the eyelids, and another be applied at any other part of the person, a peculiar flash or luminous appearance will be perceived the moment the plates are put into connection with the poles of a battery. The sensation will be reproduced, but with less intensity, the moment the connection is broken. A like effect, but less intense, is produced, when the current is transmitted through the cheek and gums.

499. **Excitation of the nerves of hearing.** — If the wires connected with the poles of a battery be placed in contact with

he interior of the two ears, a slight shock will be felt in the head
it the moment when the connection is made or broken, and a roar-
ng sound will be heard so long as the connection is maintained.

500. **Supposed sources of electricity in the animal organisation.** — Although Galvani's theory of animal electricity did
not survive its author, the supposition that there exists in the
organisation of animals a source of electrical action has never
been abandoned. Humboldt and Pfaff discovered traces of electrical development in connecting the nerve and muscle of a frog.
Reoscopic tests have indicated the presence of a current, when
two remote portions of a nerve, or of the muscle belonging to it,
are brought into connection. Dr. Donné of Paris thinks that
there is a source of electrical excitement between the inner and
outer skins. He placed the inner and outer skins of the mouth
in connection by a platinum wire, upon which the presence of a
feeble current was detected by a reoscope. Dr. Wilson Philip
showed that in certain cases a voltaic current might perform the
functions of the nerves. Having destroyed the action of some of
the nerves leading to the stomach of a dog, he restored their
suspended action by connecting the severed ends with a voltaic
current.

501. **Electrical fishes.** — The most conspicuous example of
the development of electricity in the animal organisation is presented by certain species of fish. Of these *electrical fishes* there
are seven genera : —

1. Torpedo narke risso.	5. Silurus electricus.
2. „ unimaculata.	6. Tetraodon electricus.
3. „ marmorata.	7. Gymnotus electricus.
4. „ galvanii.	

No observations, sufficiently exact and extensive, have yet
applied the data necessary to determine the source of the vast
quantities of electricity, which these creatures are capable of developing at will. There is nothing in the phenomena observed
which countenances the supposition, that the electricity is the
result either of mechanical, thermal, or chemical causes analogous
to those which have been already explained. When it is therefore
stated to arise from a physiological action peculiar to the organisation of the animal, a name is merely given to an unknown
agency. In the absence, therefore, of any reasonable theory, we
are compelled to limit ourselves to a mere statement of the phenomena.

502. **Properties of the torpedo; observations of Walsh.**
—According to the observations of Walsh, who first submitted
his animal to exact inquiry, the following are its effects : —

If the finger or the palm of the hand be applied to any part of

the body of the animal out of the water, a shock will be felt si
to that produced by a voltaic pile.

If, instead of applying the hand directly, a good conductor,
as a rod of metal several feet in length, be interposed, the ι
will still be felt.

If nonconductors be interposed, the shock is not felt.

If the continuity of the interposed conductor be anyv
broken, the shock is not felt.

The shock may be transmitted along a chain of several pe
with joined hands, but in this case the force of the shock is ra
diminished as the number of persons is increased. In this
the first person of the chain should touch the torpedo on the l
and the last on the back.

When the animal is in the water, the shocks are less in
than in the air.

It is evident that the development of electricity is produce
a voluntary action of the animal. It often happens that in to
ing it no shock is felt. But when the observer irritates the an
shocks of increasing intensity are produced in very rapid su
sion. Walsh counted as many as fifty electrical discharges
duced in this way in a minute.

503. Observations of Becquerel and Breschet.—In a s
of observations and experiments made on the torpedos of Chio
near Venice by MM. Becquerel and Breschet, it was ascerta
that when the back and belly were connected by the wires
sensitive reoscope, a current was indicated as passing from
back to the belly. They also found that the animal could at
transmit the current between any two points of its body.

504. Observations of Matteucci.—In a series of experim
made on the torpedos of the Adriatic, M. Matteucci confirmed
results obtained by MM. Becquerel and Breschet, and also

ceeded in obtaining the spark from the cur
passing between the back and belly.

505. The electric organ.— In the sev
species of fish endowed with this quality,
organ in which the electric fluids are devel
differs in form, magnitude, position, and struct

506. The torpedo, *fig.* 292., is a flat, car
ginous fish which · resembles the common
Its body is smooth, and has the form of a ne
circular disc, the anterior border of whic
formed by two prolongations of the muscle w
are connected on each side with the pectoral
and which have between these organs an
space in which the electric apparatus is deposi

.   Fig. 292.

This apparatus, which is shown in *fig.* 293., is composed of a multitude of membranous prismatic tubes lying closely together, and subdivided by horizontal partitions into small cells, like those of a honeycomb, filled with mucous matter, and traversed by the ramifications of several large trunks of the pneumogastric nerves.

Four or five hundred of these prisms are commonly counted in each organ. Hunter in one case found 1182. They are nearly at right angles to the surface of the skin, to which they are strongly attached at the ends. When the structure of each of these prisms is examined, they are found to consist of a multitude of thin plates whose planes are perpendicular to the axis of the prism, separated from each other by strata of mucous matter, and forming a combination resembling the original galvanic pile.

Four bundles of nerves of considerable volume are distributed

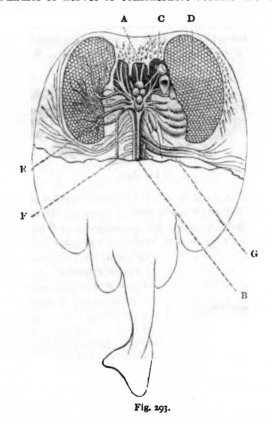

Fig. 293.

in the organ, and, according to Matteucci, the seat of the elec-trical power is at their origin.

In *fig*. 293. A is the brain, B the spinal cord, C the eye and optic nerve, D the electric organs, E the pneumogastric nerves ramifying through this organ, F the branch of these nerves constituting the lateral nerve, and G the spinal nerve.

These organs develope electricity, which is identified in all its physical properties with that of the electric or voltaic apparatus. The torpedo, though less powerful than the gymnotus, is capable, nevertheless, of rendering insensible the arms of those who touch it.

It has been lately ascertained that the electric functions of these organs have a close connection with the posterior lobe of the brain, since by destroying this lobe or dividing the nerves which proceed from it, the animal is deprived of the electric power.

Several species of the torpedo inhabit the seas that wash the coast of Europe. They have been frequently found near the shores of Vendée and Provence in France.

507. **The Silurus electricus,** *fig*. 294., another of these species, which is found in the Nile and Senegal, has a length of

Fig. 294.

from twelve to sixteen inches. The seat of its electric power seems to be a particular tissue situate between the skin and the muscles of the sides, having the appearance of a foliated cellular tissue. The Arabs give to this fish the name Raasch, an Arabic word which signifies thunder.

Fig. 295.

508. **Gymnotus electricus.—** One of the species which possess this curious physical power is the Gymnotus electricus, or electric eel, *fig*. 295. This species, which inhabits Southern America, closely resembles common eels, wanting, however, the fins at the end of the tail, and no scales being visible upon its skin, which is covered with a glutinous matter. Its length is from six to seven feet, and it is commonly met with

n the streams and ponds, which are found in various places in the
mmense plains which overspread the valleys of the Cordilleras,
he banks of the Oronoco, &c. The electric shocks which the
.nimal is enabled to give at will have an intensity sufficient to
)aralyse not only men but horses. It uses this organ accordingly,
lot only to defend itself from the attacks of its enemies, but to
:ill at a distance the fishes on which it feeds, the water being a
ufficient conductor of electricity to transmit the shock. Its first
lischarges are generally weak; but when the animal is irritated
nd roused, they become stronger, and at length acquire a terrible
ntensity. When the animal has communicated a certain number
f these shocks, it becomes exhausted, and is forced to desist,
nd it is not until after the lapse of a certain interval that it is
nabled to recommence. It would appear as though the electric
'gan, like the scientific machine, when once completely dis-
larged, requires a continued action of the exciting power, which
this case is a vital function of the animal, to recharge it.

Manner of capturing them. — The natives of the coun-
ies which the animal inhabits, avail themselves of this temporary
spension of its offensive power to capture it. Troops of wild
rses are driven into the reservoir in which the creature is
iown to prevail; immediately the horses are fiercely attacked,
ceiving a rapid succession of intense electric shocks, by which
ey are more or less stunned and paralysed, and not unfrequently
lled; but the assault has the effect of exhausting the electric
ls, and rendering them comparatively inoffensive, so that they
e easily captured, either by the net or harpoon.

Electric organs. — The apparatus by which the gymnotus
oduces these electric shocks, is extended along the entire length
the back to the tail, and consists of four longitudinal masses
nposed of a great number of membranous folds, connected by
infinite number of smaller membranes placed transversely to
m. The small prismatic cells formed by the combination of
se membranes are filled with gelatinous matter, and the whole
paratus is supplied with large nerves.

BOOK THE THIRD.

MAGNETISM.

~~~~~~~

CHAPTER I.

DEFINITIONS AND PRIMARY PHENOMENA.

509. **Natural magnets — loadstone.** — Certain ferruginous mineral ores are found in various countries, which being brought into proximity with iron manifest an attraction for it. These are called *natural magnets*, a term derived from *Magnesia*, a city of Lydia, in Asia Minor, where the Greeks first discovered and observed the properties of these minerals.

The natural magnet is also called the *loadstone*, or more properly *lodestone*, or *leadstone*, a name indicative of the guiding property of the magnet, just as the polar star was called the *lodestar*.

The natural magnet is a compound consisting of one equivalent of the protoxide and one of the sesquioxide of iron. This mineral abounds in Sweden and Norway, where it is worked for the production of the iron of commerce, yielding the best quality of that metal known.

510. **Artificial magnets.** — The same property may be imparted to any mass of iron, having any desired magnitude or form, by processes which will be explained hereafter. Such pieces of iron having thus acquired these properties are called *artificial magnets;* and it is with these chiefly that scientific experiments are made, since they can be produced in unlimited quantity of any desired form and magnitude, and having the magnetic virtue, within practical limits, in any desired degree.

511. **Neutral line or equator — poles.** — This attractive power is not diffused uniformly over every part of the surface. It is found to exist in some parts with much greater force than in others, and on a magnet a certain line is found where it disappears. This line divides the magnet into two parts or regions, in which the attractive power prevails in varying degrees, its energy augmenting with the distance from the neutral line just mentioned.

This neutral line may be called the *equator* of the magnet.

two regions of attraction separated by the equator are
ie *poles* of the magnet.

:imes this term *pole* is applied to two points, which are the
)f all the magnetic attractions, in the same manner as the
f gravity is the centre of all the gravitating forces which
ι the particles of a body.

Experimental illustration. — The neutral line and the
attraction of the parts of the surface of the magnet which
tes may be manifested experimentally as follows. Let a
whether natural or artificial, be rolled in a mass of fine
gs. They will adhere to it, and will collect in two tufts
on its surface, separated by a space
upon which no filings will appear.

This effect, as exhibited by a natural magnet of rough and irregular
form, is represented in *fig.* 296.; and
as exhibited by an artificial magnet
in the form of a regular rod or cylinder whose length is considerable
as compared with its thickness, is represented in *fig.* 297.; the equator

Fig. 296.

presented by E Q, and the poles by A and B.

Fig. 297.

The distribution of the magnetic force may also be
d as follows. Let a magnet, whether natural or artificial,
l under a plate of glass or a sheet of paper, and let iron
e scattered on the paper or glass over the magnet by
'a sieve, the paper or glass being gently agitated so as to
motion to the particles. They will be observed to affect
ır arrangement corresponding with and indicating the
ine or equator and the poles, as represented in *fig.* 298.,
ι is the equator, and A and B the poles of the magnet.

The variation of magnetic force may be ascertained
ating different parts of the surface to a small ball of iron
d by a fibre of silk so as to form a pendulum. The
ı of the surface will draw this ball out of the perpendi-
an extent greater or less, according to the energy of the

attraction. If the equator of the magnet be presented to it, no
attraction will be manifested, and the force indicated will be aug-

Fig. 298.

mented according as the point presented to the pendulum is more
distant from the equator and nearer to the pole.

515. **Curve of varying intensity.** —This varying distribution
of the attractive force over the surface of a magnet may be represented by a curve whose distance from the magnet varies proportionally to the intensity of this force. Thus if, in *fig.* 299., E Q be

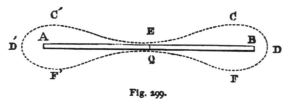

Fig. 299.

the equator and A and B the poles of the magnet, the curve E C D F
may be imagined to be drawn in such a manner that its distance
from the bar E B shall be everywhere proportional to the intensity
of the attractive force of the one pole, and a similar curve E C'D'F'
will in like manner be proportional to the varying attractions
of the several parts of the other pole. These curves necessarily
touch the magnet at the equator E Q, where the attraction is
nothing, and they recede from it more and more as their distance
from the equator increases.

516. Magnetic attraction and repulsion.—If two magnets, so placed as to have free motion, be presented to each other, they will exhibit either mutual attraction or mutual repulsion, according to the parts of their surfaces which are brought into proximity. Let B and E', *fig.* 300., be two magnets their poles

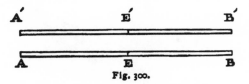

Fig. 300.

being respectively A B and A' B'. Let the two poles of each of these be successively presented to the same pole of a third magnet. It will be found that one will be attracted and the other repelled. Thus, the poles A and A' will be both attracted, and the poles B and B' will be both repelled by the pole of the third magnet, to which they are successively presented.

517. Like poles repel, and unlike attract. — The poles A and A', which are both attracted, and the poles B and B', which are both repelled by the same pole of a third magnet, are said to be *like poles;* and the poles A and B', and B and A', one of which is attracted and the other repelled by the same pole of a third magnet, are said to be *unlike poles.*

Thus the two poles of the same magnet are always unlike poles, since one is always attracted, and the other repelled, by the same pole of any magnet to which they are successively presented.

If two like poles of two magnets, such as A and A' or B and B', be presented to each other, they will be mutually repelled ; and if two unlike poles, as A and B' or B and A', be presented to each other, they will be mutually attracted.

Thus it is a general law of magnetic force, that like poles mutually repel and unlike poles mutually attract.

518. Experimental illustrations.—Let a magnetic needle, P P', *fig.* 301., be supported on a centre.

Let one of the poles A of another magnet be presented to P; it will either attract or repel P, so that the magnet P P' will turn in the one direction or the other. Suppose, for example, that it repels P; let it then be similarly presented to P', and it will be found to attract it. In this case A and P are like, and A and P' unlike poles, and, consequently, P and P' are also unlike poles.

The experiment may be further varied by presenting successively to the two poles P and P', the other pole of the magnet A; in that case it will be found that it will repel P', and attract P.

Let a piece of iron, such as a key for example, be suspended by either pole B, *fig.* 302., of a magnet. Let another magnet of similar form and equal force be presented to the former, with its unlike pole A directed towards B, and let it be moved so that A shall gradually approach B. The attraction

Fig. 301.

of B upon the key will be gradually diminished as the unlike pole approximates, and will at length become insufficient to support the key, which will

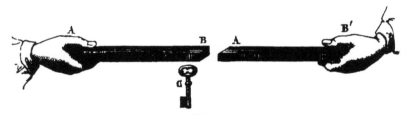

Fig. 302.

fall. In this case, the magnetic force of A counteracts that of B, and when the two poles come together their attractions will be neutralised.

519. **Magnets arrange themselves mutually parallel with poles reversed.** — If a magnet A B, *fig.* 300., be placed in a fixed position on a horizontal plane, and another magnet be suspended freely at its equator E′ by a fibre of untwisted silk, the point of suspension being brought so as to be vertical over the equator E of the fixed magnet, the magnet suspended being thus free to revolve round its equator E′ in a horizontal plane, it will so revolve, and will oscillate until at length it comes to rest in a position parallel to the fixed magnet A B; the like poles, however, being in contrary directions, that is to say, the pole A′, which is similar to A being over B, and the pole B′, which is similar to B being over A. This phenomenon follows obviously from what has been just explained; for if the magnet A′ B′ be turned to any

ction, the arm B B attracting the unlike arm B′ A′, and
ne time the arm E A attracting the unlike arm E′ B′, the
magnet A′ B′ will be under the operation of forces called
consisting of two equal and contrary forces whose
effect is to turn the magnet round E′ as a centre.
wever, the magnet A′ B′ ranges itself parallel to A B,
oles being in contrary directions, the forces exerted
ich other, since the pole A attracts B′ as much as the
:acts A′.

tic axis. — It has been already stated that certain
hin the two parts into which a magnet is divided by the
which are the centres of magnetic force, are the magnetic
straight line joining these two points is called the
xis.

ascertained experimentally. — If a magnet have a
al form, and the magnetic force be uniformly diffused
;, its magnetic axis will coincide with the geometrical
s figure. Thus, for example, if a cylindrical rod be
magnetised, its magnetic axis will be the axis of the
but this regular position of the magnetic axis does not
evail, and as its direction is of considerable importance,
ssary that its position may in all cases be determined.
be done by the following expedient : —

magnet, the direction of whose axis it is required to
be suspended as already described, with its equator
ver that of a fixed magnet resting upon a horizontal
he suspended magnet will then settle itself into such a
iat its magnetic axis will be parallel to the magnetic axis
ed magnet which is under it. Its position when thus in
n being observed, let it be reversed in the stirrup, so
ut changing the position of its poles, its under side shall
upwards, and *vice versâ.* If after this change the direc-
e bar remain unaltered, its magnetic axis will coincide
:ometrical axis ; but if, as will generally happen, it take
. direction after being reversed, then the true direction
gnetic axis will be intermediate between its directions
l after reversion.

er this more clear, let A B, *fig.* 303., be the geometrical
egularly shaped prismatic magnet, and let it be required
r the direction of its magnetic axis. Let *a, b* be the
the line M N passing through them therefore its mag-

nagnet be reversed in the manner already described over

* "Mechanics," (155.).

a fixed magnet, its magnetic axis in the new position will coincide with its direction in the first position, and the magnet when reversed will take the position represented by the dotted line, the geometrical axis being in the direction A′ B′, intersecting its former direction AB at o. The poles a, b will coincide with their former position, as will also the magnetic axis M N. It is evident that the geometric axis o A will form with the magnetic axis o a the same angle as it forms with that axis in the second position, that is to say, the angle A O M will be equal to the angle A′ o M; and, consequently, the magnetic axis M N will bisect the angle A o A′, formed by the geometric axis of the magnet in its second position.

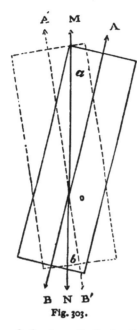

Fig. 303.

520. Hypothesis of two fluids, boreal and austral. — These various phenomena of attraction and repulsion, with others which will presently be stated, have been explained by different suppositions, one of which assumes that all bodies susceptible of magnetism are pervaded by a subtle imponderable fluid, which is compound, consisting of two constituents called, for reasons which will hereafter appear, the *austral fluid* and the *boreal fluid*. Each of these is self-repulsive; but they are reciprocally attractive, that is to say, the austral fluid repels the austral, and the boreal the boreal; but the austral and boreal fluids reciprocally attract.

521. Natural or unmagnetised state. — When a body pervaded by the compound fluid is in its natural state and not magnetic, the two fluids are in combination, each molecule of the one being combined with a molecule of the other; consequently, in such state, neither attraction or repulsion is exercised, inasmuch as whatever is attracted by one molecule is repelled by the other.

522. Magnetised state. — When a body is magnetic, the fluid which pervades it is decomposed, the austral being directed towards one side of the equator, and the boreal towards the other. That side of the equator towards which the austral fluid is directed is the *austral*, and that towards which the boreal fluid is directed is the *boreal pole* of the magnet.

If the austral poles of the two magnets be presented to each other, they will mutually repel, in consequence of the mutual repulsion of the fluids which are directed towards them; and the same effect will take place if the boreal poles be presented to each other. If the austral pole of the one magnet be presented to the boreal pole of another, mutual attraction will take place, because the austral and boreal fluids, though separately self-repulsive, are reciprocally attractive.

It is in this manner that the hypothesis of two self-repulsive and mutually attractive fluids supplies an explanation of the general magnetic law, that like poles repel and unlike poles attract. It must be observed that the attraction and repulsion in this hypothesis are imputed not to the matter composing the magnetic body, but to the hypothetical fluids by which this matter is supposed to be pervaded.

523. **Coercive force.** — The force with which the opposite fluids are combined in bodies susceptible of magnetism varies. In some the conductor is feeble, so that they are easily decomposed, and the body consequently easily magnetised. In others they are more strongly combined, resisting decomposition, and rendering magnetism more difficult.

The facility with which after decomposition they are recombined, so as to restore the body to its natural or unmagnetised state, is always proportionate to that with which they are decomposed.

This force, which resists decomposition and recomposition with more or less intensity, is called the *coercive force*. It has great intensity in highly tempered steel, which consequently, when once magnetised, retains its magnetism ; and it is scarcely sensible in soft iron, which, when magnetism is momentarily imparted to it, loses the virtue almost instantaneously.

It might be assumed hypothetically that all bodies whatever are pervaded by the two magnetic fluids in a state of combination, and that some are unsusceptible of magnetism only because no power has been discovered sufficiently energetic to overcome their coercive force, while those which are susceptible of magnetism, and which retain the virtue once imparted to them, have a coercive force sufficiently limited to allow of decomposition, but sufficiently energetic to prevent spontaneous recomposition ; and that bodies like soft iron, which are only susceptible of temporary magnetism, have so little coercive force that, when removed from the influence of the decomposing agent, the fluids are spontaneously recombined.

524. **Magnetic substances.** — The only substances in which the magnetic fluid has been decomposed, and which are therefore susceptible of magnetism, are iron, nickel, cobalt, chromium, and manganese, the first being that in which the magnetic property is manifested by the most striking phenomena.

CHAP. II.

MAGNETISM BY INDUCTION.

525. Soft iron rendered temporarily magnetic. — If the
extremity of a bar of soft iron be presented to one of the poles of
a magnet, this bar will itself become immediately magnetic. It
will manifest a neutral line and two poles, that pole which is in
contact with the magnet being of a contrary name to the pole
which it touches. Thus, if A B, *fig.* 304., be the bar of soft iron

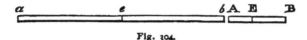

Fig. 304.

which is brought in contact with the boreal pole *b* of the magnet *a b*,
then A will be the austral and B the boreal pole of the bar of soft
iron thus rendered magnetic by contact, and E will be its equator,
which however will not be in the middle of the bar, but nearer to
the point of contact. These effects are thus explained by the
hypothesis of two fluids.

The attraction of the boreal pole of the magnet *a b* acting upon
the magnetic fluid which pervades the bar A B, decomposes it,
attracting the austral fluid towards the point of contact A, and
repelling the boreal fluid towards B. The austral fluid accordingly
predominates at the end A, and the boreal at the end B, a neutral
line or equator E separating them.

This state of the bar A B can be rendered experimentally manifest by any of the tests already explained. If it be rolled in iron
filings, they will attach themselves in two tufts separated by an
intermediate point which is free from them; and if the test pendulum (514.) be successively presented to different points of the
bar, the varying intensity of the attraction will be indicated.

If the bar A B be detached from the magnet, it will instantly
lose its magnetic virtue, the fluids which were decomposed and
separated will spontaneously recombine, and the bar will be reduced to its natural state, as may be proved by subjecting it
after separation to any of the tests already explained.

Thus is manifested the fact that the magnetism of soft iron has
no perceptible coercive force. The magnetic fluid is decomposed
by the contact of the pole of any magnet however feeble, and
when detached it is recomposed spontaneously and immediately.

526. This may be effected by proximity without contact.

e bar A B be presented at a small distance from the pole b,
manifest magnetism in the same manner; and if it be
lly removed from the pole, the magnetism it manifests will
h in degree, until at length it wholly disappears.

e end B instead of A be presented to b, the poles of the
ary magnet will be reversed, B becoming the austral, and A
eal.

series of bars of soft iron A B, A′ B′, A″ B″, *fig.* 305., be

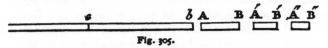

Fig. 305.

; into successive contiguity so as to form a series without
∂ contact, the extremity A of the first being presented to
eal pole b of the fixed magnet, then each bar of the series
rendered magnetic. The attraction of the boreal fluid at
ecompose the magnetic fluid of the bar A B, attracting the
fluid towards A, and repelling the boreal fluid towards B.
real fluid thus driven towards B will produce a like decom-
ı of the fluid in the second bar A′ B′, the austral fluid
:ttracted towards A′ and the boreal repelled towards B′;
e effects will be produced upon the next bar A″ B″, and

e bars be brought gradually closer together, the intensity
magnetism thus developed will be increased, and will con-
ı be increased until the bars are brought into contact.

Experimental illustration.—This may be rendered evi·
′ the simple experiment shown in *fig.* 306., where several

Fig. 306.

f soft iron are in succession suspended one from another
ıole of a magnetic bar.

Induction is the name given to this process, by which
ısm is developed by magnetic action at a distance.

Magnets with poles reversed neutralise each other.
second magnet of equal intensity with the first be laid
b, *fig.* 305., with its poles reversed, so that its austral pole

x

shall coincide with *b* and its boreal with *a*, the bars A B, A′ B′, A″ B″ magnetised by induction will instantly be reduced to their natural state, and deprived of the magnetic influence. This is easily explained. The attraction of the pole *b*, which draws towards it the austral and repels the boreal fluids of the bar A B, is neutralised by the attraction and repulsion of the austral pole of the second magnet laid upon it, which repels the austral fluid of the bar A B with a force equal to that with which the boreal fluid of the pole *b* attracts it, and attracts the boreal fluid with as much force as that with which the pole *b* repels it. Thus the attraction and repulsion of the two poles of the combined magnets neutralise each other, and the fluids which were decomposed in the bar A B spontaneously recombine; and the same effects take place in the other bars.

All these effects may be rendered experimentally manifest by submitting the bars A B, A′ B′, A″ B″ to any of the tests already explained.

530. **A magnet broken at its equator produces two magnets.** — It might be supposed, from what has been stated, that if a magnetic bar were divided at its equator, two magnets would be produced, one having austral and the other boreal magnetism, so that one of them would attract an austral and repel a boreal pole, while the other would produce the contrary attraction and repulsion. This, however, is not found to be the case. If a magnet be broken in two at its equator, two complete magnets will result, having each an equator at or near its centre, and two poles, austral and boreal; and if these be again broken, other magnets will be formed, each having an equator and two poles as before; and in the same manner, whatever be the number of parts, and however minute they be, into which a magnet is divided, each part will still be a complete magnet, with an equator and two poles.

531. **Decomposition of magnetic fluid is not attended by its transfer between pole and pole.** — It cannot, in a word, be assumed that the boreal fluid passes to one, and the austral fluid to the other side of the equator; for if this were the case, the fracture of the magnet at the equator would leave the two parts, one surcharged with austral and the other with boreal fluid, whereas by what has been just stated it is apparent that after such division both parts will possess both fluids.

532. **The decomposition is therefore molecular.** — Each molecule of the magnet is invested by an atmosphere composed of the two fluids, and the decomposition takes place in these atmospheres, the boreal fluid passing to one side of the molecule, and the austral fluid to the other. When a bar is magnetised, there-

fore, the material molecules which form it are invested with the magnetic fluids, but the austral fluids are all presented towards the austral pole, and the boreal fluids towards the boreal pole. When the bar is not magnetic, but in its natural state, the two fluids surrounding each molecule are diffused through each other and combined, neither prevailing more at one side than the other.

533. **The coercive force of iron varies with its molecular structure.**—The metal in different states of aggregation possesses different degrees of coercive force. Soft iron, when pure, is considered to be divested altogether of coercive force, or at least it possesses it in an insensible degree. In a more impure state, or when modified in its molecular structure by pressure, percussion, torsion, or other mechanical effects, it acquires more or less coercive power, and accordingly resists the reception of magnetism, and when magnetism has been imparted to it, retains it with a proportional force. Steel has still more coercive force than iron, and steel of different tempers manifests the coercive force in different degrees, that which possesses it in the highest degree being the steel which is of the highest temper, and which possesses in the greatest degree the qualities of hardness and brittleness. ·

534. **Effect of induction on hard iron or steel.** — If a bar of hard iron or steel be placed with its end in contact with a magnet, in the same manner as has been already described with respect to soft iron, it will exhibit no magnetism; but if it be kept in contact with the magnet for a considerable length of time, it will gradually acquire the same magnetic properties as have been described in respect to bars of soft iron, — with this difference, however, that having thus acquired them, it does not lose them when detached from the magnet, as is the case with soft iron. Thus it would appear, that it is not literally true that a bar of steel when brought into contact with the pole of a magnet receives no magnetism, but rather that it receives magnetism in an insensible degree; for if continued contact impart sensible magnetism, it must be admitted that contact for shorter intervals must impart more or less magnetism, since it is by the accumulation of the effects produced from moment to moment that the sensible magnetism manifested by continued contact is produced.

It appears, therefore, that the coercive energy of the bar of steel resists the action of the magnet, so that while the pole of the magnet accomplishes the decomposition of the magnetic fluid in a bar of soft iron instantaneously, or at least in an indefinitely small interval of time, it accomplishes in a bar of steel the same decomposition, but only after a long protracted interval, the decomposition proceeding by little and little, from moment to moment, during such interval.

Various expedients, as will appear hereafter, have been contrived by which the decomposition in the case of steel bars having a great coercive force is expedited. These consist generally in moving the pole of the magnet successively over the various points of the steel bar, upon which it is desired to produce the decomposition, the motion being always made with the contact of the same pole, and in the same direction. The pole is thus made to act successively upon every part of the surface of the bar to be magnetised, and being brought into closer contact with it acts more energetically; whereas when applied to only one point, the energy of its action upon other points is enfeebled by distance, the intensity of the magnetic attraction diminishing, like that of gravity, in the same proportion as the square of the distance increases.

Since steel bars having once received the magnetic virtue in this manner retain it for an indefinite time, artificial magnets can be produced by these means of any required form and magnitude.

535. **Forms of magnetic needles and bars.** — Thus a magnetic needle generally receives the form of a lozenge, as represented in *fig.* 307., having a conical cup of agate at its centre, which is supported upon a pivot in such a manner as that the needle is free to turn in a horizontal plane, round the pivot as a centre. In this case the weight of the needle must be so regulated as to be in equilibrium on the pivot.

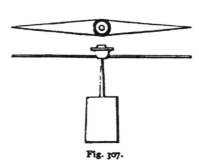

Fig. 307.

Bar magnets are pieces of steel in the form of cylinders or prisms whose length is considerable compared with their depth or thickness. In producing such magnets certain processes are necessary, which will be explained hereafter.

536. **Compound magnets** consist of several bar magnets, equal and similar in magnitude, being placed one upon the other with their corresponding poles together.

537. **Effects of heat on magnetism.** — Since the elevation or depression of temperature by producing dilatation and contraction affects the molecular state of a body, it might be expected to modify also its magnetic properties, and this is accordingly found to be the case.

538. **A red heat destroys the magnetism of iron.** — The *elevation* of temperature and the molecular dilatation consequent

upon it destroys the coercive force, and allows the recombination of the magnetic fluid. When after such change the magnet is allowed to cool, it will continue divested of its magnetic qualities. These effects may, however, be again imparted to it by the process already mentioned.

539. Different magnetic bodies lose their magnetism at different temperatures.—Thus the magnetism of nickel is effaced when it is raised to the temperature of 660°, iron at a cherry red, and cobalt at a temperature much more elevated.

540. Heat opposed to induction. — But not only does increased temperature deprive permanent magnets of their magnetism, but it renders even soft iron unsusceptible of magnetism by induction, for it is found that soft iron rendered incandescent does not become magnetic, when brought into contact or contiguity with the pole of a magnet.

541. Induced magnetism may be rendered permanent by hammering and other mechanical effects. — If a bar of soft iron, when rendered magnetic by induction, be hammered, rolled, or twisted, it will retain its magnetism. It would follow, therefore, that the change of molecular arrangement thus produced confers upon it a coercive force which it had not previously.

542. Compounds of iron are differently susceptible of magnetism according to the proportion of iron they contain. Exceptions, however, to this are represented in the peroxide, the persulphate, and some other compounds containing iron in small proportion, in which the magnetic virtue is not at all present.

543. Compounds of other magnetic bodies are not susceptible. — Nickel, cobalt, chromium, and manganese are the only simple bodies which, in common with iron, enjoy the magnetic property, and this property completely disappears in most of the chemical compounds of which they form a part. Magnetism, however, has been rendered manifest under a great variety of circumstances connected with the development of electricity which have been already explained.

544. Consequent points. — In the production of artificial magnets, it frequently happens that a magnetic bar has more than one equator, and consequently more than two poles. This fact may be experimentally ascertained by exposing successively the length of a bar to any of the tests already explained. Thus, if presented to the test pendulum, it will be attracted with a continually decreasing force as it approaches each equator, and with an increasing force as it recedes from it. If the bar be rolled in iron filings, they will be attached to it in a succession of tufts separated by spaces where none are attached, indicating the equators. If it be placed under a glass plate or sheet of paper on which fine iron filings are sprinkled, they will arrange themselves according to a series of concentric curves, as represented in *fig.* 308.

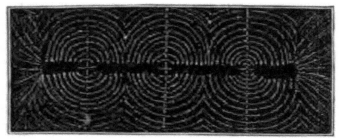

Fig. 308.

It is evident that the magnetic bar in this case is equivalent to a succession of independent magnets placed pole to pole.

The equators in these cases are called *consequent points.*

CHAP. III.

TERRESTRIAL MAGNETISM.

545. **Analogy of the earth to a magnet.** — If a small and sensitive magnetic needle, suspended by a fibre of silk so as to be free to assume any position, which the attractions that act upon it may have a tendency to give to it, be carried over a magnetic bar from end to end, it will assume in different positions different directions, depending on the effect produced by the attractions and repulsions exercised by the bar upon it.

Let *a b, fig.* 309., be such a needle, the thread of suspension o *e* being first placed vertically over the equator ᴇ of the magnetic bar ᴀ ʙ. The austral magnetism of ᴀ ᴇ will attract the boreal magnetism of *b e*, and will repel the austral magnetism of *a e*; and in like manner the boreal magnetism of ʙ ᴇ will attract the austral magnetism of *a e*, and will repel the boreal magnetism of *b e*. These attractions and repulsions will moreover be respectively equal, since the distance of *a e* and *b e* from ʙ ᴀ and ʙ ᴇ are equal. The needle *a b* will therefore settle itself parallel to the bar ᴀ ʙ, the pole *a* being directed to ʙ, and the pole *b* being directed to ᴀ.

If the suspending thread o *e* be removed towards ᴀ to ᴘ *e*, the attraction of ᴀ upon *b* will become greater than the attraction of ʙ upon *a*, because the distance of ᴀ from *b* will be less than the distance of ʙ from *a*; and, for a like reason, the repulsion of ᴀ upon *a* will be greater than the repulsion of ʙ upon *b*. The needle *a b* will therefore be affected as if the end *b* were heavier

n a, and it will throw itself into the inclined position represented in the
ure, the pole a inclining downwards.

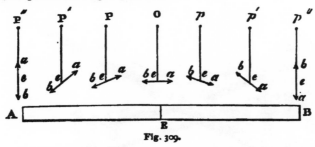

Fig. 309.

it be carried still further towards A, the inequality of the attractions
repulsions increasing in consequence of the greater inequality of the
nces of a and b from A and B, the inclination of b downwards will be
ortionally augmented, as represented at P'. In fine, when the thread of
ension is moved to a point P'' over the pole A, the needle will become
ical, the pole b attracted by A pointing downwards. If the needle be
ied in like manner from E to B, like effects will be manifested, as repre-
ed in the figure, the pole a inclining downwards, arising from the same
es.

. magnetic needle similarly suspended, carried over the surface
he earth in the directions north and south, undergoes changes
lirection such as would be produced, on the principles ex-
ned above, if the globe were a magnet having its poles at
:ain points, not far distant from its poles of rotation.   To
ler this experimentally evident, it will be necessary to be pro-
:d with two magnetic instruments, one mounted so that the
ile shall have a motion in a horizontal plane round a vertical
i, and the other so that it shall have a motion in a vertical plane
nd a horizontal axis.

46. **The azimuth compass** is an instrument consisting of a
;netic bar or needle balanced on a vertical pivot, so as to be
ible of turning freely in a horizontal plane, the point of the
ile playing in a circle, of which its pivot is the centre. It is
ously mounted and designated, according to the circumstances
purpose of its application. When used to indicate the relative
·ings or horizontal directions of distant objects, whether ter-
rial or celestial, a graduated circle is placed under the needle
concentric with it. The divisions of this circle indicate the
:ings of any distant object, in relation to the direction of the
ile, *fig.* 310.

ie most efficient form of azimuth or variation compass, as it is otherwise
d, is shown in *fig.* 310. The needle B B' is enclosed in a copper case with
iss top, the rim of which supports a telescope F F', which plays in a

vertical circle so as to be capable of being directed to any celestial or terrestrial object. The frame can be turned round the centre of the box so

Fig. 320.

that any azimuth can be given to the telescope. The azimuth angle through which the telescope is turned is indicated by the graduated circle surrounding the compass. In fine, the inclination of the telescope to the horizon, or, what is the same, the altitude of the object to which it is directed, is shown by the graduated arc m.

Screws N N are placed in the feet, by which the instrument is levelled; and a spirit level E is suspended upon the axis of the telescope by which the instrument is adjusted.

By comparing the direction of any celestial object, whose real azimuth is known, with the direction of the needle, its apparent azimuth will be found, and the difference between the apparent and real azimuth is in that case the variation of the compass.

The pivot in this form of compass is rendered vertical by means of a plumb line or spirit level.

547. **The azimuth compass used at sea** has the pivot supporting the needle fixed in the bottom of a cylindrical box, closed at the top by a plate of glass, so as to protect it from the air. The magnetic bar is attached to the under side of a circular card, upon which is engraved a radiating diagram, dividing the circle into thirty-two parts called *points*. The compass box is suspended so as to preserve its horizontal position undisturbed by the motion of the vessel, by means of two concentric hoops called *gimbals**, one a little less than and included within the other. It is supported at two points upon the lesser hoop, which are diametrically opposite, and this lesser hoop itself is supported by two points upon the greater hoop, which are also diametrically opposite, but at right angles to the former. By these means the box, being at liberty to swing in two planes at right angles to each other, will maintain itself horizontal, and will therefore keep the pivot supporting the needle vertical, whatever be the changes of position of the vessel.

This arrangement is represented in *fig.* 311., a vertical section of the compass box being given in *fig.* 312.

The sides of the cylindrical box are *b b'*, its bottom *f f'*, and the glass which covers it *v*. The magnetic bar or needle is supported on a vertical pivot by means of a conical cup, and can be raised and lowered at pleasure

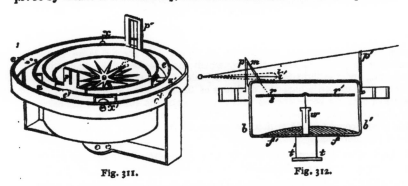

Fig. 311.   Fig. 312.

by means of a screw *w*. The compass card is represented in section at *r r'* *fig.* 312., and the divisions upon it marked by radiating lines called the *rose* are represented in *fig.* 311.

* " Mechanics " (549.).

Two narrow plates, p and p', are attached to the sides of the box so as to be diametrically opposed. In p there is a narrow vertical slit. In p' there is a wider vertical slit, along which is stretched vertically a thin wire. The eye placed at o looks through the two slits, and turns the instrument round its support until the object of observation is intersected by the vertical wire, extended along the slit p'. Provisions are made in the instrument by which the direction thus observed can be ascertained relatively to that of the needle. The angle included between the direction of the observed object, and that of the needle, is the *bearing* of the object relatively to the needle.

The compass box is suspended within the hoop $e\,e'$, at two points $z\,z'$ diametrically opposed, and the hoop $e\,e'$ is itself suspended within the fixed hoop $c\,c'$, at two points $x\,x'$, also diametrically opposed, but at right angles to $z\,z'$.

The ordinary mariner's compass enclosed in its case, called a binnacle, is shown in *fig.* 313., where K is a plate of ground glass for the purpose of

Fig. 313.

admitting light to the instrument at night. A strong lamp with a reflector is placed opposite this, by which the interior of the box is illuminated, and the light is reflected to a plate of talc, or other semi-transparent substance, on which the divisions of the compass are marked. A line marked over the box coincides with the course of the vessel, and the helmsman so regulates it that this line shall form an angle with the north pole of the needle equal to that which the course of the vessel is required to have with the meridian.

548. **The dipping needle,** *fig.* 314., consists of a magnetic needle A B, supported and balanced on a horizontal axis, and playing therefore in a vertical plane. The angles through which it turns are indicated by a graduated circle D D, the centre of which coincides with the axis of the needle, and the frame which supports it has an azimuthal motion round a vertical axis, which is indicated and measured by the graduated horizontal circle F F.

The instrument is adjusted by means of a spirit level, and regulating screws Q Q inserted in the feet.

549. **Analysis of magnetic phenomena of the earth.** — Supplied with these instruments, it will be easy to submit to observation the magnetic phenomena manifested at different parts of the earth.

Fig. 314.

If the azimuth compass be placed anywhere in the northern hemisphere, at London for example, the needle will take a certain position, forming an angle with the terrestrial meridian, and directing one pole to a point a certain number of degrees west of the north, and the other to a point a like number of degrees east of the south. If it be turned aside from this direction, it will, when liberated, oscillate on the one side and the other of this direction, and soon come to rest in it.

Since an unmagnetised needle would rest indifferently in any

direction, this preference of the magnetised needle to one particular direction, must be ascribed to magnetic force exerted by
the earth attracting one of the poles of the needle in one direction,
and the other pole in the opposite direction. That this is not the
casual attraction of unmagnetic ferruginous matter contained
within the earth, is proved by the fact that, if the direction of the
needle be reversed, it will, when liberated, make a pirouette upon
its pivot, and after some oscillations resume its former direction.
This remarkable property is reproduced in all parts of the earth,
on land and water, and equally on the summits of lofty mountains,
in the lowest valleys, and in the deepest mines.

550. **The magnetic meridian** is the direction thus assumed
by the horizontal needle in any given place.

The direction of a needle which would point due north and
south is the *true meridian*, or the *terrestrial meridian* of the place.

551. **The declination or variation** is the angle formed by the
magnetic meridian and the *terrestrial meridian*.

The declination is said to be *eastern* or *western*, according as the
pole of the needle, which is directed northwards, deviates to the
east or to the west of the terrestrial meridian.

552. **Magnetic polarity of the earth.** — To explain these
phenomena, therefore, the globe of the earth itself is considered as
a magnet, whose poles attract and repel the poles of the horizontal
needle, each pole of the earth attracting that of an unlike name,
and repelling that of a like name. If, therefore, the northern pole
of the earth be considered as that which is pervaded by boreal
magnetism, and the southern pole by austral magnetism, the
former will attract the austral and repel the boreal pole, and the
latter will attract the boreal and repel the austral pole of the
needle. Hence it will follow that the pole of the needle which is
directed northwards is the austral, and that which is directed
southwards is the boreal pole.

553. **Variation of the dip.** — It was shown in (545.) that when
a needle which is free to play in a vertical plane was carried over
a magnet, it rested in the horizontal position only when suspended
vertically over the equator of the magnet, and its austral and
boreal poles were inclined downwards, according as the needle
was suspended at the boreal or austral side of the equator, and
that this inclination was augmented as the distance from the
equator at which the needle was suspended was increased. Now
it remains to be seen whether any phenomenon analogous to this
is presented by the earth.

For this purpose let the dipping needle, *fig.* 314., be arranged with its
axis at right angles to the direction of the needle of the azimuth compass.
It will then be found, that in general the dipping needle will not rest in a

horizontal position, but will assume a direction inclined to the vertical line, as represented in the figure, one pole being presented downwards, and the other upwards. The angle which the lower arm of the needle makes with the horizontal line is called the *dip*.

If this apparatus be carried in this hemisphere northwards, in the direction in which a horizontal needle would point, the austral pole will be inclined downwards, and the dip will continually increase ; but if it be carried southwards, the dip will continually diminish. By continuing to transport it southwards, the dip continually diminishing, a station will at length be found where the needle will rest in the horizontal position. If it be carried further southwards, the boreal pole will begin to turn downwards ; in other words, the dip will be south instead of north, and as it is carried further southwards, this dip will continue to increase.

If the needle be carried northwards, in this hemisphere the dip continually augmenting, a station will at length be attained where the needle will become vertical, the austral pole being presented downwards, and the boreal pole upwards. In the same manner, in the southern hemisphere, if the needle be carried southwards, a station will at length be attained where it will become vertical, the boreal pole being presented downwards, and the austral pole pointing to the zenith.

Complete analogy of the earth to a magnet.—By comparing these results with those which have been already described in the case where the needle was carried successively over a magnetic bar, the complete identity of the phenomena will be apparent, and it will be evident that the earth and the needle comport themselves in relation to each other exactly as do a small and a great magnet, over which it might be carried, the point where the needle is horizontal being over the magnetic equator, and those two points where it is vertical being the magnetic poles.

554. **The magnetic equator.**—The needle being brought to that point where it rests horizontal, the magnetic equator will be at right angles to its direction. By transporting it successively in the one or the other direction thus indicated, the successive points upon the earth's surface where the needle rests horizontal, and where the dip is nothing, will be ascertained. The line upon the earth traced by this point is the magnetic equator.

555. **Its form and position not regular.**—This line is not, as might be expected, a great circle of the earth. It follows a course crossing the terrestrial equator from south to north, on the west coast of Africa, near the island of St. Thomas, at about 7° or 8° long. E., in a direction intersecting the equator at an angle of about 12° or 13°. It then passes across Africa towards Ceylon, and intersects that island near the point of the Indian promontory. It keeps a course from this of from 8° to 9° of N. lat. through the Indian Archipelago, and then gradually declining towards the

line again intersects it at a point in the Pacific Ocean in long. 170° W., the angle at which it intersects the line being more acute than at the other point of intersection. It then follows a course a few degrees south of the line, and striking the west coast of South America near Lima, it crosses the South American continent, attaining the greatest south latitude near Bahia; and then again ascending towards the line, traverses the Atlantic and strikes the coast of Africa, as already stated, near the island of St. Thomas.

The magnetic equator, unlike the ecliptic, is not any regular curve, but follows the course we have just indicated in a direction slightly sinuous.

556. **Variation of the dip going north or south.** — It has been explained, that proceeding from north or south, from the magnetic equator, the needle dips on the one side or on the other, the dip increasing with the distance from the magnetic equator to which the needle is transported north or south.

557. **The lines of equal dip**, therefore, may be considered as bearing the same relation to the magnetic equator which parallels of latitude bear to the terrestrial equator, being arranged nearly parallel to the former, though not in a manner so regular as in the case of parallels of latitude.

558. **Magnetic meridians.** — If the horizontal needle be transported north or south, following a course indicated by its direction, it will be carried over a magnetic meridian. These magnetic meridians, therefore, bear to the magnetic equator a relation analogous to those which terrestrial meridians bear to the terrestrial equator, but, like the lines of equal dip, they are much more irregular.

559. **Method of ascertaining the declination of the needles.** — Astronomy supplies various methods of determining in a given place the declination of the needle. It may be generally stated that this problem may be solved by observing any object whose angular distance from the true north is otherwise known, and comparing the direction of such object with the direction of the needle. Let P, *fig.* 315, be the place of observation; let P N be the direction of the true north, or, what is the same, the direction of the terrestrial meridian; and let P N' be the direction of the magnetic needle, or, what is the same, the magnetic meridian. The angle N P N' will then be the declination of the needle, being the angle formed by the terrestrial and magnetic meridians (551.).

Fig. 315.

Let o be any object seen on the horizon in the direction P o; the angle o P N is called the true azimuth of this object, and the angle o P N' is called its magnetic azimuth. This magnetic azimuth may always be observed by means of an azimuth compass.

If, then, an object be selected whose true azimuth is otherwise known, the declination of the needle may be determined by taking the difference between the true and magnetic azimuths of the object.

There are numerous celestial objects of which the azimuths are either given in tables, or may be calculated by rules and formulæ supplied by astronomy; such, for example, as the sun and moon at the moments they rise or set, or when they are at any proposed or observed altitudes. By the aid of such objects, which are visible occasionally at all places, the declination of the needle may be found.

560. **Local declinations.**—At different places upon the earth's surface the needle has different declinations. In Europe its mean declination is about 17°, increasing in going westward.

561. **Agonic lines.**—There are two lines on the earth's surface which have been called *agonic lines*, upon which there is no declination; and where, therefore, the needle is directed along the terrestrial meridian. One of these passes over the American and the other over the Asiatic continent, and the former has consequently been called the *American* and the latter the *Asiatic agonic.* These lines run north and south, but do not follow the course of meridians. It has been ascertained that their position is not fixed, but is liable to sensible changes in considerable intervals of time.

562. **Variation of declination.**—In proceeding in either direction, east or west from these lines, the declination of the needle gradually increases, and becomes a maximum at a certain intermediate point between them. On the west of the Asiatic agonic the declination is west, on the east it is east.

At present the declination in England is about 24° W.; in Boston in the U. States it is 5½° W. Its mean value in Europe is 17° W. At Bonn it is 20°, at Edinburgh 26°, Iceland 38°, Greenland, 50°, Konigsberg, 13°, and St. Petersburg 6°.

The following table, however, will exhibit more distinctly the variation of the declination in different parts of the globe. The longitudes expressed in the first column are measured westward from the meridian of Paris, and the declinations given in the second column are those which are observed on the terrestrial equator, those in the third column corresponding to the mean latitude of 45°.

Table of the Declinations of the Magnetic Needle in different Longitudes, and in Lat.=0 and Lat.=45°.

Longitudes West of the Meridian of Paris.	Declinations.		Longitudes West of the Meridian of Paris.	Declinations.	
	Lat.=0.	Lat.=45°.		Lat.=0.	Lat.=45°.
0	19° W	22° W	190	9° E	11° E
10	19 W	25 W	200	8 E	8 E
20	16 W	26 W	210	5 E	4 E
30	11 W	25 W	220	3 E	2 E
40	4 W	24 W	230	2 E	1 E
50	3 E	24 W	240	0	1 W
60	5 E	20 W	250	0	0
70	8 E	11 W	260	1 E	3 E
80	10 E	3 W	270	3 E	4 E
90	10 E	4 E	280	0	4 E
100	8 E	11 E	290	0	4 E
110	6 E	17 E	300	2 W	2 E
120	5 E	18 E	310	7 W	1 W
130	5 E	19 E	320	11 W	5 W
140	6 E	19 E	330	13 W	10 W
150	6 E	19 E	340	17 W	14 W
160	7 E	19 E	350	18 W	17 W
170	9 E	17 E	360	19 W	21 W
180	10 E	14 E			

563. **Isogonic lines** are lines traced upon the globe at a point at which the magnetic needle has the same declinations. These, as well as the *isoclinic lines*, or lines of equal dip, are irregular in their arrangement, and not very exactly ascertained.

564. **Local dip.** — The local variations of the dip are also imperfectly known. In Europe it ranges from 60° to 70°. In 1836 the dip observed at the undermentioned places was as follows:—

Pekin	-	-	-	-	-	-	54° 49′
Rome	-	-	-	-	-	-	61° 42′
Brussels	-	-	-	-	-	-	68° 32′
St. Petersburg	-	-	-	-	-	-	71° 0′
St. Helena	-	-	-	-	-	-	14° 50′
Rio de Janeiro	-	-	-	-	-	-	13° 30′

565. **The position of the magnetic poles,** or the points where the dip is 90°, is determined with considerable difficulty, inasmuch as for a considerable distance round that point the dip is nearly 90°. Hansteen considered that there were grounds for supposing that there were two magnetic poles in each hemisphere. One of these in the northern hemisphere he supposed to be west of Hudson's Bay, in 80° lat. N., and 96° long. W.; and the other in Northern Asia, in 81° lat. N., and 116° long. E. The two southern magnetic poles he supposed to be situate near the southern pole. This supposition, however, appears to be at present abandoned, and the observations of Gauss lead to the conclusion that there is but one magnetic pole in each hemisphere.

In the northern voyages made between 1829 and 1833, Sir

James Ross found the dipping needle to stand vertical in the neighbourhood of Hudson's Bay at 70° 5′ 17″ lat. N., and 114° 55′ 18″ long. W. The dipping needle, according to the observations of Sir James Ross, was nowhere absolutely vertical, departing from the vertical in all cases by a small angle, amounting generally to one minute of a degree. This, however, might be ascribed to the error of observation, or the imperfection of instruments exposed to such a climate.

The existence of the magnetic pole, however, at or near the point indicated, was proved by carrying round it at a certain distance a horizontal needle, which always pointed to the spot in whatever direction it was carried. Gauss has fixed the position of the magnetic pole in the southern hemisphere by theory at 72° 35′ lat. S., and 152° 30′ long. E.

566. **The magnetic poles are not therefore antipodal,** like the terrestrial poles; or, in other words, they do not form the extremities of the same diameter of the globe: they are not even on the same meridian. If Gauss's statement be assumed to be correct, the southern magnetic pole is on a meridian 152° 30′ E. of the meridian of Greenwich, and therefore 207° 30′ W. of that meridian, whereas the northern magnetic pole is on a meridian 114° 55′ 18″ W. The angle, therefore, between the two meridians passing through the two poles will be about 92½°. It would follow, therefore, that these points lie upon terrestrial meridians nearly at right angles to each other, and that upon these they are at nearly equal distances from the terrestrial poles; the distance of the northern magnetic pole from the northern terrestrial pole being nearly 20°, and the distance of the southern magnetic pole from the southern terrestrial pole being about 17½°.

567. **Periodical variations of terrestrial magnetism.** — It appears, from observations made at intervals of time more or less distant for about two centuries back, that the magnetic condition of the earth is subject to a periodical change; but neither the quantity nor the law of this change is exactly known. It was not until recently that magnetic observations were conducted in such a manner, as to supply the data necessary for the development of the laws of magnetic variation, and they have not been yet continued a sufficient length of time to render these laws manifest.

Independently of observation, theory affords no means of ascertaining these laws, since it is not certainly known what are the physical causes to which the magnetism of the earth must be ascribed.

In the following table are given the declinations of the needle observed at Paris between the years 1580 and 1835, and the dip between the years 1671 and 1835.

Y

568. Table of Declinations observed at Paris.

. Year.	Declination.	Year.	Declination.
1580	11° 30′ E	1817	22° 19′ W
1618	8	1823	22 23
1663	0	1824	22 23
1678	1 30 W	1825	22 22
1700	8 10	1827	22 20
1780	19 55	1828	22 5
1785	22	1829	22 12
1805	22 5	1832	22 3
1813	22 28	1835	22 4
1814	22 34	1851	20 25
1816	22 25		

Table of the Dip observed at Paris.

Year.	Dip.	Year.	Dip.
1671	75°	1820	68° 20′
1754	72 15′	1821	68 14
1776	72 25	1822	68 11
1780	71 48	1823	68 8
1791	70 52	1825	68 0
1798	69 51	1826	68 0
1806	69 12	1829	67 41
1810	68 50	1831	67 40
1814	68 36	1835	67 24
1816	68 40	1841	67 9
1818	68 35	1851	66 39
1819	68 25		

569. **The intensity of terrestrial magnetism,** like that of a common magnet, may be estimated by the rate of vibration which it produces in a magnetic needle submitted to its attraction. This method of determining the intensity of magnetic force is in all respects analogous to those, by which the intensity of the earth's attraction is determined by a common pendulum.* The same needle being exposed to a varying attraction, will vary its rate of vibration, the force which attracts it being proportional to the square of the number of vibrations which it makes in a given time. Thus, if at one place it makes ten vibrations per minute, and in another only eight, the magnetic force which produces the first will be to that which produces the second rate of vibration, as 100 to 64.

570. In this manner it has been found that the intensity of terrestrial magnetism is least at the magnetic equator, and that it increases gradually in approaching the poles.

571. **Isodynamic lines,** are lines upon the earth where the magnetic intensities are equal, and resemble in their general arrangement, without however coinciding with them, the isoclinic curves or magnetic parallels of equal dip.

572. **Their near coincidence with isothermal lines.**—It

* "Mechanics" (505.).

found that there is so near a coincidence between the
nic and the isothermal lines, that a strong presumption is
hat terrestrial magnetism either arises from terrestrial
that these phenomena have at least a common origin.

Equatorial and polar intensities. — It appears to
om the general result of observations made on the inten-
errestrial magnetism, that its intensity at the poles is to
sity at the equator nearly in the ratio of 3 to 2.

Effect of the terrestrial magnetism on soft iron. — If
; were wanted to complete the demonstration that the
the earth is a true magnet, it would be supplied by the
roduced by it upon substances susceptible of magnetism,
ch are not yet magnetised. It has been already shown
:n a bar of soft iron is presented to the pole of a magnet
·al magnetism is decomposed, the austral fluid being at-
to one extremity, and the boreal fluid repelled to the
ı that the bar of soft iron becomes magnetised, and con-
ɔ as long as it is exposed to the influence of the magnet.
a bar of soft iron be presented to the earth in the same
precisely the same effects will ensue. Thus, if it be held
irection of the dipping needle, so that one of its ends shall
:nted in the direction of the magnetic attraction of the
will become magnetic, as may be proved by any of the
magnetism already explained. Thus, if a sensitive needle
nted to that end of the bar which in the northern hemi-
s directed downwards, austral magnetism will be mani-
:he boreal pole of the needle being attracted, and the
pole repelled. If the needle be presented to the upper
:he bar, contrary effects will be manifested; and if it be
d to the middle of the bar, the neutral line or equator
indicated. If the bar be now inverted, the upper end
:esented downwards, and *vice versâ*, still parallel to the
needle, its poles will also be inverted, the lower, which
ly was boreal, being austral, and *vice versâ*.
ı bar be held in any other direction, inclined obliquely to
ıing needle, the same effects will be manifested, but in a
:ee, just as would be the case if similarly presented to an
magnet; and, in fine, if it be held at right angles to the
ı of the dipping needle, no magnetism whatever will be
:d in it.

Its effects on steel bars. — If the same experiments be
th bars of hard iron or steel, no sensible magnetism will at
leveloped; but if they be held for a considerable time in
ɔ position, they will at length become magnetic, as would
ınder like conditions with an artificial magnet. Iron and

steel tools which are hung up in workshops in a vertical position are found to become magnetic, an effect explained by this cause.

576. **Diurnal variation of the needle.** — Besides the changes in the magnetic state of the earth, the periods of which are measured by long intervals of time, there are more minute and rapid changes, depending apparently upon the vicissitudes of the seasons and the diurnal changes.

The magnitude of the diurnal variation depends upon the situation of the place, the day, and the season, but is obviously connected with the function of solar heat. At Paris it is observed that during the night the needle is nearly stationary; at sunrise it begins to move, its north pole turning westwards, as if it were repelled by the influence of the sun. About noon, or more generally between noon and three o'clock, its western variation attains a maximum, and then it begins to move eastward, which movement continues until some time between nine and eleven o'clock at night, when the needle resumes the position it had when it commenced its western motion in the morning.

The amplitude of this diurnal range of the needle is, according to Cassini's observations, greatest during summer and least during winter. Its mean amount for the months of April, May, June, July, August, and September is stated at from 13 to 15 minutes; and for the months of October, November, December, January, and March, at from 8 to 10 minutes. There are, however, occasionally, days upon which its range amounts to 25 minutes, and others when it does not surpass 5 or 6 minutes. Cassini repeated his magnetic observations in the cellars constructed under the Paris observatory at a depth of about a hundred feet below the surface, and therefore removed from the immediate influence of the light and heat of the day. The amplitude of the variations and all the peculiarities of the movement of the needle here, were found to be precisely the same as at the surface.

In more northern latitudes, as, for example, in Denmark, Iceland, and North America, the diurnal variations of the needle are in general more considerable and less regular. It appears, also, that in these places the needle is not stationary during the night, as in Paris, and that it is towards evening that it attains its maximum westward deviation. On the contrary, on going from the north towards the magnetic equator the diurnal variations diminish, and cease altogether on arriving at this line. It appears, however, according to the observations of Captain Duperrey, that the position of the sun north or south of the terrestrial equator has a perceptible influence on the oscillation of the needle.

On the south of the magnetic equator the diurnal variations are produced, as might be expected, in a contrary manner; the northern pole of the magnet turns to the east at the same hours that, in the northern hemisphere, it turns to the west.

It has not yet been certainly ascertained whether in each hemisphere these diurnal variations of the needle correspond in the places where the eastern and western declinations also correspond.

The dip is also subject to certain diurnal variations, but much smaller in their range than in the case of the horizontal needle.

As a general result of these observations it may be inferred, that if a magnetic needle were suspended in such a manner as to be free to move in any direction whatever, it would, during twenty-four hours, move round its

uspension in such a manner as to describe a small cone, whose
be an ellipse or some other curve more or less elongated, and
is the mean direction of the dipping needle.

disturbances in the magnetic intensity. — The in-
well as the direction of the magnetic attraction of the
t given place are subject to continual disturbances, in-
:ly of those more regular variations just mentioned.
listurbances are in general connected with the electrical
ie atmosphere, and are observed to accompany the phe-
:f the aurora borealis, earthquakes, volcanic eruptions,
cissitudes of temperature, storms, and other atmospheric
:es.

nfluence of aurora borealis. — During the appearance
:ora borealis in high latitudes, a considerable deflection
:dle is generally manifested, amounting often to several
So closely and necessarily is magnetic disturbance
with this atmospheric phenomenon, that practised ob-
n ascertain the existence of an aurora borealis by the
s of the needle, when the phenomenon itself is not

CHAP. IV.

MAGNETISATION.

rnetisation is founded upon the property of induction
When one of the poles of a magnet is presented to any
h is susceptible of magnetism, it will have a tendency to
: the magnetic fluid, attracting one of its constituents
ing the other. If the coercive force by which the fluids
ned be greater than the energy of the attraction of the
o decomposition will take place, and the body to which
ated will not be magnetised, but the coercive force with
fluids are united will be rendered more feeble, and
will be more susceptible of being magnetised than

:ver, the energy of the magnetic be greater than the
'orce, a decomposition will take place, more or less in
i as the force of the magnet exceeds in a greater or less
: coercive force.

rtificial magnets. — It has been already explained,
soft iron is almost, if not altogether, divested of coercive
hat a bar of this substance is converted into a magnet

instantaneously when the pole of a magnet is presented to it; but the absence of coercive force, which renders this conversion so prompt, is equally efficacious in depriving the bar of its magnetism the moment the magnet which produces this magnetism is removed. Soft iron, therefore, is inapplicable when the object is to produce permanent magnetism. The material best suited for this purpose is steel, especially that which has a fine grain, a uniform structure, and is free from flaws. It is necessary that it should have a certain degree of hardness, and that this should be uniform through its entire mass. If the hardness be too great, it is difficult to impart to it the magnetic virtue; if not great enough, it loses its magnetism for want of sufficient coercive force. To render steel bars best fitted for artificial magnets, it has been found advantageous to confer upon them in the first instance the highest degree of temper, and thus to render them as hard and brittle as glass, and then to anneal them until they are brought to a straw or violet colour.

581. **Best form for bar magnets.** — The intensity of artificial magnets depends also, to some extent, upon their form and magnitude. It has been ascertained, that a bar magnet has the best proportion when its thickness is about one fourth and its length twenty times its breadth.

582. **Horse shoe magnets.** — These magnets are shaped as represented in *fig.* 316. When magnets are constructed in this form, the distance between the two poles ought not to be greater than the thickness of the bar of which the magnet consists. The surface of the steel forming both bars, in horse shoe magnets, should be rendered as even and as well polished as possible.

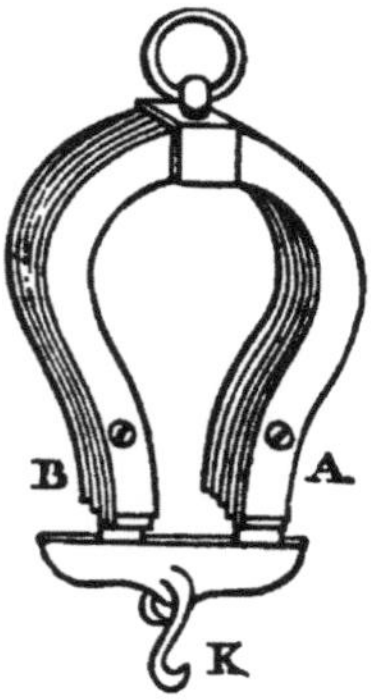

583. **The methods of producing artificial magnets by friction** commonly practised, are called the *method of single touch*, and the *method of double touch*.

584. **Method of single touch.** — The bar A'B', *fig.* 317., which is to be magnetised, is laid upon a block of wood L projecting at each end a couple of inches.

Fig. 316.

Under the ends are placed the opposite poles A and B of two powerful magnets, so as to be in close contact with the bar to be magnetised. The influence of the pole A will be to attract the boreal fluid of the bar towards the end B', and to repel the austral fluid towards the end A'; and the effect of the pole B will be similar, that is to say, to repel the boreal fluid towards the end B', and to attract the austral towards the end A'. It is evident, therefore, that if the coercive force of the magnetism of the bar A'B' be not greater than the force of the magnets A and B, a decomposition will take ce by simple contact, and the bar A′ B′ will be converted into a magnet, ving its austral pole at A′ and its boreal pole at B′; and, indeed, this will

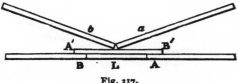

Fig. 317.

ccomplished even though the coercive force of the bar A′ B′ be consider-, if it be left a sufficient length of time under the influence of the gnets A and B.

ut without waiting for this, its magnetisation may be accomplished 1ediately by the following process. Let two bar magnets a and b be ed in contact with the bar A′ B′ to be magnetised, near its middle point, without touching each other, and let them be inclined in opposite ctions to the bar A′ B′, at angles of about 30°, as represented in the re. Let the bar which is applied on the side B′ have its austral pole, and t which is applied on the side A′ its boreal pole, in contact with the bar ′; and to prevent the contact of the two bars a and b, let a small piece of d, lead, copper, or other substance not susceptible of magnetism, be placed ween them. Taking the two bars a and b, one in the right and the other he left hand, let them now be drawn in contrary directions, slowly and formly along the bar A′ B′, from its middle to its extremities, and being 1 raised from it, let them be again placed as before, near its middle point, drawn again uniformly and slowly to its extremities; and let this ess be repeated until the bar A′ B′ has been magnetised.

t is evident that the action of the two magnetic poles a and b will be to ompose the magnetic fluid of the bar A′ B′, and that in this they are d by the influence of the magnets A and B, which enfeeble, as has been ady shown, the coercive force.

This method is applicable with advantage to magnetise, in the st complete and regular manner, compass needles, and bars ose thickness does not exceed a quarter of an inch.

;85. **Method of double touch.** — When the bars exceed this ckness, this method is insufficient, and the method of double ch is found more effectual.

he bars A and B, *fig.* 318., are placed as before, inclined at an angle 1 each other, contrary poles being presented downwards. A small k of wood L is placed between them, so as to keep the poles at a fixed ance asunder, and they are maintained in their relative positions by 1g attached to a block of wood. The bar a b to be magnetised is sup-ed at the ends as before, by the contrary poles of two bar magnets. The ined bars being placed at the centre of the bar a b, they are moved to-1er first to one extremity b, and then back along the length of the entire to the other extremity a. They are then again drawn over the bar to b, so backwards and forwards continuously until the bar is magnetised. operation is always terminated when the bars have passed over that ′ of the bar a b opposite to that upon which the motion commenced. s if the operation commenced by moving the united bars A B from the centre to the end *b*, it will be terminated when they are moved from the extremity *a* to the middle.

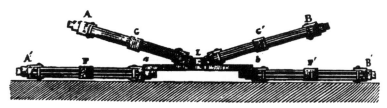

Fig. 318.

586. Inapplicable to compass needles and long bars. — By this method a greater quantity of magnetism is developed than in the former, but it should never be employed for magnetising compass needles or bars intended for delicate experiments, since it almost always produces magnets with poles of unequal force, and frequently gives them consequent points (544.), especially when the bars have considerable length.

587. Magnetic saturation. — Since the coercive force proper to each body resists the recomposition of the magnetic fluids, it follows that the quantity of magnetism which a bar or needle is capable of retaining permanently, will be proportional to this coercive force. If, by the continuance of the process of magnetisation and the influence of very powerful magnets, a greater development of magnetism be produced than corresponds with the coercive force, the fluids will be recomposed by the mutual attraction until the coercive force resists any further recomposition. The tendency of the magnetic fluids to unite being then in equilibrium with the coercive force, no further recomposition will take place, and the bar will retain its magnetism undiminished. When the bar is in this state, it is said to be magnetised to *saturation*.

It has been generally supposed that when bars are surcharged with magnetism they lose their surplus and fall suddenly to the point of saturation, the recomposition of the fluids being instantaneous. M. Pouillet, however, has shown that this recomposition is gradual, and after magnetisation there is even in some cases a reaction of the fluids, which is attended with an increase instead of a diminution of magnetism. He observes that it happens not unfrequently that the magnetism is not brought to permanent equilibrium with the coercive force for several months.

588. Limit of magnetic force. — It must not be supposed that by the continuance of the processes of magnetisation which have been described above, an indefinite development of magnetism can be produced. When the resistance produced by the coercive force to the decomposition of the fluids becomes equal to the decomposing power of the magnetising bars, all further increase of magnetism will cease.

It is remarkable that if a bar which has been magnetised to saturation by magnets of a certain power be afterwards submitted to the process of magnetisation by magnets of inferior power, it will lose the excess of its magnetism and fall to the point of saturation corresponding to the magnets of inferior power.

589. **Influence of the temper of the bar on the coercive force.** — Let a bar of steel tempered at a bright red heat be magnetised to saturation, and let its magnetic intensity be ascertained by the vibration of a needle submitted to its attraction. Let its temper be then brought by annealing to that of a straw colour, and being again magnetised to saturation, let its magnetic intensity be ascertained. In like manner, let its magnetic intensities at each temper from the highest to the lowest be observed. It will be found that the bars which have the highest temper have the greatest coercive force, and therefore admit of the greatest development of magnetism; but even at the lowest tempers they are still, when magnetised to saturation, susceptible of a considerable magnetic force.

Although highly tempered steel has this advantage of receiving magnetism of great intensity, it is, on the other hand, subject to the inconvenience of extreme brittleness, and consequent liability to fracture. A slight reduction of temper causes but a small diminution in its charge of magnetism, and renders it much less liable to fracture.

590. **Effects of terrestrial magnetism on bars.** — It has been already shown that the inductive power of terrestrial magnetism is capable of developing magnetism in iron bars, and, under certain conditions, of either augmenting, diminishing, or even obliterating the magnetic force of bars already magnetised. In the preservation of artificial magnets, therefore, this influence must be taken into account.

According to what has been explained, it appears that if a magnetic bar be placed in the direction of the dipping needle in this hemisphere, the earth's magnetism will have a tendency to attract the austral magnetism downwards, and to repel the boreal upwards. If, therefore, the austral pole of the bar be presented downwards, this tendency will preserve or even augment the magnetic intensity of the bar. But if the magnet be in the inverted position, having the boreal pole downwards, opposite effects will ensue. The austral fluid being attracted downwards, and the boreal driven upwards, a recombination of the fluids will take place, which will be partial or complete according to the coercive force of the bar. If the coercive force of the bar exceed the influence of terrestrial magnetism. the effect will be only to diminish the magnetic intensity of the bar: but if not, the effect will be the recomposition of the magnetic force and the reduction of the bar to its natural state: but if the bar be still held in the same position, the continued effect of the terrestrial magnet will be again to decompose the natural magnetism of the bar, driving the austral fluid downwards and repelling the boreal upwards, and thus reproducing the magnetism of the bar with reversed polarity.

591. **Means of preserving magnetic bars from these effects by armatures or keepers.** — When the magnetic bars to be preserved are straight bars of equal length, they are laid parallel to each other. their ends corresponding, but with poles reversed, so that the austral pole of each shall be in juxtaposition with the boreal pole of the other, as represented in *fig.* 319.

A bar of soft iron, called the *keeper* or *armature*, is applied as represented

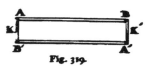

Fig. 319.

at K, in contact with the two opposite poles A and B', and another similar bar K' in contact with A' and B, so as to complete the parallelogram. In this arrangement the action of the poles A and B' upon the keeper K is to decompose its magnetism, driving the austral fluid towards B' and the boreal fluid towards A. The boreal fluid of K exercises a reciprocal attraction upon the austral fluid of A, and the austral fluid of K exercises a corresponding attraction upon the boreal fluid of B'. Like effects are produced by the keeper K' at the opposite poles A' and B. In this manner the decomposition of the fluids in the two bars A B and A' B' is maintained by the action of the keepers K and K'.

If the magnet have the horse shoe form, this object is obtained by a single keeper, as represented in *fig.* 316. The keeper K is usually formed with a round edge, so as to touch the magnet only in a line, and not in a surface, as it would do if its edge were flat. It results from experience that a keeper kept in contact in this manner for a certain length of time with a magnet, augments the attractive force, and appears to *feed*, as it were, the magnetism.

592. **Magnetism may be preserved by terrestrial induction.** — Magnetic needles, suspended freely, so as to obey the attraction of terrestrial magnetism, do not admit of being thus protected by keepers; but neither do they require it, for the austral pole of the needle being always directed towards the boreal pole of the earth, and the boreal pole of the needle towards the austral pole of the earth, the terrestrial magnet itself plays the part of the keeper, continually attracting each fluid towards its proper pole of the magnet, and thus maintaining its magnetic intensity.

593. **Compound magnets.** — Compound magnets are formed by the combination of several bar magnets of similar form and equal magnitude, laid one upon another, their corresponding poles being placed in juxtaposition.

pound horse shoe magnet, such as that represented in *fig.* 316., is
in like manner of magnetised bars, superposed on each other, and
in form, their corresponding poles being placed in juxtaposition.
ars, whether straight or in the horse shoe form, are separately mag-
before being combined by the methods already explained.

case of the horse shoe magnet a ring is attached to the keeper, and
to the top of the horse shoe, *fig.* 316., so that the magnet being sus-
from a fixed point, weights may be attached to the keeper tending to
it from the magnet. In this way horse shoe magnets often support
to twenty times their own weight.

pound magnets are sometimes constructed in the form of
bars: such an apparatus, consisting of twelve bars disposed
layers of four bars each, is shown in *fig.* 320.

Fig. 320.

king compound magnets each component bar is separately tempered
netised, the whole being afterwards combined by screws or bolts.
tal force of such a combination is always less than the sum of the
its component magnets, owing to the mutual action of the magnets
other. This effect is, to some extent, mitigated by making the
ars somewhat shorter than the central ones.

A natural magnet, mounted so as to develop its power by
the effect of induction, is shown in *fig.*
321. A, B represent the positions of
its poles; E and F are two masses of
soft iron, which adhere to it by virtue
of the magnetic force. By the effect
of these, the magnetism is augmented,
for the magnetism developed in E
and F decomposes by its reaction an
increased quantity of magnetism in A,
B, which again reacting on A, B, produces a further development of magnetic power, and so on. The keeper
G being of soft iron, increases this
reciprocal action.

595. **Magnetised tracings on a
steel plate.** — If the pole of a magnet be applied to a plate of steel of
about one tenth of an inch thick and
of any superficial magnitude, such as
a square foot, and be moved slowly
upon it, tracing any proposed figure,

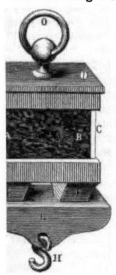

Fig. 321.

the line traced upon the steel plate will be rendered magnetic, as will be indicated by sprinkling steel filings upon the plate. They will adhere to those points over which the magnet has been passed, and will assume the form of the figure traced upon the plate.

596. **The influence of heat upon magnetism**, which was noticed at a very early period in the progress of magnetic discovery, has lately been the subject of a series of experimental researches by M. Kupffer, from which it appears that a magnetic bar when raised to a red heat does not lose its magnetism suddenly at that temperature, but parts with it by slow degrees as its temperature is raised. This curious fact was ascertained by testing the magnetism of the bar, by the means explained in (569.), at different temperatures, when it was found that at different degrees of heat it produced different rates of oscillation of the test needle.

It was also ascertained that, in order to deprive a magnetic bar of all its magnetism when raised to a given temperature, a certain length of time was necessary. Thus a magnetic bar plunged in boiling water, and retained there for ten minutes, lost only a portion of its magnetism, and after being withdrawn and again plunged in the water for some length of time, it lost an additional portion of its attractive force; and by continuing in the same manner its immersion for the same interval, its magnetic force was gradually diminished, a part still, however, remaining after seven or eight such immersions.

A magnetic bar, when raised to a red heat, not only loses its magnetism, but it becomes as incapable of receiving magnetism from any of the usual processes of magnetisation, as would be any substance the most incapable of magnetism.

597. **Astatic needle.** — All magnets freely suspended being subject to the influence of terrestrial magnetism, the effects produced upon them by other causes are necessarily compounded with those of the earth. Thus, if a magnetic needle be exposed to the influence of any physical agent, which, acting independently upon it, would cause its north pole to be directed to the east, the pole, being at the same time affected by the magnetism of the earth, which acting alone upon it would cause it to be directed to the north, will take the intermediate direction of the north-east. When, in such cases, the exact effect of the earth's magnetism on the direction of the needle is known, and the compound effect is observed, the effect of the physical agent by which the needle is disturbed may generally be eliminated and ascertained. It is, nevertheless, often necessary to submit a magnetic needle to experiments, which require that it should be rendered independent of the directive influence of the earth's magnetism, and expedients have accordingly been invented for accomplishing this. A needle

which is not affected by the earth's magnetism is called an *astatic eedle.*

A magnetic needle freely suspended over a fixed bar magnet will have a tendency, as already explained, to take such a position that its magnetic axis shall be parallel to that of the fixed magnet, he poles being reversed. Now if the fixed magnet be placed with its magnetic axis coinciding with the magnetic meridian, the poles being reversed with relation to those of the earth, its directive influence on the needle will be exactly contrary to that of the arth. While the earth has a tendency to turn the austral pole of the needle to the north, the magnet has a tendency to turn it o the south. If these tendencies be exactly equal, the needle will totally lose its polarity, and will rest indifferently in any direction in which it may be placed.

As the influence of the bar magnet on the needle increases as ts distance from it is diminished, and *vice versâ*, it is evident that it may always be placed at such a distance from it, that its directive force shall be exactly equal to that of the earth. In this case, the needle will be rendered astatic.

A needle may also be rendered astatic by connecting with it a second needle, having its magnetic axis parallel and its poles reversed, both needles having equal magnetic forces. The compound needle thus formed being freely suspended, the directive power of the earth on the one will be equal and contrary to its directive power on the other, and it will consequently rest indefinitely in any direction.

It is in general, however, almost impracticable to ensure the exact equality of the magnetism of two needles thus combined. If one exceed the other, as is generally the case, the compound will obey a feeble directive force equal to the difference of their magnetism.

598. **The law of magnetic attraction** and repulsion is the same as that of gravitation; that is, these forces increase in the same proportion as the square of the distance of the centre of attraction or repulsion diminishes. This has been established by experiments of two kinds, one of which is made upon the principle of the pendulum, and the other by an instrument invented by Coulomb, called the balance of torsion, which was applied with great success to the measurement of various other physical forces.

To determine the law of magnetic attraction by the principle of the pendulum, a magnetised needle properly suspended is first put in a state of oscillation subject only to the earth's magnetism, and the rate of its oscillation is observed. It is then submitted to the combined effects of the attraction of a magnet and that of the earth, and the rate of its vibration is again observed, from which the sum of the forces of the magnet and the earth is deduced. The magnetic force of the earth, being computed from the first observation, is then subtracted from the sum of the magnetic forces of the earth, and the magnet deduced from the second observation, the remainder being the force exerted by the magnet. This experiment being repeated in placing the magnet at different distances from the needle, it is found that its force, whether attractive or repulsive, varies inversely as the square of the distance.

599. **The balance of torsion** as applied to the measurement of magnetic forces consists of a cage of glass, *fig.* 322., having a cover

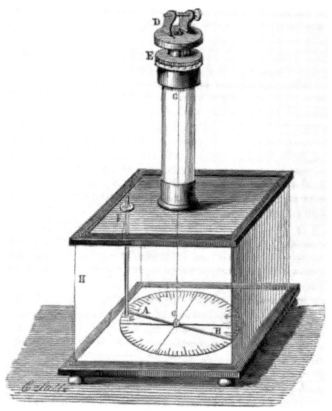

Fig. 322.

which can be removed at will, in which two holes are made; one near the edge, in which is inserted the magnetic bar F G submitted to experiment; and the other in the centre, in which is inserted a glass tube, through which an extremely fine silver wire passes, to

er end of which is suspended a magnetic needle A B: this
wire is rolled upon a horizontal pin at the top, which is
by a screw having a milled head, so that by rolling or un-
the wire the needle A B may be raised or lowered.

rrangement at the top of the glass tube by which the wire is sus-
consists of two pieces, one of which D turns in a hole made in the
f the other E. The piece D is attached to the cylindrical piece
which the wire passes, and by turning it round its centre the wire
ng the needle A B is also turned. The head of the piece E is gra-
and that of D carries upon it an index mark, which being brought
ero of the division on E, will afterwards show the angle through
ie piece D and the wire with it are turned.

et us suppose that the austral pole of the magnet G is brought down
raduated circle upon the base of the instrument, and that the austral
' the suspended needle is brought near to it. The pole of the magnet
i repel that of the needle, and the wire by which the needle is sus-
will suffer a torsion or twist in the direction in which the needle
When the tendency of the wire to untwist itself shall be equal to the
i force exerted by G upon A, the needle will rest. By turning the
he needle may then be moved, so that the pole A shall be brought
xquired distance from G, and the force of torsion of the wire will be
the force of magnetic repulsion between G and A. But the force of
s always proportional to the angle of torsion; that is, the angle
which the head D has been turned from that position in which the
ion it coincided with the zero of the scale upon E. This angle can,
, be read off, and the intensity of the repulsion corresponding to the
between G and A can be thus found.

same manner the intensity of the repulsion at any other distance,
ir less between G and A, can be determined, and it will accordingly
that these intensities will be inversely as the square of the distance
G and A.

iplify the explanation, we have omitted here the consideration of the
i of the magnetism of the earth upon the needle. This, however, is
itermined previously to the action of the magnet F G. Supposing
;net to be raised so as to leave the pole A under no other influence
t of the earth, the amount of torsion necessary to retain the pole A
in position against the magnetism of the earth can be ascertained in
ner explained above. The magnet F G being then lowered, the
necessary to retain the pole A in the same position can be deter-
nd this latter torsion is that which will equilibrate with the repul-
veen G and A.

The inductive force of the earth, considered as a mag-
ll decompose the natural magnetism of all bodies which
ot sufficient coercive force to resist its influence. Such
when placed in the northern hemisphere, will be so affected
i austral fluid will be attracted towards the boreal pole of
th, that is, in the direction of the lower pole of the dipping
and the boreal fluid will be repulsed towards its upper
All such bodies, therefore, will be rendered temporarily
ic, and will acquire a polarity corresponding in its direction

to that of the dipping needle. If their coercive force be sufficiently feeble, and their force be favourable to the development
of the magnetic effects, these effects can be rendered manifest by
presenting a compass needle to different parts of the body so
affected. If it be presented to the part corresponding with the
lower pole of the dipping needle in the northern hemisphere, the
austral pole of the compass needle will be attracted and the boreal
repelled; and if it be presented to the region corresponding with
the upper pole of the dipping needle, effects the reverse of these
will be produced.

601. **Experimental illustration.**—Let a rod of soft iron be
suspended vertically at any part of the earth where the dip is nearly
90°, and it will be found that the bar will be rendered magnetic, the
lower end having the properties of an austral, and the upper end of a
boreal pole, as may be rendered manifest by presenting a magnetic
needle, freely suspended, to the one and the other, and the direction
of which will be immediately affected in accordance with the properties of these poles respectively.

That the polarity of the bar is not proper to it, but merely induced upon it by the magnetism of the earth, may be demonstrated
by placing the bar first at right angles to the magnetic meridian,
so that both ends of it shall be similarly affected, when all magnetism will disappear, and the test needle, when presented to it,
will suffer no change of direction. But if its primitive position
be reversed, the end which was downwards and had austral polarity being presented upwards, it will be found not only to have
lost the austral, but to have acquired boreal polarity; while the
lower end previously turned upwards, which possessed boreal
polarity, will now have the properties of austral polarity.

602. Thus it appears that all bodies having so feeble a coercive
force as to allow of any degree of decomposition of their natural
magnetism, will, in the northern hemisphere, acquire a polarity
in the direction of the dipping needle, the austral pole being
directed obliquely downwards; and in the southern hemisphere,
the boreal pole being similarly directed, and the obliquity of such
polarity following the direction of the dipping needle, will decrease,
as the place of observation is nearer to the magnetic equator, the
line upon which the dipping needle is horizontal.

603. **The temporary magnetism becomes permanent**
under the influence of a great variety of effects, mechanical, physical, and chemical, which have a tendency to augment the coercive force of the body while it possesses magnetic polarity.
Thus if a bar of soft iron when suspended vertically, as described
above, and therefore rendered magnetic by the earth, be submitted
to percussion or hammering at either end, it will acquire a certain

ercive force which will resist the recomposition of the magnetic uids, and the bar will accordingly retain a certain degree of its olarity after it has been removed from the vertical position.

In like manner, if a bundle of straight pieces of soft iron wire, m or twelve inches in length, being suspended vertically, and erefore rendered magnetic, be twisted so as to form a sort of ire rope, the whole mass will retain its polarity when removed om the vertical position, the torsion conferring upon it a coercive rce sufficient to resist the recomposition of the fluids.

In the same manner various chemical effects, such as oxidation, ermal changes, and other physical incidents, are capable of so ffecting the coercive force as to cause the temporary magnetism roduced by terrestrial induction to become permanent.

604. These circumstances explain various effects which are well nown, such as the magnetisation of iron tools and implements uspended in workshops; and to the same cause may most pro-ably be ascribed the production of natural magnets. The sub-tances of which these are composed, at former epochs in the istory of the earth were probably in such a state of aggregation s to deprive them of so much of their coercive force, that the arth conferred upon them temporary magnetism, which at a osterior epoch was rendered permanent by a change in their ggregation, which increased the coercive force.

605. **Compensators for ships' compasses** are expedients by hich the errors of the compass needle produced by the attractions nd repulsions of such magnetic substances as may be contained in he vessel are neutralised or corrected.

The errors of the compass needle must proceed from one or nore of three causes : —

1°. From the inductive influence of the needle itself upon odies composed of iron around it, and the reciprocal action of he bodies thus magnetised by induction upon the needle. This ause of disturbance, which can never be very intense, can always e neutralised by removing all substances susceptible of magnetism o such a distance from the compass needle as to render the effects f such induction insensible.

2°. The needle may be disturbed by the permanent magnetism f masses of iron, which either enter into the construction of the essel, or form part of its armament or cargo. This cause of dis-urbance being permanent in its character, so long as the structure f the vessel, its armament, and cargo remain unchanged, can, hen once detected, be always allowed for, so that the error of the ompass may be corrected.

If the influence of terrestrial magnetism upon the vessel be upposed to cease or to be neutralised, the compass needle would be affected by no other influence than that of the magnetism of the vessel and its contents; and in obedience to that influence, it would assume a certain determinate direction, making a definite angle with the keel of the vessel; and it would retain this position relatively to the keel, however the direction of the keel itself might be changed. Thus, if the vessel were made to revolve horizontally round a vertical line through its centre, the compass needle would revolve with it without suffering any change of direction relatively to the keel.

Now let us suppose the vessel to have that position in which the direction given to the needle by the magnetism of the vessel shall coincide with the magnetic meridian. In that case, since the magnetism of the vessel and the magnetism of the earth give the needle the same direction, there will be no deviation. But if the vessel be then made to revolve horizontally round its centre, the line of direction of its magnetic influence will revolve, making a constantly varying angle with the magnetic meridian. The magnetism of the vessel would therefore cause the needle to deviate from the magnetic meridian, through a gradually increasing angle, on that side towards which the line of direction of the influence of the vessel turns. This deviation would increase to a certain limit; after which it would again decrease, and the needle would return to the magnetic meridian, when the vessel would have made half a revolution, after which it would deviate to the other side of the magnetic meridian, would attain a certain limit, after which it would again return in the other direction, and again coincide with the magnetic meridian, when the vessel would have completed its revolution.

If, therefore, the vessel be thus made to revolve horizontally round its centre, and the arc through which the needle oscillates on the one side and the other be observed, the line which bisects this arc will be the direction which would be given to the compass needle by the magnetism of the vessel acting upon it, independently of the magnetism of the earth; and this deviation being known, the correction necessary for the magnetism of the vessel would be obtained, since the line of direction of the magnetic meridian will in all cases be that of the bisecting line.

606. **Barlow's compensator.** — 3°. The third and most difficult cause of error of ships' compasses is due to the temporary magnetism impressed upon the masses of iron contained in the vessel by the inductive action of the earth. This is the more difficult to determine and correct, inasmuch as its effects are not only much greater than those proceeding from the other causes, but are subject to incessant variation, according to the position which the vessel assumes with relation to the direction of the

arth's magnetism. When the vessel is made to turn as above lescribed, horizontally, round its centre, the bodies it contains, vhich are susceptible of magnetism, suffer a varying action, according to the various positions they assume relatively to the lirection of the earth's magnetism. But in making one complete revolution, they assume every possible variety of position, and receive from the earth's magnetism every possible variety of effect.

Let us suppose, then, the vessel placed within a few hundred yards of the shore, and two observers to be stationed one at the compass in the vessel, and the other with a compass on the shore, being provided with instruments by which the relative directions of the two needles to those of the line joining the two observers can be accurately observed. Now if the magnetism of the vessel exerted no disturbing action the direction of the two needles would be parallel, since the direction of the earth's magnetism will be sensibly the same at two places so near each other. But it will be found, on the contrary, that the needle on the vessel will deviate from parallelism with the needle on the shore by a certain angle, and this angle can be measured by the combined observations at the two stations, and when measured the error or deviation of the needle in that particular position of the vessel will be known. The direction of the keel of the vessel being then changed, the deviation corresponding to its new position will be found in the same manner; and the vessel being thus gradually made to revolve round its centre, the deviation of the needle from the magnetic meridian corresponding to the direction of the keel at each observation will be determined, and its deviations for all intermediate directions may be computed by the method of interpolation.

This being done, the ship's compass is brought on shore and placed upon a wooden pillar, capable of being turned round its vertical axis. In the side of this pillar a number of holes placed vertically one under another are made, into which a copper rod can be inserted, carrying at its extremity two circular discs of iron, about a foot in diameter, and having such a thickness as would weigh 3 lbs. per square foot. These plates of iron will produce a disturbing effect upon the compass needle at the top of the wooden pillar, similar in kind to that produced by the vessel; and this disturbance may be made to vary in degree by transferring the copper rod, carrying the iron discs from hole to hole in the wooden pillar, so as to vary its distance from the compass needle. By a series of trials such a position may be given to it that, when the wooden pillar is made to turn through one complete revolution, the compass needle shall make precisely the same series of deviations as that which it makes upon the deck during one complete revolution of the vessel.

Now let us suppose that the compass thus supported with the iron discs, adjusted as here stated, is transported on board the vessel, it is evident that the disturbing effect which produces the deviation of the needle will be doubled, since the needle is at once affected by the induced magnetism of the vessel, and by that of the iron discs. To determine, therefore, the deviation of the needle at any moment, it is only necessary to observe its direction, first, when the copper rod with the discs is inserted in the pillar; and, secondly, when it is not so inserted. The difference between the two directions will then be the amount of the deviation.

BOOK THE FOURTH.

ACOUSTICS.

~~~~~~~~

CHAPTER I.

THEORY OF UNDULATIONS.

607. **A vast mass of discoveries** produced by the labour of modern inquirers in several branches of physics, and more especially in those where the phenomena of sound, heat, light, and the other imponderable agents are investigated, have conferred upon the physical theory of undulations much interest and importance.

608. **Undulations in general.** — When a mass of matter, whatever be its form or conditions, being in a state of stable equilibrium, is disturbed, either collectively or in the internal arrangement of its constituent parts, by any external force which operates upon it for a moment, it will have a tendency to return to the state from which it was disturbed, and will so return, provided the disturbing force have not permanently deranged its structure. After it has returned to the position of equilibrium, it will have a tendency, by reason of its inertia, to depart from such position again, and to make an excursion in a contrary direction, and so continually to pass on the one side and the other of this position, with an alternate motion more or less rapid, until, at length, by the resistance of the medium in which it is placed, and other causes, it is gradually brought to rest, and settles finally in its previous position of stable equilibrium.

Alternate motions, thus produced and continued, are variously expressed by the terms *vibrations*, *oscillations*, *waves*, or *undulations*, according to the state and form of the body in which they take place, and to the character of the motions.

One of the most familiar and generally known examples of this class of motion has already been noticed in the case of the pendulum. There the oscillation is produced by the alternate displacement of the entire mass of the body, which partakes in the common motion of vibration.

609. **Formation of a wave.** — It does not always follow,

however, that the particles of the vibrating body thus share in a common motion. If an elastic string be extended between two fixed points, and be drawn laterally from its position of rest by a force applied at its middle point, it will return to that position of rest and pass beyond it, and will thus alternately oscillate on the one side and on the other of such a position. In this case the oscillatory motion bears a close analogy to that of the pendulum, as will be more fully noticed hereafter.

Let A B, *fig.* 323., be a flexible cord attached to a fixed point at B, and held by the hand at A. If this cord be jerked smartly once or twice up and down by the hand at A, it will immediately change its form, and an apparent movement will be produced, passing from the end A towards the end B, similar to that of waves upon water. The first effect of the motion will be to cause the cord to assume the curved form A s o, rising above the position of equilibrium. This will be succeeded by a corresponding curved form o s' P, depressed to the same extent below the position of equilibrium. If the cord be jerked but once, then the point o will appear to advance towards B, the elevation A s o following it, and the depression of o s' P preceding it, so that the appearances produced successively will be those represented in *figs.* 323, 324, 325, 326.

The curve A s o s' P is called *a wave*.

The point A s o, which rises above the position of equilibrium, is called the *elevation of the wave*, s being the summit or point of greatest elevation.

The curve o s' P is called the *depression of the wave*, the point s' being that of greatest depression.

The distance s Q of the highest point above the position of equilibrium is called the *height of the wave;* and in like manner the distance s' Q' of the lowest point of the depression below the position of equilibrium is called the *depth of the wave*.

The distance A P between the beginning of the elevation and the end of the depression is called the *length of the wave;* the distance A o the *length of the elevation*, and o P that of the *depression*.

It is found that such a wave, on arriving at the extremity B, as represented in *fig.* 326., will return from B to A, as represented in *figs.* 327, 328, 329, 330., in the same manner exactly as it had advanced from A to B.

Having thus returned to A, it will begin another movement towards B, and so proceed and return as before.

610. **Waves progressive and stationary.** — A wave which thus moves in some certain direction, is called a *progressive undulation*.

Let a cord be extended between two fixed points, A and B,

fig. 331., and let it be divided into any number of equal parts, three for example, at c and d. Let the points c and d be tem-

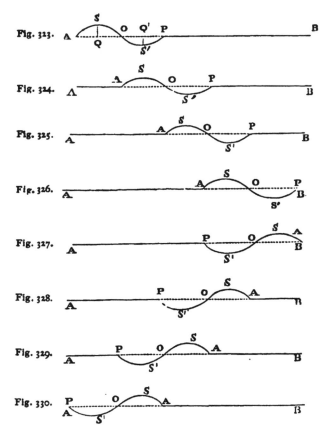

Fig. 323.

Fig. 324.

Fig. 325.

Fig. 326.

Fig. 327.

Fig. 328.

Fig. 329.

Fig. 330.

porarily fixed, and let the three parts of the cord be drawn from

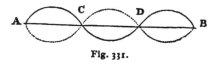

Fig. 331.

their position of rest in contrary directions, so that the cord will assume the undulating form represented in the figure. If the parts of the cord be simultaneously discharged, each part will vibrate between the fixed points c and d, the adjacent vibrations being always in contrary directions.

Now let the points c and d be liberated. No change will then take place in the vibratory motion of the cord, and it will therefore alternately throw itself into the positions represented in the figure by the continuous line and the dotted line. But as it con-

inues to vibrate, the parts c and d, although free, will be
tationary, and waves will be formed, whose elevation and depression will be alternately above and below the lines joining the
points a, c, d, and b.

Such an undulation not having any progressive motion, is accordingly called a *stationary undulation.*

The points c and d of the wave, which never change their
position, are called *nodal points.*

This species of undulation may be considered to be produced by
the alternate elevation and depression of the several parts of the
cord above and below its position of equilibrium.

As the circumstances attending, and the laws which govern, the
vibrations or undulations of bodies vary with the state in which
they are found, according as they are solid, liquid, or gaseous, it
will be convenient to consider such effects as exhibited in these
states severally.

611. **Vibrations of cords and membranes.**—Solid bodies
exhibit the phenomena of vibration in various forms and degrees,
according to their figure and to the degree of their elasticity.
Cords and wires have their elasticity developed by tension. The
same may be said of bodies which have considerable superficial
extent with little thickness, such as thin membranes like paper or
parchment. When these are stretched tight and struck, they will
vibrate on the one side and on the other of their position of equi-
ibrium, in the same manner as a stretched cord.

Elastic substances, whatever be their form, are susceptible of
vibration, the manner and degree of this varying in an infinite
variety of ways, according to the form of the body, and to the
manner in which the force disturbing this form and producing the
vibration is applied.

612. **Apparatus of August.** — Those solids whose breadth or
thickness is very small in proportion to their length,
such as thin rods, cords, or wires, are susceptible of
three kinds of vibration, which have been denominated the transverse, the longitudinal, and the
torsional.

An apparatus to exhibit these effects experimentally, contrived by Professor August, is represented in *fig.* 332. This apparatus consists of a
piece of brass wire formed into a spiral, one end of
which is attached to a frame from which it is suspended, and the other end supports a weight by
which it is strained. The transverse vibrations are
produced by fixing the lower end of the wire by
means of the movable clamp represented in the

Fig. 332.

figure. The wire is then drawn aside from its position of equilibrium and suddenly let go, after which it vibrates on the one side and on the other of this position.

To show the longitudinal vibrations, the weight suspended from the wire is drawn downwards by the hand, the wire yielding in consequence of its spiral form. When the weight is disengaged, the wire draws it up, the spiral elasticity being greater than the weight. The weight, however, rises in this case above the position of equilibrium, then falling returns to it; but in consequence of its inertia descends below it, and thus alternately rises above and falls below this position, until at length it comes to rest.

The torsional vibrations are shown by turning the weight round its vertical diameter. When so turned and let go, it will turn back again until it attains its position of equilibrium; but by reason of its inertia it will continue to turn beyond that position until stopped by the resistance of the wire, when it will return, and thus alternately twist round in the one direction and in the other, until it comes to rest.

613. **Elastic strings.** — Of the various forms of solid bodies susceptible of vibration, that which is attended with the greatest interest and importance is an extended cord; inasmuch as it not only produces the phenomena in such a manner and form as to render the laws which govern them more easily ascertained, but also constitutes the principle of an extensive class of musical instruments, and is therefore of high importance in the theory of musical sounds.

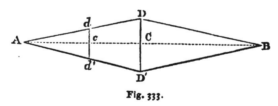

Fig. 333.

Let A B, *fig.* 333., be such an extended string. If it be drawn aside at its middle point c from its position of equilibrium, so as to be bent into the form A D B, and then disengaged, it will in virtue of its elasticity return to the position A C B; the point D approaching c with an accelerated motion, exactly in the same manner as the ball of a pendulum approaches the centre point of its vibration. Having arrived at the position A C B, the string in consequence of its inertia will be carried beyond that position, and will arrive at a position A D′ B on the other side of A C B, nearly at the same distance as A D B was. The motion of the middle point c from c to D′ is gradually retarded, until it entirely ceases at D′, precisely similar to the motion of the ball of a pendulum in ascending from the middle point to the extreme limit of its vibration. All these observations will be equally applicable to any other point of the string, such as c, which oscillates in like manner between the points d and d′. All the circumstances which were explained in the case of the pendulum, and which showed that the oscillations, whether made through longer or shorter arcs, were made in the same time, are equally applicable to this case of a vibrating string. Thus, the force which impels any point, such as D, towards the line A B, increases as the distance of D from the line A B increases. Therefore, the greater the extent of the excursion which the string has to make, the greater in proportion will be the force which will impel it; and consequently, the time of vibration will be the same, although the amplitude of the vibrations be greater. It is, therefore, the general property of all extended strings, when put in vibration, that they will oscillate on either side of their position of rest in equal times, whether the amplitude of the vibrations is great or small. It follows from this, that the time of oscillation will be the same during the continuance of the vibration of the same string, although the amplitude of the oscillations it performs be continually diminished.

These observations, with the necessary qualifications, are applicable to all vibrating bodies. In all cases, the force tending to bring them back to the position of equilibrium is great, in proportion to the extent of their departure from it; and, consequently, the time of oscillating on either side of their position of equilibrium will be the same, although the amplitude of each oscillation is variable.

614. **Their laws.** — The following laws which govern the vibration of strings have been demonstrated by theory and verified by experiment.

Let N express the number of vibrations per second which the string makes.
Let L express the length of the string.
Let s express the force with which the string is stretched.
Let D express the diameter of the string.

I. **The number N will be inversely proportional to L, other things being the same.** — That is to say, the number of vibrations made by a string per second will be increased in the same proportion as the length of the string is diminished, and *vice versâ*, the tension of the string and its thickness remaining the same.

II. **The number N varies in the proportion of the square root of s, other things being the same.** — That is to say, the number of vibrations performed by a string per second will be increased in proportion to the square root of the force which stretches the string. If the string be extended by a fourfold force, the number of vibrations which it performs per second will be doubled; if it be extended by a ninefold force, the number of vibrations it performs per second will be increased in a threefold proportion, and so on.

III. **The number of vibrations performed per second is in the inverse proportion of the diameter of the string, other things being the same.**—That is to say, if two strings composed of the same material be stretched with the same force, one having double the diameter of the other, the latter will perform twice as many vibrations per second as the former.

The three preceding rules may be expressed in combination by the following formula:—

$$ N = a \times \frac{\sqrt{s}}{L\,D}, $$

in which a is a number depending on the quality of the material of the string, and which will vary in the formula if two different strings be compared together.

It follows, from this formula, that

$$ a = \frac{N\,L\,D}{\sqrt{s}} $$

The constant number a, therefore, is found by dividing the product of the numbers expressing the vibrations per second, the length of the string, and its thickness by the square root of that which expresses the force by which the string is extended.

The manner in which the preceding laws may be verified by experiment will be explained hereafter.

The constant number a will depend upon the physical properties of the material of which the string is composed. It will, therefore, be the same for all strings of the same material and structure, but will differ when strings of a different material or different structure are composed together.

615. **Elastic plate.** — If an elastic rod, being fixed at one end and free at the other (*fig.* 334.), be drawn aside from its position of equilibrium and let go, it will pass into a state of vibration, an its vibrations will be isochronous, for the reasons which have be explained in a general manner. With rods of the same mater and structure the rate of vibration will depend on the length s thickness, but will be independent of the breadth.

With the same length the number of vibrations per second be proportional to the thickness.

With the same thickness the number will be inversely as square of the length.

Chaldni verified these laws by experiments made on thin More recently, however, M. Baudrimont showed, by experi made on plates of glass, zinc, copper, rock crystal, and woo

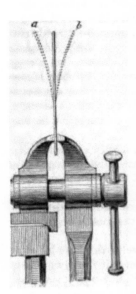

Fig. 334.

the results. ceased to be in accordance with the law in certain cases, especially when the thickness exceeds 4 or 5 twelfths of an inch. It must also be understood that these laws are only applicable so long as there are no nodal points.

616. **Elastic wires.**—The vibrations produced by elastic wires fixed at one end are not, like the vibrations of a common pendulum, generally made in the same plane; in other words, the free extremity of the wire does not describe a circular arc between its extreme positions. It appears to be impressed with, at the same time, two vibratory motions in planes at right angles to each other, and moves in a curve produced by the composition of these motions. These effects are rendered experimentally

it in a beautiful manner, by the following expedient. Let elastic steel wires, knitting needles, for example, be fixed at l in a vice or in a board, and let small balls of polished steel, of reflecting light intensely, be attached to the vibrating Each of these small polished balls will reflect to the eye a t point, and when they are set in motion this brilliant point oduce a continued line of light, in the same manner and ie same principle on which the end of a lighted stick made to revolve appears one continued circle of light.* Now, he needles are put into a state of vibration, the brilliant vill appear to describe a complicated curve, exhibited to the an unbroken line of light reflected from the polished ball.

Nodal points. — Elastic rods are susceptible of the sta-undulations already described, as well as strings. The oints in the one and the other can be ascertained experi-y by placing the vibrating string or wire in a horizontal , and suspending upon it light rings of paper. They will wn off so long as they rest upon any part of the string or cept the node; but when they come to a node, they will there unmoved, although the vibration of the string or iy continue.

experiment may be easily performed upon a string stretched

* Optics (373.).

in a horizontal position. If such a string be taken between the fingers at two points, each distant by one fourth of its length from the two extremities, and being drawn aside in opposite directions, be disengaged, it will vibrate with a stationary undulation, the nodal point being in the centre, and each half of the string vibrating independently of the other. If a light paper ring be suspended on such a string at the middle point, it will remain unmoved; but if drawn aside from the middle point, it will be thrown off and agitated until it returns to that point, where it will again remain at rest.

618. **Nodal lines.**—A solid, in the form of a thin elastic plate, made to vibrate, will also be susceptible of stationary undulations, and will have a regular series of nodal points. Such a plate may be considered as consisting of a series of rods or wires, placed in contact and connected together, and the series of their nodal points will form upon the plate a series of nodal lines.

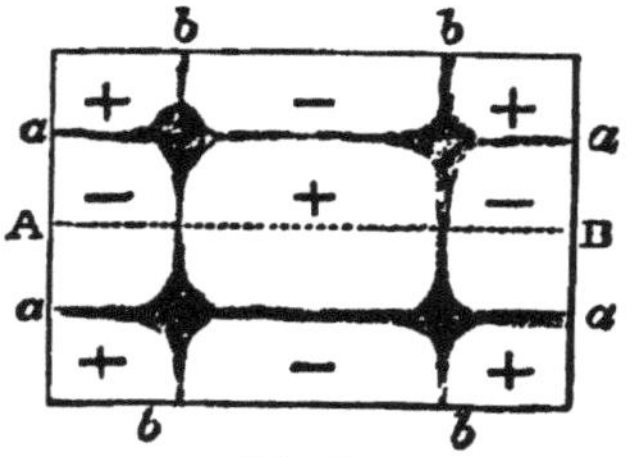

Fig. 335.

To render these nodal lines experimentally apparent, it is only necessary to spread upon the plate a thin coating of fine sand; when the plate is put into vibration, the sand will be thrown from the vibrating points, and will collect upon the nodal lines, and affect an arrangement of which an example is given in *fig.* 335. This will be more fully explained hereafter when we treat of *sound.*

619. **Undulation of liquids.**—**Circular waves.**—If a vessel containing a liquid remain at rest, the liquid being subject to no external disturbance, the surface will form a uniform level plane. Now, if a depression be made at any point of this surface by dropping in a pebble, or by immersing the end of a rod, and suddenly withdrawing it, a series of circular waves will immediately be formed round the point, as a centre, where such depression is made, and each such wave will expand in a progressively increasing circle, wave following wave until they encounter the bounding sides of the vessel.

620. **Apparent progressive motion of waves an illusion.**— In this phenomenon a curious deception is produced. When we perceive the waves thus apparently advancing, one following another, we are irresistibly impressed with the notion that the fluid itself is advancing in the same direction; we consider that the same wave is composed of the same water, and that the entire surface of the liquid is in progressive motion. A little reflection, however, on the consequences of such a supposition will prove

that it is unfounded. The ship which floats on the waves of the sea is not carried forward with them; they pass beneath her in lifting her on their summits, and in letting her sink into the abyss between them. Observe a sea-fowl floating on the water, and the same effect will be seen. If, however, the water itself partook of the motion of the waves, the ship and the fowl would each be carried forward with a motion in common with the liquid. Once on the summit of a wave, there they would constantly remain; or if once in the depression between two waves, they would likewise continue there, one wave always preceding and the other following them.

It is evident, therefore, that the impression produced, that the water is in progressive motion, is an illusion. But, it may be asked, to what then does the progressive motion belong? That such a progressive motion does take place in something, we have proof from the evidence of sight; and that no progressive motion takes place in the liquid we have still more unquestionable evidence. To what, then, does the motion belong? We answer, to the form of the surface, and not the liquid composing it.

To render intelligible the manner in which the waves upon a

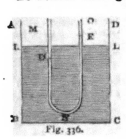

Fig. 336.

liquid are produced, let A B C D, *fig.* 336., be a vessel containing a liquid whose surface when at rest is L L. Let us imagine a siphon M N O inserted in this vessel, filled with water to the same level as the vessel. It is evident that the water included within the siphon will hold the same position precisely as the water of the vessel which the siphon displaces. If we suppose a piston inserted in the leg M N to press down the water from the level L L to the depth D', the water in the leg N O will rise to the height F. If the piston be suddenly withdrawn, the water in the leg M N will again rise, and the water in the leg N O will fall, the surfaces D' and E will return to the common level L L, but they will not remain there, for, in consequence of the inertia, the ascending motion of the column D and the descending motion of the column E will be continued, so that the surface D' will rise above L L, and the surface E will fall below it, and having attained a certain limit, they will again return respectively to the level L L, and oscillate above and below it until, by friction and atmospheric resistance, they are brought to rest at the common level L L.

Now if we imagine the siphon to be withdrawn, so that the water which occupies its place may be affected by the same pressure at D', the same oscillation will take place; but, at the same time, the lateral pressure which is obstructed by the sides of the siphon will cause other oscillations, by the combination of which the phenomenon of a wave will be produced.

Let A B C D, *fig.* 337., be an undulation produced on the surface of a liquid. This undulation will appear to have a progressive motion from A towards x.

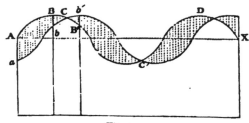

Fig. 337.

Let us suppose that in the interval of one second the summit of the wave B is transferred to *b'*. Now let us consider with what motion the particles forming the surface of the water are affected during this interval.

The particle at B descends vertically to *b*, while the particle B' ascends vertically to *b'*. The several particles of the wave in the first position between B and C descend in the vertical lines represented by dotted lines in the figure to the several points of the surface between *b* and C. At the same time, the several points of the surface of the wave in its first position between C and B' rise in vertical lines, and form the surface of the wave in its second position between C and *b'*.

In like manner, the particles of the wave in the first position between B' and C' rise in vertical lines, and form the surface of the wave in its new positions between *b'* and C'.

In the same manner, during the same interval the particles of liquid forming the surface B A descend in vertical lines and form the surface *b a*.

Thus it appears that in the interval of one second the particles of water forming the surface A B C *fall* in vertical lines, and those forming the surface C B' C' *rise* in vertical lines, and at the end of a second the series of particles form the surface *a b* C *b' c'*.

In this manner, in the interval of one second, not only the crest of the wave is transferred from B to *b'*, but all the parts which form its profile are transferred to corresponding points holding the same relative position to the new summit *b'*. Thus we see that the *form* of the wave has a progressive motion, while the particles of water composing its surface have a vertical motion either upwards or downwards, as the case may be.

621. **Stationary waves.**—Hence it appears that each of the particles composing the surface of a liquid is affected by an alternate vertical motion. This motion, however, not being simultaneous but successive, an effect will be produced on the surface *which* will be attended with the form of a wave, and such wave

will be progressive. The alternate vertical motion by which the particles of the liquid are affected will, however, sometimes take place under such conditions as to produce, not a progressive, but a stationary undulation. This would be the case if all the particles composing the surface were simultaneously moved upwards and downwards in the same direction, their spaces varying in magnitude according to their distance from a fixed point.

To explain this, let us suppose the particles of the surface of a liquid between the point $a e$, *fig. 338.*, to be simultaneously moved in vertical lines

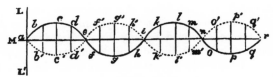

Fig. 338.

upwards, the centre particle c being raised through a greater space than the particles contiguous to it on either side. The heights to which the other succeeding particles are raised will be continually diminishing, so that at the end of a second the particles of liquid which, when at rest, formed the surface $a e$, will form the curved surface $a b c d e$.

In like manner, suppose the particles of the surface $e i$ to be depressed in vertical lines, corresponding exactly with those through which the particles $a e$ were elevated. Then the particles which originally formed the surface i would form the curved surface $e f g h i$, and they would become the depression of a wave. Thus the elevation of the wave would be $a b c d e$, and its depression $e f g h i$.

Having attained this form, the particles of the surface $a b c d e$ would fall in vertical lines to their primitive level, and having attained that point, would descend below it; while the particles e, f, g, h, i, would rise to their primitive level, and having attained that position, would continue to rise above it. In fine, the particles which originally formed the surface of the undulation $a b c d e f g h i$ would ultimately form the surface $a' b' c' d' e' f' g' h' i$ represented by the dotted line.

Having attained this form, the particles would again return to their primitive level, and would pass beyond it, and so on alternately.

In this case, therefore, there would be an undulation, but not a progressive one. The nodal points would be e, i, n, r, and these points during the undulation would not be moved; they would neither sink nor rise, the undulatory motion affecting only those between them.

This phenomenon of a stationary undulation produced on the surface of a liquid may easily be explained, by two systems of progressive undulation meeting each other under certain conditions, and producing at the points we have here called nodal points the phenomenon of interference, which we shall presently explain.

Stationary undulations may be produced on a surface of liquid confined in a straight channel by exciting a succession of waves, separated by equal intervals, moving against the end or side of the channel, and reflected from it. The reflected waves, combined with the direct waves, will produce the effect here described.

It may also be produced by exciting waves in a circle from its central point. These waves being reflected from the circular surface, will produce another series, which, combined with the former would be attended with the effect of a stationary undulation.

622. **Depth of waves.** — When a system of waves is produced upon the surface of a liquid by any disturbing force, a question arises to what depth in the liquid this disturbance of equilibrium extends. It is possible to suppose a stratum of the liquid at any supposed depth below which the vertical arrangement would not be continued. Such a stratum may be regarded as the bottom of the agitated part of the fluid.

The Messrs. Weber, to whose experimental inquiries, in this department of physics, science is much indebted, have ascertained that the equilibrium of the liquid is not disturbed to a greater depth than about three hundred and fifty times the altitude of the wave.

623. **Reflection of waves.** — If a series of progressive waves impinge against any solid surface, they will be reflected, and will return along the surface of the fluid as if they emanated from a centre equally distant on the other side of the obstructing surface.

To explain this, it is necessary to consider that when any part of a wave encounters the obstructing surface, its progress is retarded, and the particles composing it will oscillate vertically in contact with the surface, exactly as they would oscillate if they had at this point been first disturbed. They will therefore, at his point, become the centre of a new system of waves, which will be propagated around it, but which will form only semicircles, since the centre of undulation will be against the obstructing surface, which will, as it were, cut off half of each circular undulation. As the several points of the wave meet the obstructing surface in succession, other series of semicircular waves will be formed, and we shall see that by the combination of these various systems of semicircular waves, a single wave will be formed, the centre of which will be a point just so far on the other side of the obstructing surface, as the original centre was on the side of the fluid.

Let c, *fig.* 339., be the original centre of undulation, and let

ave w w issuing from it move towards the obstructing surface
The first part of this wave which will meet the obstructing

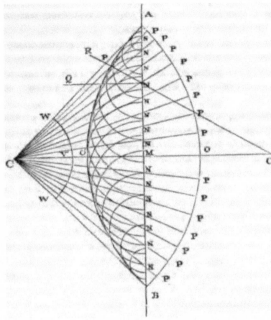

Fig. 339.

'ace will be the point v, which moves along the line c m per-
dicular to it.   After this, the other points of the wave on the
side and on the other will successively strike it.
et us take the moment at which the surface is struck at the
its b and a equally distant from the middle point m by two
ts of the wave.   All the intermediate points between b and a
have been previously struck ; and if the wave had not been
rcepted by the obstructing surface, it would at the moment
hich it strikes the points b and a have had the form of the
ular arc a o b, having the original point c as its centre.
ut as the successive points of the wave strike the surface a b,
y will, according to what has been explained, each become the
tre of a new wave which will have a semicircular form ; and to
rtain the magnitude of such wave at the moment the original
e strikes the point a and b, it is only necessary to ascertain
distance through which each semicircular wave will expand,
the interval between the moment at which the vertex of the
inal wave strikes the point m, and the moment at which the
extremities of the wave strike the points a and b.   It is

A A

evident that if the wave had not been interrupted at M, its vertex would have been moved on to O; and as the new wave reflected from M will have the same velocity, it follows that at the moment the original wave would have arrived at O, the reflected wave will have expanded through a semicircle whose radius is M O. Therefore, if we take the point M as a centre, and a line equal to M O as a radius, and describe a semicircle, this semicircle will be the position of the new wave formed with M as a centre, at the moment that the extremities of the original wave struck the points A and B.

In like manner, it may be shown that if P be the position, which the point of the original wave which struck N would have attained had it not been interrupted, the distance from which the semicircular wave having N as a centre would have expanded in the same time will be determined by describing a semicircle with N as a centre, and N P as a radius. In the same manner it may be shown that the forms of all the semicircular waves, produced with the points N of the obstructing surface between A and B as centres, will be determined by taking the several parts of the radii C P, which lie beyond the obstructing surface as radii, and the points N where they cross the obstructing surface as centres. This has been accordingly done in the diagram, by which it will be perceived that the space to the left of the obstructing surface is intersected by the numerous semicircular waves which have been formed. But it appears also that the series of points where they intersect each other most closely is that of a circular arc A o' B, having for its centre the point c', whose distance behind the surface M is equal to the distance of the centre C before it, so that C M shall be equal to c' M. The effect will be, that a circular wave A o' B will be formed, the intersection of the semicircles within this being so inconsiderable as to be imperceptible. This wave A o' B will accordingly expand from the surface A B towards C on the left in the same manner as the wave A O B would have expanded on the right towards c', if it had not been interrupted by the obstructing surface.

If any radius of the original wave, such as C P, and the corresponding radius C P' of the reflected wave be also drawn, these two radii will evidently make equal angles with the line C M C' which is perpendicular to the obstructing surface; and consequently, if from the point N a line N Q be drawn parallel to C M, and therefore perpendicular to A B, the lines C N and N R will form equal angles with it.

624. **Law of reflection.** — The angle C N Q is called *the angle of incidence* of the wave, and the angle Q N R is called *the angle of reflection;* and hence it is established as a general law, that in the

reflection of waves from any obstructing surface, the angle of incidence is equal to the angle of reflection, — a law which has already been shown to prevail when a perfectly elastic body is reflected by a perfectly hard surface.

When a wave strikes a curved surface, it will be reflected from it in a different direction, according to the point of the surface at which it is incident. It will be reflected from such point in the same direction as it would be if it struck a plane which coincides with the curved surface at this point.

625. **Waves propagated from the foci of an ellipse.** —

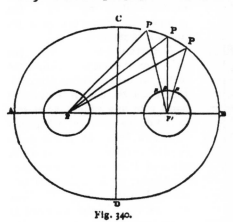

Fig. 340.

There are two species of curves, which in those branches of physics which involve the principles of undulation are attended with consequences of considerable importance. These figures are the ellipse and the parabola. *Fig.* 340. represents an ellipse : A B is its major axis, and C D its minor axis ; F F′ are two points upon its major axis called its foci, which have the following property. If lines be drawn from the foci to any point P in the ellipse, these lines will form equal angles with the ellipse at P, and their lengths taken together will be equal to the major axis A B.

A remarkable consequence of this property follows, relative to undulations having for their centres one or other of the foci. If a series of progressive circular waves, propagated from the focus F as a centre, strike the surface, they will be reflected from the surface at angles equal to those at which they strike it, because, by the law which has been already established, the angles of reflection will be equal to the angles of incidence. If, then, we suppose several waves of the same system diverging from the focus F, to strike successively the elliptical surface at the point P, they will be reflected in the direction P F′ towards the other focus. But as all the points of the same wave move with the same velocity, they will describe equal spaces in the same time. Let the points *p p p* upon the lines P F′ be those at which the points of the wave will arrive simultaneously. It then follows, that the lines F P and P *p* will, taken together, be equal, being in each case the spaces described in the same time by different points of the same wave.

If, then, these equal lengths ꜰ ᴘ p be taken from the lengths ꜰ ᴘ ꜰ′, which are also equal to each other, as has been already explained, the remainders ꜰ′ p will necessarily be equal; therefore the points p will lie at equal distances from ꜰ′, and will therefore form a circle round ꜰ′ as a centre.

Hence it follows, that each circular wave which expands round ꜰ will, after it has been reflected from the surface of the ellipse, form another circular wave round ꜰ′ as a centre.

626. **Waves propagated from the focus of a parabola.** —

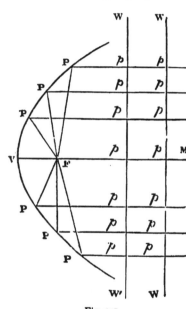

The curve called a parabola is represented in *fig.* 341. The point ᴠ is its vertex, and the line ᴠ ᴍ is its axis.

A certain point ꜰ upon the axis near the vertex, called the focus, has the following property. Let lines be drawn from this point ꜰ to any points such as ᴘ in the curve; and let other lines be drawn from the points ᴘ severally parallel to the axis ᴠ ᴍ, meeting lines w w′ drawn perpendicular to the axis, and terminated in the curve. The lines ꜰ ᴘ and ᴘ p will be inclined at equal angles to the curve at the points ᴘ, and the sum of their lengths will be everywhere the same; that is, if the length of the line ꜰ ᴘ be added to the length of the line ᴘ p, the same sum will be obtained whichever of the points ᴘ may be taken; and this will be the case whatever line w w′ be drawn perpendicular to ᴠ ᴍ.

Fig. 341.

It follows from this property, that if the focus of a parabola be the centre of a system of progressive waves, these waves, after striking the surface, will be reflected so as to form a series of parallel straight waves in the direction of the lines w w′, and moving from ꜰ towards ᴍ.

This may be demonstrated in precisely the same manner as it has been proved in the case of the ellipse that the reflected waves form a circle round the focus ꜰ′; for the lines ꜰ ᴘ and p ᴘ, *fig.* 341., forming equal angles with the curve, will necessarily correspond with the direction of the incident and reflected waves, and the sum of these lines being the same wherever the point ᴘ may be situated, the several points of the same wave striking different points of the parabola will arrive together at the line w w', inasmuch as they move with the same velocity, and have equal spaces to move over.

On the other hand, it follows, by precisely similar reasoning, that if a series of parallel straight waves at right angles to v M, moving from M towards v, should strike the parabolic surface, their reflections would form a series of circular waves of which the focus F would be the centre.

If two parabolas, A v B and A' v' B', *fig.* 342., face each other so

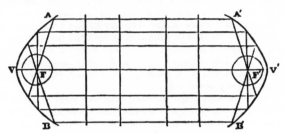

Fig. 342.

as to have their axes coincident and their concavities in opposite directions, a system of progressive circular waves issuing from one focus F, will be followed by a corresponding system, having for the centre the other focus F'. The waves which diverge from F, after striking on the surface A v B, will be converted into a series of straight parallel waves moving at right angles to v v', and towards v'. These will strike the surface A' v' B', and after being reflected from it will form another series of circular waves, having the other focus F' as their common centre.

A circular wave, if its extent be not great compared with the length of its radius, may be considered as practically coinciding with a parabolic surface whose focus is at the middle point of the radius of the circular surface.

For example, let A B, *fig.* 343., be a circular arc, whose centre

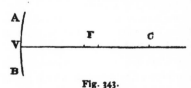

Fig. 343.

is c, and whose middle point is v. Let F be the middle point of the radius c v. Then A B may be considered as so nearly coinciding with a parabola whose focus is F, and whose vertex is v, that it will possess all the properties ascribed to the parabola; and consequently spherical surfaces, provided their extent be small compared with their

A A 2

diameters, will have all the properties here ascribed to parabolic surfaces.

627. **Experimental illustration.**—All these effects have been beautifully verified by experiment by means of expedients contrived by the Messrs. Weber, whose arrangements, nevertheless, for this object admit of still further simplification.

1. Let a trough of convenient magnitude be partially filled with mercury, so as to present a surface of that fluid of sufficient extent. Let a piece of writing paper be formed into a funnel, with an extremely small opening at the point, so as to allow a minute stream of mercury to flow from it. Let a piece of sheet iron, having a perfectly plane surface, be now immersed vertically in the mercury, and let a small stream descend from the funnel at any point upon the surface of the mercury in the vessel. A series of progressive circular waves will be produced around the point where the mercury falls, which will spread around it. This will strike the plane surface of the sheet iron, and will be reflected from it, forming another series of circular waves, whose centre will be a point equally distant on the other side of the sheet iron, as already described.

2. Let a piece of sheet iron be bent into the form of an ellipse, such as that represented at *fig.* 340.; and let the position of the foci be indicated by a small wire index attached to it. Let this be immersed in the mercury in the trough; and let the funnel be brought directly over the point of the index which marks the position of one of the foci. When the mercury is allowed to fall, a series of circular waves will be produced round that focus, and, striking on the surface of the iron, will be reflected from it, forming another series of circular waves, of which the other focus is the centre, as already expressed.

3. Let a piece of sheet iron be bent into the form of a parabola, as represented in *fig.* 341., the position of the focus being, as before, marked by an index. If this be immersed in the mercury, and the stream be let fall from the funnel placed at the point of the index, a series of circular waves will be produced around the focus, which, after being reflected from the parabolic surface, will be converted into a series of parallel straight waves at right angles to its axis, as already explained.

4. Let two pieces of sheet iron formed into parabolic surfaces, with indices showing the foci, be immersed in the mercury in such a position that their axes shall be in the same direction, and their concavities facing each other. From the funnel let fall a stream upon one focus F, *fig.* 342. Circular waves will be formed which, after reflection from the adjacent parabola, will become parallel waves, and after a second reflection from the opposite parabola will again become circular waves with the other focus as a centre.

5. If pieces of sheet iron be bent into the form of small circular arcs whose length is small compared with their radius, the same effects will be produced as those which were produced by parabolic surfaces.

628. **Interference.** — When two waves which proceed from different centres encounter each other, effects ensue which are of considerable importance in those branches of physics whose theory is founded upon the principles of undulation.

I. If the elevation of one wave coincides with the elevation of another, and the depressions also coincide, a wave would be produced, the height of whose elevation, and the depth of whose depression, will be equal to the sum of the heights and depths of the elevation and depression of the two waves which are thus, as it were, superposed.

II. If, however, the elevation of one wave coincide with the depression of the other, and *vice versâ*, then the effect will be a wave whose elevation will be equal to the difference of the elevations, and whose depression will be the difference of the depressions of the two waves which thus meet.

III. If, in the former case, the heights and depressions of the waves superposed be equal, the resulting wave will have double the height of the elevation, and double the depth of the depression.

IV. If the heights and depressions be equal in the second case, the two waves will mutually destroy each other, and no undulation will take place at the point in question; for the difference of elevations and the difference of depressions being nothing, there will be neither elevation nor depression.

In fact, in this latter case, the depression of each wave is filled up by the elevation of the other.

This phenomenon, involving the effacement of an undulation by the circumstance of two waves meeting in the manner described, is called in the theory of undulation an *interference*, and is attended with remarkable consequences in several branches of physics.

629. **Experimental illustration.** — The two systems of waves formed by an elliptical surface, and propagated, one directly around one of the foci, and the other formed by reflection around the other, exhibit, in a very beautiful manner, the phenomena not only of reflection, as has been already explained, but also of interference, as has been shown with remarkable elegance by the Messrs. Weber already referred to. These phenomena are represented in *fig.* 344., where *a* and *b* are the two foci. The strongly marked circles indicate the elevation of the waves formed around each focus, and the more lightly traced circles indicate their depression. The points where the strongly marked circles intersect the more faintly marked circles, being points where an elevation coincides with a depression, are consequently points of interference, according to what has been just explained. The series of these points form lines of interference, which are marked in the diagram by dotted lines, and which, as will be seen, have the forms of ellipses and parabolas round the same foci.

630. **Inflection of waves.** — If a series of waves encounter a solid surface in which there is an opening through which the waves may be admitted, the series will be continued inside the

opening, and without interruption; but other series of progressive waves having a circular form will be generated, having the edge of the opening as their centres.

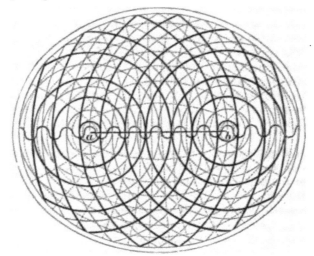

Fig. 344.

Let M N, *fig.* 345., represent such a surface, having an opening

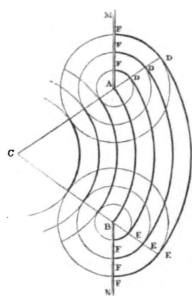

Fig. 345.

whose edges are A and B, and let C be a centre from which a series of progressive circular waves is propagated. These waves, entering at the opening A B, will continue their course uninterrupted, forming the circular arcs D E. But around A and B as centres, systems of progressive circular waves will be formed which will unite with the waves D E, completing them by circular arcs D F and E F, meeting the obstructing surface on the outside; but these circular waves will also be formed throughout the remainder of their extent, as indicated in the figure, on both sides of the obstructing surface, and intersecting the original system of waves propagated from the centre c. They will also form, with these, series of points of interference according to the principles already explained.

The effects here described as produced by the edges of an opening through which a series of waves is transmitted are called *inflection*, and they form an important feature in several branches of physics whose theory is based upon the principles of undulation.

631. The undulations produced upon a large scale in the oceans, lakes, rivers, and other large collections of water upon the surface of the globe, are attended with important effects on the economy of nature. Without these the ocean would be soon rendered putrid by the mass of organised matter which would be mingled with it, and which would chiefly float at its surface.

The principal physical cause which produces these undulations, where they take place on a moderate scale, is the motion of the atmosphere, but on a large scale they are produced by the combined effects of the attraction of the sun and moon exerted upon the surface of the ocean. The immense undulations excited by these attractions produce the phenomena of the tides which are explained in our Handbook of Astronomy.

632. **Undulation of air and gases.** — If any portion of the atmosphere, or any other elastic fluid diffused through space, be suddenly compressed and immediately relieved from the compressing force, it will expand in virtue of its elasticity, and, like all other similar examples already given, will, after its expansion, exceed its former volume to a certain limited extent, after which it will again contract, and thus oscillate alternately on the one side and on the other of its position of repose.

We may consider this effect to be produced upon a small sphere of air having any proposed radius, as, for example, an inch.

Let us suppose that it is suddenly compressed, so as to form a sphere of half an inch in radius, and being relieved from the compressing force it expands again, and surpassing its former dimensions, swells into a sphere of an inch and a half. It will again contract and return to the magnitude of a sphere, with a radius somewhat greater than half an inch, and will again expand, and so oscillate, forming alternately spheres with radii less and greater than an inch, until at length the oscillation ceases, and it resumes permanently its original dimensions. These oscillations will not be confined to the single sphere of air in which they commenced; the circumambient air will necessarily follow the contracting sphere when first compressed, so that a spherical shell of air which lies outside the sphere will expand, and become less dense than in its state of equilibrium.

When the central sphere again expands, this external spherical shell will contract, and will become more dense than in its state of equilibrium. This shell will act in a similar manner upon another spherical shell outside it, and this upon another outside it, and so forth.

If then we suppose a number of successive spheres surrounding the point of original compression, we shall have a series of alternate spherical shells of air, which will be condensed and expanded in a greater degree than when in a state of repose. This condensation and expansion thus spreading spherically round the original centre of disturbance, is in all respects analogous to a series of circular waves forming round the central point upon the surface of a liquid, the elevation of the wave in the case of the liquid corresponding to the condensation in the case of the gas, and the depression of the wave corresponding to the expansion of the gas.

633. **Propagation of wave through an elastic fluid.** — We will limit our observations in the first instance to a single series of particles of air, expanding in a straight line from the centre of disturbance A, *fig.* 346., towards T. Let s A represent the space through which the disturbing force acts, and let us imagine this air suddenly pressed from s to A by some solid surface moving against it, and let us suppose that this motion from s to A is made in a second. Now, if air were a body devoid of elasticity, and like a

Fig. 346.

perfectly rigid rod, the effect of this motion of the solid surface from s to A would be to push the remote extremity T through a space to the right corresponding with and equal to s A.

But such an effect does not take place, first, because air is highly elastic, and has a tendency to yield to the force exerted by the solid surface upon it, which moves from s to A; and secondly, because to transmit any effect from A to a remote point, such as T, would require a much greater interval of time than that which elapses during the movement of the surface from s to A. The effect, therefore, of the compression in the interval of time which elapses during the motion from s to A, is to displace the particles of air which lie at a certain definite distance to the right of A. Let the distance, for example, be AB. All the particles, therefore, of air which lie in succession from A to B will be affected more or less by the compression, and will consequently be brought into closer contiguity with each other; but they will not be equally compressed, because to enable the series of particles of air lying between A and B to assume a uniform density requires a longer time than elapses during the motion of the solid surface from s to A. At the instant, therefore, of the arrival of the compressing surface at A, the line of particles between A and B will be at different distances from each other; and it is proved, by mathematical principles, that the point where they are most closely compressed is the middle point m, between A and B, and therefore, departing from this middle point m, in either direction, they are less and less compressed.

The condition, therefore, of the air between A and B is as follows. Its density gradually increases from A to m, and gradually decreases from m to B. Now, it is also proved that the effect of the elastic force of the air is such that, at the next moment of time after the arrival of the compressing surface at A, the state of varying compression which has been just described as prevailing between A and B will prevail between another point in advance of A, such as A', and a point B' equally in advance of B, and the point of the greatest compression will, in like manner, have advanced to m', at the same distance to the right of m. In short, the conditions of the air between A' and B' will be in all respects similar to its condition the previous moment between A and B; and in like manner, in the next moment, the same condition will prevail between the particles A'' and B'' to the right of A' and B'. Now, it must be observed that as this state of varying density prevails from left to right, the air behind it, in which it formerly prevailed, resumes its primitive condition. In a word, the state of varying density which has been described as prevailing between A and B at the moment the compressing surface arrived at A will, in the succeeding moments, advance from left to right towards T, and will so advance at a uniform rate; the distance between the points A B, A' B', and A'' B'', &c. always remaining the same.

634. **Aërial undulations.** — This interval between the points A and B is called a *wave* or *undulation*, from its analogy, not only in form, but in its progressive motion, to the waves formed on the surface of liquids, already described; the difference being, that in the one case the centre of the wave is the point of greatest elevation of the surface of the liquid, and in the other case it is the point of greatest condensation or compression of the particles of the air. The distance between A and B, or between A' and B', or between A'' and B'', which always remains the same as the wave progresses, is called the *length of the wave*.

In what precedes we have supposed the compressing surface to advance from s to A, and to produce a compression of the air in advance of it. Let us now suppose this surface to be at A, the air contiguous to it having its natural density.

If the wave *proceed contrariwise* from A to s, the air which was contiguous to it at A will rush after it in virtue of its elasticity, so that the air to the right of A will be disturbed and rendered less dense than previously. An effect will be produced, in fine, precisely contrary to that which was produced when the wave advanced from s to A; the consequence of which will be that a change will be made upon the air between A and B exactly the reverse of that which was previously made, that is to say, the middle point *m* will be that at which the refraction will be greatest, and the density will increase gradually, proceeding from the point *m* in either direction towards the points A and B.

The same observations as to the progressive motion will be applicable as before, only that the centre of the progression *m*, instead of being the point of greatest, will be the point of least density.

635. **Waves condensed and rarefied.** — The space A B is also in this case denominated a wave or undulation. But these two species of waves are distinguished one from the other by being denominated, the former a *condensed wave*, and the latter a *rarefied wave*. Now, let it be supposed that the compressing surface moves alternately backwards and forwards between s and A, making its excursions in equal times. The two series of waves, as already defined, will be produced in succession. While the condensed wave moves from s towards T, the rarefied wave immediately follows it, and in the same manner this rarefied wave will be followed by another condensed wave, produced by the next oscillation, and so on.

The analogy of these phenomena to the progressive undulation on the surface of a liquid, as already described, is obvious and striking.

What has been here described with reference to a single line of particles extending from the centre of the distance A in a particular direction, is equally applicable to every line diverging in every conceivable direction around such centre, and hence it follows that the succession of condensed and rarefied waves will be propagated round the centre, each wave forming a spherical surface, which is continually progressive and uniformly enlarges, the wave moving from the common centre with a uniform motion.

636. **Velocity and force of aërial waves.** — The velocity with which such undulations are propagated through the atmosphere depends on, and varies with, the elasticity of the fluid. The degree of compression of the wave, which corresponds to the

ieight of a wave in the case of liquids, depends on the energy of
;he disturbing force. All the effects which have been described
n the case of waves formed upon the surface of a liquid are
:eproduced, under analogous conditions, in the case of undulations
:ropagated through the atmosphere.

637. **Interference of aërial waves.** — Thus, if two series of
waves coincide as to their points of greatest and least condensa-
;ion, a series will be formed whose greatest condensation and
rarefaction is determined by the sum of points, as prevailing in the
separate undulations; and if the two series are so arranged that the
points of greatest condensation of the one coincide with the
greatest rarefaction of the other, and *vice versâ*, the series will
have condensations and rarefactions determined by the difference
of each of the-separate series; and, in fine, if in this latter case
the condensations and rarefactions be equal, the undulations will
mutually efface each other, and the phenomena of interference,
already described as to liquids, will be reproduced.

As the undulations produced in the air are spread over spherical
surfaces having the centre of disturbance as a common centre, the
magnitude of these surfaces will be in the ratio of the squares of
:heir radii, or, what is the same, of the squares of their distances
from the point of central disturbance; and, as the intensity of
:he wave is diminished in proportion to the space over which it is
liffused, it follows that the effects or energy of these waves will
liminish as the squares of their distances from the centre of
:ropagation increases.

CHAP. II.

PRODUCTION AND PROPAGATION OF SOUND.

:38. **Sound** is the sensation produced in the organs of hearing
rhen they are affected by undulations transmitted to them through
he atmosphere. These undulations are subject to an infinite
ariety of physical conditions, and each variety is followed by a
lifferent sensation.

The atmospheric undulations which thus produce the sensation
f sound, are themselves excited usually by the vibration of some
lastic bodies, whose condition of equilibrium is momentarily dis-
urbed, and which impart to the air in contact with them undula-
ions which correspond with and are determined by such vibration.
:he vibrating bodies which thus impart undulation to the air

are called *sounding* or *sonorous bodies;* and the air is said to be a *propagator* or *conductor* of sound, and is sometimes called a *soni-ferous medium.*

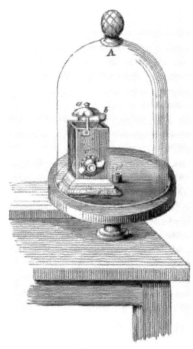

Fig. 347.

The sounding body does not, however, invariably act in a direct manner upon the air which conveys the undulation to the organ of hearing. It often happens that the vibrations of the sounding body are first imparted to other bodies susceptible of vibration, and after passing through a succession of these, the undulation is finally imparted to the air, which is invariably the last medium in the series, and that from which the organ of hearing receives it.

639. That the presence of air or other conducting medium is indispensable for the production of sound, is proved by the following experiment.

Let a small apparatus (*fig.* 347.) called an alarum, consisting of a bell *a*, which is struck by a hammer *b*, moved by clockwork, be placed under the receiver of an air pump, through the top of which a rod slides, air-tight, the end of the rod being connected with a detent which governs the motion of the clockwork connected with the hammer. This rod can, by a handle placed outside the receiver, be made to disengage the detent, so as to make the bell ring whenever it is desired.

This arrangement being made, and the alarum being placed within the receiver, upon a soft cushion of wool *e*, so as to prevent the vibration from being communicated to the pump plate, let the receiver be exhausted in the usual way. When the air has been withdrawn, let the bell be made to ring by means of the sliding rod. No sound will be heard, although the percussion of the tongue upon the bell, and the vibration of the bell itself are visible. Now if a little air be admitted into the receiver, a faint sound will begin to be heard, and this sound will become gradually *louder* in proportion as the air is gradually readmitted.

In this case the vibrations which directly act upon the ear are not those of the air contained in the receiver. These latter act upon the receiver itself and the pump plate, producing in them sympathetic vibration; and those vibrations impart vibrations to the external air which are transmitted to the ear.

If in the preceding experiment a cushion had not been interposed between the alarum and the pump plate, the sound of the bell would have been audible, notwithstanding the absence of air from the receiver. The vibration in this case would have been propagated, first from the bell to the pump plate and to the bodies in contact with it, and thence to the external air.

Another more simple method of performing this experiment is shown in *fig.* 348. A bell is suspended within a glass globe, in the neck of which there is a stopcock. The air being exhausted from this globe by a syringe or by the air pump, the sound of the bell will be inaudible, and will become audible and gradually louder by admitting the air by slow degrees.

Persons shut up in a close room are sensible of sounds produced at a distance outside such room; and they may be equally sensible of these, even though the windows and doors should be absolutely air-tight. In such case the undulations of the external air produce sympathetic vibration on the windows, doors, or walls by which the hearers are enclosed, and then produce corresponding vibrations in the air within the room by which the organs of hearing are immediately affected.

Fig. 348.

640. **Sound progressive.**— It has been shown that the propagation of undulations through the atmosphere is progressive; and if it be admitted that such undulations are the agencies by which the sense of hearing is affected, it will follow that an interval of time, more or less, must elapse between the vibration of the sounding body and the perception of the sound by a hearer, and that such interval will be proportionate to the distance of the hearer from the sounding body, and to the velocity with which sound is propagated through the intervening medium. But this progressive propagation of sound can also be directly proved by experiment.

Let a series of observers, A, B, C, D, &c., be placed in a line, at distances of about 1000 feet asunder, and let a pistol be discharged at P, about 1000 feet from the first observer.

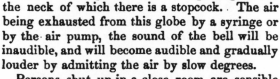

P————A————B————C————D————E————F

This observer will see the flash of the pistol about one second before he hears the report. The observer B will hear the report one second after it has been heard by A, and about two seconds after he sees the flash. In the same manner, the third observer at C will hear the report one second after it has been heard by the observer at B, and two seconds after it has been heard by the observer at A, and three seconds after he perceives the flash. In the same way, the fourth observer at D will hear the report one second later than it was heard by the third observer at C, and three seconds later than it was heard by the observer at A, and four seconds after he perceives the flash.

Now it must be observed, that at the moment the report is heard by the second observer at B, it has ceased to be audible to the first observer at A; and when it is heard by the third observer at C, it has ceased to be heard by the second observer at B, and so forth. It follows, therefore, from this, that sound passes through the air, not instantaneously, but progressively, and at a uniform rate.

641. **Breadth of sonorous waves.**—As the sensation of sound is produced by the wave of air impinging on the tympanum of the ear, exactly as the momentum of a wave of the sea would strike the shore, it follows that the interval between the production of sound and its sensation, is the time which such a wave would take to pass through the air from the sounding body to the ear; and since these waves are propagated through the air in regular succession, one following another without overlaying each other, as in the case of waves upon a liquid, the breadth of a wave may always be determined if we take the number of vibrations which the sounding body makes in a second, and the velocity with which the sound passes through the air. If, for example, it be known that in a second a musical string makes 500 vibrations, and that the sound of this string takes a second to reach the ear of a person at a distance of 1000 feet, there are 500 waves in the distance of 1000 feet, and consequently each wave measures two feet.

The velocity of the sound, therefore, and the rate of vibration, are always sufficient data by which the length of a sonorous wave can be computed.

642. **Distinction between musical sounds and ordinary sounds.**—It has not been ascertained, with any clearness or certainty, by what physical distinctions vibrations which produce common sounds or noises are distinguished from such as produce musical sounds. It is nevertheless certain, that all vibrations, in proportion as they are regular, uniform, and equal, produce sounds proportionably more agreeable and musical.

Sounds are distinguished from each other by their *pitch* or *tone*, in virtue of which they are high or low; by their *intensity*, in virtue of which they are loud or soft; and by a property expressed in French by the word *timbre*, which we shall here adopt in the absence of any English equivalent.

643. **Pitch.**—The pitch or tone of a sound is grave or acute. In the former case it is low, and in the latter high, in the musical scale. It will be shown hereafter that the physical condition which determines this property of sound is the rate of vibration of the sounding body.

The more rapid the vibrations are, the more acute will be the sound. A bass note is produced by vibrations much less rapid than a note in the treble. But it will also be shown that the length of the sonorous waves depends on the rate of vibration of the body which produces it : the slower the rate of vibration, the longer will be the wave, and the more grave the tone.

All vibrations which are performed at the same rate produce waves of equal length and sounds of the same pitch.

644. **Loudness.**—The intensity of a sound, or its degree of loudness, depends on the force with which the vibrations of the sounding body are made, and consequently upon the degree of condensation produced at the middle of the sonorous wave. Waves of equal length, but having different degrees of condensation at their centres, will produce notes of the same pitch, but of different degrees of loudness, in proportion to such degrees of condensation.

645. **Timbre.** — The timbre of a sound is not easily explained, and still less easily can the physical conditions on which it depends be ascertained. If we hear the same musical note produced with the same degree of loudness in an adjacent room successively upon a flute, a clarionet, and a hautboy, we shall, without the least hesitation, distinguish the one instrument from the other. Now this distinction is made by observing some peculiarity in the notes produced, yet the notes shall be the same, and be produced with equal loudness.

This property, by which the one sound is distinguished from the other, is called the *timbre*.

646. **In the same medium, all sounds have the same velocity.** — That this is the case, is manifest from the absence of all confusion in the effects of music, at whatever distance it may be heard. If the different notes simultaneously produced by the various instruments of an orchestra moved with different velocities through the air, they would be heard by a distant auditor at different moments, the consequence of which would be, that a musical performance would, to the auditors, save those in immediate proximity with the performers, produce the most intolerable confusion and cacophony; for different notes produced simultaneously, and

which, when heard together, form harmony, would at a distance be heard in succession; and sounds produced in succession would be heard as if produced together, according to the different velocities with which each note would pass through the air.

647. **Velocity.**—The velocity of sound varies with the elasticity of the medium by which it is propagated. Its velocity, therefore, through the air will vary, more or less, with the barometer and thermometer.

The experimental methods which have been adopted to ascertain the velocity of sound are similar in principle to those which have been briefly noticed by way of illustration. The most extensive and accurate system of experiments which have been made with this object, were those made at Paris by the Board of Longitude in the year 1822. The sounding bodies used on this occasion, were pieces of artillery charged with from two to three pounds of powder, which were placed at Villejuif and Montlhéry. The experiments were made at midnight, in order that the flash might be more easily and accurately noticed. They were conducted by MM. Prony, Arago, Mathieu, Humboldt, Guy Lussac, and Bouvard. The result of these experiments was, that when the barometer was at 29·8 inches, and the thermometer at 61°, the velocity of sound was 1118·4 feet per second.

According to the theory of Laplace, the velocity of sound increases at the rate of 1·11 feet per second for every degree in the rise, and decreases at the same rate for each degree in the fall of the thermometer. Hence it appears that the velocity of sound at 32° is 1086·2 feet per second. For all practical purposes, it is sufficiently exact to take 1120 feet as the velocity of sound at 62°, and allow thirteen inches for every variation of a degree in temperature.

648. **Distance measured by sound.**—The production of sound is in many cases attended with the evolution of light, as, for example, in firearms and explosions generally, and in the case of atmospheric electricity. In these cases, by noting the interval between the flash and the report, and multiplying the number of seconds in each interval by the number of feet per second in the velocity of sound, the distance can be ascertained with great precision. Thus, if a flash of lightning be seen ten seconds before the thunder which attends it is heard, and the atmosphere be in such condition that the velocity of sound is 1120 feet per second, it is evident that the distance of the cloud in which the electricity is evolved must be 11200 feet.

Among the numerous discoveries bequeathed to the world by Newton, was a calculation, by theory, of the velocity with which sound was propagated through the air. This calculation, based upon the elasticity and temperature of the air, gave as a result about one sixth less than that which resulted from experiments.

This discrepancy remained without satisfactory explanation until it was solved by Laplace, who showed that it arose from the fact that Newton had neglected to take into account, in his computation, the effects of the heat developed and absorbed by the alternate compression and rarefaction of the air produced in the sonorous undulations. Laplace, taking account of these, gave a formula for the velocity of sound which corresponds in its results exactly with experiment.

649. **All gases and vapours conduct sound.** — As all elastic fluids are, in common with air, susceptible of undulation, they are equally capable of transmitting sound.

This may be rendered experimentally evident by the following means. Let the alarum be placed under the receiver of an air pump, as already described, and let the receiver be exhausted. If, instead of introducing atmospheric air into the receiver, we introduce any other elastic fluid, the sound of the alarum will become gradually audible, according to the quantity of such fluid which is introduced under the receiver. If a drop of any liquid which is easily evaporated be introduced, the atmosphere of vapour which is thus produced will also render the alarum audible.

650. The same sounding body will produce a louder or lower sound, according as the density of the air which surrounds it is increased or diminished. In the experiment already explained, in which the alarum was placed under an exhausted receiver, the sound increased in loudness as more and more air was admitted within the receiver. If the alarum had been placed under a condenser, and highly compressed air collected round it, the sound would be still further increased.

When persons descend to any considerable depth in a diving bell, the atmosphere around them is compressed by the weight of the column of water above them. In such circumstances, a whisper is almost as loud as the common voice in the open air, and when one speaks with the ordinary force it produces an effect so loud as to be painful.

On the summit of lofty mountains, where the barometric column falls to one half its usual elevation, and where therefore the air is highly rarefied, sounds are greatly diminished in intensity. Persons who ascend in balloons find it necessary to speak with much greater exertion, and, as would be said, louder, in order to render themselves audible. When Saussure ascended Mont Blanc, he found that the report of a pistol was not louder than a common cracker.

651. **Effect of atmospheric agitation on sound.** — Violent

winds and other atmospheric agitations affect the transmission of sound. When a strong wind blows from the hearer towards the sounding body, a sound often ceases to be heard which would be distinctly audible in a calm. A tranquil and frosty atmosphere placed over a smooth and level surface is favourable to the transmission of sound. Lieutenant Forster held a conversation with a person on the opposite side of the harbour of Port Bowen, in the third polar expedition of Sir Edward Parry, the distance between the speakers being more than a mile.

It is said that the sound of the cannon at the battle of Waterloo was heard at Dover, and that the cannon in naval engagements in the Channel have been heard in the centre of England.

652. Liquids are also capable of propagating sound. Divers can render themselves audible at the surface of the water; and stones or other objects struck together at the bottom produce a sound audible at the surface.

It appears from the experiments of M. Colladon, made at Geneva, that sounds are transmitted through water to great distances with greater force than through air. A blow struck under the water of the Lake of Geneva was distinctly heard across the whole breadth of the lake, a distance of nine miles.

Solid bodies, such as walls or buildings interposed between the sounding body and the hearer, diminish the loudness of the sound, but do not obstruct it when the sound is made in air; but it appears from the experiments of M. Colladon, that the interposition of such obstacles almost destroys the transmission of sound in water.

653. **Sounds which destroy each other.** — When two series of sonorous undulations propagated from different sounding bodies intersect each other, the phenomena of interference explained in the theory of undulation are produced, and an ear placed at such a point of interference will not be affected by any sense of sound, so long as the two sounding bodies continue to vibrate; but the moment the vibration of either of the two is discontinued, the other will become audible. Thus, it appears that two sounds reaching the ear together, instead of producing, as might be expected, a louder sound than either would produce alone, may altogether destroy each other and produce silence.

This phenomenon is precisely analogous to the case of two series of waves formed upon the surface of the same liquid, at a point where the elevation of a wave of one series coincides with the depression of a wave of the other.

If two sounding bodies were placed in the foci of an ellipse, as represented in *fig.* 340., an ear placed on any of the lines of interference there indicated would be conscious of no sound; but the moment that either of the two sounding bodies became silent, the other would be heard; or if the ear of the listener were removed to a position midway between two lines of interference, then both sounds would be heard simultaneously, and combined would be louder than either alone.

654. **Experimental illustration.**—This phenomenon of interference may be produced in a striking manner by means of the common tuning fork, used to regulate the pitch of musical instruments.

Let A and B, *fig.* 349., be two cylindrical glass vessels, held at right angles to each other, and let the tuning fork, after it has

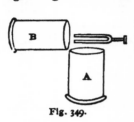

Fig. 349.

been put in vibration, be held in the middle of the angle formed by their mouths. Although, under such circumstances, the vibration of the tuning fork will be imparted to the columns of air included within the two cylinders, no sound will be heard; but if either cylinder be removed, the sound will be distinctly audible in the other. In this case, the silence produced by the combined sounds is the consequence of interference.

Another example of this phenomenon may be produced by the tuning fork itself. If this instrument, after being put into vibration, be held at a great distance from the ear, and slowly turned round its axis, a position of the prongs will be found at which the sound will become inaudible. This position will correspond to the points of interference of the two systems of undulation propagated from the two prongs.

655. **Examples.** —Solids which possess elasticity have likewise the power of propagating sound. If the end of a beam composed of any solid possessing elasticity be lightly scratched or rubbed, the sound will be distinct to an ear placed at the other end, although the same sound would not be audible to the ear of the person who produces it, and who is contiguous to the place of its origin.

The earth itself conducts sound, so as to render it sensible to the ear when the air fails to do so. It is well known, that the approach of a troop of horse can be heard at a distance by putting the ear to the ground. In volcanic countries, it is said that the rumbling noise which is usually the prognostic of an eruption is first heard by the beasts of the field, because their ears are generally near the ground, and they then by their agitation and alarm give warning to the inhabitants of the approaching catastrophe. Savage tribes practise this method of ascertaining the approach of persons from a great distance.

656. Velocity of sound in different media. — The velocity with which sound is propagated through different media varies with their different physical conditions.

In the following table are given the velocities with which sound is propagated through the several liquids therein named, the temperature being 50°.

TABLE.

Velocities of Sound of Liquids at 50° Fahr.

Names.	Specific Gravity.	Compressibility under one Atmosphere in Millionths of primitive Volume.	Velocity of Sound in Feet per Second.
Sulphuric ether - - -	·712	131·35	3409
Alcohol - - - -	·795	94·95	3390
Hydrochloric ether - -	·874	84·25	3814
Essence of turpentine - -	·870	71·35	4180
Water - - - -	1·000	47·85	4707
Mercury - - - -	13·544	3·38	4869
Nitric acid - - - -	1·403	30·55	5036
Water of ammonia (saturated) -	·900	38·05	6044

Table showing the Velocities of Sound as propagated by various solid Substances.

Names.	Velocities (that through Air being 1).	Names.	Velocities (that through Air being 1).
Whalebone - - -	6·66	Mahogany wood ⎫	
Tin - - - -	7·50	Ebony	
Silver - - - -	9·00	Hornbeam	
Walnut ⎫		Elm ⎬ - - 14·40	
Yew ⎪		Alder	
Brass ⎬ - - 10·66		Birch ⎭	
Oak ⎪		Lime ⎫	
Plum-tree ⎭		Cherry ⎬ - - - 15·00	
Tobacco-pipes - - ⎰ 10·00		Willow ⎭	
⎱ 12·00		Pine - - - 16·00	
Copper - - - 12·00		Glass ⎫	
Pear tree ⎱		Iron ⎬ - - - 16·66	
Red beech ⎰ - - 12·50		Steel ⎭	
Maple - - - 13·33			

657. Effects of elasticity of air. — The velocity with which sound is transmitted through the air varies with its elasticity; and where different strata are rendered differently elastic by the unequal radiation of heat, the agency of electricity, or other causes, the transmission of sound will be irregular. In passing from stratum to stratum differing in elasticity, the speed with which sound is propagated is not only varied, but the force of the intensity of the undulations is diminished by the combined effects of reflection and interference, so that the sound, on reaching the ear, after passing through such varying media, is often very much diminished.

The fact, that distant sounds are more distinctly heard by night than by day, may be in part accounted for by this circumstance, the strata of the atmosphere being during the day exposed to vicissitudes of temperature more varying than during the night.

658. **Biot's experiment.** — The relative velocities of sound, as transmitted by air and by metal, are illustrated by the following remarkable experiment of Biot: — A bell was suspended at the centre of the mouth of a metal tube 3000 feet long, and a ring of metal was at the same time placed close to the metal forming the mouth of the tube, so that when the ring was sounded its vibrations might affect the metal of the tube; and when the bell was sounded, its vibrations might affect only the air included within the tube. A hammer was so adapted as to strike the ring and the bell simultaneously. When this was done, an ear placed at the remote end of the tube heard the sound of the ring, and after a considerable interval heard the sound of the bell.

659. **Chladni's experiments.** — The solids composing the body of an animal are capable of transmitting the sonorous undulations to the organ of hearing, even though the air surrounding that organ be excluded from communicating with the origin of the sound.

Chladni showed that two persons stopping their ears could converse with each other by holding the same stick between their teeth, or by resting their teeth upon the same solid. The same effect was produced when the stick was pressed against the breast or the throat, and other parts of the body.

If a person speak, directing his mouth into a vessel composed of any vibratory substance, such as glass or porcelain, the other stopping his ears, and touching such vessel with a stick held between his teeth, he will hear the words spoken.

The same effect will take place with vessels composed of metal or wood.

If two persons hold between their teeth the same thread, stopping their ears, they would hear each other speak, provided the thread be stretched tight.

660. **Loudness dependent on distance.** — In has been shown that while the pitch of a sound depends upon the length of the sonorous wave, or, what is the same, the number of waves which strike the ear per second, the loudness depends on the degree of condensation or rarefaction produced in each such wave; but the loudness is also dependent on the distance of the hearer from the sounding body; and therefore, when it is stated that it is proportional to the condensation and rarefaction of the sonorous waves, the estimate must be understood to be applied to sounds heard at the same distance from their origin.

In explaining the general theory of undulations, it has been shown that as the undulation spreads round the centre from which it emanates, its intensity diminishes as the square of the distance is augmented; and this general principle consequently becomes applicable to sonorous undulations; and, therefore, when other things are the same, the intensity or loudness of the sound diminishes in the same proportion as the square of the distance of the hearer from the sounding body is augmented. Thus in a theatre, if the linear dimensions be doubled, other arrangements being the same, the loudness of the performers' voices, as heard at any part of its circumference, will be diminished in a fourfold proportion.

CHAP. III.

PHYSICAL THEORY OF MUSIC.

661. **The monochord.** — Of the various forms of apparatus which have been contrived for the production of musical sounds with a view to the experimental illustration of their theory, that which is best adapted for this purpose are those which, under various denominations, consist of strings submitted to tension

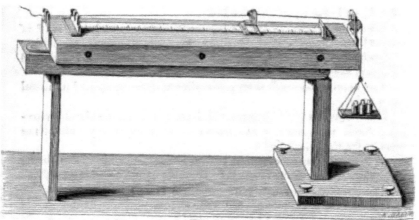

Fig. 350.

over a sounding board. An instrument of this form, consisting of a single string, and called a *monochord* or *sonometer*, is represented in *fig.* 350. It consists of a string of catgut or wire attached to a fixed point, carried over a pulley, and stretched by a known weight. Under the string is a hollow box or sounding board, to the frame of which the pulley is attached. The string rests upon two bridges, one of which is fixed, and the other can be moved with a sliding motion to or from, so as to vary at pleasure the length of the part of the string included between the two bridges.

A divided scale is placed under them, so that the length of the vibrating part of the string may be regulated at pleasure. By varying the weight, the tension of the string may be increased or diminished in any desired proportion. This may be accomplished with facility by circular weights which are provided for the purpose, and which may be slipped upon the stem of the weight. By means of this apparatus, the relation between the various notes of the musical scale and the rate of vibration by which they are respectively produced, have been ascertained.

662. Its application to determine the rates of vibrations of musical notes. — It has been shown that the rate of vibration of a string such as that of the monochord is inversely as its length, other things being the same. Thus, if its length be halved, its rate of vibration is doubled; if its length be diminished or increased in a threefold proportion, its rate of vibration will be increased or diminished in the same proportion; and so forth.

Let the bridges be placed at a distance from each other as great as the apparatus admits, and let the weight which stretches the string be so adjusted, that the note produced by vibrating the string shall correspond with any proposed note of the musical scale; such, for example, as ♦ , the low c of the treble clef. This being done, let the movable bridge be moved towards the fixed bridge, continually sounding the string until it produces the octave above the note first sounded, that is, until it produces the middle c ♦ of the treble.

If the length of the string be now ascertained by reference to the scale of the monochord, it will be found to be precisely one half its original length.

663. A double rate of vibration produces an octave. — Hence it follows, that the same string will sound an octave higher if the length is halved. But it has already been shown that the rate of vibration will be doubled when the length of the string is halved. Hence it follows, that two sounds, one of which is an octave higher than the other, will be produced by vibrations, the rate of which will be in the proportion of 2 to 1; and, consequently, the length of the undulation producing the lower note will be double that of the undulation producing the higher note.

664. **Rates of vibration for other intervals.** — If, instead of moving the bridge to the point necessary to produce the octave to the fundamental note C, it be moved to such positions that the string shall produce the successive notes of the scale between it and its octave, the lengths of the string being noted by reference to the scale, it will be found that they will be respectively those which are inscribed below the annexed scale under the notes severally. The length of the string producing the fundamental note C is assumed to be 1, the fractions expressing, with reference to this length, the lengths which are found to produce the successive notes of the scale severally.

Let the seven successive notes of the gamut be expressed as follows : —

ut	re	mi	fa	sol	la	si	ut
C	D	E	F	G	A	B	C
1	$\frac{8}{9}$	$\frac{4}{5}$	$\frac{3}{4}$	$\frac{2}{3}$	$\frac{3}{5}$	$\frac{8}{15}$	$\frac{1}{2}$

The names given by continental writers to these seven notes are those written beneath them in the upper line — ut, re, mi, fa, sol, la, si, ut ; but those by which they are most generally known in England are the letters of the alphabet inscribed in the lower line, the fundamental note being C, and the succeeding ones designated by the letters inscribed beneath them.

Let us suppose, then, that the monochord produces this fundamental note C, and that the movable bridge be then advanced towards the fixed bridge so as to shorten the string until it produces the note D. It will be found that its length will be reduced ⅛th, and that, consequently, the length necessary to produce the note D will be ⁸⁄₉ths of that which produces the note C. Let the bridge be now advanced until the string sound the note E; its length will then be ⅘ths of that which produces the fundamental note. In the same manner, being further shortened, let it produce the note F; its length will be ¾ths of its original length. In the same manner, the lengths of the string corresponding to each of the successive notes of the gamut, will be found to be expressed by the fractions which are written in the above diagram under the notes severally.

But since the number of vibrations per second is, by the principles already established, in the inverse ratio of the length of the string, it follows, that if the number of vibrations per second corresponding to the fundamental note C be expressed by 1, the number of vibrations per second corresponding to the other notes successively will be as follows : —

ut	re	mi	fa	sol	la	si	ut
C	D	E	F	G	A	B	C
1	$\frac{9}{8}$	$\frac{5}{4}$	$\frac{4}{3}$	$\frac{3}{2}$	$\frac{5}{3}$	$\frac{15}{8}$	2

The meaning of which is, that in producing the note D, nine vibrations will be made in the same time that eight are made by the note C. In like manner, when the note E is sounded, five of its vibrations correspond to four of C, four vibrations of F correspond to three of C, three vibrations of G correspond to two of C, five vibrations of A correspond to three of C, fifteen vibrations of B correspond to eight of C, and, in fine, two vibrations of the octave C correspond to one of the fundamental C.

The relative numbers corresponding to the notes of one octave being known, those of the octaves higher or lower in the musical scale can be easily calculated.

It appears from what has been already proved that the note which is an octave higher than the fundamental note is produced by a rate of vibration twice as rapid: and this principle would equally apply to any other note. We shall, therefore, always find the rate of vibration of a note which is an octave above a given note by multiplying the rate of vibration of the given note by 2; and, consequently, to find the rate of vibration of a note an octave lower, it will only be necessary to divide the rate of vibration of the given note by 2. If, therefore, it be desired to find the rate of vibration of the series of notes continued upwards beyond the series given in the preceding diagram, it will only be necessary to multiply the numbers in the preceding series by 2.

665. **Physical cause of harmony.** — If these results be compared with the effect produced upon the ear by the combination of these musical notes sounded in pairs, we shall discover the physical cause of those agreeable sensations denominated harmony, and the opposite sensations denominated discord.

The most perfect harmony is that of the octave, which is so complete as to be nearly equivalent to unison. Now the fundamental note C produced simultaneously with its octave is attended by two series of vibrations, of which two of the octave correspond to one of the fundamental note. It follows, therefore, that the commencement of every alternate vibration of the upper note coincides with the commencement of a vibration of the lower.

Next to the octave, the most agreeable harmony is that of the fifth, which is produced when the fundamental note C is sounded simultaneously with G. Now it appears by the preceding results that three vibrations of G are simultaneous with two of C. It follows, therefore, that every third vibration of G commences simultaneously with every second vibration of C. The coincident vibrations, therefore, are marked by the commencement of every second vibration of the fundamental C, whereas, in the octave, a coincidence takes place at the commencement of every vibration.

The coincidences, therefore, are more frequent in the octave than in the fifth, in the proportion of 1 to 2.

The next harmony to that of the fifth is the fourth, which is produced when the fundamental note C is sounded simultaneously with F. Now it appears from the preceding results that four vibrations of F are simultaneous with three of the fundamental note. and, consequently, that there is a coincident vibration at the commencement of every third vibration of the fundamental note. The coincident vibrations are, therefore. less frequent than in the fifth in the proportion of 3 to 2 : and less frequent than in the octave in the proportion of 3 to 1.

The harmony which comes next in order to the fourth is that of the third, produced when the fundamental note c is sounded simultaneously with E. Now it appears from the preceding results that five vibrations of E are made simultaneously with four of c; and that, consequently, there is a coincidence at every fourth vibration of the fundamental note. The coincidences, therefore, in this case are less frequent than in the fourth, in the ratio of 3 to 4, less frequent than in the fifth in the proportion of 2 to 4, and less frequent than in the octave in the proportion of 1 to 4.

Scale exhibiting the Effect of Binary Combinations of the Fundamental Note with a Series of Three Octaves continued severally upwards and downwards.

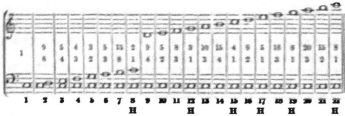

The figures which are placed over each combination express the number of vibrations which in each case take place simultaneously, and the name of the interval, as it is technically called in music, is written under the lower line. Thus, the interval between the fundamental note c and the note B is a seventh; and the figures above indicate that fifteen vibrations of B are made in the same time as eight vibrations of c. In the same way, the interval between c and F in the treble is called an eleventh; and the figures indicate that eight vibrations of F are made while three of c take place.

666. **Physical cause of the harmonics of the harp or violin.** — On inspecting the numbers which in the preceding scale indicate the relative rates of vibration of these pairs of musical sounds, it will be observed that there are certain combinations in which a complete number of vibrations of the upper note are made in the time of a single vibration of the lower note. These are distinguished by the letter H written under the interval. The first is the octave, in which two vibrations of the upper note correspond to one of the lower; the second is the twelfth, in which

three vibrations of the upper note correspond to one of the lower; the third is the fifteenth, in which four vibrations of the upper note correspond to one of the lower; the fifth is the nineteenth, in which six vibrations of the upper correspond to one vibration of the lower; and, in fine, the seventh is the twenty-second, in which eight vibrations of the upper correspond to one vibration of the lower.

These combinations (which possess other and important properties) are called *harmonics*.

One of the most remarkable properties of the harmonics is, that if the fundamental note be produced by sounding the open string, a practised ear will detect in the sound mingled with the fundamental, the several harmonics to it, and more especially those which are in nearest accord with the fundamental note. Thus the octaves will be produced; but these are so nearly in unison with the fundamental note that the ear cannot distinguish them. The twelfth, or that which has three vibrations for one of the fundamental note, is distinctly perceptible to common ears. The more practised can distinguish the seventeenth, or that which vibrates five times more rapidly than the octave; and some pretend to be able to distinguish the vibrations of the nineteenth, which vibrates six times for one of the fundamental note.

667. **Experimental verification by Sauveur.**— These phenomena have been explained and verified in a satisfactory manner by Sauveur, who showed that when a string is put into vibration it undergoes subordinate vibrations, which take place in its aliquot parts. Thus, if an edge touch the string gently, when in vibration, at its middle point, as represented in *fig.* 351., each half will continue to vibrate independently.

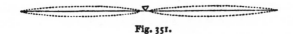

Fig. 351.

If the edge be in like manner applied at one third of the length, the vibration will still continue, each third part vibrating independently of the other; and in fine, the condition of the entire string when left to vibrate freely, is represented in *fig.* 352.,

Fig. 352.

where the subordinate vibrations produced in the aliquot parts of the string are represented.

668. **Limit of the musical sensibility of the ear.** — Since

the pitch of a musical note depends on the number of vibrations produced per second, it follows that whenever two notes are produced by a different number of vibrations per second, they will have a corresponding musical difference. Now a question arises as to the limits of the power of the ear to distinguish minute differences of this kind. For example, it may be asked whether two musical notes produced by vibrations differing from each other by only one in a million, that is to say, if, while one string make a million of vibrations, another string shall make a million and one, is the ear capable of perceiving that one note is more acute than the other? It is certain that no ear could discover such a difference, although it ·is equally certain that such a difference would exist. The question then is, what is the limit of sensibility of the ear.

If two strings of the same wire were extended by equal weights on the monochord, and the movable bridges brought to coincide, so that the strings would be of precisely equal length, then it is certain that when struck they would produce the same note, since all the conditions affecting the vibration of the string would be identical. Now, if one of the bridges be moved slowly, so as gradually to lengthen the vibrating part of the string, the limit may be found at which the ear will begin to be sensible of the dissonance of the notes. The point thus determined may fix the limit of the sensibility of the ear.

The comparative lengths of the two strings in such a case would indicate the different rates of vibration of which the ear is sensible.

Sensibility of practised organists. — The result of such an experiment would of course be different for different ears, according to their natural sensibility, and to the effects of cultivation in improving their musical perception. Practised organists are able to distinguish between notes which differ in their vibrations to the extent of one in eighty.

Thus, if a string of the monochord have 20 inches between the bridges, and the other 20¼ inches, their rates of vibration being then in the proportion of 80 to 81, the difference would be distinguishable. Such an interval between two musical sounds is called a *comma*.

But when the difference of the rates of vibration are much less than this, they cannot be distinguished by the ear. The notes on common square pianos are each produced by two strings, and on grand pianos by three strings struck simultaneously by the same hammer. In tuning the instrument, these strings are tuned separately, until they are brought as nearly to the same pitch as the ear can determine. When struck together, however, a slight dissonance will in general be perceptible, which is adjusted by tuning one or the other until the sounds are brought into unison.

Since, however, such unison is only determined by the ear, and since the sensibility of that organ is limited, it follows that the unison thus obtained can never be perfect otherwise than by chance.

669. **Methods of determining the absolute number of vibrations producing musical notes.** — We have hitherto noticed only the relative rates of vibration of different musical notes. If the absolute number of vibrations per second, corresponding to any one note of the scale, were known, the absolute number of vibrations of all others could be computed. Thus, the note which is an octave higher than the note proposed, would be produced by double the number of vibrations per second ; a note one fifth above it would be produced by a number of vibrations per second found by multiplying the given number by 3 divided by 2, and so on. In a word, the number of vibrations per second necessary to produce any given note would be found by multiplying the number of vibrations per second necessary to produce the fundamental note by the fractions given in (664.) corresponding to the proposed note.

670. **The Sirène.** — An instrument of great ingenuity and beauty, called the *Sirène*, has been supplied by the invention of M. Cagniard de la Tour, for the purpose of ascertaining the whole number of vibrations which correspond to any proposed musical sound.

A tube of about four inches in diameter, represented at $f f'$, *fig.* 353., to which wind can be supplied by means of a bellows or otherwise through a pipe $y y'$, is terminated in a smooth circular plate $v v'$, stopping its end. In this plate, and near its edge, a number of small holes are pierced very close together, and disposed in a circular form, as represented in *fig.* 354., the perforations being made, not perpendicular to the plate, but in an oblique direction through it. Another plate of equal magnitude $u u'$, and having a circle of holes precisely similar, is fixed upon this so as to be capable of revolving with any required velocity round its centre. As it revolves, the holes in the upper plate $u u'$ correspond in certain positions with the holes in the lower plate $v v'$; but in intermediate positions, the holes in the lower plate not corresponding with those in the other plate, the exit of the air from the tube $f f'$ is stopped. If, then, we suppose the upper of these two plates to revolve upon the lower, a current of air being supplied to the tube $f f'$ through $y y'$, the air will escape where the holes in the superior plate correspond in position with those in the lower plate, but in intermediate positions it will be intercepted. The effect will be, that when the superior plate moves with a uniform velocity, there will be a series of puffs of wind allowed to escape from the holes of the inferior plate through those of the superior plate in uniform succession with equal intervals of time between them. This succession of puffs will produce undulations in the air surrounding the instrument, and when their velocity is sufficiently increased these undulations will produce a sound. If the motion be uniform, this sound will be maintained at a uniform pitch; but as the motion of the plate

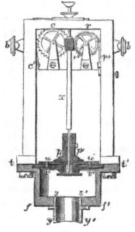

Fig. 353.

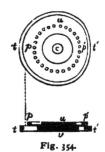

Fig. 354.

is increased, the pitch will become more elevated; and, in short, such a velocity may be given to the superior plate as to make the instrument produce a sound of any desired pitch, acute or grave.

A small apparatus is connected with the superior plate, by which its revolutions are counted and indicated. This apparatus consists of a spindle x, *fig.* 353., which carries upon it a worm or endless screw, which drives the teeth of a small wheel r, connected by pinions and wheelwork with another wheel c. These wheels govern the motion of hands upon small dials d d', *fig.* 355. These hands being brought to their respective zeros at the commencement of the experiment, their position at the end of any known interval will indicate the number of puffs of air which have escaped from the holes of the revolving plate u u' in the interval, and will consequently determine the number of undulations of the air which correspond to the sound produced.

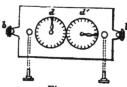

Fig. 355.

A perspective view of this instrument is shown in *fig.* 356.

Experiments. —Various series of interesting experiments have been performed with this instrument by its inventor, which have shown that it not only indicates the pitch of the note produced, but also that the *timbre* of the sound has a relation to the thickness of the revolving plate, and of the fixed plate over which it turns, and with the space between the holes pierced in these plates. These conditions, however, have not been investigated with sufficient precision to supply any general principles. M. Cagniard de la Tour thinks, nevertheless, that when the interval between the

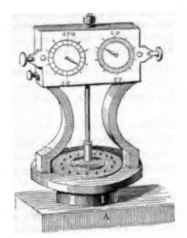

Fig. 356

holes pierced in the plates is very small, the sound approaches to that of the human voice, and when they are very considerable it approaches to that of a trumpet.

671. **Savart's apparatus.**— Another instrument for the experimental determination of the number of vibrations corresponding to a note of any proposed pitch is due to M. Savart, whose experimental investigations have thrown so much light upon the physics of sound.

This apparatus, which is represented in *fig.* 357., consists of a frame *a a* constructed in a very solid manner, supporting a large wheel *b* connected, by an endless band *x*, with a small grooved

Fig. 357

wheel fixed upon the axis of another large wheel *d'*, which is formed into teeth at its edge. These teeth strike successively a piece of card or other thin elastic plate presented to them, and fixed upon the frame *a a*, as represented in *fig.* 358. The successive impulses given to the card produce corresponding undulations in the air, the effect of which is a musical sound.

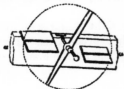

Fig. 358.

The number of undulations per second thus produced in the air will correspond with the number of teeth of the wheel *d'* which pass the edge of the card in a second. Now, if the number of turns per second given to the primary wheel *b* be known, the relative magnitudes of this wheel and the small wheel attached to the axis of d', will determine the number of revolutions per second given to the wheel d', and, consequently, the number of teeth of the latter, which, in a second, will strike the edge of the card. In this way, undulations of the air can be produced at the rate of 25000 per second.

The sounds produced by this means are said to be clear, continued, and distinct, and easily brought into unison with any musical instrument, since they can be produced at a uniform pitch for any desired interval of time.

Since by the stroke of each tooth of the wheel d', the card is made to move first downwards and then upwards, or *vice versâ*, it is clear from what has been explained that, for each tooth of the wheel d' which passes the card, a condensed and a rarefied wave of air will be produced.

In the sound, therefore, which results there will be as many double vibrations, that is to say, undulations, including each a condensed and rarefied wave, as there are teeth of the wheel d' which pass the card; and to ascertain the number of such double vibrations corresponding to any note, it will be only necessary to observe the number of teeth of the wheel d' which passes the card when the sound produced by the instrument is brought into unison with the proposed note.

672. **The absolute rates of vibration of musical notes ascertained.**—By accurate experiment, made both with the Sirène and with the instrument of M. Savart, it has been found that the A of the treble clef or ♭═══ is produced by imparting undulations to the air at the rate of 880 single vibrations, or 440 double vibrations, per second. By single vibration is here to be understood condensed waves only, or rarefied waves only; and by double vibration, the combination of a condensed and rarefied wave. It is more usual to count the vibrations, taking the latter, or the double vibration, as the unit, and we shall therefore here adopt this nomenclature; and it may therefore be stated, in this sense, that the A of the diapason, the note usually produced by the sounding fork for determining the pitch of musical instruments, is produced by imparting to the air 440 undulations per second.

It must be stated, however, that some slight departure from this standard prevails in different established orchestras. Thus, it is estimated that the pitch of this note in the under-mentioned orchestras, is produced by the number of vibrations per second exhibited below:—

Orchestra of Berlin Opera	-	-	437·32
„ Académie de la Musique, Paris	-	-	431·34
„ Opéra Comique, Paris	-	-	427·61
„ Italian Opera, Paris	-	-	424·14

The number of vibrations corresponding to all the other notes of the musical scale may be computed by the result here obtained, combined with the relative numbers of vibrations given in (664.). Thus, if it be desired to determine the number of vibrations per second corresponding to the fundamental note [♪], it will be only necessary to divide 440, the number of vibrations of the note [♪], by the fraction ♩, or what is the same, to divide it by 10, and multiply the quotient by 3. The number of vibrations, therefore, per second which will produce the note [♪] will be 44×3 =132.

673. **Tuning fork.**—To determine the pitch at which instruments should be tuned, and to be enabled, as it were, to transport a given pitch from place to place, an instrument called a *tuning fork* or *diapason* has been contrived. This instrument is an elastic steel bar, bent into the form of a fork, and mounted upon a handle. If either of its prongs be smartly struck upon any hard surface, they will both begin to vibrate, and if held near the ear, will produce the perception of a musical note; and so long as the fork remains unaltered, this note will be always the same. It may be also put in vibration by drawing up between the prongs any bar thicker than the space between them, as shown in the figure. The sound will be rendered more audible if the handle of the fork, while in vibration, be pressed upon any sonorous body such as a board or thin box.

In its original construction, the fork is regulated so as to produce

a particular note, usually [♪]

When tuning forks are required, having somewhat a higher or lower pitch, it has been generally found necessary to provide a separate fork for each pitch, By an ingenious contrivance, however, Mr. Daniel Klein, of the establishment of Mr. Erard, at Paris, has found means to vary within the necessary limits the pitch of the same fork. He accomplishes this by means of a small brass clamp, which slides upon one of the prongs, as shown in *fig.* 359., and which can be fixed in its position by means of a clamping screw: by varying the place of this upon the prong, the pitch of the fork can be raised and lowered. Marks are engraved upon the prong, showing the

Fig. 359.

position which the clamp must have, so as to correspond with the pitch adopted by each of the principal orchestras.

674. **Range of musical sensibility of the ear.** — On a seven octave pianoforte the highest note in the treble is three octaves above , and the lowest note in the bass is four octaves below it. The number of complete vibrations corresponding to the former must be, therefore,

$$440 \times 2 \times 2 \times 2 = 3520;$$

and the number of vibrations per second corresponding to the latter is

$$\frac{440}{2 \times 2 \times 2 \times 2} = \frac{440}{16} = 27\tfrac{1}{2}.$$

Now, since all ordinary ears are capable of appreciating the musical sounds contained between these limits, it is clear that the range of perception of the human ear is greater than that of such an instrument, and that, consequently, this organ is capable of distinguishing sounds produced by vibrations varying from 27 to 3520 per second.

675. It has been generally assumed that the lowest of these notes constituted the most grave musical sound of which the ear is sensible; but Savart has shown, by a series of experiments remarkable for their conclusiveness, that the organ of hearing has a wider range of sensibility. For this purpose he substituted for the toothed wheel d', *fig.* 357., a simple bar of iron or wood, which was made to revolve round its centre in the same manner as the toothed wheel. Two plates of wood were placed on each side of the bench, as represented in *fig.* 358., and were so adjusted that the revolving bar passed nearly in contact with them. At each transit of the bar near their edges an explosive sound was produced, of deafening loudness. The loudness was found to be a maximum when the distance of the bar from the edges of the plates was from the 4000th to the 8000th of an inch. When the bar was moved very slowly, these were recognised by the ear as distinct and successive sounds; but when a velocity was imparted to it which produced from seven to eight sounds per second, the sound became continuous, and was recognised as a musical note of great depth in the scale. It was rendered evident, therefore, from this experiment, that the ear is capable of appreciating musical sounds produced by from seven to eight complete vibrations per second.

676. To determine, on the other hand, the limit of the sensibility of the ear for acute musical sounds, Savart increased the

diameter of the wheel d', *fig*. 357., so as thus to impart a more rapid motion to the teeth. In this way he found that musical sounds were distinctly recognised produced by 24000 complete undulations per second.

By this experiment it was, therefore, established that the range of sensibility of the ear for musical sounds extended from 7 vibrations to 24000 per second.

Savart, however, maintains that these limits are not the extreme ones of the susceptibility of the ear.

677. Length of the waves corresponding to musical notes. — It has been already shown, that by the combination of the velocity of sound with the rate of undulation, the length of the sonorous waves corresponding to any given note can be determined.

Thus, if we know that 440 undulations of the note ϕ strike the ear in a second, and also that the velocity with which this undulation passes through the air is at the rate of 1120 feet per second, we may conclude that in 1120 feet there are 440 complete undulations; consequently, that the length of each such undulation is

$$\frac{1120}{440} = 2\cdot54 \text{ feet.}$$

By a like calculation, the length of the sonorous waves corresponding to all the musical notes can be determined.

To find the length of the sonorous waves corresponding to the highest and lowest notes of a seven octave pianoforte, we are to consider that the highest note has been shown to be produced by 3520 vibrations per second; the length of each variation will, therefore, be

$$\frac{1120}{3520} = 0\cdot318.$$

The number of vibrations corresponding to the lowest note is 27·5; the length, therefore, of the sonorous undulation will be

$$\frac{1120}{27\cdot5} = 40\cdot73 \text{ feet.}$$

To find the length of the vibrations corresponding to the gravest note produced in Savart's experiments, we must divide 1120 by 7; the quotient will be 160 feet, which is the length of the undulation required.

678. Application of the Sirène to count the rate at which the wings of insects move. — The buzzing and humming noises produced by winged insects are not, as might be supposed, vocal sounds. They result from sonorous undulations imparted to the air by the flapping of their wings. This may be rendered evident by observing, that the noise always ceases when the insect alights on any object.

The Sirène has been ingeniously applied for the purpose of as

certaining the rate at which the wings of such creatures flap. The
instrument being brought into unison with the sound produced
by the insect indicates, as in the case of any other musical sound,
the rate of vibration. In this way it has been ascertained that
the wings of a gnat flap at the rate of 15000 times per second.
The pitch of the note produced by this insect in the act of flying
is, therefore, more than two octaves above the highest note of a
seven octave pianoforte

CHAP. IV.

VIBRATIONS OF RODS AND PLATES.

679. **Vibration of rods.** — Among the numerous results of the
labours of contemporary philosophers, some of the most beautiful
and interesting are those which have attended the experimental
researches of Savart, made with a view to determine the phenomena of the vibration of sonorous bodies, some of which we have
already briefly adverted to. Although these researches are too
complicated, and the reasoning and hypotheses raised upon them
are not sufficiently elementary to be introduced with any detail
into this volume, there are nevertheless some sufficiently simple to
admit of brief exposition, and so interesting that their omission,
even in the most elementary treatise, would be unpardonable.

The vibration of thin rods, whether they have the form of a
cylinder or a prism, or that of a narrow thin plate, may be considered as made transversely or longitudinally. If they are made
transversely, that is to say, at right angles to the length, they will
be governed by nearly the same principles as those which have
been already explained as applicable to elastic strings.

680. Let us suppose a glass tube, about seven feet long, and
from an inch to an inch and a half in diameter, to be suspended in
equilibrium at its middle point. Let one half of it be rubbed
upon its surface, in the direction of its length, with a piece of damp
cloth. The friction will excite longitudinal vibration, that, with
a little practice, may be made to produce a musical sound, which
will be more or less acute, according to the force and rapidity of
the friction.

It will be found that the several sounds which will be successively produced by thus increasing the force of the friction,
will correspond with the harmonics already explained in (666.);
that is to say, the rate of vibration of the lowest of these tones

.ng expressed by 1, that of the next above it will be expressed
2, and will therefore be the octave; the next will be expressed
3, and will therefore be the twelfth; and the next by 4, which
ll therefore be the fifteenth.

If the same experiment be performed with long rods of any
·m, and of any material whatever, the same result will be
ticed.   When rods of wood are used, instead of a moistened
th, a cloth coated with resin may be employed.   It is found
at rods, composed of the same material, will always emit the
ne notes, provided they are of the same length, whatever be
eir depth, thickness, or form, provided only that their length be
nsiderable compared with their other dimensions.

681. **Marloye's harp.**—This instrument, represented in *fig.*
·O., consists of twenty thin deal cylindrical rods of decreasing

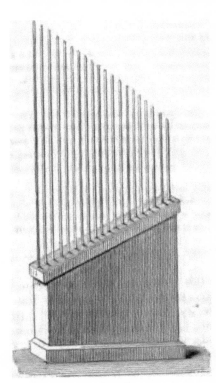

length, and so regulated
that the notes they pro-
duce shall be those of the
musical scale, the half notes
being distinguished by coloured rods like the black
keys of a pianoforte.

The rods are sounded by
pressing them between the
finger and thumb, previously
rubbed with powdered rosin,
and drawing the fingers longitudinally upon them.   An
effect is produced having some
resemblance to that of the Pan ·
dean pipes.

682. **Nodal points.** —
Were it possible to render
visible the state of vibration of each point of the
surface of these rods, it
would be found that the
degree of vibration would
vary from point to point,
and that at certain points
distributed over the sur-
face of these rods there
would be no vibration.
These nodal points, as they

Fig. 360.

ve been called, are distributed according to certain lines sur-
unding the rods.

But it is evident that motions so minute and so rapid as these vibrations, cannot be rendered directly evident to the senses.

683. The following ingenious method of *feeling* the surface while in vibration, and ascertaining the position of the nodal lines, was practised with signal success by Savart. A light ring of paper was formed, having a diameter considerably greater than that of the tube or rod. This ring was suspended on the tube, as represented in *fig.* 361.

The tube, which we shall suppose here, as before, to be formed of glass and of the same dimensions as already explained, being suspended on its

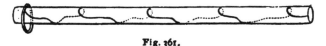

Fig. 361.

central point, and put in vibration, as already described, by friction produced upon that half of the tube on which the ring is not suspended, it will be found that the vibration of the tube will give the ring a jumping motion which will throw it aside, and cause it to move to the right or left, as the case may be, until it shall arrive at a point where it shall remain at rest, its motion as it approaches this point being gradually diminished. At this point it is evident that there is no vibration, and it is, consequently, a nodal point.

Let this point be marked upon the glass with ink, and let the tube be then turned a little round on its axis, so as to bring the point thus marked a little aside from the highest position which it held when the ring rested upon it. Let the tube be now again put in vibration, so as to produce the same note as before. The ring will be again moved, and will find another point of rest.

Let this point be marked as before, and let the tube be again turned, and let the same process be repeated, so that a third nodal point shall be determined. By continuing this process, a succession of nodal points will be found following each other round the tube, and thus a nodal line will be determined.

This process may be continued until the entire course of the nodal line shall be discovered.

Experiments conducted in this way have led to the discovery that the nodal lines surrounding the tube have a sort of spiral or screw-like form, represented in *fig.* 361. The course is not that of a regular helix, since it forms, at different points of the surface of the tube, different angles with its axis, whereas a regular helix will at every point form the same angle; but this variation of the inclination of the nodal line to the axis is not irregular, but undergoes a succession of changes which are constantly repeated, so that each revolution of the nodal line is a repetition in form of the last.

If the ring be now suspended on the other half of the tube, a similar nodal curve is formed, which is not, however, a continuation

of the former. The two spirals seem to have a common origin at
the end, and to proceed from that point, either in the same or
contrary directions, towards the other end of the tube.

684. Savart examined also the position of the nodal line on the
inner surface of the tube, by spreading upon it grains of sand, or
a small bit of cork. These were put in motion in the same manner
as the ring of paper by the vibration, and were brought to rest on
arriving at a nodal point. A series of nodal lines similar to the
exterior system was discovered.

When the friction is increased so as to make the tube sound the
harmonics to the fundamental note, the spirals formed by the nodal
line are reversed two, three, or four times, according to the order
of the harmonic produced.

685. In the case of prismatic rods or flat laminæ, the nodal
curves are still spirals, but more irregular and complicated than
in the case of tubes or cylinders.

The vibrations of thin plates were produced and examined by
the following expedients:—An apparatus was provided, represented in *fig.* 362. A small piece of metal *a*, having a form slightly

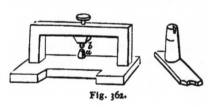

Fig. 362.

conical, is fixed in the bottom
of a frame, and at its upper
surface a piece of cork, or
buffalo skin, is fixed to intercept vibration. A corre-
sponding cylinder is moved
vertically, directly above it,
by a screw, which plays in

the frame *b*, and which is also covered at its extremity with a piece
of cork.

When the screw is turned, the two extremities can be brought
into contact, so as to press between them with any desired force
any plate which may be interposed.

An elastic plate, the vibration of which it is desired to observe,
is inserted between them, and held compressed at any desired
point by turning the screw. The plate thus held can be put in
vibration by means of a violin bow, which being drawn upon its
edge, clear musical sounds may be produced, and brought into
unison with those of a pianoforte, or other musical instrument.

To ascertain the state of vibration of the different points of the
surface of the plate, sand or other light dust is spread upon it, to
which motion is imparted by the vibrating points. Those points
which are at rest, and which are therefore nodal points, impart no
motion to the grains of sand which lie upon them, and those which
are upon the vibrating points are successively thrown aside, until

they reach the lines of repose or nodal lines, where at length they settle themselves.

When a musical sound of a uniform pitch has, therefore, been continued for any length of time, the disposition of the grains of sand upon the plate will indicate the position and direction of the nodal lines.

686. **Lateral vibrations of rods or plates.** — An easy experimental method of determining the laws which govern these, is indicated in *fig.* 363   The rod or plate being held at one end by a vice, the length of the rod may be varied at pleasure.

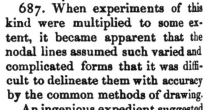
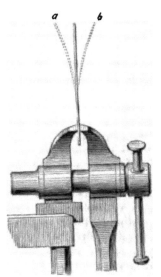

687. When experiments of this kind were multiplied to some extent, it became apparent that the nodal lines assumed such varied and complicated forms that it was difficult to delineate them with accuracy by the common methods of drawing.

An ingenious expedient suggested itself to Savart, by which facsimiles of all these figures were obtained. Instead of sand, he used litmus mixed with gum, dried, reduced to a fine powder, and passed through a sieve, so as to obtain grains of equal and suitable magnitude. This coloured and hygrometric powder he spread upon the vibrating plates, and when it had assumed the form of the nodal lines, he applied to the plates with gentle pressure damp

Fig. 363.

paper, to which the coloured powder adhered, and which, therefore, gave an exact impression of the form of the nodal lines.

In this manner he was enabled to feel, as it were, the state of vibration of the different parts of the plate, and to ascertain with precision the lines of no vibration, or the nodal lines, which separated from each other those parts of the plate which vibrated independently.

In this way many hundred experiments were made, and exact diagrams obtained representing the condition of the vibrating plates.

688. One of the consequences which most obviously followed from these experiments was, that the nodal lines became more and more multiplied the more acute the sound was which the plate produced. This consequence was one which might have been

icipated from the analogy of the nodal lines of the plate to
nodal points of the elastic string. It has been already shown,
t with a single nodal point in the middle of the string, the oc-
ᵫ to the fundamental note is produced; that when two nodal
nts divide the string into three equal parts, the twelfth is pro-
:ed; that when three nodal points divide the string into four
.al parts, the fifteenth is produced, and so on. What the sub-
isions of the string are to the notes produced by its vibrations,
subdivisions of the surface of the vibrating plate by the nodal
:s, are to the note which it produces; and it was consequently
ural to expect, that the higher the note produced, the more
ltiplied would be the divisions of the plate.

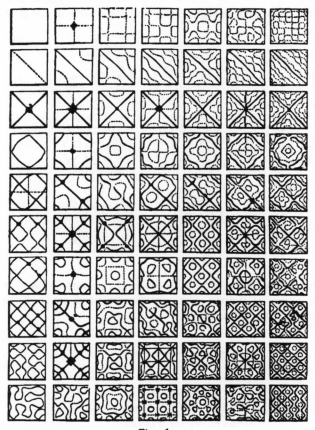

Fig. 364.

89. Curious forms of the nodal lines.—But a circumstance
:nding these divisions not less curious than their number was

their form, for which no analogy existed in the vibration of strings.
It would be impossible here to give any definite notion of the
infinite variety of which these nodal figures are susceptible; they
change not only with the pitch of the note produced, but also with
the form and material of the plate, and the position of the point
at which it is held in the instrument, represented in *fig.* 362. It
will not, however, be without interest to give an example of the
variety of figures presented by the nodal lines produced upon
the same square plate. These are represented in the series of
figures 364.

Similar experiments, made on circular plates, showed that the
nodal lines distributed themselves either in the direction of the
diameter, dividing the circle into an equal number of parts, or in
circular forms, more or less regular, having the centre of the plate

Fig 365.

at their common centre, or, in fine, in both of these combined. In
the annexed series of figures 365. are represented some of the
varieties of form thus obtained.

CHAP. V.

VIBRATIONS OF FLUIDS.

690. **Fluids,** whether in the liquid or gaseous state, have been
hitherto considered merely as conductors of sound, their sonorous

undulations having been derived from the vibratory impulses of solid bodies acting upon them.

Fluids themselves, however, are capable of originating their own undulations, and consequently must be considered not merely as conductors of sound, but likewise as sonorous bodies.

If the Sirène of Cagniard de la Tour, already described, be submerged in water, and made to act as it has been described already to act in air, the pulsations of the water will produce a sound. In this case, the origin of the sound is the action of the liquid upon itself. The successive movements of the liquid through the holes in the circular plate of the Sirène are the origin of the sonorous undulations which are transmitted through the liquid.

Sounds produced by communication. — It is well known that vocal sounds are increased in loudness and force when they are produced at the mouth of any cavity of sufficient extent, depth, and proper form. In that case the vibrations imparted by the vocal organs to the air contiguous to the mouth are propagated to the air in the cavity, the vibrations thus communicated increasing in a very remarkable manner the loudness of the sound.

Vitruvius relates that in the ancient theatres, which were of vast magnitude, this expedient was adopted to give increased force to the voice of the actor, round whom hollow vessels were disposed in the decorations of the scene, so as to elude the notice of the audience, which, by the communicated vibrations of the contained air, rendered the voice of the actor distinctly audible in the remotest parts of the theatre.

In modern opera houses, the stage itself, when mounted with a flat scene at the back, has this effect, and in certain parts of the house the audience can hear the voice of the prompter almost as distinctly as the notes of the artist. The prompter's seat is roofed with a sort of arched hood, from the surface of which the sounds he produces are reflected to the flat scene at the back of the stage, from which they are again reflected to those parts of the house where they are heard. The practical proof of the truth of this explanation will be found in the fact, that the prompter immediately ceases to be heard when the flat scene is withdrawn, and the entire depth of the stage thrown open.

To reduce the phenomena of communicated vibrations to more regularity, Savart contrived the apparatus shown in *fig.* 366., consisting of two cylinders sliding one within another, like the tubes of a telescope, one of which is open at both ends, and the other only at one end. By drawing the closed cylinder in and out, the depth of the open cylinder can be varied at pleasure. The cylinders are mounted upon a cradle or hinge joint upon the summit of a vertical pillar fixed in a bar, which slides horizontally in its base. A vase made of bell metal is mounted on a vertical pillar, at a height corresponding with that of the mouth of the

Fig. 366.

cylinder, so that the latter can be moved to or from the vase at pleasure, and can be inclined so that the mouth shall be more or less obliquely presented to the vase.

If the vase be put in vibration, either by the blow of a hammer or by drawing over its edge the bow of a violin, a musical sound will be produced, which, being communicated to the air in the cylinder, will impart vibration to it. But to render this fully effective, it is necessary to vary the length of the cylinder by drawing the closed cylinder in and out, until it has that length which corresponds to the note produced by the vase.

691. **Wind instruments.** — Innumerable examples might be found of sonorous undulations produced by air upon air. The Sirène itself, which has been already explained, forms an example of this, and at the same time indicates the manner in which the pulsations are imparted to the air. All wind instruments whatever are also examples of this. The air, by the impulses of which the sonorous undulations are produced, proceeds either from a bellows, as in the case of organs, or from the lungs, as in the case of ordinary wind instruments. The pitch of the sound produced depends partly upon the manner of imparting the first movement to the air, and partly on varying the length of the tube containing the column of air to which the first impulse is given.

When the tube, as is generally the case in instruments of music, has a length which is considerable in proportion to its diameter, the gravest note which it is capable of producing is determined by a sonorous undulation of its own length. By varying the embouchure, and otherwise managing the action of the air on entering the tube, notes may be produced which are harmonics to the fundamental notes determined by the length of the tube.

When these harmonics are produced, nodal points will be formed in the column of air included in the tube; and if the tube were divided, and capable of being detached at these nodal points, the removal of a part of the tube would not alter the pitch of the note produced.

In wind instruments in which various notes are produced by the opening and closing of holes in their sides by means of the fingers or keys, there is a virtual variation in the length of the sounding part of the tube, which determines the pitch of the various notes produced. In some cases, the length of the tube is varied, not by apertures opened and closed at will, but by an actual change of length in the tube itself. Examples of this are presented in some brass instruments, and more particularly in the trombone.

692. Although the length of the column of the air included in the tube of a wind instrument alone determines the pitch of the note, its *timbre* depends in a striking and important manner upon the material of which the tube is composed.

693. It is well known that organ builders find that the quality of tone is so materially connected with the quality of the material composing the tube, that a very slight change in the alloy composing a metal tube would produce a total change in the quality of the tone produced. The excellence of an organ depends in a great degree upon the skill with which the material of the tubes, whether wood or metal, is selected.

694. **Organ pipes.** — The general principles explained in the preceding paragraphs are illustrated in a striking manner by the effects of organ pipes. These are of two sorts, called *mouth pipes* and *reed pipes*.

A mouth pipe consists of a *foot*, which is a hollow cone receiving the wind by which the pipe is sounded, from an air chest, in which the air is compressed by a bellows. To this foot is attached the body of the pipe, which is either square or round, the length always having a considerable proportion to its diameter. At the place where the body of the pipe is connected with the foot, there is an arrangement by which the quality of the sound produced by the pipe is determined.

This arrangement consists of an oblique opening a' (*fig.* 367.) leading from the foot c' by which the air enters, immediately above which is a lateral opening in the body of the pipe bounded by an edge b', against which the air escaping from a' strikes. The edges a' and b' are called the lips, a' being distinguished as the lower and b' the upper. A front view of the pipe, showing the upper lip b, the lower lip a, and the foot c, is shown in *fig.* 368.

Organ pipes are generally either square or circular in their transverse section; the wooden pipes being square and the metal circular. A section of a square pipe is given in *fig.* 369., and front and side views of a circular pipe are given in *figs.* 370, 371.

In *fig.* 372. the embouchure is so formed that the upper lip *b* is movable, so that the effects of varying the magnitude of the opening can be ascertained experimentally.

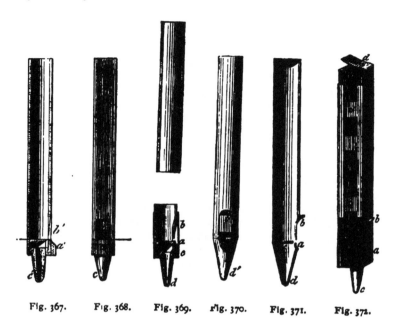

Fig. 367.   Fig. 368.   Fig. 369.   Fig. 370.   Fig. 371.   Fig. 372.

The air entering through *c* rushes through the mouth, where it encounters the edge of the upper lip *b*, which partially obstructs it. The part which passes up the pipe produces a momentary compression of the column of air within the pipe against which the increased elasticity reacts, and this goes on producing in the whole length of the pipe an alternate compression and expansion, from which results a specific sound.

The pitch of the pipe is ascertained experimentally by the bellows and air chest, shown in *fig.* 373. The bellows is worked by means of a pedal, the air being driven up to the air chest through the pipe. The air chest is pierced with a dozen holes, which are stopped by valves, opened by a row of keys.

When it is desired to try a pipe, the foot of the pipe is inserted in one of the holes; and when the corresponding key is pressed down, the valve being opened and air admitted to the pipe, the note is produced. Two or more such pipes may be placed upon the air chest, so as to be sounded together, and tuned one with another, in the same manner as are the notes of a pianoforte.

The quality and timbre of the note produced will vary with the form of the lips and magnitude of the mouth. Thus the mouth represented in *fig.* 369. is different from that shown in *fig.* 368.

So long, however, as the length of the tube remains unaltered, the note produced can undergo no other change than that of passing

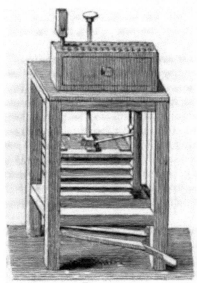

to a higher or lower octave. If the tube be opened at the upper end, and the air admitted slowly into it, a certain note will be produced called its fundamental note, being the lowest which it is capable of producing. If the force of the air be increased, or the magnitude of the mouth or form of the lips be varied, the note produced may change; but such change will always be to one, two, or more octaves above the fundamental note. Thus, if the

fundamental note be 🎼 ,

by increasing the force of the wind or modifying the mouth or lips, the pipe will produce

Fig. 373.

🎼 ; and a further modification of the same conditions will cause it to produce 🎼 , and so on; but no modification which can possibly be produced, either in the force of the wind or in the form of the mouth or lips, can ever make the pipe produce any intermediate note, or any octave lower than the fundamental note.

If the diameter of the pipe be greater than the tenth or twelfth part of its length, it will be very difficult or wholly impracticable to produce from it the fundamental note, the note produced being always one or more octaves above it. This is the reason why organ pipes necessarily are diminished in their diameters, in the same proportion as they are diminished in their lengths.

The length of a pipe which is open at the upper end, is that of the sonorous wave, which corresponds to its fundamental note. If the octave to the fundamental note be sounded, two sonorous waves will be produced in the pipe, and the note produced will be the fundamental note of a pipe of half the length. If the note produced be two octaves above the fundamental note, three waves will be produced in the pipe, and the note will be the fundamental note of a pipe one third of the length, and so on.

If the pipe be closed at the top, the series of octaves produced by similarly varied conditions will be the alternate octaves; the first being the second above the fundamental note; the second the fourth, and so on.

The points of separation of the sonorous waves thus produced in each case in the column of air enclosed within the pipe can be demonstrated experimentally by means of a pipe constructed like that represented in *fig.* 372., in which, by means of sliding pieces, openings can be made at any desired points in the length of the tube. When an opening is made at the point of separation of the successive undulations, such opening will produce no change in the note. Thus, when the note produced is an octave above the fundamental note, an opening may be made at the middle point of the length. If it be two octaves, openings may be made at the two points, which divide the whole length into three equal parts, and so on.

The smallest metal pipes are made of tin, and are open at the top, producing the highest notes. The larger metal pipes are made of pewter, the shortest being open, and the longest stopped; the medium ones being partly stopped.

695. **Reed pipes.** — A reed is, in general, a thin oblong plate of some vibratory material, attached to an opening in such a manner that a current of air can pass into the opening, grazing, as it passes, the edges of the reed.

Let g, *fig.* 374., represent, for example, an oblong plate of zinc or copper about an eighth of an inch in thickness, along the centre of which an oblong aperture is cut. At one end e of this aperture a thin and very elastic plate of metal ef is fastened, which nearly but not altogether covers the aperture. Air rushing through the space around the edges of ef, will cause it to vibrate, and this vibration will be imparted to the air in contact with it. This is the most simple form of reed, and the sound may be produced with it by merely applying the plate g to the lips and forcing the breath through the opening.

The reed commonly used in organ pipes depends upon the same principle, but is otherwise arranged. The parts are shown in *fig.* 375., consisting of two tubes d and c joined end to end, and separated by a piece a, which stops the passage between them. The reed b passes under this piece a. This part of the pipe is represented in detail in *fig.* 376., where the oblong opening covered by the reed a, and the sliding piece b connected with the rod c, by which the length of the reed can be regulated at pleasure, are shown. The reed covers in this case an oblong opening in a prismatic metal tube supposed to be closed at its lower end. The opening establishes a communication between the two tubes placed above and below the stopper. The reed in its natural position very nearly closes the oblong opening; that is to say, it fits it, so that when pushed in or drawn out, it grazes with its three free edges the borders of the opening; when it is put in vibration, therefore, it opens and closes the aperture alternately.

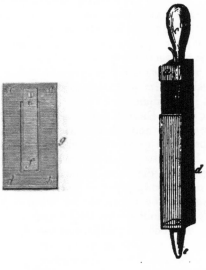

Fig. 374.   Fig. 375.

In certain pipes there are reeds somewhat differently constructed, which give a particular quality to the note. One of these is represented in *figs.* 377, 378, 379., and it differs from the former

Fig. 376.   Fig. 377.   Fig. 378.   Fig. 379.

inasmuch as the reed does not pass through the aperture, but presses upon its edges.

The mouth pieces of bassoons, hautboys, clarionets, &c., are only different forms of the application of the reed. In these cases, the pressure of the lips determines the length of the vibrating part of the reed, just as the piece *b* does in *fig.* 376., and in *fig.* 378.

696. The height of an organ is usually expressed and determined by the length of its longest pipes, or those which produce its longest notes. Among the existing instruments of this class, the most celebrated is that of Haarlem, built, in 1748, by Christian Müller; its height is 103 feet, and its breadth 50 feet. The great organ has 16 stops; the upper one 15; and the quire one 14; and there are 15 stops connected with the pedals. It includes 5000 pipes; each pair of bellows is 9 feet long and 5 feet broad.

In the cathedral of Ulm is an organ whose largest pipe is 93 feet high, and 13 inches diameter.

697. The three largest English organs are those in York Minster, Birmingham Town Hall, and Christchurch, London. The York organ has 24 stops in the great organ, and 10 in the quire organ. The pedal organ has 10 stops; two octaves, varying from 32 feet to 8 feet; 32 feet open diapason in metal, wood, and trumpet. There are in the organ 4089 pipes, in 50 ranks.

The Birmingham organ contains the following stops : three open diapasons to 16 feet c; double and stop diapason; two principals of metal, and two of wood; a twelfth and two fifteenths of metal, and one of wood. A reed fifteenth, 4 feet; posaun, 16 feet; trumpet, 16 feet; clarion, 8 feet; sesquialtra, 4 ranks; mixture, 4 ranks; two octaves of German pedals, 32 feet metal; open diapason to 8 feet c; 32 feet wood, ditto; 2 octaves of pedal trumpets, 16 feet to 8 feet c.

There are a variety of other practical details in this magnificent instrument which we have not space here to enumerate.

698. The sound produced by a jet of hydrogen, directed in a glass tube, forms a remarkable example of the manner in which the sonorous undulations of air would be produced by movements originating in air itself.

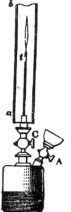

This apparatus, the explanation of the principle of which is due to M. de la Rive, consists of a small glass vessel in which hydrogen is generated in the usual way, by the action of acid on zinc or iron. A funnel and stopcock A, *fig.* 380., are provided, by which the supply of the acid may be renewed. A pipe proceeds from the centre of the top of the vessel furnished with a stopcock c, in which a small tube is inserted terminating in a very small aperture, from which a fine jet of the gas escapes when the stopcock is opened, and a sufficient pressure produced by the accumulation of gas within the vessel. The jet proceeding from *t* in this manner being inflamed, a glass tube of considerable length and having a diameter of about two inches is held over it, so that the jet is made to burn at some distance above the lower end of the tube. A musical sound will thus proceed from the air within the tube, the intensity of which will depend upon the length of the tube.

Fig. 380.

' This effect is explained as follows: The vapour which is the first product of the combustion of the hydrogen fills a portion of the tube above the flame, and excludes from it the air, but the cold of the tube soon condenses this vapour, and a vacuum is produced, into which the air rushes with a rapid motion. This effect being repeated by the continuance of the combustion of the hydrogen, a corresponding undulation is produced in the column of air in the tube, and a musical sound is the result.

699. **Echoes.**—It has been already shown, that when undulations propagated through a fluid encounter a solid surface, they will be reflected from it, and will proceed as though they had originally moved from a different centre of undulation.

Now, if this take place with the sonorous waves of air, such waves encountering the air will produce the same effect as if they proceeded, not from the surrounding body which originally produced them, but from a sounding body placed at that centre from which the waves thus reflected move. Upon these principles echoes are explained.

If a body, placed at a certain distance from the hearer, produce a sound, this sound would be heard first by means of the sonorous undulations which produced it proceeding directly and uninterruptedly from the sonorous body to the hearer, and afterwards by sonorous undulations which, after striking on reflecting surfaces, return to the ear. The repetition of the sound thus produced is called an *echo*.

To produce an echo it will be necessary, therefore, that there shall be a sufficient magnitude of reflecting surface, so placed with respect to the ear, that the waves of sound reflected from it shall arrive at the ear at the same moment, and that their combined effect shall be sufficiently energetic to affect the organ in a sensible manner.

If, for example, the sounding body be placed in a focus F of an ellipse, as represented in *fig.* 381., the hearer being at the other focus F', the sound will be first heard by the effect of the undulations, which are produced directly along the line F F', from one focus to the other. But it will be heard a little

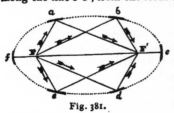

Fig. 381.

later by the effect of the waves, which, diverging from the sounding body at F, strike upon the elliptic surface, and are reflected to the other focus F', where the hearer is placed. The interval which elapses between the sound and the echo in this case will be the time which sound takes to move through the difference between the direct distance F F', and the sum of the two distances at any point in the ellipse from the foci F F'. It has been already explained that the sum of these two distances is always the same wherever the point of reflection may be, being equal to the major axis of the ellipse. It is for this reason that all the reflected rays of sound from every part of the ellipse will meet the ear placed at ᴦ′ at the same moment, since they will take the same time to move over the same distance. If the reflected surface were not elliptical, or if, being elliptical, the hearer were not placed at the focus ᴦ′, then the sum of the distances of the different points of the reflecting surface from the ear would be different, and the reflected rays of sound arriving from different points of the surface, would reach the ear at different moments of time. In this case, each ray of sound would be too feeble to produce sensation, or a confused effect would be produced.

It is not necessary that the elliptic surface reflecting the sound should be complete. If different portions of the reflecting surface, *a, b, c, d, e, f, fig.* 381., be so placed that they would form part of the same ellipse, they will still reflect the rays of the sound to the other focus of the ellipse; and if they are so numerous or extensive as to reflect rays of sound to the ear in sufficient quantity to affect the sense, an echo will be heard.

700. If surfaces lie in such a position round the points ᴦ and ᴦ′, that these points shall be at the same time the foci of different ellipses, one greater than the other, a succession of echoes will ensue, the sounds reflected from the greater elliptic surface arriving at the ear later than those reflected from the lesser. The interval between the successive echoes in such a case would be the time which the sound takes to move over a space equal to the difference between the major axes of the ellipses.

If a person who utters a sound stand in the centre s of a circle, *fig.* 382., the circumference of which is either wholly or partly

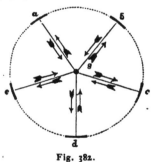

Fig. 382.

composed of surfaces, such as *a, b, c, d, e,* which reflect sound, he will hear the echo of his own voice; as in this case the sonorous undulation, which proceeds from the speaker encountering the reflecting surfaces in a direction perpendicular to them, will be reflected by them back to the speaker, as represented by the arrows, and will reach his ear after an interval corresponding to that which sound requires to move over twice the radius of the circle. If the speaker in such a case be surrounded by surfaces composing either wholly or partly two or more circles, of which he is the common centre, then he will hear a succession of echoes of his own voice, the interval between them corresponding to the time which sound would take to move over twice the difference between the successive radii of the circles.

If a speaker stand at s, *fig.* 383., midway between two parallel walls ᴀ and ʙ, these walls may be considered as forming part of a circle of which he is the centre, and they will reflect to his ear the

sounds of his own voice, producing an echo.   In this case the position of the speaker s being equally distant from A and B, the sounds

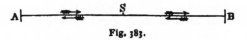

Fig. 383.

reflected from these surfaces will return to his ear simultaneously,
and produce a single perception.   But a part of the undulation
reflected from B, not intercepted by the speaker at s, will arrive at
A, and will be reflected from A and again arrive at s, where it will
affect the ear.   The same may be said of the sounds reflected from
A, which, proceeding to B, will be again reflected to s; and as the
distances moved over by the sounds thus twice reflected are equal,
they will arrive simultaneously at s, and would then produce a
second echo.   This second echo, therefore, will proceed from the
successive reflections of the sound by the two walls A and B, and
the interval between it and the first echo will be the time which
sound takes to move over twice the distance s A, or the whole
distance between the two walls.

Thus, if the two surfaces A and B were distant from each other
1120 feet, then the interval between the utterance of the sound ,
and the first echo would be one second, and the same interval
would take place between the successive echoes.

If the speaker, however, be placed at a point s, *fig.* 384., which
is not midway between the two walls A and B, the echo proceeding

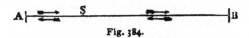

Fig. 384.

from the first reflection by the wall A will be heard before the echo
which proceeds from the reflection by the wall B, and in this case
a single reflection from each wall will produce two echoes.

If we suppose a second reflection from each wall to take place,
two echoes will be again produced.   So that with two reflections
from each wall four echoes will be heard; and in general the
number of echoes which will be heard will be double the number
of reflections.

701. It may be asked, why the number of reflections, in such
case, should have any limit?   The answer is, that the reflected
waves are always more feeble than the direct waves; and that
consequently intensity, or loudness, is lost by each reflection, until
at length the waves become so feeble as to be incapable of affecting the ear.   A speaker can articulate so as to be distinctly
audible at the average rate of four syllables per second.   If,

therefore, the reflecting surface be at the distance of 1120 feet, the echo of his own voice will be perceived by him at the end of two seconds after each syllable is uttered; and since, in two seconds, he can utter eight syllables, it follows that he can hear, successively, the echo of these eight syllables; if he continue to speak, the sounds he utters will be confused with those of the echo.

The more distant the reflecting surfaces are, the greater will be the number of syllables which can be rendered audible by the ear.

It is not necessary that the surface producing an echo should be either hard or polished. It is often observed at sea, that an echo proceeds from the surface of the clouds. The sails of a distant ship have been found also to return very distinct echoes.

702. **Remarkable cases of multiplied echoes.** — Numerous examples are recorded of multiplied repetitions of sound by echoes. An echo is produced near Verdun by the walls of two towers, which repeats twelve or thirteen times the same word. At Adernach, in Bohemia, there is an echo which repeats seven syllables three times distinctly. At Lurleyfels, on the Rhine, there is an echo which repeats seventeen times. The echo of the Capo di Bove, as well as that of the Metelli of Rome, was celebrated among the ancients. It is matter of tradition that the latter was capable of repeating the first line of the Æneid, which contains fifteen syllables, eight times distinctly. An echo in the Villa Simonetta, near Milan, is said to repeat a loud sound thirty times audibly. An echo in a building at Pavia is said to have answered a question by repeating its last syllable thirty times.

703. Whispering galleries are formed by smooth walls having a continuous curved form. The mouth of the speaker is presented at one point of the wall, and the ear of the hearer at another and distant point. In this case the sound is successively reflected from one point of the wall to another until it reaches the ear.

704. Speaking tubes, by which words spoken in one place are rendered audible at another distant place, depend on the same principle. The rays of sound proceeding from the mouth at one end of the tube, instead of diverging, and being scattered through the surrounding atmosphere, are confined within the tube, being successively reflected from its sides, as represented in *fig. 385.*; so that a much greater number of rays of sound reach the ear at the remote end, than could have reached it if they had proceeded without reflection.

Speaking tubes, constructed on this principle, are used in large buildings where numerous persons are employed, to save the time which would be necessary in dispatching messages from one part of the building to another. A speaking tube is sometimes used on shipboard, being carried from the captain's cabin to the topmast.

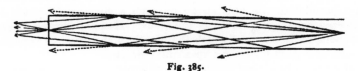

Fig. 385.

A like effect is produced by the shafts of mines, walls, and chimneys, as well as by pipes used to convey heated air or water.

705. The speaking trumpet is another example of the practical application of this principle. A longitudinal section of this instru-

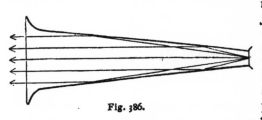

Fig. 386.

ment is represented in *fig.* 386. The force of the trumpet is such, that the rays of sound which diverge from the mouth of the speaker are reflected parallel to the axis of the instrument. The trumpet being directed to any point, a collection of parallel rays of sound moves towards such point, and they reach the ear in much greater number than would the diverging rays which would proceed from a speaker without such instrument.

A speaking trumpet as used on board ship is represented in *fig.* 387.

Fig. 387.

706. A hearing trumpet, represented in *fig.* 388., is, in form and application, the reverse of the speaking trumpet, but in principle the same. The rays of sound proceeding from a speaker more or less distant, enter the hearing trumpet nearly parallel; and the form of the inner surface of such instrument is such that, after one or more reflections, they are made to converge upon the tympanum of the ear.

Fig. 388.

If a sounding body be placed in the focus of a

parabola formed of any material capable of reflecting sound, the rays which issue from it will, after reflection, proceed in a direction parallel to the axis of the parabola. This will be apparent from what has been explained in (626.); and if, on the other hand, rays parallel to the axis strike on such a surface, they will be reflected converging towards the focus. Hence it appears that a parabola, in the focus of which the mouth of the speaker is placed, would be a good form for a speaking trumpet.

If a watch be placed in the focus of a parabolic surface, such as a metallic speculum of that form, an ear placed in the direction of its axis will distinctly hear the ticking, though at a considerable distance; but if the parabolic reflector be removed, the ticking will be no longer heard.

CHAP. VI.

THE EAR.

707. Theory of the organ not understood. — The form and structure of the eye is so evidently adapted to the physical properties of light, and the purpose for which each of its parts is adapted can be so clearly demonstrated, that it might naturally be expected that a similar conformity could be shown to prevail between the form and structure of the ear, and the physical properties of sound. With the exception, nevertheless, of one or two exterior arrangements in the organ of hearing, the peculiar and complicated form and structure of its internal parts have not hitherto been shown by any satisfactory or conclusive reasoning to have any relation to the principles of acoustics. In treating, therefore, of the ear considered merely as a branch of applied physics, little more remains than to describe its parts as anatomists have demonstrated them, indicating the obvious relation which the exterior and more simple parts have to the laws of acoustics.

708. Description of the ear. — The ear consists of three distinct parts differing altogether each from the other in their form. They are denominated by anatomists the *external ear*, the *middle ear*, and the *internal ear*, being placed in that order, proceeding inwards from the external and visible part of the organ.

709. The external ear. — The part of the external ear which is visible outside the skull, behind the joint of the lower jaw (*fig.* 389.), is called the *pinna* or *auricle*.

710. Concha. — The several parts of the auricle marked in the

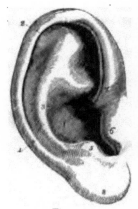

Fig. 389.

figure by the numbers 1, 2, 3, &c., are distinguished by specific names in anatomy. With the exception, however, of the cavity 7, called the *concha*, none of these parts can be considered as having any important acoustic properties. The depression 2, called the fossa of the helix, and the surrounding cartilage 1, called the helix, may possibly have some slight effect in reflecting the rays of sound towards the concha 7, and thence into the interior of the ear. If such, however, were the purpose, it would be much more effectually answered by giving to this part of the organ a form more closely resembling that of the wide end of a trumpet. As the external ear is actually constructed, the only part which perfectly answers this purpose is the concha.

711. **External meatus.**—Proceeding inwards from the concha, the remainder of the external ear is a tube something more than an inch long, the diameter of which becomes rapidly smaller from the concha inwards; its calibre, however, is least about the middle of its length, being slightly augmented between that point and its connection with the middle ear. Its section is everywhere elliptical, but in the external half the greater diameter of the ellipse is vertical, and in the internal, horizontal. This tube does not proceed straight onwards, but is twisted so that the distance from the concha to the point where it enters the middle ear is less than the total length of the tube. The external part of the tube is cartilaginous like the external ear, but its internal part is bony; the bony surface, however, being lined by a prolongation of the skin of the auricle.

712. **Membrane of tympanum.**—The internal extremity of this tube is inserted in an opening leading into the middle ear, which is inclined to the axis of the tube at an angle of about 45°. Over this opening, which is slightly oval, an elastic membrane called the *membrane of the tympanum* is tightly stretched like parchment on the head of a drum.

In *fig.* 390. the several parts of the ear are shown divested of the surrounding bony matter; and to render their arrangement more distinct, they are exhibited upon an enlarged scale. The concha, with the tube leading inwards from it marked *a*, terminates at the inner end, as already stated, in the tense membrane of the tympanum placed obliquely to the axis of the tube. The resemblance of this tube with the concha to the speaking or hearing trumpet is evident, and the physical purposes which it fulfils are obviously the same, being those of collecting and conducting the

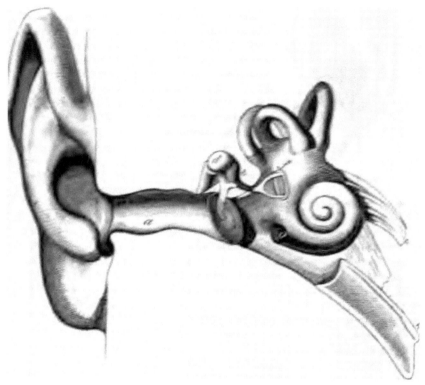

Fig. 390.

sonorous undulations to the membrane of the tympanum, which will vibrate sympathetically with them.

713. **The middle ear** is a cavity surrounded by walls of bone, which, however, are removed in *fig.* 390, to render visible its internal structure. An opening corresponding to the membrane of the tympanum is made in the external wall, and the external part of the inner ear shown in the figure is part of its inner wall. The inner and outer walls of this cavity are very close together; but the cavity measures, vertically as well as horizontally, about half an inch, so that it may be regarded as resembling the sounding board of a musical instrument, composed of two flat surfaces, placed close and nearly parallel to each other, the superficial extent of which is considerable compared with their distance asunder.

714. **Eustachian tube.** — This cavity is kept constantly filled with air, which enters it through a tube *b*, called the *eustachian tube*, which opens into the pharynx, forming part of the respiratory passages behind the mouth. Without such a means of keeping the cavity supplied with air, having a pressure always equal to that of the atmosphere, one or other of two injuries must ensue : either the air in the cavity, having a temperature considerably above that of the external air, would acquire a proportionally in-creased pressure, which would either rupture the membrane of the tympanum, or give it undue tension ; but if this did not take place, the air confined in the cavity would be gradually absorbed by its walls, and would consequently be rarified, in which case the pressure of the external atmosphere, being greater than that of the air in the cavity, would force the membrane of the tympanum inward, and would ultimately rupture it. By means of the eusta-chian tube, however, a permanent equilibrium is maintained be-tween the air in the cavity and the external air, just as is the case in a drum, or in the sounding board of a musical instrument, where apertures are always provided to form a free communication with the external air.

The middle ear is sometimes called the tympanum or drum, but sometimes these terms are applied to what we have above called the membrane of the tympanum, and in that case the cavity included between the walls of the middle ear is called the tym-panic cavity.

715. **Fenestræ ovalis and rotunda.** — In the inner wall of this cavity there are two principal foramina, a greater and a lesser ; the former being called, from its oval shape, the *fenestra ovalis*, and the latter the *fenestra rotunda ;* the former is shown at *f*, in *fig.* 390., and the latter at *o*. Over both of these elastic membranes are tightly stretched, as the membrane of the tym-panum is over the inner end of the external meatus.

716. **Auricular bones.** — Between the membrane of the tym-panum and the membrane of the fenestra ovalis there is a chain, consisting of three small bones articulated together, and moved by muscles having their origin in the bones which form the walls of the cavity. These three bones are shown in *fig.* 390., at *d*, *e*, and *f*. The first *d* is called, from its form, the *malleus*, or hammer ; the end of its handle is attached to the membrane of the tympanum near its centre ; its head, which is round, is inserted in a corre-sponding cavity of the second bone *e*, called the *incus*, or anvil ; and the smaller end projecting from this, articulated with the third bone *f*, called the *stapes*, or stirrup, from the obvious ana-logy of its form. The base of this stirrup corresponds in magni-tude and form with the fenestra ovalis, in which it is inserted,

keeping, as it would appear, the membrane which covers that aperture in a certain state of tension upon it. The handle of the malleus being firmly attached to the centre of the membrane of the tympanum, draws that membrane inwards, so as to render it more or less convex, or rather conical, towards the tympanic cavity.

The muscles which act upon these small bones are supposed to have the property of giving greater or less tension to the two membranes which they connect, so as to render them more or less sensitive to the sonorous undulations propagated through the external ear. When the sounds are loud the muscles render the membranes less sensitive, and when they are low they render them more so. According to this supposition, when we listen attentively to low sounds, we not only concentrate the attention of the mind upon them, but we also act upon the nerves which govern the muscles inserted in the chain of auricular bones, and thereby increase the sensitiveness of the organ.

It must be observed, however, that this is a mere hypothesis, no such action of these bones and muscles having been established as a matter of fact.

717. The use of the auricular bones is supposed to be the transmission of the pulsations imparted by the sonorous undulations from the membrane of the tympanum to the membrane of the fenestra ovalis. It has been ascertained, however, that if the membrane of the tympanum were altogether destroyed, the sense of hearing would still remain, though it would not be so perfect. It must therefore be inferred that the auricular bones are not the only means of transmitting the sonorous undulations to the internal ear, the air contained in the middle ear being itself sufficient for that purpose.

It cannot be doubted that the membrane which covers the fenestra rotunda has some share in producing the sensation of sound; and if so, the chain of bones can have no effect upon it, the undulations being merely propagated to it by the air contained in the middle ear.

718. **The internal ear.** — We now come to consider the internal ear, which is, in fact, the true and only organ of the sense of audition, the external and middle ears being merely accessories by which the sonorous undulations are propagated to the fluids included in the cavities of the internal ear.

The internal ear is a most curious and, as it must be acknowledged, a most unintelligible organ, also called, from its complicated structure, the *labyrinth*. Its channels and cavities are curved and excavated in the hardest mass of bone found in the whole body, called the *petrous* or bony part of the skull. It is shown in *fig.* 390., as if all the surrounding mass of bone except that which forms the immediate surfaces of the cavities were cut away.

719. **Vestibule.** — It will be seen that this labyrinth consists of three distinct parts: a middle chamber, called the *vestibule*, in the exterior wall of which the fenestra ovalis *f* is formed, and into the internal wall of which the auditory nerve *n* is admitted.

720. **Semicircular canals.** — At the posterior and upper part of the vestibule are three curved tubular cavities, called the semicircular canals, and distinguished by anatomists as the *anterior, posterior,* and *superior semicircular canals,* according to their relative positions.

721. **Cochlea.** — On the interior and anterior side of the vestibule, near the fenestra rotunda, is a cavity formed like a spiral tube, called, from its resemblance to the cavity within the shell of a snail, the *cochlea,* the Latin word for that animal. The semicircular canals, and the cochlea, have severally free communication with the vestibule.

722. **The auditory nerve.** — The auditory nerve arrives at the bony wall of the internal ear, through a passage called by anatomists the internal auditory meatus. Before entering the foramina provided for its admission into the internal ear, it separates into two principal branches, one of which is directed to the vestibule and the other to the cochlea, which are thence called, respectively, the *vestibular* and *cochlear nerves.*

723. **The membranous canals.** — Within the three semicircular canals are included flexible membranous pipes of the same form, called the membranous canals. These pipes include within them the branches of the auditory nerve, which pass through the semicircular canals, and they are distended by a specific liquid called *endolymph* in which the nervous fibres are bathed. The bony canals around these membranous canals are filled with another liquid called *perilymph,* which also fills the cavities of the vestibule and the cochlea. It appears, therefore, that all the cavities of the internal ear are filled with liquid, and it must, accordingly, be by this liquid that the sonorous undulations are propagated to the fibres of the auditory nerves. The liquid being incompressible, the pulsations imparted either by the auricular chain of bones, or by the air included in the cavity of the middle ear, or by both of these, to the membranes which cover the fenestra ovalis and the fenestra rotunda, are received by the liquid perilymph within these membranes, and propagated by it and the endolymph to the various fibres of the auditory nerve.

This arrangement will be rendered more clearly intelligible by reference to *fig.* 391., which is a perspective magnified view of the

labyrinth.— the canals, vestibule, and cochlea being laid open so
as to display their interior.

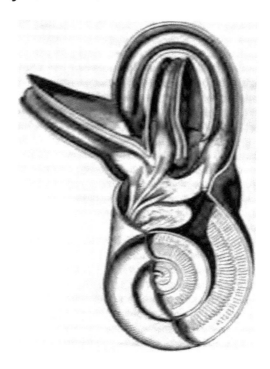

Fig. 392.

724. **The lamina spiralis.** — The spiral tube of which the
cochlea is formed makes $2\frac{1}{2}$ revolutions round its geometrical axis,
and it is everywhere divided through its centre by a thin plate
called the *lamina spiralis*, upon the surface of which the fibres of
the cochlear nerve are spread. The internal structure of the
cochlea will be rendered more intelligible by reference to *fig.* 392.,
where 1 represents the central bone round which the spiral winds,
and 2 the lamina spiralis, which follows the course of the spinal
canal.

A section of the cochlea made by a plane passing through its
axis, showing the course and distribution of the nervous fibres, is
given in *fig.* 393., where 1 is the principal auditory nerve, 2 the
nerves in the lamina spiralis, 3 the central nerve of the cochlea,
and 4 the vestibular nerve.

To render still more apparent the distribution of the cochlear
branch of the nerve upon the lamina spiralis, a perspective view

of this lamina with the nervous fibres spread upon it, divested of the surrounding part of the cochlea, is given in *fig.* 394.*

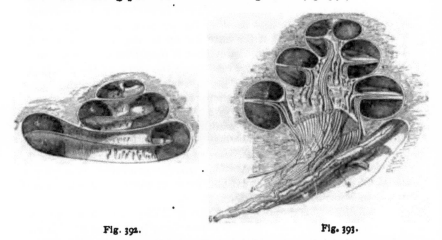

Fig. 392.   Fig. 393.

The form and magnitude of the external ears of many species of animals is more favourable for auscultation than the human ear.

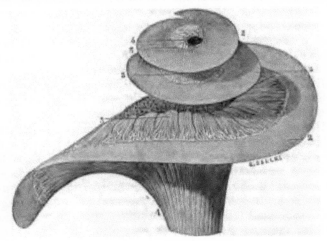

Fig. 394.

It will be evident, for example, that all ears formed like those of the horse are better adapted for the collection of the sonorous undulations.

* This figure is reproduced by permission of the author and publisher from the original, made from a preparation by Professor Sappey, of Paris, and published in his Descriptive Anatomy.

725. **Theory of the tympanum.** — The physical theory of the tympanum, though much better understood than that of the internal parts of the organ, is still but imperfectly comprehended It is evident that one at least of its purposes is to propagate the sonorous undulations of the external air to the membranes of the internal ear; and it is probable that it may also have some effect, not yet fully understood, in modifying the force of the vibrations.

It has been demonstrated by Savart that a membrane tightly extended over an opening, as parchment is on a tambourine or drum head, will be thrown into vibration by a sound produced near it. If fine sand be sprinkled upon a drum head, it will be agitated and thrown into various forms by a sound produced near it, the particles jumping upwards as if they were repelled by the parchment. But no such effect will be produced if a piece of card or board be laid upon the same opening, unless a sound of extreme loudness be produced.

It will also be found that the susceptibility of such a membrane to enter into vibration will vary according to its tension. It may, therefore, be inferred that the membrane of the tympanum will be thrown into vibrations by the sonorous pulsations of the external air. These vibrations will be imparted more or less to all objects with which the tympanum is connected, and so much the more so as these objects are more vibratory, and as the tympanum itself is rendered more vibratory by its tension. Thus all the masses of bone surrounding the middle ear, the labyrinth, and the auditory nerve, will be thrown into vibration.

It is evident also that the membranes extended over the fenestræ of the labyrinth, will be thrown into vibration by the pulsations of the air included in the middle ear.

However useful the membrane of the tympanum and the auricular bones, which are connected with the fenestra ovalis, may be, they are not indispensable to the exercise of the sense of hearing. When the membrane of the tympanum has been ruptured, the air included in the middle ear communicating freely with the external ear, the pulsations of the external air are propagated to the membranes of the labyrinth, without other modification than such as they may receive from the concha and the auditory canal.

But even if the auditory canal were closed, the pulsations of the external air would be propagated with more or less effect to the air in the middle ear, through the pharynx and the eustachian tube.

726. But of all parts of the organs of sense, that which has most completely resisted all attempts at explanation upon physical principles is the structure of the labyrinth. Why its complicated

cavities should have the peculiar form and disposition given to them has not been explained.

727. Organ of hearing in birds.—Although the sense of hearing may exist in the absence of some of these parts, its efficiency will be impaired; and we find accord-

ingly, as we descend in the scale of organisation, that these parts disappear one by one in animals which are less and less elevated in the series. With birds, for example, the auricle is altogether wanting, and the external ear is reduced to the auditory meatus. The cochlea also loses its spiral form, and the tapering tube is straight instead of being coiled round a cone, and is proportionally shorter than with superior animals, as will appear by the outline of the bony labyrinth of the barn owl shown in *fig.* 395., where 2 is the vestibule, and 3 the cochlea divested of the spiral form.

Fig. 395.

728. Reptiles.—In reptiles generally the external auditory meatus is wanting, and the ear commences with the membrane of the tympanum, which is its exterior part. The structure of the tympanic cavity is also simplified.

729. Fishes.—In most species of fishes both the external and middle ears are wanting, and the organ is reduced to the labyrinth, which consists of a membranous vestibule surmounted by three semicircular canals, having below it a little sack, which appears to supply the place of the cochlea. The auricular apparatus is placed in the lateral part of the great cavity of the skull.

730. Lower species.—In descending still lower in the scale of organisation, all traces of the semicircular canals and the cochlea are effaced, and the organ is reduced to a membranous vestibule, consisting of a little sack filled with a liquid, in which the last fibres of the acoustic nerve are diffused. Such a vestibule seems to be an essential element of the ear, never being absent so long as that organ has any existence.

731. Cochlear branch the true auditory nerve.—The experimental researches of M. Flourens have led to the conclusion that the cochlear branch of the nerve is the only part which is absolutely essential to the sense of hearing; the parts which traverse the semicircular canals, and are diffused through the vestibule, being merely accessory. That eminent physiologist showed, by a numerous course of experiments on mammifers and birds, that the removal of the vestibular nerves, and those of the membranous canals, never destroyed the sense of hearing; but that, on the other hand, the removal of the cochlear branch invariably produced absolute deafness, even though the vestibular and other branches of the nerve remained unimpaired.

It was inferred from these remarkable experiments that the nervous cord, which passes into the internal ear from the internal meatus, is not a single nerve, but consists of two, one of which only, being that which passes into the cochlea, is the true auditory nerve, and that the other branches have functions connected with the movements of the body, which are detailed at considerable length in M. Flourens's experiments.*

* " Recherches Expérimentales sur le Propriétes et les Formations du Système Nerveux dans les Animaux Vertébrés," par M. P. Flourens, ch. xxvii. xxviii. xxix. Paris 1842.

INDEX.

THE END.